HOT SHOTS

HOT SHOTS

CELEBRATING THIRTY YEARS OF THE SHORT MYSTERY FICTION SOCIETY

EDITED BY

JOSH PACHTER

To all who write, read, and love short mystery fiction

TABLE OF CONTENTS

Foreword

I didn't publish my first piece of professional fiction until I was forty-one years old—roughly a quarter of a century older than Josh Pachter, the editor of this volume, was when he made his first sale to *Ellery Queen's Mystery Magazine.*

Not long afterwards, I discovered the Short Mystery Fiction Society, a group of writers, readers, editors, publishers, and others interested in crime and mystery short stories. Today, I'm honored to be serving as the president of SMFS, and I'm thrilled that this anthology, celebrating the organization's first thirty years, is being published during my tenure.

Mind you, I can't take much credit for the existence of this book. For that, we have to thank Mark Schuster (the SMFS member and officer whose dedication and research skills resulted in a definitive history of the Derringer Awards, which the SMFS has presented since 1998) and Josh (a hugely accomplished writer and editor who took on the daunting task of combing through that history, tracking down stories, contacting authors, and ultimately compiling this extraordinary selection of winners).

Before I started publishing fiction, I had the same internal image of "an author" that many people probably do, a crude idea of a solitary figure, working in isolation in some austere cell, living in a beautiful but perhaps lonely world of words. The greatest surprise and most profound pleasure of my writing life has been discovering that this isn't the case—or at least it doesn't have to be. I thought the most satisfying part of being a writer would be simply seeing my name on published stories—and this does remain a thrill, every single time. As it turns out, though, what's been even more rewarding is finding myself part of a vibrant, caring, and enthusiastic community.

That community takes a number of forms—conferences and emails, webinars and collaborations—but the SMFS has been one of the most important for me. Through it I've met, worked with, and formed friendships with amazing people, including some of the most skilled and prolific writers working in the field today. You're going to meet a lot of them in the following pages.

These are tough times for writers, especially for writers of short fiction. A lot of markets have disappeared or shriveled under the digital age's continual assault on readers' attention spans. We have more forms of entertainment than ever before to compete with, and the threat of AI looms. It's gratifying and inspiring that, in this cultural atmosphere, a group like SMFS has survived for three decades.

I'm confident that, whatever shiny new distractions emerge, there will always be those of us who understand and appreciate the unique qualities and delights to be found in short mystery fiction. The authors you're about to encounter honor and build on the legacy of Poe and Doyle, Chandler and Hoch, Christie and Highsmith. That legacy is in good hands. I firmly believe that many of the best writers who have ever worked in this genre are writing now. For evidence of that, just turn the page.

If you enjoy these stories—and I can't imagine that you won't—I hope you'll join us in the SMFS, if you haven't already.Just Google "Join Short Mystery Fiction Society," type your email address in the little window, and click "Join." Membership is free and open to everyone…and you just might make some of the best friends you'll ever have.

In the meantime—happy reading!

Joseph S. Walker
   Bloomington, Indiana
   September 13, 2025

Introduction

As current SMFS president Joe Walker explains in his foreword to this anthology, the Short Mystery Fiction Society traces its formal beginnings back to 1996, and the Derringer Awards were born two years later, in 1998. There were five award categories that inaugural year—Best Flash Story (200-400 words), Best Short Short Story (400-1200 words), Best Short Story (1200-5000 words), Best Novella (more than 10,000 words), and Best First Short Story—along with the first-ever Derringer tie, with stories by Kris Neri and Barbara White-Rayczek each receiving a Best Short Story Derringer. (Wait, what about stories ranging from 5001 to 10,000 words? To quote the legendary Elwood P. Dowd: "Not knowing, I cannot say.")

In 1999, Kris Neri's win for Best Short Short made her the first-ever repeat winner, and Edward D. Hoch became the first recipient of the Society's Golden Derringer for Lifetime Achievement.

In 2000, an award for Best First Short Story was given for the second and last time, and in 2001, there was an award for Best Puzzle Story for the first and only time.

In 2002, the Society gave out its first Silver Derringer for Editorial Excellence, awarded posthumously to Cathleen Jordan to honor her years as the editor of *Alfred Hitchcock's Mystery Magazine.* (It wasn't until 2025 that a second Silver Derringer was awarded, this time to Janet Hutchings in recognition of her thirty-four years at the helm of *Ellery Queen's Mystery Magazine.*)

The current set of four competitive categories—Best Flash Story, Best Short Story, Best Long Story, and Best Novelette—made its debut in 2008, with Richard Helms becoming the first person to win two Derringers in the same year, for Best Long Story under his own name and Best Novelette for a story published as by Eric Shane. (Eight years later, John M. Floyd would also rack up a pair of wins in the same year.)

In 2009, the Golden Derringer was renamed the Edward D. Hoch Memorial Golden Derringer for Lifetime Achievement and awarded to Clark Howard, who'd won a competitive Derringer in 2004.

In 2010, the Society initiated its Short Mystery Fiction Hall of Fame to honor "deceased writers' impact on the mystery and crime short story." The first inductee was—inevitably—Edgar Allan Poe, and membership in the Hall was subsequently awarded to Sir Arthur Conan Doyle, R. Austin Freeman, Baroness Orczy, G.K. Chesterton, Raymond Chandler, Agatha Christie, Dorothy L. Sayers, Dashiell Hammett, Ellery Queen, Cornell Woolrich, Stanley Ellin, Ed Hoch, Rex Stout, and, in 2025, O. Henry.

The first time the same person won a competitive Derringer *and* the Golden in the same year was 2020…and the double winner that year was, ahem, me. In addition to Clark Howard, seven other people have won the Golden Derringer and at least one competitive Derringer in *different* years: Doug Allyn, Michael Bracken, Brendan Dubois, John Floyd, Henry Slesar, Art Taylor, and me (since I also won one in 2025). And there are a dozen Golden Derringer winners who haven't—at least not yet!—won a competitive Derringer: Lawrence Block, Martin Edwards, Loren D. Estleman, Barb Goffman, Ed Gorman, Ed Hoch, John Lutz, James Powell, Bill Pronzini, Robert Randisi, Ruth Rendell, and S.J. Rozan.

In 2025, after considerable discussion by the membership, a Best Anthology Derringer was introduced on a two-year trial basis.

As of this writing, the all-time competitive Derringer champions are Doug Allyn and John Floyd, with six wins apiece—and the prolific Mr. Floyd is the only person who's won Derringers in five different categories (Best Short-Short, Best Flash, Best Short, Best Long, and Best Novelette). After Doug and John comes Art Taylor with four wins, and then Michael Bracken, Rob Lopresti, Earl Staggs, and Stacy Woodson, each with three.

Of the one hundred and twenty Derringers that the Society has awarded during its first thirty years (not counting Golden and Silver Derringers and the new Best Anthology Derringer), far and away the most significant *source* of winning stories has been *Ellery Queen's Mystery Magazine*, with twenty-one winners. In second place is *Alfred Hitchcock's Mystery Magazine* with nine, and the various *Best New England Crime Stories* anthologies and *Murderous Intent* are tied with six winners each. (Interestingly—at least to me!—all six of *Murderous Intent's* winning stories appeared during the first three Derringer cycles, *four* of them during the *first* year the Derringers were awarded!)

In 2015, Untreed Reads published *Flash and Bang: A Short Mystery Fiction Society Anthology*, edited by J. Alan Hartman and featuring nineteen previously unpublished stories by members of the group. Since then, the idea of putting out another anthology has come up several times, but it's never quite happened until now.

During the summer of 2024, it was pointed out on the SMFS's listserv that the Society's thirtieth anniversary was rapidly approaching. I proposed an anthology of Derringer-winning stories to Joe Walker and offered to put it together, and Joe gave me the green light. Thanks to the tireless efforts of Assistant Derringer Awards Coordinator Mark Schuster, I had access to a comprehensive listing of all previous winners, and I selected one story to represent each year.

Because this was going to be a volume featuring close to thirty stories, I regretfully made the decision *not* to include any of the Best Novelette winners—but you'll find Mark's list of winners at the back of the book, and I encourage you to put on your deerstalker and Inverness cape and do your best to track them down; there are some *wonderful* novelettes out there, as well as all the other winners not to be found in these pages, and they are *all* well worth your attention.

As I chose the stories for this anniversary volume, I made an effort to include a roughly equal number of male and female authors and came pretty close to succeeding. I would have loved to have been able to give significant representation to writers of color and from the LGBTQIA+ community, too, but there sadly don't seem to have *been* many members of either constituency among the winners…a situation I fervently hope will change as we move forward.

I was able to contact most of the original authors (or their literary agents or heirs) for permission to reprint the stories collected in this volume. In a small number of cases, however, a concerted good-faith attempt to locate the current owner of a story's copyright was ultimately unsuccessful. Any information that might lead us to the copyright holders of those stories would be greatly appreciated.

As contributors to my series of "inspired by" anthologies know, I am a (and some would say a *very*) hands-on editor. Since all of the stories featured here have not only been previously published but are also award recipients, though, I have done *very* little tinkering with the texts as they were submitted to me, mostly restricting myself to correcting occasional typos and maintaining consistency of spelling, punctuation, grammar, and formatting. These stories didn't *need* much in the way of editing, anyway— they are tales that have not only *received* awards recognition but have *deserved* it, and I hope you'll enjoy reading them as much as I have.

Happy thirtieth anniversary, SMFS! Here's to the *next* thirty years!

Josh Pachter
    Midlothian, Virginia
    September 13, 2025

L.A. Justice

by Kris Neri
(Best Short Story, 1998)

I've come to expect the unexpected from my parents. After decades of being billed as "Hollywood's madcap couple," those lovable loonies—Martha Collins and Alec Grainger—wouldn't recognize the real world if it bit them. But Mother's doozy of a predawn telephone call surprised even me.

"Tracy!" she hissed. "There's a man in my bed."

Now I ask you, is that something a mother should say to her impressionable thirty-four-year-old child? I told her as much.

I might have been less flippant, had I known the man was dead.

With Dad away on location and their latest housekeeper having quit, I'd anticipated frequent appeals from Mother—only I figured they'd be more mundane. You'd think I'd learn. I broke countless laws racing from my Studio City condo to their Beverly Hills home and arrived to find Mother waiting in the open doorway. Seeing her fighting back tears, I wanted to take her in my arms and kiss the hurt away, like she used to do for me—until I realized it wasn't the presence of the dead guy that upset her.

"Tracy, darling," she mourned, "you're not dressed."

Stealing a glance to make sure in my haste that I hadn't left the house naked, I saw that I was wearing my favorite battered sweats, just as I thought. Mother, of course, was decked out well enough to appear on *The Tonight*

Show. To say our standards differ is the understatement of the century.

"Excuse me, Mother. I didn't know that finding a stiff in your bed constituted a formal affair."

Still, I might have popped for underwear if death had come calling at a saner hour. I'm not a morning person at the best of times, but with my husband Drew out of town for some lawyer do, I'd severed the scant hold the nine-to-five world has on me and frittered the night away sucking down Häagen-Dazs and taking in a *Remington Steele* marathon. I'd had less than an hour's sleep when that panicky call came through.

"Mother, forget about me. Who died? How—?" I caught sight of the living room through the open archway. Every piece of furniture had been knocked over and torn apart. "What did you do? Host your last tornado or wrap party here?"

"That's how I found it. It's how the whole house looks."

So someone had been searching for something. My hope that this might just be a practical joke was starting to seem foolish. I raced up the stairs to the master bedroom.

Nope, no one was laughing. Tossed on the bed like a ragdoll in a dumpster was a twenty-something man. Despite an unfortunate tendency to flashy clothes, he must have been a looker before someone blew off the top of his head and death turned his skin a trifle pasty. The proverbial tall, dark, and handsome—if it isn't too tacky to check out a corpse.

"Well, there's nothing we can do but call the police."

Mother's martyred sigh overflowed with exasperation. "Tracy, *I* could have done that. Why do you think I called *you*?"

I knew why. Because she bought into the myth that I, as a mystery writer, could solve cases on my own. Don't laugh—I believed it, too. But still, real people can't operate like the amateur detectives in books. Or so Drew keeps telling me.

"Tracy, if you call the police, they're sure to put your old mother in jail."

She only refers to herself as "old" when she wants something, so I didn't take her seriously. "Why would they do that? You couldn't have known this clown."

"Oh, but I did," she insisted. "Paulo Luca was my…protégé."

"Your—? Oh, God! Do you mean to tell me that, while my father is slaving away on some remote location shoot, you're messing around with a kid a quarter of your age?"

"Half!"

We compromised on a third. "But you've given him money?"

Reluctant nod. "And that van we had. I was even planning to take him to Cannes with me next week. Oh, you wouldn't understand."

I understood, all right. She'd paid a young man to flatter her, to make her feel young. And I thought all the old fools were men.

"Jeez, Mother." I spotted a gun tossed on the floor.

"Don't pick it up!"

"The idea never occurred to me. What idiot—?" *Oops*, I thought, looking into the face of Fury. "Don't tell me you haven't played the patsy in enough pictures to know you *never—*"

"You're obviously confusing me with some B-movie queen."

Right.

"Besides, it's my gun. My fingerprints must be on it. I practiced at the range just yesterday."

"You have a gun? I'm a mystery writer, and I don't have one. Are you any good?"

"Crack shot."

"Really? I've always figured I'd close my eyes and—"

"Tracy, aren't we getting off-track?"

It's called denial. I absently slumped onto the bed; before leaping away, my hand brushed Paulo's.

"Jeez, he's warmer than I am."

"I don't think he'd been…you know—when I came home."

"But you must have an alibi. Where were you at this hour?"

"At Franny's."

Terrific. You might remember Francesca Grant. She played the secondary lead in a few of Mother's pictures. They have dinner together about once a month and watch tapes of their old movies. Too bad she has Alzheimer's.

By morning, Franny wouldn't remember how many toes she had.

"We fell asleep in front of the set. When I woke up, I just put a blanket over her and left."

"Franny's companion?"

"Already asleep in her room."

The hole Mother was in just kept getting deeper. I glared at the cause. "Where did you pick up old Paulo?"

"Don't make it sound sordid. I met him through his uncle, Antonio, a charming gentleman and quite good looking for his age."

That meant he was at least ten years younger than she was.

"It was all very proper, Tracy."

"As long as you overlook that dead boy toy on your—wait a minute. Paulo's uncle isn't Antonio *Luca*, is he? Hangs around Folio's Ristorante downtown?"

"He is there a lot."

"No! Don't you read the papers? Antonio Luca is reputed to be the most notorious crime boss on the West Coast."

"There is no mob in L.A. Everyone knows that."

"Fine. You wanna tell him, or should I?"

Talk about giving new meaning to the old rock-and-a-hard-place squeeze. At least the cops would ask questions; Luca's crowd wasn't known for due process.

"Uh, darling. I'm afraid you haven't heard the worst."

"It can't get any worse, Mother," I snapped.

"When I came home, there was a message on the machine from your father. They've changed his shooting schedule. He'll be home later this week, instead of next month. In time to go with me to Cannes."

So she not only wanted me to do the impossible, she wanted it fast.

For once, Mother withered under my glare. Biting her lip indecisively, stripped of all her protective affectations, I had her right where I'd always wanted her. It broke my heart. Despite the stormy roller coaster she insisted on making of their marriage, she adored Dad. And so did I. What choice did I have?

I still longed to taunt her, to demand how she would have coped with both Paulo and Dad in Cannes. But what would be the point? Consequence was too abstract a concept for Mother to deal with when life was tickling her nose. Maybe some people really are so far outside the norm that they can't be held to conventional standards.

I'd have to remember that for my own defense, when Drew lowered the boom on me.

I finally agreed to put Paulo on ice. Literally. Mother's neighbor was away and had left an emergency key with my parents. Happily, she had a walk-in freezer.

"How are we going to get him there, Tracy?"

I wanted to throw him over the fence, but she wouldn't hear of it. Since Paulo had thoughtfully left the van in the driveway before buying country real estate, I said we'd take that and asked her for the keys.

"I don't have them, dear. I gave Paulo the only set."

"So get them."

"I'm not going to touch him. You get them."

"Oh, for chrissakes."

I patted Paulo down, but there weren't any keys in his pockets. Figured. If his killer hadn't found what he was looking for here, he'd try Paulo's place. I ordered Mother to get over her squeamishness and help me drag Paulo to the van. He wasn't a small man, and he was starting to like the position he'd been left in too much to change.

"But, darling, how will you start the van without keys?"

"Don't worry, I'll hotwire it."

She shot me a look across the bow of her protégé. "Surely a response to warm any mother's heart. Don't even tell me where you picked up that little skill."

I hate it when she acts like a normal mother. Who was she trying to kid? She hadn't winced at making me an accessory.

We wrestled Paulo into the back of the van. The engine started up as easily as my parents' cars always had when I was in high school and they refused to let me borrow them.

"Oh, Tracy, where did I go wrong? How did you develop this skewed sense of right and wrong?"

My tongue still hurts where I bit it.

"What would your father think?"

I thought she had a lot of nerve bringing Dad into it, considering what was decomposing just a few feet behind us. But maybe she really felt lost in this crisis without him. They had been together through a lot of married years. For that matter, they were together when they were divorced, and even, let's face it—when they were married to other people.

Now, I was thrilled Drew wasn't there to witness this caper. He was too much the Officer of the Court to condone our turning the victim into a popsicle. If he ever learned of it, there would be no living with him. Doubtless a moot point, since Mother and I were unlikely to emerge from this skirmish in any better shape than Paulo.

"I could sure use a drink," Mother announced, after we left Paulo in his new home.

"Don't get comfortable, Mother. We're only half finished." I reminded her that we still had to put the house in order. "If either the police or the mob drop by, this place has to look like nothing happened here."

Mother affected a yawn. "Tracy, dear, you know how much I'd love to help, but when a woman reaches my age, she needs her sleep. You'll understand, someday."

I understood now—she was sticking me with a mess second only to the one left by the Northridge earthquake. I spent hours cleaning up and burning the bedspread in the fireplace. Finally, I took the shower I so desperately needed and found myself standing knee-deep in water that wouldn't drain.

While I leaned over the side of the tub with Drāno corroding my hands as I wrestled with the drain cover, Mother appeared in the doorway, wearing a satin negligee and an honest-to-God feather boa.

"Mother, you're awake. I can't tell you how much I miss the privileged life of a celebrity child."

"If you cursed quieter, I wouldn't be. For a sweet young thing, you sure have a smutty mouth."

"Yeah, yeah. Get me a screwdriver, willya?"

"Where might something like that be?" she asked.

"Never mind. I've got it." No wonder the water wouldn't drain. Stuffed down the pipe was a narrow cloth bag that had to be over a foot long. "Unless you've taken to hiding things in your plumbing, this must be what Paulo's killer was looking for." I ripped open the stitches at the top and dumped some of the contents into my hand. What a disappointment. "Who would hide this? It's just a bag of gravel."

Mother laughed, a trifle hysterically. "Gravel? Darling, those aren't stones—they're uncut diamonds."

"Diamonds?" I rolled one around in my hand.

"Good ones, too, by the look of them. There must be over a hundred of them, each as big as your eyeball."

I'd heard organized crime frequently converted large amounts of cash into diamonds for easier movement across borders. Bet I knew whose suitcase had been targeted to carry them to Cannes. How could I tell her it was a set-up?

"Are you thinking what I'm thinking?" Mother asked.

Maybe she'd figured it out herself.

"I don't know," I said cautiously. "What are you thinking?

"How we'll wow them at the next Academy Awards."

Funny. I was wondering who my real parents were.

"Tell me again why we're doing this?" Mother asked, when I parked near Folio's Ristorante. "If you ask me, we should be as far away from this place as possible."

"I already told you. You're going to go in there and give the performance of your life, so—"

"Oh, this won't be the performance of my life. That would be either—"

"Mother! You have to convince Luca you don't know where Paulo is, so they look *elsewhere* for him."

"Oh. And why are you riding shotgun?"

"Because there's a good chance someone in Luca's circle will know you're lying, and I'm counting on reading that thought on his face."

Now I understood how Paulo had conned Mother. If he was anything like his uncle, the boy had been smooth. Of course, it may not have been passed by either genes or association. Luca introduced us to his son Denny and one of his "boys," Tom Ricci.

Denny was like a big, dumb dog, eager to please his old man but clumsy. The way his tongue lolled on his drooping lower lip, he even looked like a panting dog. But Ricci bore watching. While he was as flashy and as much a stereotypical thug as Paulo had been, right down to the ornate pinky rings, I saw unexpected depth in his dark eyes.

"Always a pleasure to see you, Martha, and to meet your charming daughter, but I thought you would be with Paulo," Luca said in his exquisite accent.

"You mean Paulo isn't here?" Concern tugged at Mother's features. "Oh, dear. I hope nothing has happened to him. We were planning a trip. To Cannes, you know."

I caught the look that passed between Luca and his henchmen. They knew very well.

"When Paulo didn't return my phone calls, naturally I thought—" Her voice caught.

I could see the wheels turning in Luca's eyes. They were his diamonds, all right.

"Now, Pop, don't jump to no conclusions. You know Paulo knew how much this trip to Cannes meant to…uh…him," Denny ended stupidly. "He wouldn't just take off."

While Denny and Luca went through the charade of speculating where Paulo might be, strictly for our benefit, Tom studied Mother thoughtfully, like he was trying to place this new piece into the puzzle. He knew Paulo was dead, I was sure of it.

People—especially those of a certain age who spent their youth idolizing Martha Collins, the Star—will do anything for her. The elderly locksmith who re-keyed her house the last time she blew up at Dad didn't blink at loaning me his picks. I should have held out for a lesson. We thought we were so clever when we tailed Tom Ricci to that flophouse. But if the lock on his door was any harder to pick, the caper was going to end in that hall with the rats and roaches.

"Hurry, Tracy. Who knows how long he'll be gone."

"Got it!"

Ricci's room surprised me. Not only was it too clean for that dump, there was a monastic simplicity that didn't jibe with his taste in apparel.

"I'll search, while you watch the door, Mother. If you see him coming, we'll dive into the closet."

Seemed like a good plan. Too bad one of us couldn't stick to it. She kept coming up behind me and looking over my shoulder. The third time, I was about to chew her out, only she noticed something.

"Oh, look. That drawer has a false bottom. I had a hidden panel like that put into a night table when you were little and liked to snoop through my things."

I remembered that. I used to check it out all the time. I pressed the hidden lever, but it stuck.

"Uh, Tracy…"

"Not now, Mother, I can't get this thing—there it goes."

"Darling," she went on, in her best movie-star tone, "you remember meeting this lovely man, Tom Ricci, don't you?"

I whirled around. Some gatekeeper. Ricci had not only slipped past her, he'd pulled his gun on us. I smiled knowingly and gestured with the wallet I'd found in the hidden space.

"No, Mother, I remember meeting Special Agent Thomas Ricci of the FBI."

"I don't understand, Tom," Mother said. "What does it mean to be in 'deep cover'?"

Please tell me I'm adopted.

"Martha, it just means I'm a man without a life."

Talk about sobering remarks. And subtle changes. Tom looked just as much the wiseguy as ever, but the honest expression of the real man dominated his appearance now. Along with his pain.

"Tracy, I believed in this when I started, but I don't know who the good guys are, anymore. All my superiors seem to care about is nailing Luca. I'm supposed to ignore whatever anyone else does. I've looked the other way so many times, I can't live with myself."

"You knew about Paulo's murder?"

"Sure. I followed Denny to your mom's house."

"Denny?" I'd obviously missed one of those telling expressions. Maybe because Denny's face was as expressive as cheesecake. "Why would he kill Paulo, his own cousin?"

"You've seen what he's like. His old man never trusts him with anything important. Paulo was the heir apparent. Denny probably figured he'd steal Luca's diamonds and branch out on his own, but Paulo outsmarted him."

"Surely now they'll let you out," I insisted. "They'll need your testimony."

He snorted. "You think that was the first murder I've kept quiet about?" Tom insisted he knew of two other murders Paulo had committed, and he'd actually helped Denny buy guns, arrange for a bomb, and deal drugs. "Maybe if I could have tied Luca to any of it, but—"

He shrugged. "Look at it from my bosses' perspective. With Paulo gone and Denny so hopeless, I'm going to be worth more to Luca than ever. They'll never let me go, now."

"Oh, my," Mother murmured.

Tom shook his head. "I've got a wife and kids I hardly ever see, and for what? I tell ya, Tracy, if I had some money, I'd just walk away and start life over somewhere else."

"And so you shall, dear boy," Mother said and patted his hand. "My daughter will make it possible."

Huh? They both looked at me expectantly. Why me? I mean, he was this tough Federal cop, hardened by years of deep cover within the mob. Who was I? Just Tracy Eaton, mystery writer and detective wannabe. What did they expect me to do?

"Tom, I know you're sick of duplicity, but…well, how do you feel about shell games?"

Tom's eyes brightened. "Tracy, you find me a big enough shell, and I'll be glad to be your pea."

It's hard to feel like you're commanding a well-trained army when your troops act more like the Keystone Kops. If it had been fun lugging Paulo down the stairs, rescuing him from the neighbor's freezer after he took shape, so to speak, was just too many laughs for me. Do frozen corpses weigh more, or was I just getting really sick of Paulo?

"Hold up your end, Mother. If he hits the driveway, you're picking up the pieces."

"Tracy, really—how callous. The dead deserve our respect," that maternal paragon insisted.

Like it had been my idea to stash him. My offensive imagery seemed to do the trick, however. Mother developed surprising strength for an old lady, slipping Paulo into the van like he'd been greased.

"I still don't see why we had to move him," Mother grumbled, after we tucked the van back in her yard. "You saw how little Myrna keeps in that freezer. She might not have found him for years."

Mother was obviously being respectful to the dead again. And as forgetful as ever.

"The objective isn't to delay the discovery of the murder, it's to shatter all connection with you. To muddy the water so much both that both the police and the mob will have to accept the scenario we leave behind."

"Oh, right. Well, not to worry. Tom will take care of that. I have every confidence in the dear boy."

Judging by her flush, I suspected she was auditioning another protégé. I wished I shared her confidence. Tom worried me. He was at the end of his tether, dangerous at this point in the operation, when keeping his two masters happy had never been more crucial. Luca seemed frantic. Tom reported that he kept barking orders and making Tom chase down every rumor in search of his diamonds. Poor Tom also had to find the man we needed and squeeze him just enough so he'd accept a deal—and then he had to sell the Bureau on it.

I kept telling myself there was nothing to worry about. That having held on this long, Tom wouldn't quit now. But when he still hadn't shown up at Mother's house more than two hours after he said he would, I figured he had fallen off the tightrope. While debating whether Mother and I should make ourselves scarce, I heard a soft knock on the door.

"Where were you?" Mother roared with uncharacteristic vengeance when Tom entered.

Her anxiety probably had less to do with Tom's delay than the fact that Dad had called again while we waited. The lies seemed to come easily enough to her—she calls that acting—but Dad's return had been bumped up to the day after tomorrow. Now we had no margin for error. If Tom failed to finish his part of the operation tonight, we'd never make it.

"Tom?" I asked tentatively.

"It took longer than I thought, okay? But everything's set. With a little luck, we'll pull it off."

I would have felt better if he hadn't looked like a man who'd left all his luck behind him.

Tom remembered to leave a message for Luca. "Yo, Antonio," he said, assuming his thug persona for the last time. "I found Paulo. He just had mechanical trouble in that van Martha Collins gave him. Him and me are gonna stop at your old warehouse, where he hid the…merchandise, and we'll see you for breakfast."

I hotwired the van again, and we drove Paulo through the darkened streets of the abandoned warehouse district in search of Luca's building. Since Tom cradled on his lap the device he had picked up tonight, Mother unlocked the door and lit the light bulb hanging from the ceiling. I drove the van in.

Tom's hands shook so badly, he couldn't connect the wires as he'd been instructed to. I moved him aside. I raised my face for one last look at him, longing for some assurance that Luca hadn't turned him. But Tom was already backing toward the door.

I brought the wires together.

My heart stopped.

Despite the eerie silence, I didn't hear the click that Tom said I would when the connection was made. No time to try it again. I sprinted out the door at what must have been world-record pace, to the place where Tom had taken refuge and was now trying to convince Mother to sacrifice the knees of her hose.

I threw her to the ground and covered her body with my own and held her there, squirming, while thunder ripped through earth and sky, till the last of the fragments of metal and mortar and flesh and bone rained down on us.

"Police still have no leads on the van that exploded in the warehouse district yesterday," the news anchor reported. "Not enough remains of the bodies for formal identification, but the victims are believed to be Paulo Luca and Thomas Ricci, reputed gangland figures. The men were reportedly carrying a small shipment of uncut diamonds."

Mother and I watched the news in a VIP lounge at the airport, while we waited for Dad's plane.

"In a related story, the body of a man identified as Dennis Luca, son of reputed underworld kingpin Antonio Luca, was found dead this morning of execution-style gunshots. Mr. Luca's role in the killing is under investigation."

Mr. Luca's role made me sick. I remembered staking out Folio's. We had to make sure the message we'd sent reached Luca. I wasn't certain whether I'd know on sight, after having blown it with Denny. But there was no question. When Luca left the restaurant, his Continental charm had evaporated, leaving a bitter old man. A man who, when faced with the most critical decision of his life, elected to be a businessman, not a father.

Seeing him and understanding that he'd condemned his own son to death, I knew that despite my protestations, I never really wanted to be anyone else's daughter. I felt a little misty suddenly, and I wanted to hug Mother.

But why was she shaking her head?

"Sloppy, Tracy," she said. "Such a poor plan. What were you thinking?"

"Excuse me?"

"Admit it, darling, luck played the primary role. You couldn't be sure the bomb builder would tell Antonio it was *Denny* who commissioned the bomb. Nor could you count on it working so well the police wouldn't guess there'd been only *one* body in the van and would have to rely on Tom's telephone message to make the identification."

That wasn't luck, it was Tom's final arrangement with the Bureau. He delivered Luca on a murder charge, and they leaned on the police to make the identification quickly. Now Tom was safe somewhere in the loving arms of his family with enough of a nest egg to keep their ship from running aground, once they found a fence. Exactly as I'd planned. My only regret was doubting him.

"And your moral judgment—really, darling. You let criminals settle the score. Is that what you call justice?"

I felt my blood pressure rising. "Come on, Mother, this is L.A. You know the wheels of justice grind chunky style here. How many trials have we seen where obviously guilty defendants not only got off, the jury practically threw them a testimonial dinner? This way, Denny got the verdict he deserved."

"Well, all I can say is I hope your father never learns of it. He'd be so disappointed."

So that was what this was about. She should have trusted me more. I had my own secret, didn't I? Fortunately, Drew wasn't expected for another couple of days. Plenty of time for the dust to settle, so I could sweep it under the rug.

"Tracy, why are you always so out of step with conventional society?"

I just shook my head. But if you find that question equally perplexing, I suggest you catch a glimpse of Mother at next year's Academy Awards. Take special note of the baubles. Rocks as big as your eyeballs.

Why, indeed?

Pretty Kitty

by Joyce Holland
(Best Flash Story, 1999)

"Don't even think about it, Puss," I said to the little ball of black fur poised to jump onto my lap. "I keep telling you, I am not a cat person!" I opened the newspaper and shook it threateningly.

"Ah, shut up, Lew," Maggie said, slapping our plates and two glasses of milk on the table. "I pay for the stupid cat food! And I'm sick of living hand to mouth. We can't even afford a six-pack of beer, for crying out loud!"

I stared at my plate. The cat's food looked better. "I'm not very hungry, but this looks great," I lied, hoping to stop an onslaught of endless nagging. Maggie was still on the ragged edge of pretty, but the years were taking their toll. Or the meanness. Nothing made her happy lately. Probably had a new boyfriend. Funny thing was, I didn't really care anymore. Kinda wished one would take her off my hands. I'd give the poor sucker a medal if he could last a year.

The telephone rang, and Maggie sprang to her feet.

The feisty feline took advantage of the distraction to jump onto the table. I reached to lift her down, but the little devil humped her spine and backstepped around the salt and pepper shakers.

"At least drink your milk," Maggie hollered at me, as she dashed to answer the phone in the hall.

I turned and watched her go, wondering who was calling. The fuzzball seized the opportunity, took two quick steps, and stuck her nose in my glass.

She sniffed experimentally.

The hell with this, I decided. *It's her cat, let* her *share with it, if she wants.* I set the kitty back on the floor, changed my milk for Maggie's, then drank the whole thing. Anything to keep the peace. A beer would have been nice.

Maggie came back and started to eat, watching me with an oddly intense stare. "Wrong number," she said. She picked up her milk and took a long swig—then suddenly grasped her throat and slid off her chair to the floor.

"You switched the glasses!" she cried through clenched lips.

Speechless, I watched her death throes.

The kitten jumped in my lap, curled up, and began to purr.

"Maybe I could *become* a cat person," I said, gently stroking her glossy fur. "Pretty kitty."

Just a Man on a Sidewalk

by Carol Kilgore
(Best Flash Story, 2000)

"Psst. Hey, mister!"

He looked around, but no one else was in sight. Should he acknowledge the loud whisper? Or should he ignore it?

"Psst. Mister. With the hat. Mister!"

He couldn't ignore it now. The door of the van opened, and two men with stocking masks jumped out, hauled him inside, and dumped him unceremoniously on his duff. The van screeched off down the deserted street, as his captors blindfolded him and tied his hands behind his back.

"What on earth do you fellows want with me?" he asked.

Laughter all around. "As if you didn't know, mate. Bloke doesn't think we know who he is." That set off another round of laughter.

While his captors were busy laughing, he was busy testing the rope binding his wrists. It was a little loose, and he knew if he kept working at it, he would be able to free himself.

A new voice cut in, a voice harder than the others. "How much will they pay to get you back?"

"I'm sure I don't know what you're talking about."

"Andrew Charles Webley. That's what I'm talking about. You. The chairman of the largest bank in London."

"Well, that *is* me. But I am no longer chairman of the bank."

"You expect us to believe that?" Another round of laughter followed.

"Believe what you want. It's true. I was let go just this morning."

"You're lying. You take this route to your office every single day."

The man sighed. "That's correct. I do. However, the board met in secret last night and voted me out. They called me early this morning, and I was on my way to gather some personal belongings. Call the bank, if you don't believe me." After he spoke the last sentence, he heard the electronic beeping of a cell phone.

He listened in silence while the man with the hard voice made the call to the bank. He knew his dismissal had been confirmed when curses bounced around the van.

"Turn right at the next corner and stop," the voice barked.

The van made the turn and stopped. Andrew Charles Webley was pushed out onto the sidewalk. He heard his umbrella and briefcase hit the cement beside him. He continued to work at the rope and soon slipped one hand free. Then he pulled off the blindfold before removing the rope from his other wrist. He found himself only about a mile from where the van had picked him up.

He glanced at his watch and began walking quickly toward the intersection where he could get a taxi. He still had time to make his flight to Rio. Had his captors bothered to check his briefcase, they would have discovered enough cash for him to make the trip comfortably, a few bonds, and a list of foreign bank accounts. The board had been on the right track suspecting him of embezzlement.

The Cabin Killer

by Henry Slesar
(Best Puzzle Story, 2001)

There weren't many major crimes in Pinetree Mountain, and Sheriff Brawley liked it that way. But when he saw the body of the pretty young woman, his kindly blue eyes turned to steel.

His deputy, Stan, took the static-filled call at 2:15 PM that summoned them to the Miles place on Moccasin Road. The reason for the static became clear when they arrived five minutes later and saw Peter Miles standing alongside a red Jaguar, holding a cellular phone in one hand, a scotch on the rocks in the other.

Even though the Miles family lost most of their money, they still kept a hunting lodge, and Brawley kept up with their affairs. He knew that Peter, the most frequent visitor to the cabin, was about to marry the daughter of a beer baron, a happy ending for an impoverished playboy.

"In here," Peter said. He led them to a door that had been forcibly opened, the knob hammered off. Inside, he pointed to the open bedroom door and finished his drink in a gulp.

The victim was no more than twenty, beautiful even in death. The cause of death was obvious. The hunting knife had been buried deep in her chest.

Stan's knees went liquid. Brawley sent him out to look around the area and then asked Peter the obvious question.

"No," he answered fervently, "I didn't know her! I saw her at the Moosehead Inn once or twice, serving drinks, but all I ever said to her was, 'Another scotch, please!'"

"Let me introduce you," Brawley said drily. "Her name's Alma Wilson. Been working at the Moosehead about a year."

Peter shuddered. "I didn't even know she was in the bedroom when I arrived."

"When was that?"

"Only ten minutes ago! I found the door open, but the cabin's always being broken into. The place has been shut up all winter, so there were things to do. I switched on the electricity, opened the windows to air the place out. I had a bottle in my car, and God knows I needed a drink when I saw…this. I called the police at once."

There was a commotion at the door. Stan was pushing two men ahead of him, one holding a shotgun with a dented butt, one with a loaded tool belt.

"Found these guys outside, Sheriff. Josh Morton and Gary Logan."

"Hello, Josh," Brawley said to the bearded young man. "How's the hunting today?"

Josh Morton scowled, aware that the season hadn't begun. "Just target shooting, Sheriff. Ain't killed nothing."

"And how about you, Gary? Driving that new pickup. Wouldn't be picking up girls, by any chance?"

The second man looked at his muddy boots. "Just delivering some firewood, that's all."

"I want you fellas to take a look at something in the bedroom. Hold on to your breakfast."

Sheriff Brawley didn't know which one said the name first.

"Alma Wilson!"

"You've seen Alma plenty of times. You two are always hanging out at the Moosehead, aren't you?"

Josh Morton gulped. "Where else can you go in this town?"

"In fact, Alma was one of the big attractions. Some of the customers even dated her. Didn't you, Josh?"

"Couple of times. When she ditched her old boyfriend." He looked slyly at the man beside him.

"She didn't ditch me," Gary Logan shouted. "I didn't want no part of Alma Wilson! She went out with every guy in town!"

By the time the coroner arrived, Sheriff Brawley had finished a thorough search. It would have discouraged a cop of lesser intuition. Except for a patch of dry mud in the living room, everything was clean and tidy, the kitchen spotless, the cupboards and closets bare, the fireplace filled with unburned birch logs.

But Brawley knew he had the murderer just the same.

Who was the murderer, and what clue gave him away? Read the final paragraph in Appendix C (page 267).

All the Fine Actors

by Earl Staggs
(Best Short Story, 2002)

He'd been sitting on the hot tarred roof for an hour, with his rifle across his lap. His back ached from pressing against the stubby concrete safety wall edging the front of the building, and his face and scalp itched from perspiration under the blond wig and beard. Campaign speeches rose with their own tinny echo from a PA system rigged up for the street rally below. The mayor was talking now, promising better schools, lower taxes, and anything else the crowd wanted to hear.

"Good for you, Mr. Mayor," the shooter mumbled to himself. "Now shut up, so I can do what I have to do and get off this stinking roof."

As if he'd heard the plea, the mayor began what sounded like a wrap-up to his part of the program.

"…so I hope you good folks know you can count on me. I know I'll be counting on you…."

Using his rifle for support, the shooter twisted himself around and rose into a crouching position just below the top of the short wall that had become like a second spine over the last hour or so, then inched his head up to have a look. Four stories down, the street was cordoned off at one end by police cars and an ambulance and by a mobile TV van at the other. Blue and white lettering on the van said *Channel Five Eyewitness News*.

"…to put your confidence in me once again with your vote come Election Day."

Some two hundred people stood shoulder to shoulder in the street, surrounding a speaker's platform erected in the middle of the block for the occasion. Twenty more sat in two rows of folding chairs on the platform, facing the building the shooter had chosen for his own part of the program. At the lectern, the short, balding, pear-shaped mayor, sharply dressed in a dark suit and red necktie, raised both arms high in the air and gave the crowd his best smile as they erupted into a round of shouting and applause.

The shooter lifted his rifle, gently rested its barrel across the top of the wall, and snugged the stock into his shoulder. He sighted his scope on the mayor's chest for a second, then slowly panned left. Sheriff Sanford Thornberry, broad-shouldered and ruggedly handsome, sat there tall and straight in his perfectly fitted tan uniform, reading something. His speech. Beside him, an attractive, leggy blonde in a white suit and pink blouse did her best to appear interested in what was going on. Mrs. Sheriff. Next to her, Chief Deputy Ansel Williams squirmed in his chair, as though he wasn't at all comfortable being there. He was a tall man like the sheriff and wore the same uniform, but his sloping shoulders and bulging gut made it look like a misfit. Businessmen in suits and more uniformed deputies filled the chairs in the second row.

The mayor waved his arms up and down in a motion to quiet the crowd and leaned toward the microphone.

"And now it gives me great pleasure to introduce the man who has served as your sheriff for two terms and needs your vote for another one—"

The shooter pulled a handkerchief from his back pocket and wiped perspiration from his forehead and eyelids.

"—the man who's done more to clean up this county than anyone else—"

He lowered his cheek to the stock of his rifle again, adjusted the scope slightly with two fingers, and waited.

"—the best sheriff we've ever had around here, and a man I'm proud to call my very good friend, your sheriff and mine…Sanford L. Thornberry!"

The crowd exploded into a thunderous round of applause as the sheriff stood, shook hands with the mayor, and stepped up to the microphone. The man on the roof waited until the noise of the crowd died down before he squeezed the trigger. He watched just long enough to see the sheriff grab his chest and fall, then hurried across the rooftop to the stairwell door, his rifle in one hand, a briefcase in the other.

He took the first flight of steps quickly, stopping at the third-floor landing long enough to disassemble the rifle and place it in the briefcase along with the wig and beard. On his way down two more flights, he wrestled off the dark T-shirt that covered the short-sleeved dress shirt and necktie underneath. At the exit door on the first level, he stopped to stuff the T-shirt in the briefcase and took time to run a comb through his short dark-brown hair. He stepped out of the building onto a side street, looking like any thirty-five-year-old bank manager or insurance salesman out for a midday stroll. If anyone had happened to spot him on the roof, their description would be useless.

He weaved his way through the frenzied, horrified crowd in the street and up to the speaker's platform. Sheriff Thornberry lay on his stomach beside the lectern. A ragged blotch of crimson stained the wood planks beneath his chest. The mayor had removed his suit jacket and placed it over the sheriff's head and upper body. Within minutes, an ambulance worked its way through the crowd, and a team of paramedics lifted the sheriff onto a stretcher and carried him away.

The shooter scanned the people still milling around on the platform until he met another pair of eyes looking back. A nod passed between them. The brief nod acknowledged that everything had gone as planned. It was also an unspoken confirmation of the prearranged meeting to complete the transaction. The old warehouse at the edge of town. Nine o'clock tonight.

The shooter turned and made his way back through the crowd and walked a block away to his car. The easy part was over. The hard part lay ahead. Most of the time, the final part went as planned, but sometimes his clients got cute and decided to change the arrangements. Something in that pair of eyes told him this would be one of those times. He checked his watch. Ten past four. Nearly five hours to wait.

He drove slowly and casually around town to kill the first hour, then stopped at the Four Star Cafe. By now, he figured the news would be well spread. He was right. Inside the narrow restaurant, six locals stood like a cluster of statues at the end of the long counter. Six more sat motionless at small round tables along the opposite wall. A distressed young anchorwoman, blond and long-faced, spoke from a TV set hanging on the back wall next to the kitchen door. The shooter settled onto a stool at the end of the counter close to the front door, unnoticed, and joined the silent audience.

"Hundreds watched in shock and horror as Sheriff Sanford L. Thornberry, apparently dead from a single gunshot to the chest, was taken away to Memorial Hospital. Chief Deputy Ansel Williams spearheaded an immediate search of the area to locate the person who fired the shot. Pete Crosby is on the scene now. Pete, can you tell us anything new on this terrible tragedy?"

"Sally, I'm here with Deputy Ansel Williams, who is in charge of the investigation. So far, the person or persons responsible have not been apprehended. Is that correct, Deputy Williams?"

Williams stepped into camera view, looking even more nervous and uncomfortable than he had sitting on the speaker's platform. "We're still searching the area," he said stiffly, leaning back from the microphone the reporter had thrust within inches of his face. "Whoever did this won't get away, I promise you that."

Crosby asked, "Did anyone see who fired the shot?"

"Uh, no," Deputy Williams replied, finally looking at the camera. "As of yet, we have not found a witness who saw anything. We're still combing the area and will continue to do so."

The reporter had another question ready. "What about roadblocks? Is it possible the shooter has gotten out of town this soon?"

Williams shifted his weight and looked from side to side, as though he wanted to finish the interview and get on with more important duties. "We can't rule out any possibility at this point, but we've been in contact with the state police, and roadblocks are being established."

The shooter grinned to himself. *Roadblocks. Yeah, right, deputy. Tie up traffic for fifty miles around. Only an amateur would try to run. The best place to hide is in plain sight.*

Crosby was saying now, "Sally, I see Mayor Thompson over here. Let me see if I can talk to him. Mayor Thompson, can we talk to you for a minute?" Crosby walked to his left with the microphone, leaving Deputy Williams where he stood.

The mayor turned to face the camera and ran a hand over his bald scalp as Crosby asked, "Mayor, what do you have to say about this shooting?"

The mayor looked at the camera for a moment, then closed his eyes, lowered his head, and wagged it slowly from side to side. "What do I have to say?" he muttered sadly. "What can I say? One of the finest men I've ever known has been shot down in broad daylight, right here in the center of town." He looked straight into the camera then with a determined, tight-jawed expression. "I'll say this. We're going to do everything possible to find out who's responsible. I'm personally taking charge of the investigation, and no stone will be unturned until justice is done."

The shooter nearly snickered out loud. *Very dramatic, Mr. Mayor. You should be on the stage. But then,* he thought, *all politicians are actors in a way.*

"Thank you, Mayor Thompson," the reporter said, "and now back to you in the studio, Sally."

"Thank you, Pete Crosby, for that on-the-scene report." Sally stared into the camera now from her anchor desk in the studio. "Angela Thornberry, wife of the slain sheriff, was driven away from the scene immediately after the shooting and made no comment. We're attempting to get an interview with her, to get her reaction to the events of the day."

Good for you, Sally, the shooter thought. *Don't you love to stick a microphone in someone's face and ask how it felt to see a loved one gunned down? Reporters!*

The TV screen played a scene taped earlier of Mrs. Thornberry being led to and helped into the back seat of a police car. She appeared unsteady on her feet, and her movie-star face was a smear of tears and mascara. She looked into the camera for a second and mouthed something through trembling lips as she collapsed into the car seat.

The shooter rolled his eyes. *A bit over the top, but not a bad performance overall. Quite good, as a matter of fact.* He wondered if Mrs. Sheriff had ever been an actress.

The waitress, standing below the TV at the far end of the counter, turned her head in the shooter's direction and noticed him. He gave her a nod and a pleasant look as an invitation. She was a short, plump woman in her late thirties, with a pleasantly pretty face now pulled tight with obvious grief. Over her left breast, her dark blue polo shirt displayed four embroidered white stars in a crescent pattern over the name *Mitzi*. She came to his end of the counter with a glass of water in her hand.

"This county's never going to be the same without San Thornberry," she said, shaking her head as she placed the glass in front of him. Her voice quivered, as though she needed to cry. She pulled an order pad and a short pencil from a back pocket of her tight jeans and looked at him with her best effort at a friendly smile. "What can I get you?"

"Did you know him well?" the shooter asked.

After a deep breath and a loud exhale, she said, "All my life, just about. We grew up together, went all through school together. We even dated a few times, before he went away in the Marines."

"And after the Marines?"

Mitzi sighed and tried the friendly smile again. It was weak. "Oh, he was hooked up with that Angela by then. We stayed friends, though. He came in here a lot, and we talked. It's not going to be the same around here without him." She turned her attention back to the TV.

"How's the chocolate cake?" the shooter asked.

"Huh?" Her eyes were glued to the screen

"That chocolate cake down there looks good." He had decided not to eat a big meal until after the meeting later that night.

She looked back at him blankly for a second, then down the counter, where a three-layer chocolate cake sat under a clear plastic cover. "Oh. It's good. Homemade. Want a piece?"

"Please," he said and watched her walk over to get it. No acting job here, just genuine emotion over the loss of an old friend. He wished he could say something to relieve the grief she felt. He couldn't, of course, but he felt sorry for her. He wondered for a second what it would be like to spend time with people like Mitzi instead of people playing roles to serve their own purposes. He knew he couldn't do that, either. Not with what he did for a living.

After serving his cake, Mitzi went back to the other end of the counter.

Anchorperson Sally's face filled the screen now. "Sanford Thornberry had been sheriff of Wyncombe County for two terms," she said, "and according to local polls was well on his way to being reelected to an unprecedented third term. Recently, he announced that he was close to making arrests after a long investigation into an alleged drug-smuggling operation that has plagued the county for several years."

Right, Sally, the shooter thought. *He was close, all right. Too close. That's why I'm here.*

He ate his cake slowly and caught snatches of conversation from the others in the restaurant.

"If you ask me," one elderly woman sitting alone at one of the tables along the wall said, "that snobby wife of his had something to with this. Everyone knows she's been running around with the mayor. San Thornberry must've been blind."

"That's just rumor, Mattie," a fat man two tables away said, "and you should be careful what you say about people."

A young man sitting farther down the counter and wearing a baseball cap joined in. "It was the damn Mexicans, if you ask me, the ones bringing the drugs up here. San never should've messed with them."

Mitzi glared at the man. "Well, somebody needed to do something about the drugs. It's all over town, and you know it."

"Knowing it and stopping it's two different things," the man shot back. "You don't mess with the Mexican mafia."

"Shut up, Howard," Mitzi said. "You think you know everything. The mafia's Italian, not Mexican."

"Oh, no?" Howard shot back. "You just start messing around with the drug business, and you'll find out if there's a Mexican mafia or not."

The shooter finished his cake, put enough money on the counter to cover it plus a generous tip for Mitzi, and left the Four Star Cafe as unnoticed as he'd come in. He drove to his motel and locked himself in his room. Six o'clock. Three more hours to go. By now, he was certain the person he was meeting would pull something. It was only a feeling, but a very strong one, and he was seldom wrong about people. With the ones he dealt with, there was no honor left. *Honor!* He snorted at the thought and lay across his bed to plan his moves for later.

The old cinderblock warehouse sat by itself on the outskirts of town, with boarded windows and faded letters across the front saying *Johnson Bros. Moving and*, the rest of it washed away by wind and rain. Beside it, a large parking lot had gone mostly to potholes and weeds, surrounded by squatty trees and overgrown brush. The lot was empty, except for an old moving van, rusted and sagging on flat tires against the building wall. It was eight o'clock and quite dark, and the shooter sat parked in his car half a block away.

At ten past eight, a dark minibus stopped on the street in front of the warehouse. Seven men piled out. They talked for a few minutes before three of them climbed back in the minibus. The other four walked to the ancient moving van in the parking lot beside the warehouse, opened the back door, and climbed in.

At eight forty, a car pulled into the parking lot, drove to the back, and stopped. Three men got out. One man went left, one went right. The driver stayed by the car, leaned against the fender, and lit a cigarette.

The scene was set.

The shooter drove down the street and pulled into the parking lot. He stopped halfway across the lot, his car facing the other one. He got out and walked over to stand with his back against the old moving van.

Deputy Sheriff Ansel Williams pushed himself off the fender of his car, tossed his cigarette to the ground, and smiled. "You're a little early."

"No sense putting it off," the shooter said. He shot looks right and left for the two other men. The one on the left was crouched behind overgrown brush, the other one was out of sight behind the warehouse. "Let's finish our business and get it over with. The sheriff is dead, like you wanted. Give me the rest of my money, and I'm on my way."

Williams held his smile for a moment, then wiped a hand across his mouth. "I gotta hand it to you, pal. Hell, you walked right over and mingled with the crowd like you belonged there. Very slick."

"You're pretty slick yourself, pal. With Thornberry out of the way, you'll get the sheriff's job and keep your drug business with the Mexicans going strong."

Williams' eyes opened wide. "How…how did you know about that? I never told you about that."

The shooter glanced right and left again. The two men hadn't made a move yet. Probably waiting for a signal. "Just a wild guess. I picked up a little scuttlebutt around town. Doesn't make sense you'd want your boss taken out just to get his job. Had to be more to it than that."

Williams smiled again. More like a smirk. "Don't matter if you know now. You're not going to be telling anybody about it."

"No problem there. Just pay me what you owe me, and I'm outa here for good. What happens around here means nothing to me."

"Yeah, well," Williams said. He rubbed a hand across his chest slowly and deliberately. The signal.

The shooter heard movement on his right first, then the left. The two men stepped out into the open, and both had guns in their hands. Dark-skinned Latinos. Howard's Mexican mafia. And they had him in a crossfire. He sized them up quickly. The one on the right, stocky and solid, about forty, eyes grim, mouth tight. He'd been around, a pro, wouldn't shoot unless he had to, wouldn't buck the odds. The other one younger, maybe twenty, anxious eyes darting around, licking his dry lips, came here to shoot—and he would, no matter what.

Williams took a step forward. "About the rest of your money, I'm, uh, afraid there's been a little change in the plan. Sure, I had to protect my business interests with my friends across the border. And I wanted the sheriff's job, but there's no guarantee I'd get it. Not without a little insurance. Too bad you won't hear the scuttlebutt around town tomorrow. With all the publicity about me taking down the man who killed San Thornberry,

I'll pull every vote in the county."

"That's quite a plan, Williams. You hire me to take out Thornberry, then you kill me and become the local hero. Looks like I underestimated you."

The shooter reached behind himself and rapped his knuckles against the side of the van. Three times. "Only problem is, you underestimated me. Did you really think I'd be stupid enough to come out here by myself?"

Williams cocked his head, confused. "What are you talking about?"

The shooter didn't answer. He didn't have to. The back door of the moving van swung open, and four men in uniforms jumped out. At the same time, the dark minibus that had been parked in front of the warehouse spun into the parking lot and skidded to a halt beside the shooter's car. Three more cops scrambled out with shotguns.

The first man out of the moving van, Sheriff Sanford Thornberry, shouted, "It's over, Ansel. Tell your men to lose the weapons and get their hands in the air."

Williams stood frozen in place, shocked and unbelieving. "San? What the hell—?"

The shooter's attention was on the young gunman on his left, hoping he wouldn't shoot but knowing he would. When the kid raised his automatic, the shooter dove forward, rolled on his shoulder and came up on one knee, his gun extended in both hands. "Don't do it!" he shouted, but the kid sprayed a dozen wild rounds before a bullet from the shooter's gun hit him in the gut, dead center. The kid froze for an instant, crumpled to his knees, then fell face down.

The shooter jerked his head to the right. The older gunman's hands were in the air, his weapon at his feet, a grin of resignation pulling up one side of his face. He looked back at the kid, now writhing on the ground and uttering painful groans mixed with sobbing. "Stupid," the shooter muttered under his breath.

By then, Sheriff Thornberry's deputies had reacted and raced up to surround Williams and the older gunman.

San Thornberry marched straight to Williams. "You went too far, Ansel," he said, furiously jabbing a finger at his chief deputy. "I knew you were in on the drug business, but I didn't have enough proof. When the Feds told me you hired a man to get me out of the way, we put this little show together. Now I can nail you for the drugs and conspiracy to commit murder."

Williams stared at the shooter. "Feds? You mean this guy's a Fed? Jesus! A Fed."

The shooter stood up and dusted himself off. He gave Williams a mock salute. "You have to be careful who you hire these days, pal." He then stepped back and watched the sheriff and his men do their job. Within a few minutes, Deputy Williams and the older thug were handcuffed and loaded into the minibus. Someone had called for an ambulance for the wounded kid lying on the ground. Its siren grew louder in the night air.

The shooter removed the small recording device from beneath his shirt and handed it to the sheriff.

"I'm glad that's over," Thornberry said. "I don't mind telling you, I've been nervous as a cat all day. It's an odd feeling being shot at, even when you know it's blanks."

"You pulled it off just fine, Sheriff," the shooter said.

"Not really. I almost forgot to break the fake blood capsule when I fell, and I was scared as hell somebody would see me laying there breathing. Good thing they got me out of there in a hurry."

"You can thank your mayor for that," the shooter said. "He had the ambulance crew all set to move in fast. He did his part well. So did your wife, by the way. I hope it wasn't too tough on her."

Thornberry threw his head back and laughed. "Are you kidding? She said she hasn't had so much fun in years. She used to be an actress, you know."

The shooter smiled. "How about that?"

"Oh, yeah," said the sheriff. "She wants to go back to it after the kids are grown. So what about you, now? I guess you'll be heading back to FBI headquarters."

The shooter shook his head. "I never go there. I'll be heading home to Florida, try to get in a week or two of fishing."

"Then what?"

"Then someone else'll decide to solve a problem the easy way. They'll start asking around for someone to do the job, the word'll get to us, and I'll have another assignment."

The two men shook hands, and the shooter drove away. He had a long drive back to Florida, but he'd be home in time for the redfish to start biting in Green River. The big grouper would be hitting off Cedar Key in a day or two. He grinned as he pulled onto the interstate. *Very predictable, fish, once you get to know them.*

Just like people.

Closure

by Dave White
(Best Short Story, 2003)

"Where were you?" Omar said, his voice like a needle in my ear. We were sitting on the New Jersey Turnpike, heading north. Traffic was slow, grinding, and typical for any weekday morning. People were making their way to their jobs, most heading toward New York City. We were heading toward the city as well. But unlike the commuters going through their daily routine, I wasn't exactly sure what I was doing, except getting into a conversation I wasn't sure I wanted to be in.

"What?"

"That morning. Where were you?"

Brake lights flashed in front of me, and I responded in kind.

"I was sitting in this car, watching a hotel on Route 1. I was waiting for a banker to come out with his girlfriend. His wife hired me. I had the radio on, and they started talking about it. They stopped the commercials, the music, everything."

A day earlier, Omar Hassan stumbled into my office, although I didn't know his name at the time. It was mid-afternoon, around three or four, and his breath smelled like bourbon. His eyes opened and closed, deep brown puddles that looked exhausted. He hadn't shaved, and a dark shadow was forming over his olive skin. His oil-black hair was sticking out left and right. He ran a hand through it, but that didn't help. He wore a striped

34

button-down shirt open at the collar and khakis. He slumped in the client chair I had.

"Jackson Donne?" he asked.

I said that I was.

He nodded and introduced himself and said, "I need help."

"Most people who come in here do," I said.

He sighed, rubbing his chin. I was hoping he wouldn't vomit, but I casually slid my trashcan in his direction. Just in case.

He pressed his index finger and thumb against the bridge of his nose. "I lost my wife in the Trade Center," he started. "She worked on the ninetieth floor of Tower One. I don't know. I didn't hear from her. I didn't know anything. They haven't found her yet. I don't know. I wish they would."

He paused, as if waiting for me to say something. What was there to say?

"Everything was just starting go well. I was getting back to work. I was going out with friends. I felt a little bit human again. And then…and then yesterday the phone rang. Some guy, I don't know, sounded my age. He said he had information about my wife. He wants me to pay for it. He wants ten thousand dollars. I took the money out of the bank this morning. All I have left is the money I need to pay you."

"Me?"

"Yeah. I don't know what this guy knows about my wife. It could be someone trying to hustle me. But I want to believe it could be real. Maybe she slept with someone else; maybe she was cheating on me. Maybe he knows some little tidbit about her that I should never know. But I have to know. I have to have more of her. I need it. And then there's that part of me…"

His voice trailed off, and he put his head in his hands. "Maybe she's still alive. Maybe he knows where she is. God, I know it sounds stupid. I want to believe she got out of that wreckage and just needed some time alone. I need to do this—no matter what it costs me."

He put his head down, and I gave him a minute to collect himself. He didn't cry.

"What would you like me to do?" I asked.

He coughed. "I'm scared. I've never done anything like this. This guy wants me to meet him with the money tomorrow at ten. He said I should drive up to Liberty State Park and meet him where the ferry used to leave for the Statue of Liberty. Have you ever been there?"

I nodded. It was a stone's throw from where the Towers used to be. Every kid had been there, if they'd been to the Statue of Liberty. A ferry would take people from the pier on the Jersey side to Ellis Island. Since September, the ferries hadn't run, and the tourist attractions were closed, although the news was they would reopen soon.

Omar continued. "I can't go alone. It's too close to where it all happened. I'm scared, and I need someone there."

"So you want to hire me? What about friends?"

"I can't ask them. I'm too embarrassed."

"Have you spoken to the police? The park will be crawling with them anyway, the way security is now."

Omar laughed. "The police? You think the police are going to help me? I'm just what they're looking for, the ones they are keeping their eyes open for. I need someone who has nothing to do with this."

I sighed. I agreed. Omar wrote me a check and left. I went to the bank and cashed it.

The next morning was unseasonably warm for November, the temperature in the low seventies. I wore a light windbreaker and my Yankees cap. It was the kind of morning that held promise. The sky was clear, the sun was out, and there was a slight breeze. It felt like only good things could happen today. Still, there was a knot in the pit of my stomach.

I stood on George Street, waiting for Omar, wanting to enjoy the morning. I sipped coffee and watched everyone walk by. Omar and I decided to get to the park an hour early. That way, I could scout around and find the best vantage point. This whole thing seemed hastily planned. There were too many problems. The park could be too crowded. I didn't want to be firing off shots into a park filled with morning joggers and dog walkers. Not to mention several cops. Yet I brought my gun. I felt more comfortable with it.

Too many holes, but there wasn't much time, and this was the best I could come up with.

Jackson Donne, bodyguard extraordinaire.

Omar showed up as I was tossing my coffee cup into the trash. He was dressed about the same as last night, but his face was shaved and his hair was combed. He carried a large brown paper bag and two cups of coffee in a plastic tray. More caffeine would make me jumpy and wouldn't help my stomach, but I accepted one of the cups when he offered. We got into my Prelude, and I started it up. I took Route 18 north to the Turnpike.

Omar didn't talk much for the first few miles. He sat and sipped his coffee, watching the road ahead of us. He didn't seem nervous; he seemed contemplative. He didn't shake, he didn't breathe deeply; he just sat.

I drove with my hands at ten and two, tightly wrapped, with my knuckles turning white. Blame it on the caffeine.

We stared at the bumper on a Mercedes for a long time. We crawled along, past the *New York Times* distribution center, the only sound the hum of car engines. I tried the radio, but couldn't find anything interesting, just a lot of talk about Ground Zero. Like nothing else in the world had happened since. Neither of us needed that. It was time to make some mix tapes.

"Where were you?" Omar said, his voice like a needle in my ear.

"What?"

"That morning, where were you?"

"I was sitting in this car, watching a hotel on Route 1. I was waiting for a banker to come out with his girlfriend. His wife hired me. I had the radio on, and they started talking about it. They stopped the commercials, the music, everything."

"So what happened?"

I looked at Omar. He wasn't looking at me. His eyes were on the glove box.

"With the case," he said. "What happened with the case?"

"The banker came out ten minutes later. I took a few pictures of him with the girl and went and got them developed."

"So you kept working?"

"Yeah."

There was a break in the left lane, and I took advantage. I was able to speed ahead about fifty feet, then slammed on the brakes again.

"Did you deliver the pictures to your client?"

"Yeah."

"That day?"

"No. I had to wait for the pictures to be developed." I wondered what he was getting at.

"You could have gone to a one-hour place."

"Yeah. I could have." But I didn't.

He nodded as if satisfied. Traffic opened up a bit at the next rest stop, and I was able to push the Prelude to fifty. Mind you, the speed limit's sixty-five, but it was a start.

"My last few moments with her weren't special, hardly memorable. I wish they were. But that morning was just so typical. She left for work at six. I kept sleeping. I didn't have to get up until eight. I worked at nine. So I slept through her leaving." He sighed. "I wish I could say anything. Like we had a fight, and now I feel guilty for never saying goodbye. Or that we made love and she left and was late to work. Just to spend some time with me. But there wasn't anything. She kissed me on the cheek, and I mumbled a goodbye. Another Tuesday."

In all the time he'd spoken, he'd never once referred to his wife by her name. It was a defense mechanism, I suppose, a way not to let it get too close. I had done the same when I lost my fiancée in a car accident. How long had it been since Omar said her name to anyone?

"I listened to a CD as I drove to work. I'm a nurse at Robert Wood Johnson. I got in that morning just in time to see the second plane hit. I knew. I knew she was there, and I knew she was probably dead." He coughed into his fist.

"She never called from her cell phone to tell me anything. Not like you hear on the news. I never heard from her. I don't know. For the next few hours, I couldn't function. I couldn't work. We had a knife wound come in. Required immediate surgery. We almost lost him, because I couldn't move quick enough. I couldn't do what was asked of me. I took a leave of absence on September 13th. I went back last week."

He was quiet a moment, watching the traffic.

Then he said, "You said you didn't deliver those photos that day. You could have. Were you trying to save someone from more pain?"

He looked at me. I didn't say anything.

"I'm sorry," he said. "I just needed to get that off my chest."

At first, it surprised me. I didn't expect him to tell me anything about the day he lost his wife. It seemed something so deeply personal. But then again, he trusted me to keep him alive. Why wouldn't he trust me with his secrets?

Traffic finally cleared near Newark Airport. As airplanes landed and took off, I sped up to seventy. Omar Hassan didn't say much for the rest of the trip. I took the correct exit and followed the signs to a parking lot about half a mile from where we needed to be. I turned the car off and opened my door.

"Stay here for fifteen minutes or so and then make your way up. I'm going to walk up there and check things out. If I'm leaning against the railing, things are fine. If I'm anywhere else, stay in the car."

He nodded. I left him there.

I walked along the brick sidewalk, watching the area around me. I could see the water and the New York skyline. Dust still seemed to float around the gap between buildings. A breeze came from the east, blowing into my face. Boats made their way up the Hudson. To my left stretched a pier, many yachts and privately owned boats waiting for weekend trips. To my right squatted a brick building, long and wide but only one story high. It was an old train station, and the broken-down tracks that weren't used anymore still sat, forgotten. The building now housed a gift shop and ticket window for the ferry. They didn't do much business now but remained open.

When I reached the building, I read a sign that was posted:

NO GUNS, KNIVES OR EXPLOSIVES BEYOND THIS POINT.
PUNISHABLE TO THE FULL EXTENT OF THE LAW.

I felt my gun against my hip. Anyone willing to bring a gun, knife, or explosive to the park wasn't going to be intimidated by a sign.

I made my way down to the water. Leaning against the metal barrier that kept people from falling in, I scanned the environment. People enjoyed the unusual November weather, jogging or walking their dogs. A few tourists fed quarters into the binoculars to get a better look at the skyline. To the north, you could see the Empire State Building, metal glistening in the sunlight, the Chrysler Building as well. I wondered what the tourists were checking out, the buildings or their own view of history.

Without binoculars, I could see the buildings that used to surround the Twin Towers, some of them still cracked and damaged. I could also see the arm of a crane used in the cleanup. I couldn't imagine what it must have been like to stand here that morning, feeding quarters to see everything. I closed my eyes. What the hell was I doing here?

Next to me, a man in jeans and an oversized Drew University sweatshirt faced the river. His hands were clenched around the railing, his knuckles white. His eyes were wide open, not blinking in the wind. I wanted to ask if he was okay, if he knew someone in the tragedy. Part of it was compassion; the rest was morbid curiosity. I looked away before he felt me staring.

My watch said it was nine thirty-five. I scanned the area again. Two cops leaned against the same railing I did, about fifteen feet south. They eyed the crowd as well. Over their shoulders I could see the back of the Statue of Liberty and Ellis Island, closed now. The ferry pier was silent, boats docked. Back toward the parking lot, a squad car circled lazily. They had this place pretty well covered. Checking one last time, no one looked suspicious to me.

I could see Omar making his way toward me, paper bag in hand. He didn't walk up next to me, which was smart. He sat on a park bench. The bag rested against his leg. The two cops watched him for a long time. An Arab-American with a bag? I'd watch him, too. When the park didn't explode, the cops went back to sunning.

The breeze made the park colder than it was in New Brunswick, but it was still a great morning. Fresh air, sunshine, and blue skies. I tried to enjoy the weather while waiting. Not knowing exactly what was going to happen didn't help. I watched a police cruiser slowly circle the lot near where I had parked. At nine fifty-nine, the man in the Drew University windbreaker walked up to Omar. I tensed. Omar looked up at the man, middle-aged and rugged. His face was bearded, his blond hair combed. There were tufts of gray at his temples. He didn't hold himself up straight. His body language made him look worn out. His mouth moved, and Omar shook his head, but I couldn't hear what was said. The breeze blew the words away from me. They kept talking, Omar shaking his head as if to say, "No, no." Not emphatically, very calmly. The man became more animated, waving his hands around. I edged closer, part to help and part to hear. Then the man reached into his pocket, and everything changed.

"On the ground! Now!" the man yelled. With the breeze, I could still hardly hear him. He pulled a revolver and pressed it to Omar's head. Omar went down to his knees.

I bounced off the railing and took a few steps forward. To my left, the cops did the same, but they had farther to come. One of them said something into his radio. Off in the distance, the cop car stopped. Its doors opened, and two more cops came running.

Omar looked at me, his eyes wild with confusion and fear. He was on his knees, kneeling execution-style in front of the gunman. The paper bag was behind the two of them, ignored. The gunman's mouth moved slowly, but I still couldn't hear him.

"Put that fucking gun down!" Both cops had their guns out. The other two were still running.

A jogger screamed, and the tourists hit the deck. I moved closer. Behind me, I could hear boats in the water and small waves splashing against the wall. One of the cops tried to whisper, but the wind caught it, and I heard it: "Maybe we should let this guy put the sand nigger down. For us."

As I edged forward, the gunman became audible. "—you to see it. Look across the river. Can you see that?"

Omar's head was in the way. I couldn't see the gun, where it was leveled, how tense the gunman's hand was. Directly in front of them, all I could see was this guy's face. It was pressed together in some emotion that wasn't happiness. It might have been concentration, but it looked more like anger. I wanted to see the gun. Was his hand on the trigger or the trigger guard?

The two running cops finally got into position behind the gunman. Their guns were out now, too. All the way down the road, past the parking lot, at the intersection where I had pulled in, another squad car blocked the road. Two other cops stood outside the car, making sure traffic stayed out of the way. A line of cars started to fill the road, backing way up to the entrance.

"Put that gun down!"

I wasn't sure how long we had been standing there. It could have been an hour.

Trying to get a better view, I moved to my left. Slowly but surely, my sightline changed, but it wasn't enough.

"Hey, asshole! Get out of the way!"

I turned slightly and realized that I wasn't the only one there. I definitely didn't want to be in the cops' line of fire. They were just as tense as everyone else. Awareness struck me like a bolt of lightning. I was the only pedestrian still standing.

"Tell me about my wife," Omar said.

"Your wife? What are you talking about?" The gunman's voice was off the wall. Wild.

"Back away! Drop the gun and back away!"

Horns honked, and brakes squealed off in the distance. I heard another boat horn.

"Why am I here? What do you know about my wife?" Omar didn't sound scared.

"I don't know anything about your wife. I know you killed my brother."

"Wh-what are you talking about?"

"How could you be so—so—so *callous*? You bastard. All for what?"

I wanted to pull my gun out. I wanted to put this guy down. But if I did that, I'd draw the cops' attention from where it needed to be. I couldn't think. I was a spectator. I might as well have been watching on television.

"Who are you?" Omar asked.

"Shut up. Shut up! It doesn't matter who I am. You don't care who I am.

All I am to you is a faceless American. Someone you hate. So you try to kill us. You killed my brother!"

Think, Jackson. Don't just stand here like an idiot. Do something. Do your job.

"I don't know your brother," Omar said.

"I have nothing left."

Finally, I thought of something to say. "Whatever your problem is, it's not Omar's fault. Someone lured him here promising information about his wife. Put the gun down."

"Who the hell are you? Get down on the ground." He took the gun off Omar for a second and pointed it at me. That was the cop's chance, but they didn't take it. They were afraid of getting me shot.

One of the cops said, "Listen to him, sir. Get on the ground and don't get yourself hurt. Don't be a hero."

I didn't listen. I just stood there. I had played my hand. I had nothing else.

The gun went back to Omar, pressing harder against his skull. His neck bent a little unnaturally.

"It's not my fault!" Omar said. "Just take the money. The money you wanted."

One of the dogwalker's dogs tried to get loose, impatient at all of this. The owner tugged on the leash hard, and the dog backed off, sat, and sniffed the ground.

"Money? I don't want your money. You shouldn't be here. It's an insult to me that you come to here to look. Why did you come here? To gloat and celebrate?"

Tears were running down this man's face, soaking his blond beard so it changed color. Omar was crying, too. The wind had blown his hair into every direction. He looked a lot like he did yesterday in my office. Disheveled, confused, and afraid.

"Last chance. Put that goddamn gun down!"

The two cops behind the gunman and Omar edged their way around toward the two cops on my left. They were getting out of the line of fire. If they had to shoot, they didn't want to be hit by one of their own.

"I had nothing to do with your brother's death. My wife, Julia, died there, too." Omar's voice was quiet, or at least it sounded that way to me. But through the wind, he could have been yelling.

"Your wife?" The gun hand shook. For a second, I thought he would drop the gun.

"Please drop it," I said. It was a whisper. The Hudson River's smell was strong. It smelled like dead fish, trash, like all sorts of sludge.

The first shot sounded like thunder. Omar fell forward and hit the ground.

Everything else moved in slow motion. My head said to run to Omar, but my instincts said otherwise. I dove to the ground. That moment was so clear. The ground was rough brick and scratched my hands as I tried to break my fall. I heard the volley of bullets, most likely coming from the police. I heard the car horns. I heard people screaming. I heard a sickening thump as a body collapsed. I pressed my face against the brick, feeling blood on my hands. And then there was silence. The smell of gunpowder and the river reached me.

The first sound I heard was someone crying, then a dog barking, the cops screaming into their radios for an ambulance. I didn't hear the words "Officer down!" The call must have been for both Omar and his assailant. I made my way to my knees.

One of the policemen—Sanders, his nametag said—was making his way around all the tourists and joggers. When he got to me, I told him I was okay. Best I could come up with.

It was a beautiful day. The sun was shining, the temperature was warm, and there was a nice breeze coming off the water. It was a great day to spend at the park. Except there were two men on the ground, cops everywhere, and ambulance sirens in the distance. There was nothing I could do. I hated the feeling, the adrenaline surge with no place to go.

I wondered if, in the split second after he shot Omar, this man who lost his brother was happy. If he'd helped himself. Did he find the payment he was looking for?

If there was any hope for either of them, the cops would be working a lot harder than they were. The ambulance, lights flashing, pulled as close as it could get. After about five minutes, EMTs dressed in dark blue coveralls and sneakers loaded both bodies into the back of the truck. EMTs have to do everything in their power to keep someone alive until they get to the hospital. Then they can be pronounced dead. These guys worked, but it didn't look like they were working hard. The doors shut, and the truck drove off.

Eventually, I gave my statement. I had to show my P.I. license more than once. They called in my name to check on me. I told them everything. Everything except for the ten thousand dollars that everyone seemed to forget. The paper bag that sat under the bench just a few feet away. When I was cleared to leave, I took the bag with me. I walked back to my car, the New York skyline standing tall behind me.

I took my time driving out of the park, wondering what I was going to do. I didn't get on the Turnpike immediately; I drove through the streets of Jersey City. Kennedy Boulevard was crowded with people, and traffic was slow. This was where the terrorists had lived, the news said repeatedly. It was a ghetto. People strolled along, shopping in a Salvation Army store, and homeless people begged for money. Buses trucked along in front of me, trying to get people from Jersey City to anywhere. I found what I was looking for.

I double-parked in front of a Red Cross advertising a September 11th Fund. I walked in with the paper bag and gave it to the woman. When she opened it, her mouth formed a *wow*. Suddenly I felt hollow and left.

The best the police could figure, it was just dumb luck. They were probably right. The man who shot Omar had a note in his pocket. He wrote about how much he missed his brother. The letter ended saying he wanted to get as close to his brother as he could. It was signed Carl Burton. Between the note and the weapon, the police guessed he'd wanted to commit suicide. Killing Omar was a fluke. Burton saw a chance to exact some measure of revenge and took it. He'd said he didn't know about the money, which led to another problem: who had called Omar?

A few weeks later, I was flipping through the *Star Ledger* and read an article about people trying to scam victims of the tragedy. Maybe that's what happened to Omar. Maybe some asshole, preying on victims, didn't show up, or maybe he was there and left when the guns were pulled. I don't know.

Everyone kept saying the world was a different place. I went about my life. I worked cases. I took walks around the Rutgers campus and watched students party, laugh, and study. I didn't see cops with rifles. I didn't walk through a metal detector. I wanted to say the world was the same. For weeks, I had said I wasn't affected by it all. A week ago, I would have said I didn't know anyone who died because of the September 11th tragedy.

I wish I could keep saying it.

Notions of the Real World

by Dorothy Rellas
(Best Mid-Length Short Story, 2004)

One afternoon in late spring, I was listening to *I Love a Mystery* on the radio when my grandmother came into the living room and switched it off.

"You have to stop listening to those mystery dramas, Callie," she said, her voice unusually harsh. "It's all pretend. A nine-year-old girl needs notions about the *real* world. I doubt you even realize we're in a war."

I sat down in my chair. I knew a lot about the war. I couldn't help it. My grandfather switched on the news every night at dinner. If the real world was Pearl Harbor and the air raids in London and people dying in Europe, I didn't much like it. The war news gave me bad dreams. I didn't have bad dreams from *Gangbusters*, *The Shadow*, or *I Love a Mystery*, which was my favorite program.

My mother had given me a diary in January for my birthday. I wrote "nothing much happened today" about a hundred times, put it in my underwear drawer, and forgot about it. After my grandmother talked to me about my pretend world, I dug out the diary and wrote "Notions of the Real World" in big letters in the back of the book. I wasn't sure what that meant, exactly, so I wrote in, "Mystery stories are not the real world."

I lost my favorite radio program in June. That had to be a picture of the real world, so I rummaged in my dresser drawer for my diary. I wrote, "*I Love a Mystery* is going off the air, starting next week."

My mother had been working in a department store in Carter, a tiny town in the middle of Minnesota's lake country, for the past year. I'd been living with my grandparents in Minneapolis.

A letter came from my mother in August. My grandmother read it and then sat down next to me on the sun porch. She told me that my mother wanted me to live with her in Carter, starting in September. I hugged myself and grinned. Although I loved my grandparents, living with them wasn't like being with my mother.

"There's something else, Callie," my grandmother said, with a serious expression on her face. "You have a new father."

On the way up to my room, I tried to make sense out of my grandmother's words. I already had a father. How could I have more than one?

I took the diary out of the bottom of my dresser, opened it to the back page, and wrote: "Sometimes, bad things happen." I'd have to ask my best friend Heidi if she knew about having more than one father. Or maybe Sister Agnes, after school started the next week. Tears trickled down my cheek when I realized I might not ever see Heidi again. And I wouldn't be going to Saint Andrew's anymore. I erased the notion and wrote a new one: "Sometimes, when bad things happen, worse things follow."

In September, my mother and a man met me at the train station in Carter. "This is my almost-grown-up daughter Callie," my mother said. She put her arm around my shoulder and looked at me with that funny expression like the one I'd seen when she talked about my father moving to California without us. "And, Callie, this is your new father, Albert Olsen."

I snuggled closer to my mother.

"I want you to call me Albert, and I hope we'll be friends," he said. "I'm a deputy sheriff in Carter. Maybe someday I'll give you a ride in my squad car."

He was older than my mother, about my grandfather's age, I figured. His voice was deep, and he sounded very serious, almost stern. He reminded me a lot of the character Jack on *I Love a Mystery*. But I'd always imagined that, even though Jack seemed tough, he was really kind and gentle. Albert Olsen, scowling down at me, didn't look gentle. I decided I didn't like him very much.

When we arrived at the boarding house where my mother and Albert lived, she showed me their room upstairs in the corner near the stairway. Then she took my arm, and we walked along the hallway.

"This is the bathroom," she said, leading me past the door, "and then Mr. Shackleford's room. He's an old man but very nice." She walked to the last room that was in the opposite corner to her room. "You're a lucky girl—a room all your own." She opened the door.

The room was the size of a closet, hardly big enough to hold the bed and small dresser, but with windows on two sides. My heart dropped. There was no radio in the room.

After we put my things in drawers and hung my dresses and coats on pegs on one wall, my mother put her hands on my shoulders. "Albert is a nice, kind man, and he's very fond of both of us."

I wondered how he could be fond of me. We'd only met an hour ago.

My mother showed me through the rest of the house. She introduced me to the other borders and Mr. Shackleford at dinner. The two men who lived in the downstairs bedrooms were young and hardly glanced at me. Mr. Shackleford had a thatch of white hair and dozens of lines on his face. But he smiled and shook my hand as though I was a grownup.

Earlier, when my mother had taken me into the parlor, I noticed a big Philco radio against one wall. At dinner, I asked Mrs. Carlquist, who owned the boarding house, if I could listen to it. She said children shouldn't be allowed in a grand room like that.

"Anyone but a fool can see she's a well-behaved child and won't hurt anything," Mr. Shackleford said.

Mrs. Carlquist wouldn't change her mind.

I cried myself to sleep that night. I already missed my grandparents and Heidi. But mostly, I would never hear *Sherlock Holmes* and *Suspense* again. Or *The 11:30 Club* every Saturday, when they played records by Duke Ellington, Glenn Miller, and Benny Goodman. And if I didn't have a radio, how would I know if *I Love a Mystery* came back?

My mother had already registered me at Carter Elementary School. I gradually learned to like the boys and girls in the fifth grade and ignore Miss Kraft's comments about being *different* because I was from *the big city*.

It started snowing in mid-October. By November, the plows came rumbling past the house almost every day. There weren't any radiators in my room, and sometimes at night, when the wind whistled through the cracks around the windows, I couldn't sleep because I was so cold.

At dinner, Mr. Shackleford, Albert, and a couple of the borders who had the downstairs bedrooms talked about how much better things were going to be in the country, what with the opening of defense plants that made things for the war effort. Sometimes Mr. Shackleford asked me what I thought about the war. I didn't tell him that I knew nothing about it anymore, because I couldn't hear H.V. Kaltenborn or Gabriel Heatter or Boake Carter on the radio. I did mention the movie we'd seen in school about the Maginot Line. We had nothing to worry about, the announcer had said, because the Germans would never be able to invade France, which meant Hitler couldn't take over Europe.

"I'm not so sure," Mr. Shackleford said.

He gave me a book written by a reporter named William L. Shirer, *Berlin Diary*. I read from it every night before I went to bed. It took me a long time, and I didn't understand all the words. After I turned off the light, I'd sit staring out the side window, thinking about what must be going on in the rest of the world. It was hard to understand it all. It was so peaceful, here in this snow-white world. I was glad I lived in Minnesota, instead of in Paris or London or Berlin. I wrote a new notion in my diary: "It's a good thing to live in America."

It was the week after Thanksgiving when I came home from school one afternoon and found Mr. Shackleford's door partly open. I checked to see if he was in the bathroom, but he wasn't. Sometimes, his door didn't catch when he closed it. I knew he didn't like anyone being able to see inside his room, so I tapped and called to him. He didn't answer, and my tapping pushed the door open. He was lying on his bed.

"Do you want me to close the door?" I asked him. I called his name louder, because he was a little hard of hearing. "I'll close the door, if you want me to."

He didn't move. I crept forward. He had his eyes closed, and his face had a funny color, kind of gray. I'd never seen anyone who died before, but I knew Mr. Shackleford was dead. That night, I added a new notion to my diary: "It's very sad when nice people die."

After that, I felt shivery when I walked past his room. I imagined that his body was still lying on the bed. I finally asked my mother if I could use the door on the side of the house, and then I'd only have to go past his room on my way to and from the bathroom. The side door was toward the back of the upstairs. It led outside to a small porch and then down creaky steps to the backyard, where there was a garage and a shed. Mrs. Carlquist gave me a key, and I put it around my neck on a string, so I wouldn't lose it.

"You've been through some rough times this year," my mother said, a few nights later. "I guess we all have," she added, getting that faraway look in her eyes, "but you're so young, it must be hard to understand it all."

She stared at me until I wondered if she was sick or if something bad had happened to Albert, like maybe a bank robber had shot him. Just thinking of his not being around anymore, like old Mr. Shackleford, made me sad. I was surprised at feeling that way. I liked him a little better now, even though when he asked me if I'd mind if he adopted me, I said "No!" very loud and ran to my room.

"I'm making a lot more money in my new job," my mother was saying, leading me upstairs to her bedroom. "I can afford to buy a few things now, especially with Albert's salary, too."

We went inside her room, and on the table was a small Zenith radio. She had tied a red ribbon around it. "It's your Christmas present—a little early, but I know how much you've missed your mystery program with the three detectives and your music. Maybe later I'll buy you a phonograph." She took the radio into my room and plugged it in.

I didn't tell her that *I Love a Mystery* wasn't on the radio anymore, and I hadn't thought she knew about *The 11:30 Club*.

It was the first time I'd actually had a radio of my own. I could turn on anything I wanted. I started listening to Edward R. Murrow reporting the air raids from London again, too. When I heard the sirens in the background, I wondered what it would be like, having to rush to an air-raid shelter whenever the German bombers flew overhead. It made me sad, just like thinking of Mr. Shackleford. Or Albert maybe someday being shot.

Just before Christmas, Van and Mae Jones moved into Mr. Shackleford's room. Mr. Jones was a lineman with the telephone company, and his wife was a waitress at Osterberg's Restaurant on Main Street. They were around my mother's age. At first, I was afraid they'd all become friends, but I heard Albert tell my mother he didn't trust Van because he acted funny. At dinner, Van waved his arms a lot and twitched and hunched his shoulders. I thought Mae Jones was very pretty, and she was always nice to me.

They had some friends, two men and a girl. One of the men, Tommy, came over every morning to pick up Van and take him to work. He was even louder and more nervous than Van. They all went out together a lot, and sometimes Tommy would come upstairs when they came home. He always smiled at me. Not like Van, who raised his left eyebrow when he saw me, half closed his eyes, and puckered up his lips. He made me feel funny.

I could hear them laughing in their room. Sometimes even Mae joined in. But when she and Van were alone, I heard her crying out or moaning. She talked so softly I couldn't understand what she said. A few times, I heard loud thumps. It sounded like someone had fallen down.

My best friend in school was Dolores Youngdahl. One time, my mother let Dolores spend the night. Van and Mae were alone, and Dolores heard the commotion from the next room.

She snickered. "You know what they're doing, don't you?"

My cousin Estelle had told me all about what grownups did. I was glad it was dark, because Dolores couldn't see me blush. I hadn't exactly understood everything that Estelle told me, but I surely didn't want anyone to know that. According to her, adults thought it was fun, and they giggled and sighed a lot, and it made them happy.

"I don't think that's what they're doing," I told Dolores. "It sounds more like someone is falling down. Listen."

We were quiet for a few minutes, and I tried to picture what the noise was like.

"As though someone is slapping someone," I said, after a particularly sharp *crack* sounded. "And I think Mae is crying."

"You can do it in different ways," Dolores said. "You should see the animals on the farm. They do some crazy things."

The next day, after Dolores left, I took my diary out. I couldn't think of anything to write that would describe what I thought I'd heard. Finally, I wrote: "Sometimes, people act like animals."

Over the next few weeks, the noises gradually became louder. A couple of times, I heard Mae cry out. I was sure she'd said, "Stop, please, Van." But when I mentioned it to my mother, she told me not to pay any attention.

"Van is going into the Navy soon," my mother said. "After they leave, maybe Mrs. Carlquist will rent to someone like Mr. Shackleford again." Albert just frowned.

I couldn't ignore them. Tommy was over a lot, Mae was crying more often, and the smacks were getting louder. One morning, I was on my way to the bathroom just as Mae came out. One of her eyes was swollen shut, and she had a big red mark on her cheek.

I wondered if I should tell Albert or call the police from the wall phone downstairs. But my mother said I must have imagined it, because whenever she saw Mae, she looked the same as usual. I wanted to remind her that we hadn't seen Mae very often lately.

One night, Mrs. Carlquist said that Mr. and Mrs. Jones wouldn't be eating with us, because they'd gone out for dinner with their friends to celebrate Van going into the service in two days. It was so quiet in their room, I fell asleep right away. But during the night, I woke up and heard voices. One of them sounded like Mae's. She stood close to the wall, so I was able to make out a few of the words.

"No, I mean it, I'm leaving."

The slap was loud. The woman cried out, not really loud, but like the puppy I had when I was a little kid that cried for his mother.

"You bitch." Van's words were clear. He was standing close to her and to the wall. There were a couple of *cracks*, loud and close together.

Those finally stopped, but someone was crying and making a funny gurgling, gasping sound. Then there was a *thud*.

"Bitch," Van said again. He sounded more than just angry. There was hate in the word.

It was quiet for a few minutes. Then I heard a dull thumping and a shuffling noise, like something was being pushed across the carpet. Finally, there was the click of the door opening and a jostling sound.

I crept out of bed and opened my door just a bit. In the moonlight that came in through the windows along the side hall, I saw the outline of a man. He was pulling something heavy behind him. When he came to the side door at the rear, he opened it and dragged whatever he had to the outside stoop. I heard a dull *thump, thump, thump* down the steps.

The clock next to the window said two thirty. My mother and Albert were too far away to hear anything, and only the empty parlor and dining room were under the side hallway. I remembered one of my notions. This was something bad, I was sure of it.

I put on my snowsuit over my pajamas, grabbed the string with the key on it, and went out to the hall. I half expected to run into Tommy or maybe one of Van's other friends on my rush to the side door. But the hall was empty. I opened the door leading outside and saw Van Jones in the moonlight. He was downstairs, carrying a bundle over his shoulder, slowly walking through the backyard toward the garage and shed. My boots were next to the door. I put them on fast and went outside, just as Van Jones went inside the shed. I sped down the steps.

It wasn't snowing, but a cold wind swooped down from the North Pole, and it went right through my snowsuit. That afternoon, one of the boys who did odd jobs for Mrs. Carlquist had shoveled the snow off the path. Shrubs bordered it, and the sidewalk was on the other side. I stayed close to the shrubs. In case Van came out of the shed, I'd have a place to dart into and hide, so he wouldn't see me. When he came outside again and started walking toward me, I hid. He slipped on the ice when he was next to me, caught himself, and said some words I'd never heard before.

Later, when I crawled back into bed, there was no noise from the room next door. I guess I slept a little, but I heard Tommy pull up at the usual time before dawn to pick Van up for work. I fell into a deep sleep after that, and my mother had to waken me for school.

I thought of Van and Mae all day. After school, I peeped inside their room, but it was empty. I tried to imagine what Jack, Doc, and Reggie would do on *I Love a Mystery*. They were brave and, most important, strong. I wasn't either one. I knew I couldn't wait for Mae to come home from work. *If* she came home. There was nothing else to do but see what Van had put in the shed. I'd have to do that before Van and Tommy returned from work. They'd take the bundle and put it in Tommy's car. Then I'd never know what had happened in Mr. Shackleford's room.

When I walked into the house, Mrs. Carlquist was just leaving.

"Going to the grocery store and then to the dairy," she said. "Think you'll be all right alone?"

I nodded, waited until she was out of sight, and then went outdoors and to the shed.

My heart was pounding when I opened the door. The bundle was a bedspread, and it was on the shed floor. I wasn't sure how I was going to unwrap it to see what was inside. I didn't want to think it could be Mae Jones. But if it was, at least she'd spent the night in the shed under the bedspread. I just hoped she wasn't hurt so bad that I wouldn't be able to get her inside the house before Van came home at four. She could go to bed for a while and have tea and rice with cream and sugar on it until she felt better. I'd even let her sleep in my bed, if she didn't want to go back to her room.

I finally managed to unwrap the bedspread enough to see. It was Mae Jones. My heart thudded, and my hands started shaking. I'd recognized that Mister Shackleford was dead as soon as I saw him. Mae's face was swollen and discolored, and I knew she was dead, too.

When I was back inside the house, I wanted to rush upstairs and write a new notion in my diary. But the clock on the dining-room buffet said three forty-five. Van and Tommy would be home at any time. The notion would have to wait.

There was a card with my mother's number at the plant and the sheriff's number on the wall over the telephone. I dragged a footstool in from the parlor and positioned it in front of the wall phone. No use calling my mother. She'd probably just tell me to mind my own business. I dialed the Sheriff's Department. A gruff voice answered, and I told him I needed to talk to Albert Olsen.

"He ain't here. Who is this?"

I was tongue-tied for a minute. Then I blurted out, "His daughter."

The front door opened, and I felt my legs go weak. Van Jones and Tommy walked in.

The man at the Sheriff's Department was still talking. "Should be back in about fifteen minutes. I'll tell him to call you," he said, his voice much softer.

"Who you talkin' to?" Van asked me.

I hung up, jumped down from the stool, and began pushing it back into the parlor. Van followed me inside and grabbed my arm.

"I asked you a question, kid. Who was that on the phone?"

Everyone said I was tall for my age, but Van towered over me. He was even taller than Albert.

"My mother," I said, trying to talk loud, so he wouldn't know how scared I was. "I have to call her if I'm in the house alone."

"Hey, little girl is all alone here," he said. In the doorway, I saw Tommy frown.

I shouldn't have told them about no one being home. My heart was really hammering now.

"Where's old lady Carlquist?"

I gulped. "She went to the grocery store. She'll be right back."

"Wanna play a little game?" he asked me.

I nodded.

"Hide in here. Be real quiet." He shoved me toward the big davenport along the wall. "We'll be watching, so don't cheat, understand?"

"What's the game?"

He looked irritated. "If you stay in here till I tell you to come out, you get a prize."

The two went into the hall, closed the door to the parlor, and a minute later I heard a key turn in the lock. I sat on the davenport and hugged myself to keep from shaking. Tommy's and Van's voices were low, and I couldn't understand what they said. But when another door closed, I knew they'd gone outside.

Through the net curtains on the front windows, I watched Tommy and Van walk to the car parked at the curb. They backed it up and around the corner onto the side street, until I couldn't see it anymore. I knew what they'd do. Put Mae Jones' body in the back seat and take her someplace. Then they'd come back for me.

My grandmother always said that, in case of big trouble, ask God for help. I started praying. When nothing happened, I walked around the room. The dining room was on the other side of one wall. From the dining-room table, I'd noticed double doors that led into the parlor. There was a rod that clicked into the floor on one, but the other had a door handle. On the parlor side, a big wardrobe hid the doors. If I could shove it aside, maybe I could get out and call my mother before Van and Tommy came back.

I put my shoulder against one side of the big piece of furniture, not really thinking I'd have the strength to budge it. But it must have been empty, because gradually it moved. I pushed it along the wall, until I could see one of the doors behind it. At the same time, I heard the phone ring.

If it was Albert, it wouldn't do any good. I'd never get the door open in time. I finally moved the wardrobe past one door and saw that, if either door could be opened, it would be the other one, the one with the handle on it. The phone stopped ringing.

I stationed myself on the other side of the wardrobe and began pushing in the opposite direction. Perspiration was rolling down my cheeks. Or maybe it was tears, because I was crying by this time. I'd seen enough movies to know that Van killed Mae by either hitting her or strangling her. I knew he'd do the same thing to me.

Little by little, the wardrobe moved across the wall, until I finally had it past the other door. I hardly breathed when I turned the handle. The door swung open, just barely grazing the end of the wardrobe. I rushed out into the hall and stared up at the phone. I didn't have the footstool, the door into the parlor from the hall was locked, and there was no key.

"Well, well, look at Miss Smarty Pants."

I wheeled around. Van was coming downstairs from his room, a suitcase in his hand, Tommy behind him.

"How'd you like to go for a little ride, kid?" He smiled at me, and for the first time I noticed his teeth were yellow.

"Grab her, Tommy," he said and headed for the front door.

Tommy took hold of my arm, and I made myself go limp. But for Tommy, it didn't matter. He was even bigger than Van, and he just picked me up.

It had started snowing, and the wind whirled the flakes around through the late-afternoon gloom. Tommy held me against him like he was carrying a bag of groceries. I could feel the cold seeping through my sweater. Halfway to the car, the wind picked up, whistling through the leafless trees in Mrs. Carlquist's front yard. One of the whistling sounds was followed by tires squealing and a sharp *crack*.

"Drop the kid," a voice boomed out. It sounded just like Jack on *I Love a Mystery*.

"What the hell's goin' on?" Tommy hugged me close and hunched down behind a snowbank.

"Put her down," the voice said again. "I've got a gun, and I'll use it if I have to."

Tommy must have been off balance, because when I began squirming around, he dropped me. I fell into snow that was colder than anything I'd ever felt in my life.

"It's the cops," Van yelled. "Get the kid into the car!"

Tommy hesitated for a second and then took off running. "Forget her! Let's get out of here!"

Two more cars shrieked to a stop in front of the house.

I stopped shaking all of a sudden and felt sleepy. I'd heard of people freezing in the snow, but I hadn't been out that long—had I? Or maybe I was fainting. Heidi had fainted in school once. Then someone wrapped a heavy jacket with fur inside around me.

"The kid all right?" a man asked.

I felt myself being picked up.

"She'll be okay." Albert's booming voice made me open my eyes. "I promised you a ride in my squad car, remember?" he said, smiling down at me. "I think we'll do that now, okay?"

I tried to nod, but he held me so close I couldn't move my head. He put me in the back seat of his squad car.

"Just lie down. I'll get you to the hospital," he said.

As soon as the car moved, I sat up. Albert drove very fast, but it didn't seem much different than riding in any car—except for the sound of the siren.

A doctor looked me over and said I was okay, so Albert drove us to the Sheriff's Department, which was in a small building next to the train depot. When we went inside, Van Jones and Tommy stood behind the counter. They had handcuffs on. Van glared at me.

"My name is Nels," the sheriff told me, after they'd taken Van and Tommy away. "Glad everything turned out all right." He frowned. "I didn't know you had a daughter, Al."

Albert turned to me and winked. "Oh, yes, and a very brave, very smart one. She telephoned and left a message to call my daughter. When I called the house and no one answered, I knew something was wrong." He kissed me on the cheek. "Now let's you and Nels and me go into the back room, and you can tell us what happened."

On the way home, Albert stopped at Fitzhugh's, and I had a strawberry soda, which was my very favorite. And at dinner, everyone asked me questions, even the two young men who lived on the first floor. It was like on *I Love a Mystery*, when Doc, Jack, and Reggie explain what happened.

When I went upstairs to my room, I took out my diary. I wondered if my grandmother would think I'd learned anything about the real world since she switched off the radio. I looked over my notions. I'd been sure that bad things happened when my mother announced that I had a new father and I had to leave St. Andrew's. But I decided Albert wasn't so bad, after all. I wrote: "Sometimes, what looks bad turns out to be good."

Then I remembered how Edward R. Murrow sounded when he talked about the people who were killed in the air raids in London, and Mr. Shackleford and Mae Jones dying. I added another notion: "Sometimes, very bad things happen to nice people."

I put away my diary. Maybe someday I'd be able to write down why it all had happened.

Viscery

by Sandy Balzo
(Best Mid-Length Short Story, 2005)

The dream was in living color, and she was gorgeous: blond, blue-eyed, and young—maybe twenty to my thirty-three. And svelte, a hundred and ten pounds against my one seventy-five.

She also was tall, though since we were horizontal it was hard to be certain about that. The top of her head came up to my nose, putting her about five inches shorter than my six-one, assuming we were lined up toe-to-toe. Which we no longer were, since she was slipping slowly down my torso, her blond hair leaving my face to brush my neck, then my chest, then my belly, then—

I woke up startled, not sure what had awakened me so abruptly but ready to wreak vengeance on whatever it was that had, whether human or mechanical.

That's when I realized I'd been drugged.

I lay still for a moment, trying hard to concentrate on the white ceiling fan above me. My vision was blurry, and my limbs felt heavy, weighted down. I tried to shift position and realized it was the covers of the bed that were pinning me. The blanket and sheet were pulled up to my neck and tucked in snug on each side, like I'd slipped into the bed unseen as it was being made.

I blinked, then blinked again, trying to clear my hazy vision. A woman loomed over me suddenly, her face close to mine, a macabre reprisal of my dream—the *early* moments of my dream, thank the Lord, for this woman was *not* the woman of my dreams.

No, this woman was very old and very ugly. White hair, faded eyes, and on one cheek a nickel-sized brown mole that looked like it could crawl away under its own power. I turned my head away as I realized with horror that she intended to kiss me. The kiss landed on my ear, rather than my lips. Repulsed even so, I rolled sideways, intending to dislodge the covers and hit the floor running.

Sluggish from the drug, I hit the floor, all right, but head-first and still tangled in the blanket. As I struggled to free myself, the woman appeared next to me, extending a pale, bony hand.

I shrank away from her touch. "What do you want?" I croaked. My voice sounded hoarse and uneven, though perhaps that was because my ears seemed stuffed with cotton.

What the hell had they given me?

And who were *they*?

And what did they want?

The last thing I remembered was kissing Sarah and our baby girl Kathleen goodbye and driving to work at the bank. My car was a just-off-the-assembly-line '62 Oldsmobile Ninety-Eight, and I clearly remembered parking it snug along the wall in the executive parking ramp, in order to leave as much space as possible between it and Hal Schultz's Caddie. Mr. Schultz was our bank president, and he had the habit of opening his Cadillac's driver-side door with the reckless abandon of the very rich and very privileged.

When I'd been driving my old '57 Chevy, I hadn't minded as much. And truth be told, it wouldn't have done my career or my Chevy any good to complain, anyway.

But now, with my promotion secure and the Buick paid for in cash, I did mind. I had bought the car with the bonus I'd gotten when I'd been named SVP. That's *Senior* Vice President, which is the step above First Vice President, which is the step above plain old Vice President, which is the step above Assistant Vice President. Sunset Bank, as a friend of mine likes to point out, has more VPs than customers.

Anyway, I'd been through all the ranks and now was second-in-command, the youngest man ever to have achieved that post, with all the stock options and indemnifications to prove it.

But I digress.

So I'd parked my car and then…what?

I didn't know.

The crone's voice interrupted my drug-induced reverie. "I'm going to help you up, and then we're going to take a bath."

That got me moving. "The hell we are," I said, shoving her hard. She fell backwards on her rump, and I managed to get myself untangled and onto my feet.

The woman crawled a couple of steps toward the door. I felt bad for pushing her, but I'd been pushed myself, far beyond my limits.

"You've hurt me, John." She said it matter-of-factly, like she was used to being hurt.

She knew my name, too, which told me that, whatever had happened, whoever had taken me, it hadn't been random. I'd been targeted for this abduction. But why?

The logical answer, of course, was my new job, the one I'd been flashing around like a giggly girl with an engagement ring: *Look at me, I'm a senior vice president! Look at my car! Look at my benefits package!*

What an idiot. Bank executives already were attractive targets for kidnappers, banks having money and all, and I'd practically stood on a street corner with my thumb stuck out, waiting to be picked up.

But vague regret over my stupidity was about as far as my brain would take me in its current addled state. And my body wasn't doing much better. In fact, the surge of energy that had gotten me upright had left me even weaker in its wake.

So much so that, while I'd been ruminating, the old lady was already up and at the door. "I'm going to have to lock you in, John. I don't want to do that."

She sounded like she meant it. Probably thinking about that bath we were missing.

"Then don't," I said, finally willing myself the four steps across the room toward her.

She stepped into the hall, putting the edge of the open door between us. "I'm sorry, but you leave me no choice."

She shook her head wearily, and her necklace and the loose flesh beneath it swung back and forth in time to the movement.

I blinked my eyes twice, and the haze cleared for a moment. Dangling on the chain around her neck was a wedding ring. *My* wedding ring. I grabbed it and yanked, breaking the chain. "That's *mine*, damn it," I yelled, suddenly beside myself with fury, a merciful break from the fear and confusion. "How dare you touch me, how dare—"

That's when I realized I was standing there in my undershorts. Not only had the old crone taken my wedding ring from my finger while I was unconscious, she had undressed me. The thought made me sick.

I raised my fist, the ring still clutched in it. I'm not sure if I really would have punched her, but she didn't give me the chance. She slammed the door in my face, and I heard the lock turn.

She didn't move away, though. "You don't need that ring," she hissed from the other side. "And your marriage? Your wife? You can forget them, too, John."

I backed away, nearly tripping over the bed in my eagerness to escape the malignancy that seemed to seep right through the door.

Jesus. Did they have Sarah, too? But where were they holding her? Did they mean to kill her? Or me? Or both of us?

I looked at the wedding ring in my hand.

Sarah. Quite literally the blue-eyed blond girl of my dreams, though that was the twenty-year-old Sarah. The Sarah I'd met in college.

Now, some nine years later, she was still just as beautiful, if a little less... uninhibited. The fact that I still dreamed of her and no one else never failed to stagger me.

Sarah. I slipped the ring on my finger. "Will I ever see you again?" I whispered.

And Kathleen. What would become of our baby, if both Sarah and I were…gone? My brother would take her in and love her, I knew. But Kathleen would grow up never knowing her parents, not able to remember so much as a trip to the zoo or a hug or a kiss from us. I imagined Kathleen poring over yellowed baby pictures, desperately trying to manufacture memories to fit the photos.

I knew I was wallowing, but even the idea of Kathleen growing up without us wasn't nearly as bad as the alternative, the thought I refused to entertain: that they had our baby, too, and meant her harm.

No. Thinking of that would do me little good and would do Sarah and Kathleen even less. But I did need to think—to think of a way out.

I sat down on the bed.

I'd been kidnapped—that much was clear. I wondered how many people had been involved. The woman had to have at least one male accomplice. Even if she had managed to undress me, she wouldn't have been able to move me while I was unconscious.

So what was her partner doing right now?

Making a ransom demand?

And what would the bank do in response?

If Schultz couldn't be bothered not to bash my car door with his every day, could he be bothered to hand over a hundred thousand—or more—in ransom?

A knock at the door made me jump up—or try to. This exertion/exhaustion was becoming a tiresome cycle. I heaved myself off the bed and toward the door. "Who's there?"

The old woman or the accomplice? The Lady or the Tiger—though in this case they both were losing propositions.

"I have your medication."

Medication? Did she really think I was going to let her drug me voluntarily?

Apparently so. "You'll feel better if you take it," the crone crooned.

I'd feel better only when I was out of there, when I'd found Sarah and knew that she and our baby were safe. But for now, I needed to play along.

The fact that the old woman wanted me to take another dose meant the current one must be wearing off. So, bad as I still felt, there wouldn't be a better time to make a break for it.

"All right," I said, purposely making my voice weak. "I *am* feeling lousy."

"Of course you are," she said, fiddling with the lock. "That's because you got so angry. You mustn't—"

She opened the door.

I stepped behind it, using the solid wood as a shield like she had, and checked behind her for her accomplice. No one.

She came in with a glass of water. I noticed it was a plastic glass, oxymoronic as that sounded, probably so I couldn't break it and gain a weapon. And God knows I'd gladly gut the hag if it would get me home.

The old woman held the glass out to me with one hand and reached into her voluminous apron pocket with the other.

That's when I struck, knocking the glass out of her hand and bolting from the room. My right hip was hurting, probably from the fall out of the bed. I could hear the old woman yelling my name as I hightailed it down the hall and into a living room.

My vision was still hazy, and I searched frantically for a door. There. On the far wall next to the television set.

I dashed across the room and undid the door chain. Then I turned the knob and pulled. The door stayed shut. I checked the lock button in the doorknob. It was popped out, meaning the door was unlocked. And the knob turned easily enough, but still the door wouldn't open. What the hell?

I jiggled the knob.

"You can't get out." The old woman was right behind me. I could feel her attic-stale breath on the back of my neck.

I pulled frantically at the door again, only then noticing a third lock. One that could be opened only with a key.

"You can't get out," the old woman repeated. "You might as well sit down on the couch. I'll get your breakfast." Then she walked away.

I slumped against the door. Somehow the fact that she could go off to make breakfast, secure in the knowledge that I was trapped, was more demoralizing than anything to date.

She came back in with a Melmac coffee cup. "Sit down on the couch," she said again.

I obeyed. I didn't know what else to do.

"Here's your coffee. Not too hot, so you won't burn yourself. Or me." A ghost of a smile, exposing her yellowing teeth and crinkling the hideous mole on her cheek. I took the coffee, and she turned and left me again.

I set the cup on the end table. Did she think I was stupid? The coffee had to be drugged.

The woman came back into the room. "You need to calm down, you know. Would you like the television on?" I didn't answer, but she crossed the room to a Zenith and punched a couple of buttons anyway. Then she went back to what I presumed was the kitchen.

That got me to thinking about where *I* might be.

Ignoring the game show on the screen, I looked around the room for a newspaper or anything that would tell me whether I was still in Sunset. At least then, assuming I could get my hands on a phone, I could give the police a place to start.

But no newspaper, no telephone, no nothing. I eyed the TV set—a station ID might give me the information I needed.

But Garry Moore presiding over *I've Got a Secret* wasn't going to help much. Pushing myself up off the couch and across the room to the television, I checked behind me for the old woman before changing the channel.

A Tom and Jerry cartoon. Kathleen's favorite, but it wasn't going to tell me where I was. I pressed on past a Nile River travelogue and *The Guiding Light*.

Then an anchorman appeared on the screen. That stopped me short. News in the morning meant something big must have happened. I started to punch the volume up, but an age-spotted hand reached in and shut the set off.

"You have no need to be watching that."

The way she said it made me certain they had no intention of letting me go. Ransom or not.

The old lady had carried in a TV table topped with a plate of bacon and eggs and set it down. I'd been so engrossed in changing channels, I hadn't even heard her. I would have to be more careful.

"Sit on the couch, and I'll put this in front of you," she said.

Again, I did what I was told. For now. My plan was to conserve my strength, so I'd be ready when an opportunity to escape presented itself. Maybe it would be when the mail was delivered, or a repairman came. Whatever, it had to be before the old lady's accomplice returned.

She set the TV table in front of me. "Should I cut up your eggs?"

She assumed I'd drunk the coffee, and the drugs were taking effect. "Yes," I mumbled, playing along. If I could get my hands on a knife, maybe I could force her to tell me where Sarah was before I made my escape.

But when she pulled the linty knife out of her apron pocket, it was a plastic non-serrated one that wouldn't cause so much as a papercut. I could do more damage with a manila file folder.

The old woman sawed the two fried eggs and bacon into a runny mess and surveyed me. "Do you need me to feed you?"

Ugh. Playing drugged or not, that was *not* going to happen. "No, I can do it." I picked up the fork.

As I did so, she grabbed my other hand. "John, I need to have that ring back."

She was talking about the wedding ring, Sarah's and mine. I tried to pull my hand away from her, but the old crone was surprisingly strong.

"I'll keep it safe for you," she promised.

Sure, by hanging it around that withered old neck of yours again, I thought. My head was pounding, and anger surged. Almost without thinking, I plunged the fork into the back of her hand as she pawed at my fingers.

She screamed and let go.

I was up like a flash, searching for another way out. Behind me I could hear the old woman, in the kitchen and on the phone, urging someone to get help. Her accomplice, of course. If I didn't get out now, I knew I never would.

The place was like a jail, though, every window barred with decorative wrought iron. The only one without the fleur-de-lis prison bars was the picture window. I would have to go through it.

Looking around the room for something to break the glass, I settled on a small armchair. Problem was, my strength was waning again, and I wasn't sure if I could pick up the chair, much less throw it through the window.

As I struggled with it, I heard the old woman behind me. By sheer strength of will—or, perhaps, sheer panic—I picked up the chair and put it through the window. As the crone's fingernails clawed at my back, I scrambled awkwardly through, landing hard on the wooden porch beyond.

I pulled myself up with the help of the porch railing. Behind me, I could hear the crone unlocking the door. She might be too old to make it through the window, but she didn't have to. She had a key to the door.

As I turned to barrel down the porch steps, the old woman already was pushing her way through the aluminum storm door. One step down, I turned and caught a glimpse of something reflected obliquely in the mirrored glass of the open door.

It stopped me cold.

Sarah.

She was standing on the porch to the right of the door, her hair covered in pellets of shattered glass. She appeared unharmed.

"Sarah." I said it aloud this time, but she didn't answer, didn't move toward me. She seemed lost. Drugged, of course.

I reached up and grabbed her by the arm. "Sarah, we have to get away from here."

Confused, she tried to twist away from me. I wondered where they had kept her, and how she had gotten away. I wondered if Kathleen was safe. But there was no time to ask now. We had to run.

I pulled at Sarah again, managing to propel her down the one step to me. But that was as far as we got. The old woman had Sarah's other arm, the two of us playing tug-of-war with my wife as the human rope.

What's worse, I was losing. With one gigantic effort, the old woman yanked Sarah back up and away from the edge of the porch.

I lost my grip and fell back, just managing to catch myself on the stair railing. My heart was thudding and my ears were ringing as I tried to climb back up. Meanwhile, the crone was trying to push Sarah into the house.

As I got to them, the ringing in my ears turned into a high-pitched wail. Was it Sarah screaming? The old woman keening insanely? I couldn't tell. Everything was bedlam.

Then, suddenly, the old woman let go of Sarah and backed off.

I didn't understand why, until I saw the police car pull up in front of the house.

It hadn't been ringing or wailing, screaming or keening I'd been hearing, but the siren of the approaching squad car. Someone must have heard the commotion and called the police. As I glanced at the house next door, I saw a curtain twitch. God bless nosy neighbors.

Two officers get out of the squad car.

I took a deep, grateful breath and went to Sarah. "Honey, it's okay. We're safe." I tried to kiss her, but she turned away.

"Let her go," from one of the cops.

I did as he asked, affected more by the look of revulsion on Sarah's face than by the barked order.

The officers came around their car, and I unsteadily descended the porch steps to meet them.

"Thank God you're here," I told an officer with sandy hair. "This woman is holding me against my will. My wife and I—"

But the burly officer grasped my arm and started to tow me toward the house. "C'mon, sir. Let's go inside."

"You don't understand," I said, trying desperately to shake him off. "I've been kidnapped. I'm John Collins, Senior Vice President of Sunset Bank."

"Sure." He kept right on walking, dragging me along with him back up the porch steps.

What in the hell was going on? I felt like I'd fallen into an episode of *The Twilight Zone*. Rod Sterling would appear any moment. Or even better, Allen Funt, ordering me to "Smile, you're on *Candid Camera!*"

I knew I wasn't thinking clearly, but I also knew I had to do something. Now.

Yanking my arm free at the top of the steps, I lost my balance and landed hard on one knee in front of Sarah. I took her hand. "Please, honey. Tell them who I am."

But, again, she wouldn't look at me.

"Sarah. Don't you know me, honey?"

The beautiful blue eyes—Sarah's eyes—turned toward me. They were filled with tears. "I know you, Daddy."

Daddy?

As the officer walked me into the house, I caught sight of a reflection in the mirrored storm door. A big, sandy-haired man in police uniform. And a shriveled, shuffling old man in his underwear.

Daddy?

Secondhand Shoe

by Patricia Harrington
(Best Flash Story, 2006)

"She has such cold eyes. Whatever do you see in her?"

Cassie overheard the new woman in her man's life and waited for Bernard to say something by way of protest. Instead, he said, "Oh, she's not so bad."

For a moment, Cassie felt blinded by his betrayal. Then an intense hatred overtook her, but not for Bernard. For *that woman*. Cassie's love for Bernard remained unabated. She wouldn't let him cast her aside like a secondhand shoe.

Cold eyes? How could he let that woman speak that way? He was such a fool. Cassie briefly closed her eyes to shut out the sight of them. Ruefully, she acknowledged that it was because of Bernard's gullibility—his simple goodness—that she loved him. That was the very quality that had attracted Cassie to him and now drew that woman, too.

Cassie couldn't stand to watch anymore and slipped away, knowing in the very reaches of her soul that she must protect Bernard from this new woman…for his own good.

Oh, why couldn't he see through her guile?

The next night, Cassie waited for the woman to pull into the driveway below the house. The woman got out of the car and walked on stiletto-thin heels, carrying a bag of groceries toward the dimly lit front porch. Cassie kept well back, hidden in the dark at the top of the stairs, coldly watching the woman approach.

When she reached the top of the stairs, her right foot poised to step onto the porch, Cassie lunged with a furious cry. The woman screamed and fell backward, her arms flailing as she twisted to catch her balance. She careened over the wrought-iron railing and then lay crumpled and silent on the sidewalk below, the groceries scattered around her.

Cassie meowed once, and then—with a low, throbbing purr—padded silently into the shadows to wait for Bernard by the back door.

Cranked

by Bill Crider
(Best Mid-Length Story, 2007)

After the meth lab exploded, Karla decided she'd walk to the truck stop.

It wasn't her fault that some moron had fired a shotgun and blown the place up. Karla had been lucky, having jumped out a window before the blast, but she'd been cut by flying glass, and the hair on the back of her head was a little bit singed.

She still looked pretty damned good, though, better than any of the skanks at the truck stop, that was for sure. She knew she wouldn't have any trouble getting a ride out of town, and she might be able to get away before anybody found out she was still alive.

She didn't think anybody else who'd been in the meth lab was alive. The place had gone up in flames just seconds after the explosion.

Karla felt a little bad about that, but none of it would've happened in the first place if that drug task-force Nazi hadn't sent her in there with a wire. Whatever had happened, she figured the whole thing was on him.

Not that he'd see it that way, the self-righteous bastard.

Karla didn't like walking in the heat and humidity. The mosquitos sang around her ears, and her whole face felt greasy. She could still smell the cat-piss odor of the meth lab, and she supposed the stink was in her clothes and hair. She didn't feel a personal feminine freshness, either.

But she had to stay off the road, so it would take her a while to get to the highway. She'd still look better than those truck-stop hoes, anyway.

She heard sirens in the distance and walked back farther into the trees. First came a sheriff's car, and before long a couple of fire trucks came tearing along the county road, dragging rooster-tails of dust behind them. Karla didn't think the fire trucks would do much good, not the way the house had been burning. As if she cared.

Lloyd hadn't taken his meds for two days, and he was feeling damned sharp, considering. He was fully dressed under the covers, except for his shoes, which were stuck under the side of the bed. He thought he was looking good, and he'd look even better when he put his teeth in.

Lloyd knew that, in his case, *better* was a relative term, but at least with his teeth in he'd look a little less like Gabby Hayes.

His daughter Lou came into the room, like she did every day when she got off work. She looked a little disappointed, as usual, that Lloyd hadn't kicked off yet.

She was a skinny blonde, but the color was out of some bottle. She'd had brown hair as a kid, but it had gone gray early, not like Lloyd's, which still had a lot of black in it even though he was seventy-six. Lou had her mother's disposition. That wasn't a recommendation.

"How're you today, Daddy?" she said, the same as every day.

Usually, Lloyd could hardly answer, because his mind was so fuzzed with the drugs. They gave them to everybody in the Home, because they liked to have the inmates nice and quiet all the time. In a lucid moment, Lloyd had just pretended to take the shit and spit it out later. After two days, he was almost back to normal.

But in Lloyd's case, *normal*—like *good*—was a relative term. Lloyd had never liked to play by the rules, which was how he'd wound up in the Home. He'd stayed drunk for a week and a half after the doctor had told him what was wrong, and Lou had gotten him committed. He'd been a handful at home, he knew that, so he didn't blame her much. By the time he was halfway sobered up, they'd got him full of the meds, and he was trapped.

He knew he hadn't led a godly life, and maybe this was his punishment for all the things he'd done before he got sent to the pen that time. He'd put that behind him after his release, but things had a way of catching up with a man.

He'd been a healthy, strong guy for most of his life, and once in the pen he'd jerked an ax handle away from a building tender who'd knocked his teeth out with it. Lloyd had cold-cocked the building tender with the ax handle and spent two weeks in the cooler, but it had been worth it. His false teeth always reminded him of that building tender, the bastard.

"Daddy?" Lou said.

Lloyd came back from wherever he'd been and looked at his daughter with what he figured was the right amount of confusion and distrust.

"Sure could use a Co' Cola," he said.

Lou looked at him sternly, the bitch. She hadn't sprung for so much as a single Co' Cola since he'd been in the Home, nor even a candy bar. Made him spend his own money, of which there was damn little left.

"Some change in the drawer," he said.

Lou sighed. She walked over to the cheap nightstand by the bed and pulled open the drawer. Three quarters lay in the bottom. She glanced down at them and then at Lloyd, who gave her a pathetic, pleading look.

"Oh, all right," she said.

She took the quarters from the drawer and left the room to go to the soft-drink machine, which was in the big rec room, quite a distance from Lloyd's own room.

As soon as she cleared the door, Lloyd sat up, turned around, and put on the old black walking shoes he'd bought at Walmart. He liked them because of the Velcro straps.

He stood up and looked over at the other bed, where a dried-up fella named Jones lay on his back with his eyes and mouth wide open. He was just about mummified. In the month and a half he'd been in the Home, Lloyd had never heard Jones say a word.

"I'm bustin' outta this joint," Lloyd told Jones.

Jones didn't respond. Maybe he really was a mummy. Lloyd didn't waste any more time on him. As he'd hoped, Lou had left her purse on the room's only chair.

Lloyd took her billfold out and helped himself to the money inside, only twenty-one dollars. It would have to do, and he figured she owed it to him.

He also helped himself to her car keys. Then he put the purse back down and went out into the hallway. He looked both ways. Nobody in sight. There was an exit door at the end of the hall to his left, and he didn't think it was alarmed. What with the drugs, nobody ever tried to leave, so there was no need to go to the trouble and expense of wiring the doors.

Lloyd walked down the hall, his rubber soles squeaking on the linoleum floor. He hesitated for a second when he came to the door, then took hold of the bar and pushed. The door opened and no alarm sounded, so Lloyd slipped out and let the door close silently behind him. He looked around the parking lot until he saw Lou's old Chevy Malibu. A piece of crap, but it was all he had.

He took his teeth out of his pocket and stuck them in his mouth, moving them around until they felt right. When they did, he gave a porcelain grin. It felt good.

Whistling "San Antonio Rose," Lloyd headed for the Malibu, grinning again as he thought of the look on Lou's face when she got back to the room and found him gone.

The grin faded when he saw that the needle on the Chevy's gas gauge was sitting on the red E. Shit. He'd have to buy gas, and he didn't have but twenty-one dollars. He could remember when you could fill the tank for a hell of a lot less than five bucks, but not anymore. Well, he'd worry about that later. He wheeled out of the parking lot and headed for the truck stop.

Royce Evans and Burl Isom were tooling along in Royce's rattletrap Dodge Ram pickup. They looked a lot like the two dumbasses in the Dodge ads on TV, but they didn't know it. They thought they looked like George Clooney and Brad Pitt in *Ocean's Twelve*, only taller.

It was the crystal that gave them that illusion, which is one reason they liked to amp up. They had plenty of other reasons, too, but that one was good enough.

Trouble was, staying amped cost money, and Royce and Burl didn't have any.

"Shit," Royce said, as he drove the Dodge into and out of a chug hole, causing him and Burl to bounce their heads off the roof. Both of them laughed like monkeys.

"Where we gonna get us some money?" Burl said, when the pickup had stopped rocking. It could have used new shocks, but fat chance that Royce would spend any money on something like that.

"Shit if I know," Royce said. "Can't get it from Karla. She's in jail."

Karla worked for a housecleaning service called the Kweens of Kleen. She'd let Royce into a couple of houses, and he'd pilfered a thing or two. Karla had taken the fall for him, which was how she'd wound up as an informant for the county's one-man drug task force.

"We ought do what Clooney would do, him and Brad Pitt," Royce said. "Knock over a casino or something."

"Closest one's Coushatta," Burl said. "We could be there in an hour, but them damn Innians would tomahawk us if we tried it."

"Fuck the Innians. We could take 'em. But we ain't got an hour to spare. Let's knock over the truck stop."

"How we gonna do that?"

"Check this out," Royce said.

He leaned over and opened the glove compartment. A Glock niner slid out and bounced off the floor of the truck.

"Holy shit," Burl said, picking it up. He looked it over and put it back in the glove compartment. "Where'd you get that thing at?"

"Stole it off a dead Innian," Royce said, and he and Burl went off on another laughing jag.

After he managed to get control of himself, Burl said, "Goddamn, Royce, you kill me. You are one funny sonuvabitch."

He reached out and slugged Royce in the right arm, and Royce lost his grip on the steering wheel. The truck slewed from one side of the road to another, the headlight beams shining into the ditches and fields.

Royce fought the wheel, but he couldn't keep the truck out of the ditch. It went down the steep side, ripping through the tall weeds, tilting dangerously. Just before it hit the bottom, Royce clamped both hands on the wheel and wrenched hard to the left. For several seconds, the truck cruised along the side of the ditch. Burl stuck his head out the window and howled like a ruptured wolf until Royce manhandled the truck back up on the road.

Royce looked over at Burl and said, "Wanna do it again?"

Burl laughed even harder than before. Finally, he wiped the tears from his eyes and said again, "Goddamn, Royce, you kill me. You are one funny sonuvabitch."

By the time she finally got to the Trucker's Heaven, Karla was frazzled, but that didn't keep her from being impressed, as she always was with the way the place looked. It was the liveliest place in the county, acres of concrete for the big trucks to park, lit up like Las Vegas. Twenty-four gas pumps for the four-wheelers in front, diesel in the back. Everything you could want in the big rambling building: restaurant where you could get a chicken-fried steak big as a pizza; a store that sold DVDs, CDs, candy, beer, jerky, you name it; showers; bedrooms where you could pick up a phone and order a massage of just about any body part; fast-food burgers and rotisserie chicken; a sound system that pumped country music into the air, twenty-four hours a day.

Karla thought the real heaven, in which she believed powerfully as only someone who never attends church can, must be a lot like that, but heaven probably didn't have quite as many truckers. That would be okay with Karla. Most of the ones she'd met in the past had been nice enough, but not all of them. You could never be sure. However, Karla had held onto her .22 pistol when the meth lab blew up, so she figured she'd be fine. She threaded her way through the cars and gas pumps and walked up to the big glass doors.

Lloyd hated Trucker's Heaven. He hated the lights and noise, which reminded him of some cheap carnival midway. It made him long for the days when he'd pull up to one of the two pumps at the Sinclair station and Harry and Larry, the Derryberry twins, would come striding out in their uniforms and gray caps with a green dinosaur on them and fill up his car, check the oil and water, air up the tires, and sweep out his old Ford with a whisk broom while Lloyd sat there in the front seat in comfort.

Now he'd have to get in line to buy gas that cost him as much as three or four good meals would have, back in the day, and he'd have to pump it himself. If the tires needed air, he'd better have some quarters, because the compressor wouldn't work without payment. And nobody was going to look under his hood, either.

It was okay, though. All he wanted to do was gas up and get out of there.

First, however, he'd have to pay. Nobody gassed up at Trucker's Heaven without sticking a credit card in the pump or paying inside first. Lloyd parked at the pump, got out, and went to pay. He figured he'd get twenty dollars' worth of gas and use the dollar that was left over for a candy bar. What he'd do for money after that, he didn't know. It might not even matter.

Royce made a hard right turn off the feeder road onto the concrete lot at Trucker's Heaven with tires squealing. He sailed into a parking spot between a Hummer and an Escalade and threw on the brakes just in time to keep from running up over the curb and into the ice machine that sat on the walk.

Neither Royce nor Burl was wearing a seatbelt. Burl slammed into the dash, which he thought was funnier than anything else that had happened so far. Royce had been braced for the stop, so he didn't quite bang his head on the steering wheel.

"Hand me that pistol," he said.

Burl couldn't stop laughing, but he managed to open the glove compartment. The pistol slid out and fell to the floor.

"Shit," Royce said. "You can't do anything right."

He leaned over and picked up the Glock.

"Lemme use it," Burl said between giggles.

"You don't have enough sense," Royce said. "Let's go."

"What about masks? We can't let 'em see our faces."

"We'll pull up our T-shirts. Like this." Royce reached a hand into his outer shirt—a green, yellow, and red aloha job that he probably thought was invisible—and pulled his T-shirt up over his nose. "See?"

Burl got the giggles so bad that he slipped off the seat onto the floor and doubled up under the dash.

"You're an asshole," Royce said. "Just for that, you can stay in the truck."

Burl nearly strangled himself as he tried to stop giggling and get back up on the seat. He pulled his T-shirt over his nose, narrowed his eyes, looked from left to right, and said, "Let's go."

"Not while you look like that. We gotta be inconspicuous."

They unmasked, got out of the truck, and stepped up on the walk. Burl looked toward the door.

"Hey, Royce, that's Karla. I thought she was supposed to be in jail."

"Damn," Royce said. "And who's that old fart with her?"

Burl shrugged. "Never saw him before."

"Maybe he's her grandpa. Well, they just better not get in our way. Come on."

"Can I put my mask on?"

"Go ahead."

Burl pulled up his T-shirt and giggled all the way to the door.

Lloyd thought the girl in front of him sure did have a nice shape, and she even said thank you when he opened the door for her. Showed she had a good upbringing.

He looked around before he went in and saw a couple of redneck idiots headed his way. One of them had his T-shirt pulled up over the lower half of his face, and the other one had something in the hand he was hiding behind his back. It sounded like one of them was giggling, but Lloyd couldn't be sure, what with the Cornell Hurd Band blasting over the speakers. Anyway, his hearing wasn't what it used to be.

Whoever they were, Lloyd wasn't going to hold the door for a couple of assholes like that. He started inside, but Royce sped up and jerked the door out of his hand.

"Get out of the way, you old fart," he said.

Lloyd didn't take that kind of shit from anybody. "Look here," he said.

"Shut the fuck up," Royce said, pulling his T-shirt up over his nose and sticking the gun in Lloyd's skinny belly. "And get the hell outta my way."

Lloyd doubled over, not because of the pistol barrel in the belly but because of what was already in there that the doctors said was going to kill him.

"Yeah," Burl said, shoving Lloyd on into the store and into a cardboard bin of bargain CDs. "Get the hell outta my way."

The bin collapsed, and Lloyd went to the floor amid a pile of plastic.

Karla looked around at the noise. "Royce? Is that you?"

"Hell, no."

Royce pointed the Glock at the man behind the high counter. "Gimme all your money."

Burl stood by, giggling.

"Burl?" Karla said. "What the hell do you two think you're doing?"

"Robbing the joint," Burl said between giggles. "How'd you know us with our masks on?"

A woman in the candy aisle overheard him and looked around. She started to scream when she saw Royce's pistol.

Royce turned and fired off a shot that went over the woman's head to shatter the glass door of one of the big refrigerators holding soft drinks, fruit juice, and water.

The man behind the counter grabbed the mic that he used to talk to the people pumping gas.

"We have a robbery in progress," he said. "Call 911. Call 911."

People all over the parking lot pulled out cell phones and started punching in the number.

"Shit-shit-shit," Royce said.

Karla thought he was wasting his breath, and so were those people making calls. All the cops in the county would still be out at the meth lab, sifting through the ashes. It would take them a while to get organized and get to the truck stop.

Three burly truckers intent on foiling the robbery started toward the front from the Hickory Holler restaurant in the back, one of them carrying a chair like it was a kid's toy.

Royce shot him. He fell against a popcorn machine, dropping the chair.

The other two men ducked into the chips and peanuts aisle.

"Goddamn," Burl said.

"Royce," Karla said, "you're cranked out of your mind. Put down that gun."

Royce wasn't listening. He turned back to the cashier and put a bullet into a carton of Marlboros on the shelf behind him.

"Gimme the money. C'mon, c'mon."

The cashier said, "We put it all in the vault slots. All's I got is about fifteen bucks."

"C'mon, c'mon."

Lloyd finally got untangled from the CD bin and knocked the CDs off him. Trucker music. Red Sovine, Dave Dudley, C.W. McCall. Lloyd figured truckers were the only ones using CB radios anymore. He stood up and said, "Hey, asshole."

Burl looked at him over the rim of his T-shirt. "Which one of us you mean?"

"You'll do," Lloyd said and kicked him in the balls.

Burl's T-shirt slipped down to reveal his whole face, but that was the least of his concerns. He grabbed his crotch and fell to his knees, trying to get his breath, tears running down his face.

Royce grabbed the money the cashier put on the counter and turned to Burl.

"Get up, dumbass. We gotta get outta here."

"No, you don't," Lloyd said. "Lemme have that gun."

"Screw you," Royce said and pulled the trigger.

The bullet missed Lloyd and blew the cotton brains out of a teddy bear in a bin of stuffed animals.

"Now look what you did," Lloyd said.

"You old bastard."

Royce was ready to pull the trigger again, but Karla said, "Don't you pull that trigger, Royce. I have a gun, and I'll shoot you in the knee if you do."

Lloyd had known the girl had a good upbringing. She was sticking up for her elders.

Royce looked at her and slammed the Glock into her wrist. She dropped the .22, and Burl picked it up as he struggled to his feet, his left hand still holding his crotch, tears running down his face.

"Shoot the old fart," Royce said, "and let's go."

He grabbed Karla's good arm and dragged her through the door.

Lloyd walked up to Burl, who was bent halfway over and trying to get his finger through the trigger guard of the .22. Lloyd took hold of the pistol and twisted it up and back. He heard Burl's finger snap. Burl fell to the floor, assumed the fetal position, and whimpered like a baby, his hands clutched together at his groin.

When Lloyd started past him, however, Burl stuck out a foot and tripped him. Lloyd staggered into the thick glass door and hit his forehead on it. He turned around and shot Burl in the ass cheek. Burl screamed like a panther.

"Jesus," the cashier said. "You're one mean old dude."

Lloyd gave him a blindingly white grin. "You ain't seen nothing yet, sonny."

Royce shoved Karla into the floorboard on the passenger side of the truck and started to back out of the parking space, but he couldn't see too well because of the Escalade on one side and the Hummer on the other.

Which is why he didn't notice the Camaro.

The driver of the Camaro didn't notice Royce, either, because he had his windows up, was talking on his cell phone, and listening to Gwen Stefani with his speakers cranked up loud enough to drown out the Cornell Hurd Band from Trucker's Heaven's speakers.

The rear of the truck hit the front of the Camaro, turning it halfway around. The driver, who had no idea what had happened, jammed his foot at the brake, missed, and hit the accelerator pedal. The Camaro shot forward and crashed into the grille of a Trans Am that's driver was filling with regular unleaded.

The Trans Am was shoved backward about ten feet, not a bad thing in itself. The bad thing was that the hose was still jammed in the filler hole and was torn from the pump. Regular unleaded sprayed all around.

An alarm sounded, Gwen Stefani said, "This my shit," and the clerk inside Trucker's Heaven hit the automatic shut-off button, but it was already too late, because the right front hubcap popped off the Camaro, spun a foot or two, and struck the concrete, sending up a couple of sparks.

And that was all it took to turn Trucker's Heaven into Trucker's Hell. Fire was all over the Camaro and the Trans Am. The guy who'd been at the pump had run out of the way, and the Camaro's driver jumped out and ran, too, as did everyone else who was at the pumps.

Karla tried to get out of the floor of the truck to see what was happening, but Royce hit her in the forehead with his fist and knocked her under the dash.

The pickup had stalled when it hit the Camaro. Royce ground on the starter but couldn't get it to catch.

"Fuck this," he said, and he looked back and saw the parking lot aflame.

He jumped out the door of the truck and ran around the Hummer, where Lloyd was waiting for him.

"Where's that lady you had with you?" Lloyd said. He had to yell it to be heard over the screams, the country music, and Gwen Stefani.

The Trans Am blew up about then, so if Royce answered, Lloyd didn't hear him. Lloyd hadn't expected an answer, however. He had a feeling that Royce hadn't had a very good upbringing and didn't respect his elders.

Royce grabbed for the Glock he'd stuck in the waistband of his pants, intending to shoot Lloyd. He wasn't likely to miss, since they were standing only about two feet apart.

Lloyd had the .22, and he wouldn't mind depriving the world of one more piece of white trash. He'd have done it, too, if he'd known how many bullets he had left. He'd already wasted one on that asshole in the store, and he didn't want to waste another.

He was standing by the freezer that held bagged ice, so he reached out his left hand and flipped the door open, swinging it as hard as he could back into Royce, who had the pistol almost out of his waistband.

When the door hit his hand, Royce pulled the trigger. His scream could be heard even above Gwen Stefani, who was declaring yet again that she wasn't no hollaback girl.

"Maybe you just shot the end of it off," Lloyd said.

He stepped over Royce, who was now lying on the none-too-clean sidewalk with blood on the front of his pants. Lloyd gave him a little kick for good measure and went to the truck. He looked in the driver's side door and saw Karla on the floor. Off to his right, another car blew up with a *fwoomp* that shook the parking lot. Lloyd could feel the heat from the fire through his clothes.

"We better get outta here," Lloyd said. "What do you think?"

"Let's go," Karla said, wiggling out from under the dash.

Lloyd pulled himself up into the driver's seat. The engine turned over the first time he tried it, and he drove past the burning cars and pulled onto the service road. Looking in the rearview mirror, he saw his daughter's Chevy consumed by flames. He hoped she had good insurance.

"Whichaway you headed?" Lloyd said.

Karla fluffed her hair. She wished she'd had time to freshen up and use the toilet. Maybe she could do that a little farther on down the road.

"I was thinking of visiting my aunt up in Paragould, Arkansas. She might give me a job in her beauty parlor. Where you going?"

"Never been to Arkansas. What's it like there?"

Karla started to answer, but she closed her mouth when she looked up and saw the sheriff's cars, a couple of fire trucks, and a DPS car headed for them, flashers going, sirens yowling.

"Don't think they'll be interested in us," Lloyd said. "There's this big fire back there behind us, and they'll be going to that."

Karla looked back just as there was another explosion. A fireball rose in the sky, and she thought it was even brighter than when the meth lab went up. She wondered if Arkansas was far enough away, but she guessed it would do.

"Arkansas is all right," she said, turning to give Lloyd a good look. "You want to go? We could have us some fun."

"Damn, girl, I'm old enough to be your granddaddy. Considering the way I spent some of my time when I was younger, I might *be* your granddaddy."

"I don't think so. My mama's not from around here. She had me up in Paragould. You never been there, have you?"

"Nope."

"Okay. So how about it?"

Lloyd stopped at a red light. When it changed to green, he turned left, drove under the highway, and turned left again. When he was headed north on the highway, he said, "You sure you want me to go along?"

"Like I said, we could have us some fun if you did."

Lloyd thought about it. "I got to tell you two things before you decide for sure. For one thing, I ain't led a blameless life."

Karla nodded. "That makes two of us. What's the other thing?"

Lloyd didn't think he'd tell her about the stomach problem. Why worry her? He wondered how much fun a man his age could stand and how long somebody who was damn near dead would last with a woman like this one. By God, maybe he'd just find out.

"Well?" Karla said. "What's the other thing?"

Lloyd gave her a grin.

"These ain't my real teeth," he said.

The Gospel According to Gordon Black

by Richard Helms
(Best Long Story, 2008)

Gordon Black was a short man with an intimidating stare. His hair and beard were completely white. He liked to accentuate his points by drawing circles in the air with his index fingers.

"We are nothing but organic flotsam, bobbing in the infinite sea of life. Don't you agree, Mr. Gold?"

"Sure," I said.

At eighty dollars an hour, plus expenses, I could agree with all sorts of garbage.

"I don't hear much conviction in your voice," Gordon Black said.

"Conviction costs extra."

"A cynic, huh?"

"If I had a nickel for every time someone's called me that, I wouldn't need to charge eighty dollars an hour."

"So you're like the psychiatrists, who nod and agree with their patients, so long as the clock is ticking?"

I made a note on the legal pad I had brought with me to Gordon Black's office: *Has had experience with psychiatrists.*

"I am for hire," I said. "I don't do this for fun."

"How do I know you can help me?"

"Beats me. I don't know yet what you want me to do."

He seemed to think for a moment.

"I've founded a new religion. Perhaps you've heard of it."

"Sorry. I let my subscription to *New Religions Magazine* lapse a couple of years ago."

He smiled.

I smiled back.

We had shared a secret joke.

I could do this all day.

"My philosophy is simple. We are nothing but temporal flesh. There is nothing before us, and nothing after we die. Our entire existence is encompassed by the time between our births and our deaths."

"Okay."

"My religion doesn't require a supreme being meting out rewards and punishments to regulate our behavior. What we do with—or to—one another is and should be regulated by the concepts of civility and mutual respect."

"What's the payoff?" I asked.

Black rubbed the side of his nose and seemed to take my moral measurements with his onyx-colored eyes.

"The…payoff, as you refer to it, is social order and peace. The reward for being a good person is being a good person. That leads to a sense of peace and contentment, feelings of goodwill, and behavior regulated by internal values rather than external judgment."

"And, in the interest of social order, what kind of behavior would you not condone?" I asked.

"Any behavior that is hurtful, damaging, or coerced."

"So, whatever two or more people want to do together—as long as they agree to it and nobody forces anybody else—you're fine with that?"

"Of course."

"And," I said, "this is different from hedonism how?"

"Hedonism?"

"An existential philosophy based on the concept of shifting moral constants and the pursuit of pleasure."

Black leaned his plush button-and-tuck leather office chair back and surveyed me again. His opinion of me was changing by the moment.

Or maybe I just saw it that way.

"An educated man? In your profession?"

"I'm only a part-time thug. I played college football. One of the few requirements of my scholarship was that I attend classes. A lot of my teammates took this as an opportunity to nap during the day. I decided I might as well pay attention and maybe learn something."

"Like hedonism?"

"There were plenty of opportunities in college to study hedonism."

"I see," he said. "Well, there may be more than a little bit of the hedonistic philosophy in my religious manifesto. I also borrowed some parts of Zen Buddhism, the Kabbalah, and some of the more naturalistic pantheistic traditions."

I had a feeling that he was playing a tape in his head and transcribing it for me. I stifled a yawn.

"What about hope?" I said.

"What about it?"

"I'm no expert, but it seems to me that one of the foundations of most religions is the aspect of hope. People adhere to a system of beliefs because it offers them some relief from their personal fears."

"Fears of what, exactly?" Black asked.

"Well...death, mostly. People tend to gravitate toward the promise of salvation. They like to think that there's something to look forward to beyond the grave. You don't offer them that."

"Self-delusion," he said, making a dismissive circle with his hand. "Fairy tales. Isn't it better to admit that we are temporal beings and savor every bit of our brief moment in the sun? Isn't it better to sample the entire buffet of experience, to delight in the wholeness of life?"

"But with respect," I said.

"Of course. Pleasure without respect is exploitation. We don't exploit others."

I made a couple more notes and looked back up at him.

"Well, this is fun," I said. "But how exactly can I help you?"

"I'm being defamed," he said. "People are spreading lies about me."

"What kind of lies?"

"They're saying that I engage in pederasty, and drug use, and the vilest things."

"Who are these people? Do you have some idea of their identities?"

"Oh, you know. The usual voices of the religious establishment. The Christian Right, all the established and entrenched faiths. They attack that which threatens them."

"That's a lot of suspects. Could you narrow it down a bit?"

"The loudest of my critics are on the Internet. I have a number of screen names I can give you."

I stopped writing and thought about it for a second.

"This sounds more like a legal problem. If you think you are being libeled, perhaps you need an attorney, not a private investigator."

"I can deal with the criticisms from the established religious camps. Now, though, I think I'm being blackmailed."

He picked up the telephone and dialed three numbers.

"Could you bring in the envelope?" he said and then hung up the phone. A moment later, a woman walked into the office.

She was tall and redheaded. Her conservative business suit struggled to conceal a very well-tended and genetically prosperous body. I could see the outline of her bra through the sheer white blouse under her tweed jacket. Her eyes were like emeralds.

"This is Emma Rhodden," Black announced. "If I am the head of my church, Emma is its heart. She is my closest confidant. This is Mr. Gold, Emma. We talked about him earlier."

She slipped her hand into mine and squeezed. Her eyes locked onto my eyes. "Mr. Gold. How nice to meet you. Thank you for helping Gordon and the Church." She handed me the envelope, then turned and left the office. She closed the door behind her.

"I bet you just respect the hell out of her," I said.

"The envelope, Mr. Gold."

I broke the seal on the manila envelope and fished inside. It contained a computer printout.

"Emma found that slid under the front door when she came into the office the other day," he said.

It was a photograph of Black. With or without respect, the act in which he was engaged was illegal in just about every state.

"It's faked, of course," he said.

"Of course."

"Very cleverly done, though. The computer programs for manipulating images become more sophisticated every year."

The attached message was straightforward: *Stop spreading your Godless beliefs, or this will be delivered to the authorities.*

"I could prove in court that the image was manufactured," Black said. "But it would be expensive, and once something like this is reported in the papers, it hardly ever matters whether you're later exonerated. People will believe what they will believe. I don't mind criticism. This, however, begs for intervention. I want you to find the people who sent this threat and stop them."

"And you think the people who have attacked you on the Internet are the best candidates?"

"They're a place to start."

I considered the implications. Starting out with a list of screen names wasn't promising. I had dealt with online companies in the past and had found them to be about as cooperative with their records as Swiss banks. Attaching names to the people who had openly criticized Gordon Black and his new religion would take some doing. I could envision hours and hours of inquiries.

At eighty dollars an hour plus expenses.

"Sure," I said. "I'll look into it."

The list Gordon Black had provided wasn't exactly a smoking gun. The Internet is full to the brim with wacky types who luxuriate in anonymity, and who believe that their firewalls actually shield them from every aspect of the real world.

That kind of presumption just bugs the hell out of me.

On the other hand, these people do know a thing or two about their medium, and one of the Prime Directives of the ether world is that one can expect complete protection of one's true identity by the ISP.

So I decided that the only way to catch a little fish was to use a larger phish.

The idea came to me halfway through my second Anchor Porter of the day, as I sat on the deck at my Montara Beach house, resting after working for three straight hours on a copy of a Hauser classical guitar I'd promised to build for a friend in Seattle. I build musical instruments as a hobby. It helps clear my mind and gives me something to do with my hands when my girlfriend Heidi is at work.

All of the screen names provided by Gordon Black shared a common factor. They all hated Gordon Black. In effect, they had become a sort of loosely connected club, which practically begged for organization. It also occurred to me that, since they had so openly expressed their opinions with Mr. Black, they might also be open to sharing their thoughts with each other.

I allowed my plan to gestate a bit as I finished the bottle of Anchor, and then I went inside to fire up my computer.

It took me a half hour to compose the phishing letter. In effect, it was a warning about the dangers of Black's New Existence Revelations Ministries and an invitation to join an email list so that the recipients could pool their resentment and the power of their voices. When it was finished, I read it over twice and had to admit that it was more than a little convincing. For a couple of moments, I wondered whether I was playing for the right team.

I saved the letter and then went to a website that hosts mail lists. It took me ten minutes to set up one called Bogus Faiths. I also toggled the box that said I had to approve each new member. That way, I could be certain that I wouldn't be jammed with applicants who might stumble on a link to my private little club. I wanted to concentrate on the names from Black's list.

Finally, I sent my phishing email to each of the people from the list.

The next morning, I booted my computer and dropped by the mail list site, to see if I'd had any nibbles from my phishing expedition.

I had expected two or three responses right away. There are some people out there who will join a chain gang if they're properly invited. I found that eight of the nine names on the list Gordon Black had given me had requested to join the list. Apparently, I had underestimated the zeal among my little mob of zealots.

Now here's the beautiful part about my plan. In order to join a list with this particular server, you had to become a member. Membership was free, because eventually the server would flood your email in-box with dozens of commercial messages a day.

When you joined the server, you had to provide your name, your address, and other vital demographic data—such as your age, income, buying habits, etc. Then, before the server passed along your response to the list owner, they'd vet you by sending an email to you, and you'd have to respond directly before you were approved to play with the rest of the kids.

Finally—and this is the beautiful part I mentioned—the server provided me with all of this information when my little phishies applied to join my list.

Within minutes, I had a printout on my desk which outlined the names, addresses, genders, ages, and buying habits of almost every screen name Black had given me. Only one name on the list—RodOfGod—had failed to take the bait.

Not too surprisingly, almost all the people on the list lived in the Bay Area. Gordon Black's church was relatively new and accordingly small. It was a safe bet that its reputation had not had time to spread near and far. One suspect, a fellow named Hiram Darles, lived in Sacramento. The rest of the addresses were in places like Sausalito, San Jose, Daly City, and San Francisco proper.

I made a list of the members arranged by farthest distance from the city inward and decided to visit as many as possible. I doubted that any would admit to sending the picture to Gordon Black, but I've also found that most extortionists prefer to operate from behind a screen. Most of them, when exposed, wilt in the light of day, especially if that light comes in the form of a six-foot guy with malice in his eyes.

I decided to skip Hiram Darles for this round. Sacramento was nowhere near the longest distance I'd driven to interview someone, but it would take the better part of a day, and I decided that it made more sense to see as many people in as short a time as possible.

The first person on the list lived in San Jose. Her name was Cynthia Raab. She lived in a one-bedroom apartment over a drugstore. Her bookshelves were lined with every known edition of the Bible, multiple volumes of Concordances and religious commentaries, and several lazy cats. The apartment smelled like urine. She didn't own a computer—she used the one at the local library. She thought Photoshop was a camera store. I scratched her off my list.

The next prospect was much more promising. He was actually a minister in Pacifica. I caught him coming out his front door.

I flashed him my ID and asked for a few minutes of his time. He was tall but lean and sort of sickly. His skin was translucent, his eyes watery. I had a hard time imagining him railing from the pulpit. His name was Avery Sipe.

"What do you want?" he asked.

"You've been sending threatening emails to Gordon Black," I said. His mouth started to form an argument, but I wasn't in the mood to listen. "Don't bother. I have the evidence."

"I wouldn't say they were threatening," Sipe said.

"We can let the courts deal with that," I said.

"The…the courts?"

I had never seen an Adam's apple bob four full inches before. I was so impressed that I almost forgot what I wanted to say.

"Mr. Black has received threats accompanied by pictures. If you sent them, now would be a good time to tell me. I'm a trained professional. If you lie, I'll know."

I gave him my menacing look, the one I save for bill collectors and yappy dogs.

He swallowed twice, shook his head. "I didn't do it," he pleaded.

"No more contact with Black," I said. "Not a peep. I know who you are, and I can come back when you least expect me. Is there anything you don't understand about that?"

He shook his head again. I nodded, turned, and walked to my car. I didn't look back. It's bad form to stare when a man soils his pants.

Heidi Fluhr and I were having dinner at my Montara Beach house. I had grilled ribeye steaks and winter vegetables, and we were enjoying them with a bottle of Corona Farms cabernet.

Heidi is an art dealer, a big healthy Northern European blonde with prodigious appetites. We had been seeing each other for almost two years. I liked it. She liked it. Beyond that, we weren't into making plans.

As we ate, I told her my plan.

"Devious," she said.

"Dang. I was shooting for ingenious and elegant."

"Have you had any responses?"

"I haven't checked yet."

"Ooh, let's go take a look. I love to watch you play detective."

I allowed Heidi to look over my shoulder as I played with my suspects' heads. I opened my computer and accessed the email list. As she kneaded my shoulders, I typed the following message:

Has anyone else been hassled by some glandular case in the last day or so? I'd love to know if any of you were accosted by this character and what he told you. I find it highly suspicious that, right after I start this list, I get boosted by a private investigator. I'm all for putting a stop to the sacrilege that Gordon Black calls a church, but I sure don't want to get in trouble with the cops.

I toggled the Send key and sat back to let the issue cook for a while.

"What now?" Heidi asked.

"Good question," I said. "Sometimes you just have to stir the stew and wait to see what comes to the surface."

"You're fucking with their heads, you mean."

"More or less. I scared a lot of people today. They're going to want to talk about that with people they think they can trust. If I'm lucky, one of them will slip and tell me what I want to know."

I was interrupted by a little gong sound, and a mail dialogue box popped up on my screen.

InHisName: *RU online?*

"One of my little phishes," I explained to Heidi. "That was quick."

I quickly typed a response.

I'm here.

InHisName: *That guy visited me 2.*

"Did he threaten you?" I mouthed as I typed.

InHisName: *Told me stop hassling Black.*

He scared me too.

InHisName: *How did he find us?*

Don't know.

InHisName: *Satan has great powers.*

Tell me about it. Wish I had some way to get Black to back off.

InHisName: *What u mean?*

Something embarrassing or incriminating.

InHisName: *Me 2. GTG.*

The dialogue box disappeared.

"GTG?" Heidi asked.

"Got to go," I said, translating. "IM-speak. Something the kids came up with."

"What do you think about this guy?"

"InHisName?"

"Yeah."

"I think the 'guy' is a sixty-year-old woman who lives in San Bruno. Her name is Kate, and she's an ex-hippie who spent most of the 1960s in Haight-Ashbury, grooving with Jerry and the Dead. She's not the blackmailer."

"So why did you bait her?"

"Excuse me?"

"That last bit about wanting something to make Black back off? You were trying to get her to admit that she had something on him."

"Not exactly."

"What, then?"

"I was planting seeds. She's part of my email list. It might look suspicious if I—as the list owner—came right out and asked if any of the members has a picture of Black with a goat, but if one of the other members brings it up, it won't look so hinky."

"And when someone comes forward?"

"Then I have my extortionist. Now, what can we do while we wait?"

"What did you have in mind?"

"We could always canoodle."

"You expect me to canoodle just because you cooked dinner?"

"Of course not. I expect you to canoodle because I am irresistibly handsome, and because I make your toes curl."

"And because you're so devious," she said.

"Yes," I added. "Devious helps."

I spent most of the night monitoring the email list. Nobody else tried to IM me, but the list was busy until after one in the morning. Sometime around midnight, my buddy Kate InHisName uploaded a message to the list:

We should fight fire with fire. Gordon Black and his blasphemers think they can scare us off with threats and intimidation. I bet he'd back off in a New York minute if he knew we could threaten him back. Maybe we could hire some kind of private investigator to get some dirt on Black....

I laughed out loud when I read that one. For a second, I considered playing both sides of the street.

Well, maybe it was only half a second. I have scruples, after all.

Heidi got up before I did, dressed, and left for her apartment. I awoke just after nine thirty. I hit the shower, got dressed and shaved, and settled down in my kitchen for some toaster waffles and a lot of hot coffee.

As I waited for the coffee to brew, I logged on to my laptop and checked the list.

Around two in the morning, one of my phishes had uploaded a message. It was short, sweet, and succinct:

I have something we could use on Black. I have pictures. Bad pictures. I don't want to share them with you, because they are evil, but he sure wouldn't want to see them made public.

Bingo.

I checked the screen name. PiusXIX. I checked it against my list. Hiram Darles. My guy in Sacramento. The only suspect from Gordon Black's list whom I hadn't personally visited yet. That was probably why he was so bold on the list.

I finished my breakfast, loaded his address into my GPS, and climbed into my car to make the trip to the state capital.

Hiram Darles lived in a small California bungalow in a neighborhood of similar houses constructed in the Roaring Twenties. The yard was well-tended, the flower beds weeded to distraction, and someone had brazed an ornate wrought-iron cross to the screen door on the shady front porch.

From the street, I could see a car parked in the single garage at the back end of the gravel driveway. I hoped that the car belonged to Darles and not his wife.

I banged on the front door and waited. After several seconds, I heard heavy footsteps nearing the door.

I waited as the person inside released three different deadbolt locks. Hiram Darles opened the door. He was about my age but had allowed himself to go to suet. His most prominent features were cheeks that puffed out like fugu and ruddy flopping jowls. His eyes seemed set back in folds of skin. He wore a pair of jeans and a WWJD sweatshirt.

"Hiram Darles?" I said, as he unlatched the screen.

I could see the color drain from his face. His cheeks went from rosy to ashen in seconds.

"Oh, my God, it's you!" he said.

He tried to slam the door, but I already had my size thirteen wedged in the jamb. I pulled the picture Gordon Black had given me from my back pocket, unfolded it, and held it up to him.

"Look familiar, Hiram?" I asked.

"Oh my God oh my God oh my God oh my God," he chanted. "You go away. I didn't give you permission to come in this house. You're trespassing."

"You're supposedly devout," I said. "I think you're supposed to forgive trespasses, aren't you? Tell me about the picture, Hiram."

"I don't know what you're talking about."

"Extortion is a crime," I said. "Right now, it's just you and me talking—just a couple of guys. But I have the Sacramento Police on my cellphone speed dial. You decide not to be friendly, and I can have them here in about five minutes. What's it going to be?"

He glanced back into the house, as if looking for someplace to hide. Looking at him, I concluded that it would have to be a really big place. Finally, he stepped out onto the porch and closed the door behind him.

"You can't come inside," he said.

"The hell I can't," I told him. "If I want to, I'll come inside, toss the place, reprogram your VCR, and neuter your cat. Do we understand each other?"

"You are a tool of Satan!" he said indignantly.

I leaned in very close to his face. His breath smelled like cheese.

I held out the photo again.

"You put this under Gordon Black's door," I said. I didn't phrase it as a question.

He nodded. I could see tears welling at the corners of his eyes.

"Mr. Black is very upset about this," I said.

"Gordon Black is a demon. He was sent by Satan to lead the unwary astray from the true path. Someone had to stop him."

"And you decided to be that person."

"No. I was chosen. I received that picture as an attachment to an email from a fellow believer. He—or she, it's impossible to tell online—said I should give it to Gordon Black as an example of the power of the Lord and the damnation that awaits him if he doesn't repent."

"Who was the person who sent it to you?"

"I can't recall. It doesn't matter. I wrote the demand at the bottom. I delivered the message. I'd do it again."

I nodded and looked away, out at the street, as I mulled my options.

Being a private cop has advantages and disadvantages. Among the disadvantages is the relative paucity of things you can do to miscreants once you track them down. I could have danced around the porch with Hiram for a couple of rounds, left him bruised and wiser, but all that would have proven was that I was bigger and meaner, and it would probably just fuel his righteous anger and justify future misbehavior.

"Here's the deal," I said, as I turned back to him. "You got lazy, and you got caught. Now I know who you are, and I know what you did, and you could go to jail for a long time for it."

"I just wanted him to stop," Hiram whined.

"I know. And I don't care. I work for Gordon Black, and Gordon Black wants this foolishness to end. So, no more messages. Save someone in your own neighborhood. If there are any more threats, I'm coming after you first. Is there anything I've said that you don't understand?"

He shook his head. A weighty tear plopped from his cheek onto the painted deck of the porch.

I folded the picture, stuffed it in my jacket pocket, and left Darles to his own private recriminations.

I met with Gordon Black later that afternoon. I handed him the list of suspects I'd culled from my phishing expedition and told him that Hiram Darles was the person who had tried to blackmail him. I urged him to go light on Darles—who, after all, was only doing what he thought was right, no matter how illegally he went about it.

To his credit, Black accepted the advice.

"You're probably right," he said. "And I'd be a hypocrite if I didn't at least try to respect his beliefs."

"Yes," I said. "We do want to avoid charges of hypocrisy."

"What is that supposed to mean?" Black asked.

"Nothing. I'll send you a bill."

Six months later, I was bucks up. I had been hired by a couple of Silicon Valley geeks to unravel an industrial-espionage case, and they had been very grateful for my results. Since I had time to kill and money to blow, I had taken Heidi on an impromptu trip to Lake Tahoe.

We had been back for a couple of days. It was Sunday. We were lounging in Heidi's Russian Hill apartment. She read the *Chronicle*'s local section as I nibbled on some toast, perused the sports pages, and considered hiring a sailboat to play on the Bay that afternoon.

"Eamon?" Heidi asked, looking up from the paper.

"Hmmm?"

"What was the name of that guy in Sacramento you nabbed for extortion last Christmas?"

I had to think hard to recall. I don't store a lot of the perps I run down in long-term memory.

"Darles," I said, after a moment. "Hymie, Horace, something like that."

"Hiram?"

"Yeah, that's it. What about him?"

She handed me the paper. It was turned to the obits.

"He's dead," she said.

I scanned the notice. Age forty-three. I thought he had looked a lot older, actually. Died suddenly. No cause listed. No survivors.

Not a lot to say for a life. Services were that afternoon at a funeral home in Sacramento.

"Probably a heart attack," I said. "The guy was a walking advertisement for statins. Hand me the funnies?"

"No."

"I can't have the funnies?"

"No, not that. I mean, 'no, it wasn't a heart attack.' Look on page three."

It took me a moment to find the fifteen-line blurb near the bottom of the page, recounting a hit-and-run two nights before. The details were sketchy, partly because Darles was a nobody and probably partly because the police didn't have much to tell the beat reporter who wrote the piece.

"Victim was Hiram Darles, age forty-three," I read. "Police are looking for a black SUV, make unknown."

"What do you think?"

"I think the SUV should be easy to find. A guy Darles' size would put a hefty dent in a Hummer."

"I mean, do you think it was intentional?"

"Why would you say that?"

"Well, he was an extortionist."

"Not a very good one. And I put him out of business. Darles was big and slow, and not very bright to boot. He probably just stepped off the wrong curb at the right time and couldn't get out of the way fast enough. You want to go sailing this afternoon?"

We did go sailing, but as we tacked around on the chop out in the Golden Gate, I couldn't get my mind off Hiram Darles.

I might not have recalled his name right off the bat, but I hadn't forgotten the fear in his eyes. Intimidation is one of the tools of my trade, but sometimes it carries a nasty personal freight charge.

When we got back to my house, I booted my computer and checked out the Bogus Faiths email list I had set up to phish for Gordon Black's haters. I hadn't taken the list down after closing Black's case, because I wanted to make sure Darles didn't grow a pair after my visit and decide to tempt fate.

After a month with no posts from him, I had finally lost interest and gone on to other projects. Somehow, though, I had never gotten around to taking down the list.

To my surprise, there were no recent posts. The last one had been about three months earlier, from the nice lady with the cats in San Jose—what was her name? Raab. After that, nothing.

It was possible, of course, that with such a small membership the list had simply petered out. I'd seen it happen before on a couple of guitar-making sites I had joined.

On the other hand, the list had been bustling when I abandoned it. My little group of suspects hadn't seemed the kind of folk to cut and run from a subject so close to their hearts. These people had been not only devout, but vocal about it. It was more than a little curious that they had gone silent.

I thought about it that evening in the shop I had set up in the living room of my Montara house as I worked on a banjo I'd agreed to build for a friend in Ukiah. Heidi lounged on the sofa in an extra-large Forty-Niners T-shirt and little else, reading a Jonathan Santlofer novel. She liked Santlofer because he was an artist as well as an author, and she had carried one or two of his pieces in her gallery over the years.

"Where are they?" I said, mostly to myself.

"Probably where you last left them," she said, without looking up.

"I was thinking about my little phishes."

"The holy rollers you conned on that email list?"

"Yeah. No messages in almost three months. Where did they go?"

"You're a detective. Why don't you—what's that thing you do?"

"Look into it?"

"Yeah. You should do that."

"You know," I said, "I think I will."

I put aside the banjo and booted the computer in the spare bedroom. It took me a moment to access my case records and to print out the list of suspects I had developed during the Gordon Black case.

I sat on the sofa, Heidi curled up against my side. I picked up the telephone and dialed Kate InHisName in San Bruno.

Annoying three-tone signal. An electronic voice advised me that the number was no longer in service.

More questions.

The old lady with the cats in San Jose—Cynthia Raab—same "no longer in service" message. I could see a free spirit like Kate pulling up stakes, but Raab seemed to have hunkered down for the remainder of her breathing time. On a hunch, I dialed Avery Sipe's number in Pacifica, just a couple of miles to the north.

Someone picked up the phone on the third ring.

"Hello?"

Female voice. Sounded like she was in her late teens or early twenties.

"Could I speak with Mr. Sipe, please?"

"Sure. Hold on."

I heard her put down the receiver. Moments later, someone picked it up again.

"This is Curtis Sipe," a man said.

"Excuse me. I was trying to reach Avery Sipe."

"I'm sorry. I'm afraid that—who's calling, please?"

"My name is Eamon Gold."

"Did you have some business with my father?"

It was time for a little fancy stepping. I didn't like the way he was referring to Avery in the past tense.

"We met about six months ago. I was just following up on our conversation."

"I see. I'm very sorry to have to tell you this, Mr. Gold, but my father… passed away."

"My goodness. When?"

"In February. It was very sudden."

I apologized for bothering him and racked the receiver.

Heidi had heard enough to distract her from Santlofer.

"Two of them are dead?" she asked.

"Maybe four. I need to do some research."

Every detective worth his license subscribes to one kind of database or another. Unlike the online search engines, these databases can provide you with information very few people want posted on their websites. With little more than a name, a date of birth, or a Social Security number, I can find out how much money you make, what kind of car you drive, and how much you paid in taxes last year.

I can also find out whether you're still walking the Earth or simply permanently inhabiting a hundred square feet of it.

I knew that Darles and Sipe were dead. I pulled up a news story on Sipe—who, it appeared, had fallen from a cliff at the beach in Pacifica in February. No biggie there. The coastline of California is pocked with literally hundreds of dangerous cliffs, and hardly a day goes by that you don't read about someone falling off one.

I checked on Cynthia Raab next. Asphyxiated in April, when her pilot light went out while she was asleep.

Kate Corrigan, the hippie in San Bruno, had been electrocuted by her hair dryer.

The list went on and on. Every member of my list had died in the six months since I had recruited them. Each death had been an apparent accident.

Sitting next to me at the computer, Heidi shivered.

"Damn, Gold. What's going on here?"

"I don't know," I said, reaching for the telephone. "But I think it's time I go back to church."

Gordon Black wasted no time escorting me into his office.

"Mr. Gold," he said, as I sat across the desk from him. "I must say, I didn't expect to see you again. I trust my check cleared?"

"Yes. This isn't a collection call."

I placed a printed summary of the fates of my phishes on his desk and watched as he read over it.

"Oh, my," he said, placing the paper down on the desk calendar. "I know how this must look...."

"Really?"

"Of course. I'm an intelligent man. I hired you to find these people and make them stop harassing me. Now they're all dead. It makes me look...well, vengeful."

"And it makes *me* look like an accomplice," I said. "I hope you haven't compromised me, Gordon."

"Not at all. I'm shocked at this news."

"Here's the deal," I told him. "Two people had access to this list. Obviously, I did. I gave you a report of my investigation after I shook Hiram Darles's tree. That report contained the names and addresses of every person I contacted. Now they're dead. I know I didn't do it. That leaves you."

"Not...necessarily," he said. "I discussed this case with several members of my staff—informally, that is—in a meeting several days after you met with

Darles."

"How many members?"

"Three. These are good people, Mr. Gold. They're my closest advisors—almost apostles, you might say. They revere me."

"Would they kill for you?"

"Now you're being melodramatic."

"Give me their names."

"Is that really necessary?"

"Nine people are dead, Mr. Black. That implies a certain necessity. One accident, I can buy. Two, a coincidence perhaps. Nine seems excessively improbable. Give me the names of the people you told, or I call the cops right now."

"I don't think so," said a woman behind me.

I turned to face Emma Rhodden, the "heart" of Gordon Black's church. She held a nasty-looking .32 caliber automatic.

"Emma?" Black said. "Put that down."

"No," she said. "I'm afraid I've already underestimated Mr. Gold one too many times."

With my back half turned to her, Emma couldn't see my right hand snake across my belly toward the shoulder holster where I kept my Browning.

Or maybe she could.

"Don't do that," she said. "My father taught me how to shoot when I was just a child. I would kill you before you turn halfway around. Pull out your gun, by the handle, with two fingers, and place it on the floor."

"Rhodden," I said, as I followed her directions. "RodOfGod. You were the name on Black's list who never joined my email group. You live in Sausalito, don't you?"

"What are you saying?" Black demanded. "Emma is completely loyal to me."

"Hiram Darles told me that someone he didn't know sent the picture he tried to use to blackmail you. Since he admitted sliding it under your door, my job was done. I didn't bother to find out who actually manufactured the picture. It wasn't part of the job I agreed to do."

"You're so smart, aren't you?" Emma said.

"Smart enough to know that you gave Darles that picture, Emma. What I can't quite figure out is why?"

"Neither can I," Black said. "Why did you do this horrible thing, Emma?"

"There is no such thing as bad publicity, Gordon. A church—any church—runs on money. Money comes from contributions. I figured that, if Darles released that picture, we'd get publicity, lots of it. Most people, people who can't understand what we're doing, would disregard us as a bunch of kooks and sex addicts. The right people, though, would flock to us in droves. Collections would skyrocket. We'd have the money to grow the way you always dreamed of growing."

"I never would have agreed to such a scheme."

"Why do you think I never told you?" Emma said. "I know how proud you are, Gordon. I knew you'd never give in to Darles's extortion. I figured that the picture would be distributed, one way or the other."

"My God," Black said, shaking his head. "You don't know what you've done. Why kill all those people?"

"Darles again. Somehow, he found his way to me. He was a computer geek. He figured out a way to get my name from the email address. When he found out that I was with the church, he threatened to expose me, beginning with the people he'd gotten to know on Gold's email list."

"Did he do it?" Black asked.

"I don't know. Because of the protocols Gold placed on the list, I couldn't find out what Darles had told them. So I had to get rid of each of the people on the list, one by one."

"It was important to make them look like accidents," I said, never taking my eyes off Emma's gun. "Murders make the front page of the newspaper. People who die in accidents barely make the obits."

"We have to get rid of him, Gordon," Emma said.

"What on Earth are you talking about?" Black said.

"I'm a liability," I said. "Emma believes that you'll forgive her. She's the heart of your ministry, after all. The head can never separate itself from the heart. I, on the other hand, can ruin everything. Emma expects that you'll overlook just one more *accident*."

"It's out of the question," Black said. "Emma, I love you as much as I've loved anyone. What you've done, though, is monstrous. You have acted without respect or tolerance for others. I'm afraid I have no alternative other than to excommunicate you from the church. Please put down the gun."

"What?" she asked. Her face looked puzzled.

"The gun. I must insist that you put it down."

"I did it all for you!"

"I regret that. I really do. I'll say it again. You must put the gun down."

"I—I can't," she whimpered.

"I imagine that the policeman behind you would demand it," Gordon said.

She gave him one look of incredulity, for only a second, before the uniformed cop who had crept up behind her leveled his own automatic and barked at her to drop her weapon. Shocked, she let go of the pistol almost instantly. It fell to the floor like a neglected stone.

As soon as she was cuffed, a plainclothes detective entered the room.

"Detective Crymes," I said, "this is Gordon Black."

"I wish I could say it's a pleasure, Mr. Black," Crymes said.

"Detective Crymes is with the Robbery-Homicide Division, Pacifica Police," I explained. "Once I figured out that you or one of your people had to have killed my phishes, I contacted him. Avery Sipe, one of Emma's victims, lived in Pacifica. That made it Detective Crymes' case."

I pulled my cell phone from my jacket pocket and held it up.

"Did you hear the entire conversation?" I asked.

"Every word," Crymes said. "Seems that Ms. Rhodden here has a lot of explaining to do. I'll still need some information from you, Eamon. Can I reach you at the Montara house?"

"Or at my office in San Francisco."

"I'll call you."

He and the uniformed cop helped Emma to her feet and escorted her out of the office to the waiting patrol car.

A week or so later, Heidi and I were at the Montara house, preparing to grill Alaskan salmon and Silver Queen corn. The mail truck drove up and left something in my mailbox.

I retrieved it and opened the envelope as I walked back to the deck.

"What's that?" she asked.

"A check," I said. "From Gordon Black. The note says he wants to reward me for saving his church."

"Is it a nice check?"

"Very nice. Feel like a trip? Someplace warm, with lots of sand and fruity drinks?"

"I could go someplace warm. I'm still not certain I understand this church of Black's."

"Maybe I'm just old and stuffy," I said, "but it seems more like a cover for Black and his followers to indulge adolescent fantasies."

"Different strokes for different folks."

"I do believe that you've just quoted the California state motto," I said.

"How long is it going to take the charcoal to be ready to grill?"

"A half hour or so. Why?"

She grinned at me, her eyes twinkling.

"Thought we might head to the back of the house for a while. Maybe get in a little…you know. Worship."

I took her hand and led her through the sliding glass doors into the house.

"Let us pray," I said.

No Flowers for Stacey

by Ruth McCarty
(Best Flash Story, 2009)

Reginald Stearns tucked himself in the shadows of the dumpster behind the Diamond Heights Mall and waited for the last store to close. He craved the nicotine rush a cigarette would bring but couldn't afford to have anyone look in his direction. He'd staked out the employee parking lot for the past two nights, noting the patterns and habits of the associates as they made their way to their cars.

The parking lot edged the crummy side of the building. Potholes and poor lighting plagued it, and he'd helped it along by breaking two more of the overhead lights. A steady stream of shoppers had left at nine, and as each store locked up for the night, Stearns had watched the employees head for their cars. The women, keys in hand, walked in pairs or groups. The men, cell phones to their ears, pressed the remotes to their cars and drove off long before their engines were warm.

Just when Stearns thought Stacey wasn't coming out, he spotted her. He watched as the tall redhead with her flicked her lighter and touched it to the cigarette already hanging from her lips. He knew she'd puff away as she walked toward her car. Stacey walked beside her, like the previous two nights. Her wavy blond hair hung loose over her leather jacket. Stearns hadn't touched her hair in such a long time. He closed his eyes, took a deep breath, and thought about her sweet smell.

She had on faded jeans and a black leather jacket, and the spike heels on her boots made her look taller than he remembered. Tall, and thin, and sexy.

They'd reached the redhead's car, and Stacey had stopped to talk with her. Stearns couldn't make out what they were saying, but he heard them laugh. After a few minutes, Stacey adjusted her pocketbook on her shoulder and started for her car. The other woman watched her, and so did Stearns.

Stacey turned and said, "I'll meet you there."

Stearns put his fingers to his temples. They were going to a bar! It had to be a bar. That's why Stacey had changed into her sexy clothes. Anger pounded through him. He'd followed the restraining order after getting out of prison. Read every paragraph with his parole officer. Every time they met, they went over it again. He hadn't tried to call her. Not at her apartment or her mother's. Only at her new job. Only once! He bit on his knuckle to keep from punching the dumpster. He'd stayed away from her. He hadn't even sent her the roses he always sent after a fight. No flowers for Stacey, they'd said!

Stacey got into her car, locked her doors, and started the engine. He saw her turn, give a thumbs-up to the redhead. Only then did the other woman drive away.

Stacey had parked her car in the same spot as the previous two nights, the nose of the car against the building, sheltered from the biting wind, perfect for his plan.

Stearns watched as the backup lights came on when Stacey put the car in reverse and then watched them go out when she put the car back in park. He smiled at the perfection of his plan. He'd taped a promotional flyer to the rear window of her Chevy, so when she looked in her mirror she couldn't see to back up. He knew she'd get out and remove it.

He started towards the car.

Stacey opened the car door and got out.

He wanted her to see him now, but she focused on getting the paper off her window and didn't look in his direction.

He stood behind her as she reached for the flyer. He grabbed for her hair and whispered in her ear, "Stacey."

An elbow jabbed him in the gut as a hand wrapped around his neck and flipped him over, flat on the ground. Stearns groaned as he looked at the object in his hand. Stacey's wavy blond hair.

A car screeched to a stop, inches from his face, and the redhead jumped out, gun pointed at Stearns, and shouted in a male voice, "Don't even move a finger. We got you this time, you bastard."

The woman dressed in Stacey's clothes smiled and said, "You have the right to remain silent...."

Famous Last Words

by Doug Allyn
(Best Long Story, 2010)

Ever wonder what you'd say? If you knew that the next words you spoke would be your very last?

Would you try to justify your life?

Would you say *I love you*? Or say a prayer?

Could you even assemble a coherent sentence?

I couldn't. And I had my chance.

A golden autumn evening, dusk settling on our little college town like a flannel comforter. Linette had picked me up after my last class, and we were stopped at a busy intersection, bickering cheerfully about whose turn it was to cook dinner, waiting for the light to change.

It suddenly dawned on me that the headlights in the rearview mirror were growing larger and brighter. Much too quickly.

The large truck coming up behind us wasn't slowing down at all. Speeding up, if anything. I expected him to pull around us, but he didn't. Just kept coming, straight on. And then it was too late.

Sweet Jesus! He was going to hit us! And I turned to Linette, wide-eyed, and said, "What the hell?"

Famous Last Words.

Not very profound. But then, I'm not the one who died.

As Linette swiveled around to look, the truck slammed into us! Instantly smashing our world into a whirling, mind-shredding maelstrom of shrieking metal, exploding airbags and howling rubber. Blasting my boxy little Toyota hybrid out into the flashing steel river of rush-hour traffic, triggering a horrendous chain-reaction accident. Panicked commuters slamming on their brakes, desperately cranking their wheels, swerving to avoid us.

And failing. My new Toyota Prius—with its state-of-the-art hybrid motor, rearview parking camera and electric cup warmers—was banged around like a ping-pong ball, hammered by at least three other cars before being literally smashed in half by a flatbed truck hauling twenty tons of rolled steel.

Our gas tank ruptured and spewed. And my clever little car exploded like a napalm bomb.

I hope to God Linette was already dead before the flames reached her.

But I don't know. And maybe that's best.

I woke slowly in a world of white. White tiled walls and ceilings. Even my pain felt white. My memory, too. A white blank. Empty as an unwritten page.

All I could remember were my last words to Linette: *What the hell?*

"Professor Frazier?"

I swiveled my head slowly. A woman was standing beside my bed. Tall and lanky, sandy hair cropped short as a boy's. Wearing a black suit and turtleneck. She was holding out an ID folder, but I couldn't focus on it.

"I'm Sergeant Shane Kovacs, Professor," she said, slipping the badge back inside her jacket. "Do you know where you are?"

"Hospital." I coughed, dry-mouthed. "University?"

She nodded, scanning my face like a form she had to fill out. "Can you tell me what happened?"

"Somebody...rear-ended us. A truck, I think."

"What kind of a truck was it?"

"Never saw it clearly. Only the headlights. Not a car or a pickup truck. The lights were too high. That's...really all I know."

"What about before the accident? Did you have trouble with anyone? Cut somebody off, blow your horn, flip 'em the finger? Anything at all?"

I stared at her, trying to make the words compute. "Road rage, you mean? No, there was nothing like that."

"It doesn't take much these days, Professor. If—"

"I teach History of Western Civilization at Hancock U, Sergeant. Linette's a librarian. We don't…squabble with strangers. Is she all right?"

Kovacs hesitated. "They didn't tell you?"

"Tell me what?"

"What was your relationship with Miss Rogers?"

"We…live together," I managed. "Two years now. Is she—?"

"I'm very sorry, Professor Frazier," Kovacs said, looking away to avoid my eyes. "Linette Rogers didn't make it. She was pronounced dead at the scene."

"God," somebody said quietly. Me, I suppose.

"Look, I'm sorry to have to push this, Professor Frazier, but a half dozen other victims were seriously injured in that accident. One of them may not survive the night. Several witnesses saw a gravel truck plow into your Toyota without slowing. If anything happened earlier that—"

"I told you, there was nothing. Why don't you ask the guy who hit us?"

"We haven't located him yet. After ramming into your car, the truck fled the scene. We found it abandoned a few hundred yards down the highway. It was stolen from a public works site. Maybe a drunk, maybe a joyrider. So if you can think of anything at all that could have triggered this—"

"I have no idea, Sergeant, but it had nothing to do with us. Linette and I were going home for dinner, for God's sake, trying to decide between pasta or Chinese. That's all I can tell you. End of story."

But it wasn't.

I checked myself out of the hospital at noon the following day. My left arm was in a sling, badly sprained, apparently when I was thrown from the car. I was bruised and battered, with a bandage covering an abrasion on my forehead. Beyond that, I was more or less intact. From what Sergeant Kovacs said, I was one of the lucky ones.

I didn't feel lucky.

I didn't feel anything. I'm a methodical sort, a scholar by trade and by nature. A bit of a plodder, I suppose. Linette used to tease me about being born with an old soul. Perhaps she was right.

I know students sometimes take my History of Western Civ class to catch up on their sleep. I'm not an inspired lecturer, or even very good at casual conversation.

But now I would have to say them. Famous Last Words. Linette's eulogy. The final synopsis of her life. She had no family, so the responsibility would fall to me.

And I wasn't up to it.

My idea of a fun Friday night is an easy chair by the fire with Xenophon's *Anabasis* (circa 400 BCE) and a snifter of Courvoisier.

Linette was the cheerful sparkplug that kept our relationship fresh and active. Drama Club, poetry nights at Barnes & Noble, faculty mixers. Most of our friends were really Linette's friends. She reveled in people and talk and laughter. And I enjoyed them simply because she did.

But the truth is, I never needed the company of other people much. Linette was my only need. The warm sun at the center of my universe.

How could I hope to sum up her life, her very essence, with a few brief words in a funeral-home chapel? For people I scarcely knew.

It would have been a snap for Linette. She was a poet, a wizard with words. Her verses could flash past like quicksilver or whisper your deepest secrets aloud in a crowded coffeehouse, soul to soul.

"Scratch a librarian, you'll find a poet working a day job," she'd say.

Which gave me an idea. Her poetry. Perhaps I could open her eulogy with one of her poems. Something light and airy and funny. A verse that would evoke her image more clearly than any clumsy words of mine.

Collecting a handful of workbooks from her desk, I carried them into my study and began scanning through them, panning for a nugget.

I found a few appropriate verses in the first book but continued, lost in her language. I had a prescription for painkillers from the hospital, but the relief I really needed was here, at my desk in this quiet room, surrounded by books, savoring the verses of the woman I loved. Hearing her voice echo in every line.

As the afternoon faded, I switched on the desk lamp but kept reading. With a growing sense of unease that had nothing to do with the gathering dusk.

Halfway through the second workbook, I stopped. And carefully closed the book. Unable to read one more word. Shaken to my core.

I'd found more truth than I'd been looking for. A bitter reality, shimmering just beneath the surface of her poetry. Shrouded in metaphor and allusion. But real, nonetheless. Beyond any doubt.

Linette had been having an affair.

If I'd been shattered by the accident and her death, I was far beyond that now. The hardwood floors of our apartment seemed suddenly insubstantial, as though I might fall through them, tumbling down and down to the fiery core at the center of the earth. To burn.

And I wanted to. To vanish. Cease to be. Anything to ease the searing agony in my heart.

I must have switched off the lamp, because the room was dark when I heard the noise. Someone rapping at the front door. I didn't answer. Couldn't.

The rapping grew more insistent, and I heard someone calling my name. When the doorknob rattled, I thought they'd go away.

Until a woman in black eased open the door to my study.

"Professor Frazier? Are you all right?"

"No. Not even close, Sergeant Kovacs. How did you get in here?"

"Picked the lock," she shrugged, stepping into my room, glancing around. "The security in these apartments is lousy."

"I'll complain to the landlord. What do you want?"

"Why didn't you answer my knock?"

"I don't want company."

"Sorry about that, but you're not the only victim involved here. Like it or not, I have more questions, and I need to show you something. Do you mind?"

Without waiting for a reply, she unsnapped a laptop computer, placed it on my desk and switched it on. "We pulled this from a surveillance camera at the intersection. It covers the crossroads and the state highway east and west." Grainy black and white images jumped across the screen, the movements herky-jerky from the stop-time photographs.

"I deleted the frames that showed what happened to your car, you wouldn't want to see them. There, that's the guy that hit you." She pointed to a massive gravel truck lumbering east in the right-hand lane. Just before it faded off the screen, the truck jerked to a halt, and the driver leapt out. Black T-shirt and jeans, baseball cap pulled low over his face. I leaned in, scanning the image intently.

"Do you recognize him?"

"His own mother couldn't recognize him from this. Don't you have anything clearer?"

"Afraid not. Big Brother's watching, but only at busy intersections. Look again."

She looped the images, rerunning them in step time, over and over. I stared at them till I thought my eyes would melt. "What's that mark on his upper arm?"

"A tattoo, I think. Possibly a scar. Can't see enough of it to tell. Why?"

For a moment, a faint flicker hovered around the outer edge of my memory....

Then vanished.

"Sorry, Sergeant, I just can't see his face clearly enough to identify him."

"That's because he never shows it. Notice how he raises his arm to shield his face as he exits the truck? Maybe that's not a coincidence."

"What do you mean?"

"Maybe he's familiar with the intersection. He could have covered his face to avoid the surveillance camera. Look, he creamed your car, then abandoned the truck roughly a quarter mile down the road at the edge of camera range. And just disappeared. No one reported seeing him walking or trying to hitch a ride after the accident."

"Then where did he go?"

"We don't know. It's possible he had a vehicle parked further on, but nobody noticed one. I think it's more likely that he ducked into the woods along the roadside. Twenty yards into the trees, a jogging path runs parallel to the highway for almost half a mile. A trail that circles directly back to the university campus."

I was staring at her. "You don't believe he's a drunk or a joyrider, do you?"

"I don't know what he is," she said flatly. "I was hoping you might be able to help."

"I don't know, either. I already told you that."

"Okay, then, let me tell you what we *do* know. For openers, nobody steals county gravel trucks. They have zero resale value, too easy to trace. Second, that truck is a serious piece of machinery, difficult to handle. But this driver plowed you into heavy traffic, peeled off, then had to swerve twice to avoid other cars before bailing out. I doubt a drunk or a joyrider could manage all that. So I think it's at least possible you were rammed deliberately. The question is, why would anyone do a thing like that to you?"

"They wouldn't."

"No? You haven't flunked anybody lately? Maybe booted 'em out of class?"

"I teach history, Sergeant. I have trouble enough generating curiosity, let alone violence."

"History *is* violence, Professor, preserved in the amber of the written word."

I stared at her, surprised. "That's quite good, Sergeant. Sun Tzu, isn't it?"

"I have no idea, I read a lot. So, no disgruntled students? Can you think of anyone else who'd want to harm you? Or Miss Rogers? Anyone at all?"

I hesitated, reading her face. A good face, actually: fine boned, squared off, and direct. Serious eyes, gray and unreadable as winter ice.

"I...think Linette may have been having an affair."

"You *think* so? Do you have any idea who the man is?"

"No. But you don't seem very surprised, Sergeant. You already knew?"

"A few of her friends hinted as much," Kovacs nodded. "They claimed not to know who the man was, either. I gather your girlfriend was...discreet about it. How did you find out?"

"I just…she wrote about it in her poetry. But only in metaphor. She doesn't mention his name. Calls him Apian."

"Ape what?"

"Apian." I spelled it. "A bee. A busy man, I suppose, a take-charge type. My opposite."

"Does that reference mean anything to you?"

"Not yet, but I'm only halfway through the notebooks. I doubt that it's important."

"Right now, we have no idea what might be important," she sighed, easing down in the chair beside my desk. "We're just tugging at strings, hoping to God something will unravel."

"I'd say you're the one who's unraveling, Sergeant. Would you like a cup of coffee? It's already made."

"What I really need is to zonk for twenty minutes," she said, massaging her eyes with her fingertips. "Haven't been to bed since this thing happened."

"You're welcome to crash on my couch—"

"I appreciate the offer, but I haven't time," she said, taking a deep breath, pulling herself together. "The first forty-eight hours are critical. I have to get back on the street. Could you even hazard a guess at who this…Apian might be?"

"No. I didn't know he existed until a few hours ago. What does it matter? What difference does it make?"

"Violent crime usually involves one of the Big Three: love, drugs, or money. Nobody made any money on this deal, and you don't strike me as the drug-dealer type. Which leaves passion. Love, hate, jealousy, in one form or another."

"I'm the wrong guy to ask about love. I clearly know very little about it."

"We're all amateurs in that game, Professor. I've been married twice. To cops, both times. Disasters, both times."

"Sorry."

"Why should you be sorry?"

"Because…you're right. Love's a marvelous thing when it works. It just doesn't seem to work out very often."

"If it did, we'd be bored out of our skulls, and all the blues singers would starve," Kovacs said wryly. "Let's hope we both have better luck next time. I've gotta go."

The runaway truck was replaying on her laptop again. I watched the driver dismount, concealing his face behind his forearm.

"That's the second time you've done that," Kovacs said quietly. "What do you see?"

"Nothing. I just…it's nothing, Sergeant. I wish I could be of more help."

"I'm the one who should apologize," she said, snapping the laptop closed, "for barging in at a bad time. I'm sorry as hell for your loss, Professor Frazier. If you think of anything, or if you just need to blow off some steam, call me, okay? Day or night. I keep odd hours. Okay?"

And then she was gone. And I was alone. In my arid, empty Brave New World.

I'd never thought of death as a new beginning, but in a way, that's exactly what it was.

My love, my old life, and most things I'd believed in were gone. Utterly destroyed. By twenty tons of steel and a few lines of poetry. Yet somehow I would still have to cope. To deal with the details of Linette's death. Her funeral, her eulogy, a burial plot….

But above all, I needed an explanation. A way to make sense of what had happened to us. Some sort of logic, Cause and Effect.

Had I failed her somehow? Caused her to stray? Had her affair brought on this tragedy? It seemed unlikely, but it was a place to start. And I'm a scholar, by nature and profession.

So I poured myself a stiff jolt of brandy and sat back down at my desk with Linette's workbooks. To begin researching a new field of study. Well, new to me, anyway.

Actually, it's one of the oldest subjects: The Architecture of Infidelity 101, Methodology and Procedures.

I opened the third notebook of verses. In it, Linette described her growing attraction, physical and spiritual, to her Apian. And her sadly reluctant withdrawal from her Lute Player. A reference to me, I suppose. I minored in medieval music at State.

Over the period of months spanned in the sonnets, she described the physical raptures of new love and…sweet Jesus, it was very difficult to focus on this. To remain objective.

As I read on, I kept having flashes of my love, naked and passionate, with another man….

Suddenly I lunged to my feet, gasping, gagging on a surge of acid bile in my throat. Swallowing hard, I managed to force it back down.

And then I forced myself back down, to take my seat in that chair again. And somehow go on. If I didn't wade through this now, ugly and painful as it was, I knew I never would.

And I desperately needed to know. To understand. Where we'd gone wrong. How we'd gone wrong. And how much of it was my fault.

So I read on. Sipping brandy against the sting of Linette's poetry. And gradually, the ache began to ease a bit, as the affair ran its course. Her wondrous Apian slowly but surely showed himself to be less perfect than she'd believed in that first glow of infatuation. He was human, after all.

And flawed. The self-confidence she'd admired so much proved to be simple arrogance. And his decisiveness left no room for dissent. He was more than strong, he was domineering.

Abruptly, her verses took on a darker tone. She met a Gray Lady. Who soon morphed into the Good Gray Wife.

Surprise, surprise. Linette's Apian was married.

She must have been aware of it, but in the heat of passion she'd brushed it aside. Until she actually *met* his Good Gray Wife. And liked her. A lot. And the consequences of her betrayal truly began to register.

Then a second jolt. Her Apian was an even greater rogue than she'd thought. He was not only cheating on his wife. He was cheating on Linette as well, with a new lover. And she felt shattered and betrayed—

Closing the book, I massaged my eyes, feeling a pain in my chest so sharp I thought I might be dying. Aching for all that was lost. For Linette and our lost love. And for her pain. And my own.

It's so unfair that love has such terrible power over us. To bathe our whole world in shimmering light or plunge it into darkness. Why can't things just...work the hell out? Lovers stay together—

Because we'd be bored out of our skulls, and all the blues singers would starve.

The thought jolted me like a slap in the face. I could almost hear Kovacs saying it. Joshing me out of a funk as Linette had done a thousand times before.

Women. Their hearts are terra incognita to me. I'll never understand them at all. Nor will any other man.

So I took a ragged breath and shook off my self-pity. I felt like a fighter who's been decked in the eighth round and still has four to go, but I couldn't quit now. I was nearing the end.

And so was the affair. As I paced the room, scanning the final verses, I realized that Linette's infatuation with her Apian lover was finally over. She told him she wanted to break it off—

And he hit her!

Damn it! I remembered a bruise on her jaw, only a week ago. She said she'd banged into a door at work, and like an idiot I'd believed her—but there was more. After calling him the coward he was, she promised to warn his Good Gray Wife....

And that was the final verse. I flipped through the rest of the pages, but they were blank. There were no more verses.

I closed the book slowly. Stunned. When Linette tried to break off the affair, her Apian reacted with violence. And then she'd threatened to tell his wife—

—and now she was dead. And a lot of people were injured. All because of an affair that had gone terribly wrong?

I didn't know that, not for sure. And it didn't matter, anyway, because I still had no idea who the man was.

But maybe I could find out. I may not be a man of action, but scholars know how to study. And learn.

I didn't need the verses now. I only needed to concentrate, to think through the situation clearly and objectively. About a woman I adored making love to another man.

It was even tougher than reading the verses.

Pacing my small office, I mulled through the minutiae of betrayal. Several verses had referred to making love in fading or waning light, so they'd probably met in the late afternoon. On Tuesdays and Thursdays, Linette's library shift ended at three-thirty. Two hours before my last class got out. She usually picked me up after—

I swallowed. After whatever happened.

She was never late. Nor could I think of many unexplained absences. Which narrowed it down to those two hours—or less, if you counted driving time.

Our apartment was a thirty-minute commute from the campus library, so for the affair to work…they must have been meeting somewhere near the university. Or at it.

Which meant her Apian might well be one of my colleagues. Perhaps even a friend…and for a split second I glimpsed the film fragment of that tattoo again. Damn it! I'd seen it somewhere before. I *knew* it! But couldn't place where….

Forget it. It would come in its own time. Or not.

Concentrate.

Linette's lover was probably someone I knew. Which was logical, if not much comfort. Picking up a class schedule from my desk, I scanned through the names and thumbnail photos, found myself imagining each of them with Linette. God. Couldn't handle that.

Pushing the images away, I chose a different approach.

I tried to recall any suspicious comments she'd made about my colleagues. It wasn't difficult. I have an excellent memory, especially where Linette is concerned. But I couldn't remember anything out of the ordinary, and none of them seemed likely candidates anyway. Most of my colleagues are as bookish as I am.

But I wasn't looking for a real person, was I? Apian would have to seem larger than life, somehow. An idealized figure. Heroic. And busy as a bee.

I quickly reduced the directory to a short list of active, energetic types: athletic coaches, administrators, board members. Then I scanned their bios, looking for some connection—

And there it was.

A powerful, very busy man. A self-made man. Who'd worked his way through college on the G.I. Bill after serving in the Navy during Operation Desert Storm, Gulf War I.

In a Construction Battalion, or C.B. More commonly known as the Seabees. Where he drove heavy equipment.

The Seabee emblem was an angry bee toting a rivet gun.

A tattoo I'd seen on the muscular bicep of Dean John Mackey, head of the university's Humanities Department.

My boss.

God. How could Linette...? No! Don't think about that. Focus. Concentrate on the problem at hand.

Dean Mackey was definitely a man I knew, though not very well. Senior administrators seldom mix with lowly profs. But I did know a thing or two about Big John.

We'd played in the same racquetball league last term. I'd even played against him a few times.

And he cheated. He'd deliberately block your path to the ball with a shoulder or even his racquet. Hell, he'd drive you through the wall, rather than concede a point.

These were just friendly pickup games. No money, no prestige, not even any spectators. No reason at all to cheat. And yet Mackey did. Regularly. He just couldn't bear to lose. At anything.

Big John's bullyboy tactics were an open joke around the locker room. But no one ever called him on it. Petty or not, Mackey was still head of the department.

Which was the second thing I knew about him. His position was political, not academic. His appointment came after a substantial donation to the school by his wife Doreen, a Dodge Motors heiress.

Dory Mackey is a few years older than John. A good, gray wife. But a proud, wealthy woman, who'd drop her husband like a hot rock if she learned he was cheating.

And Linette had promised to do exactly that. Break off the affair and warn his wife. And John Mackey was a powerful man with an ego and temper to match. He would not be discarded. Nor threatened.

So he lashed out. First with his fists, and when that didn't work—

Sweet Jesus. Big John had been at the wheel of that truck. I knew it now, beyond the shadow of a doubt.

The question was, what could I do about it?

Linette was drawn to Mackey because she saw him as a man of action. And I'm not. She was quite right about that. The little I know about violence generally involves Goths or Tartars, dead a thousand years before I was born.

But now I had to deal with the reality of real violence. A brutal killing committed by a man of wealth and influence. Who might well be beyond the reach of the law.

I could almost picture his attorneys scanning Linette's lyrics. And laughing. Her gossamer verses weren't proof of anything, and John's tattoo only confirmed his honorable military service.

If I accused the dean of the Humanities Department of murder on the strength of a few murky poems and a partial tattoo glimpsed on a grainy security-camera playback, I'd be fired, and my claims would be dismissed as the ravings of a grief-stricken cuckold.

And yet....

I could not let this pass. God knows, without Linette, I had little enough to live for. Somehow, I would have to settle up with Mackey. Or die trying.

Famous Last Words.

The funeral-home chapel was filled to capacity, standing room only, with a train of mourners spilling out onto the steps, a testament to Linette's vivacious spirit, the *joie de vivre* she'd shared with so many.

I thought Sergeant Kovacs might be there but didn't see her. I did see the man who mattered most, though. Dean John Mackey made an entrance just before the service began, accompanied by his wealthy gray wife.

I half-expected some sign of guilt or concern, but there was nothing.

Mackey was the picture of solicitude, greeting my colleagues and Linette's friends like a senior member of our bereaved family. Which he was, I suppose.

But seeing him there, with Linette's broken body boxed in a coffin, awaiting delivery to the flames, it was all I could do to keep from charging into the crowd to get my hands around his bull neck.

But I didn't. I kept my peace and my place at the edge of the dais, greeting the mourners, accepting condolences, making appropriate responses.

"Thanks for coming, I know how much Linette would appreciate it." Blah, blah, and so on. All the proper platitudes.

And all the time, waiting.

Then, suddenly, he was in front of me. Dean John Mackey. Burly and sure of himself in an impeccably tailored dark suit. Offering his sympathy like an old friend. Or trying to.

Without thinking, I locked onto his hand with more force than I knew I owned. And met his eyes. Then leaned in to whisper.

"I know what you did, you sonofabitch. Linette kept a diary, and your name's on every page. Once she's laid to rest, I'm taking it straight to the police. Brace yourself, Big John. Armageddon's coming."

Any doubts I had were erased by the mix of shock and murderous rage in his eyes. And he wasn't the only one. At his shoulder, his wife had gone pale as a ghost. She'd overheard every word.

"John, what on earth—?"

"Shut up!" he snapped. Seizing her arm, he practically dragged Dory past the startled line of mourners and out of the chapel, leaving me to deal with the curious stares of the crowd.

I didn't care. Confronting Mackey had been my last duty to Linette. Only the final words remained now. Her eulogy.

I began with one of Linette's verses, then went on, speaking from my heart. I shared my pain at her terrible loss but shared my gratitude as well. That I had been lucky enough to know this marvelous woman at all, let alone share her love. Even for a little while.

It was probably the best single address I've ever given. And it wasn't even necessary. When I finished, others rose to express their grief and mourn their fallen friend. Dozens of them. The ceremony continued long past its allotted hour. As powerful and moving a time as I've ever known.

But eventually, it drew to an end. The organist played "Amazing Grace," and everyone sang. And that was it.

Perhaps I was supposed to thank people as they left, but I was too depleted to make nice. I slipped into the minister's empty office instead, waiting for the chapel to clear out.

Then I sat silent in the chapel's front row, watching as Linette's coffin was lowered hydraulically from the dais to the crematorium below and consigned to the flames.

She'd always been an ethereal spirit. Now she was free to soar at last. A glint of quicksilver across the sky.

And I was free as well. The bitterness over her betrayal was gone. Burned away. Only her memory remained. And the ache of her loss.

Dusk was falling as I finally trudged out to my rental car. Climbing in, I lowered the windows and sat quietly a moment, breathing in deep draughts of cool autumn air, trying to fill the hollow in my heart.

Time to go. Firing up the rental, I headed home to my apartment.

I didn't make it. At an intersection, I was waiting for the light to change when a utility van suddenly roared out of a side street, screeching to a halt beside my sedan.

Its windows were down, and for a split second I stared into John Mackey's wild eyes before he raised his shotgun to fire.

I only had a split second, but this time I knew exactly what to say.

"Gun!" I shouted, diving under the dash.

In the back seat, Kovacs threw her blanket aside and came up with a pistol in her fist, blasting three quick rounds that blew out the van's side window, ripping into Mackey's shoulder.

His shotgun went off, and something slammed into the side of my head....

For the second time that week, I woke in a hospital. Groggy and aching but in less pain than before. Had no idea how long I'd been out or what time it was.

Sergeant Shane Kovacs was slumped in the chair beside my bed, her chin resting on her palm. Sound asleep. I studied her face in the pale light. A good face. Not conventionally pretty, I suppose, but strong and honest. A bit careworn, I thought….

When I woke again, she was watching me.

"We can't go on meeting like this," she said, straightening in her chair. "How do you feel?"

"Awful. What happened?"

"Mackey's shotgun blast shattered your windshield, and some of the fragments gave you a pretty good whack in the head. You've been out cold for several hours."

"What about Mackey?"

"His wounds aren't serious. He'll live to stand trial. One slug zipped through that Seabee tattoo he was so proud of. I'd call that poetic justice."

"It all happened so fast. Aren't you supposed to shout a warning? 'Stop or I'll shoot?' Something like that?"

"There was no time, his gun was up. Besides, you warned him at the funeral. He had plenty of time to change his mind. But he didn't." She leaned forward intently. "And you knew he wouldn't. That's why you asked me to hide in your car. How did you know he'd come after you?"

"Linette described him perfectly: a man of action. When I threatened him, he turned violent, as he did before. Only this time, you were there to nail him."

"And if I'd been too slow?"

"Even bookworms have to take occasional risks."

"Well, thanks to you and Linette, Mackey will be arraigned for murder and attempted murder as soon as the hospital cuts him loose. And from the screaming match they had in the emergency room, I don't think his wife will be bankrolling his defense."

"He's always claimed to be a self-made man. He certainly made this disaster on his own."

"And what about you, Professor? What will you do?"

"I haven't thought much about it. Take a few days off to pull myself together, I suppose. Then go back to teaching. I'm a scholar. A bit of a drudge, actually. Linette was right about that, too."

"I'd better get back," Kovacs said, rising to leave. "Can I offer you some friendly advice, Professor?"

"You saved my life, Sergeant Kovacs. Offer away."

"Fair enough. No disrespect intended, but for a perceptive woman, your girlfriend made some incredibly stupid moves. She idealized Mackey into some kind of conquering hero, and it cost her everything. Don't make the same mistake. Don't idealize her memory into some kind of...Apian. She deserves better than that. And so do you."

I stared at her, surprised. Meeting those intelligent gray eyes. "You're pretty perceptive yourself, Sergeant. I'll remember the advice. And you."

"Sorry if I overstepped."

"You didn't. And I'm sorry, too."

"About what?"

"That we met in such terrible circumstances. Given the ways of the world, I probably won't be seeing you again."

She hesitated in the doorway, giving me an odd, unreadable look.

"Famous last words," she said.

Pewter Badge

by Michael J. Solender
(Best Short Story, 2011)

I never killed a cop before.

She is barely taller than my fifteen-year-old daughter. The brim of her cop hat wouldn't likely hit my chin.

Muñoz. Her pewter-hued badge stated her name proudly.

I figured she's likely first-generation American. She's probably the first in her family to go to college. Officer Muñoz is certainly the first in her family to become a cop.

"OK, sir, just sit tight. I'll be right back," Muñoz said rather politely, not having the least inkling of how my knife was gonna feel in her gut when she came back with my license.

Sweat was rolling down the crack of my ass, adding to the already pasty mass of my boxers that bunched up under my jeans. It was never this humid in L.A., but the breezes in from the coast and the recent rain were enough to trigger the cactus and Joshua trees to bloom, a rarity. This was not lost on the gardeners, who hailed it at the same time the mugginess was being cursed by guys like me with no A/C in their cars.

"Yes, miss," I manage to say, trying to figure in my mind exactly how I'm gonna cut her when she comes back and orders me out of the car. She'll call for backup after she runs my driver's license.

I'm done for. Knives lose to guns every time, and all I have is my stiletto.

I can't figure out why she pulled me over. The car is registered to me, and

I know I wasn't speeding. Hell, I was playing it cool. There is no way they already found the body. I mean, he wasn't even cold yet.

What the hell is taking her? I'm watching her in the rearview, and she's on her radio, eyes straight ahead at me.

Jesus, I'm getting sick, sitting here sucking exhaust on Western. Every greaser, *chollo*, and lowrider in the city stares down at the poor pulled-over sumbitch as they pass me flashing gangbanger hand signs.

I reach down into the glove box for my smokes.

"Sir!" Her amplified loudspeaker crackles like a squawking crow through the humid midday sun. "Please keep both hands where I can see them."

I put my hands back on the wheel, but not before feeling the stiletto in my waistband. I was careful to wipe it clean of Zumi's blood, which was all over the handle and the blade. Christ, I didn't understand why Mick wanted his tongue cut out and brought back to him, but my job was not to ask questions, just to do his bidding.

Sitting in her cop car behind me, I see Muñoz working her computer. I'm dying here. I got Zumi's tongue in a zip-top bag inside a pink donut box that I took off his counter. It's sitting right there on my front seat, mocking me. I hadn't noticed until this very moment, but there's a huge bloody streak down the side of the box. A Rorschach, courtesy of Zumi, screaming at me from the side of the donut box.

Zumi was still breathing, barely, when I left him ten minutes ago. He had to have bled to death by now, and there was no way he was moving or talking to anyone after what I did to his tongue. Apparently being on Mick's payroll wasn't enough for him, he had to snitch for the vice squad, too. Mick didn't much care for that arrangement and wanted to send a signal to his other runners this kinda shit wouldn't fly.

That's where I came in. Mick's muscle. That's what they called me. Occasionally I'd slice off a finger or two, but never a tongue—and before today only one hit. Now I was about to be a cop killer. My day was not looking up.

"Sir." Muñoz was at the passenger window, and I had been so caught up, I hadn't noticed her leave her car and come up to mine. The bloody pink box was just below her chin as she leaned into my car, handing me my license.

"Yes, officer?"

"Do you know why I pulled you over?"

I see another cop car approaching in my rearview; this one pulls past us and stops in front of my car.

"No, officer. I don't think I was speeding." Like everyone in L.A. doesn't go twenty mph over the limit all the time.

The driver's door on the cop car ahead of me opens up, and a huge mofo cop, twice the size of Muñoz, gets out and starts walking back to us. I slide my hand subtly to my waist and my sharp little situation helper.

"Your tags are expired. In fact, they're two years overdue. The state needs their revenue, so we can keep these fine roads up."

The giant robocop sidles up to my side of the car and greets his fellow cop. "Hey, Carmen, what have we got here?"

I'm dead now. The pool in my shorts is now a lake.

"Expired tags. He's gonna have 'em paid for today, though, aren't you, Mr. Fraser?"

My head stops reeling. Shit, she's gonna let me go. I start to breathe again. "Yes, officer, right now. Gonna go home and write the check today."

I start my car.

The Amazonian cop says, "Hold on, buddy, are those donuts you got there? Don't you think a warning instead of a ticket deserves what's in the box for Officer Muñoz?"

I start to stutter and sputter, unable to say anything.

Muñoz looks down at the box and then up at her cop buddy. "Naw, I gotta lose a few, and you sure as hell don't need one. Have a nice day, Mr. Fraser. Get your tags taken care of."

I slowly pull out into the buzz that is Western Avenue. It's July. I'm sweating like a pig. I got some punk's tongue in a pink box sitting next to me.

I gotta get a new job.

The Touch of Death

by BV Lawson
(Best Short Story, 2012)

Larry liked being around kids at the park, watching them from his splintered bench where he had to wipe the bird shit off every morning. The parents probably thought he was one of those perv geezers, but that wasn't it at all. It was the stillness of the children that attracted him.

He'd long ago learned he couldn't shut out the sounds of death around him, so he'd learned to push them into the background, like his own "tape mix," as the young people called it. Worms desiccating in the sun, the last heartbeat of a squirrel as it turned into roadkill, the last gasp of a heart-attack patient in an ambulance speeding by. If he listened closely enough, he could even hear clots forming in the coronary arteries of pedestrians strolling along the hiking trail.

But the kids, they were young and healthy, and the only sounds he heard from them were whatever came out of their mouths. Like the tow-haired boy a few feet away, taunting a girl who was about the boy's age. Eight? Nine? Larry couldn't tell these things. The children drew closer, and Larry watched the boy as he folded the middle three fingers of his hand, leaving the thumb and pinky standing straight up, then waved the hand at the girl. "I'll put the touch of death on you," he cried.

As the little girl ran away screaming, Larry grabbed the boy's upraised hand. "Wherever did you learn that?" he asked.

"I saw it on TV." The boy squinted at Larry in the sun. "Don't you ever watch the Simpsons, mister?"

"Guess I don't." Fact was, Larry hadn't owned a TV in three decades.

"Bart put the touch of death on his sister." Larry dropped the boy's hand, so the child formed the touch again and waggled his fist. "It was a joke. He skipped out on karate class. But he wanted everyone to think he'd been there and learned something." The boy saw a woman waving to him. "My mom's calling. Gotta go."

Larry watched him skip over to his mother. Too bad she'd be dead in a few years from the cancer that was forming in her lungs.

Touch of death, my ass, he said to himself. *It's that Dim Mak crap again.* Another martial-arts joke, one that had propagated for centuries. All those schmucks kicking and flailing and chopping this way and that, as if you could teach somebody to use a "psychic vibrator" or whatever to mess with someone's life force.

A killing touch couldn't be taught like piano or French grammar. You had to be born with it. All that other nonsense was just men trying to compensate for their inadequacies, comparing dicks in the locker room.

Larry sighed and dragged his carcass off the bench. He had to go meet Samuzzo. He'd put it off as long as he could. Damn the man. Why couldn't he leave Larry alone? Why couldn't he let Larry stay retired?

Larry hailed a cab to take him to Pier 26 at the wharf, where he always insisted on meeting Samuzzo, and always in the morning. Lots of quiet water and sky, away from the boats with their dying fish that wouldn't start anchoring in until the evening.

Samuzzo, on the other hand, was a walking death machine. You could say that of anyone who'd lived as long as Samuzzo in his particular business, dispatching his competitors and betrayers neatly and efficiently. But Larry wasn't sure he'd ever met anyone else who could have chomping parasites in his gut, scars in his cirrhotic liver, and a heart doing an impression of a drunk drummer and still be alive and upright.

Samuzzo looked Larry up and down and didn't shake his hand. But he never did. The coward. "You know why I'm here, Larry. I need you to do me a favor. You'll get the usual amount."

Larry was unimpressed. "You said the last one was it, finito, end of story."

"Yeah, yeah, so I lied. This one's important, Lar." The way Samuzzo said it, "Lar" always rhymed with "prayer," which he probably thought was funny. Real hilarious.

"They're always important."

"Extra important. And if you do this one last job for me, I swear I won't bother you again. That's how important it is."

"So gimme the abridged version, Sammie. Tell me why I should care."

"Why should you care? He beats his kids bloody, that's why. Put one in the hospital, but he covered it up good. And he raped a thirteen-year-old. Covered that up, too. Me, I just want the double-crosser out of my way."

Samuzzo knew Larry's weakness. Kids. Damn the man. "Okay, I'll do it, but this has to be the last time, Sammie. I mean it."

Samuzzo also had advanced gingivitis, and when he smiled, his yellow and black teeth weren't nearly as disgusting as the sounds of the bacteria eating away at his gums. "Sure, Lar. It'll be the last."

"So who is this child-beating scum?"

"Bob Prosifka."

"The congressman?"

"That's right. Shame, too, as he was a cheap bribe."

Larry began to recall items he'd read in the papers. Hints of ethics violations, never proven. Corruption charges he'd blamed on a smear campaign. Then Larry remembered another story, about the congressman's son being taken to the emergency room after "falling down some stairs."

"Okay, but isn't he surrounded by handlers all the time?"

"Yes and no. He likes to get his own breakfast at Beaman's on Wednesdays. Walks the two blocks from his luxury apartment to get his chocolate-croissant fix. Alone."

"That's tomorrow."

"So it is. At least it will be over and done with soon, eh?" Samuzzo walked over to his waiting limo. "I've wired half to your account. The other half will arrive when I see the headline in the newspaper."

Larry realized there were many people—if they knew of the distasteful arrangement between Samuzzo the mobster and his unusual hit man—who would wonder why Larry didn't take Samuzzo out himself and be done with it. But they didn't know Larry's code. He only used his gift when he was paid to do it. And that had worked well. This way, society got rid of some lowlifes, and the money angle helped Larry avoid any more accidental deaths. He hadn't had one of those since his Army days, when he'd first gotten paid for killing.

Larry knew Beaman's and the street it was on quite well. He'd met his fourth wife there. She used to fry up his doughnuts extra crisp, because she knew he liked them that way. But Laura, like the others, left him when his secrets and his brooding got to be too much. That and the way Larry nagged them constantly not to smoke or drink or eat this or that or the other thing, because he could hear what it was doing to them inside.

Larry had a hard time sleeping that night, worrying about the logistics of the hit. He'd never done a congressman before and could envision bodyguards, guns, secretaries, mistresses, a horde of potential problems and witnesses. But in the end, it turned out to be one of the easiest ever.

Must have been a run on doughnuts that morning, because the line at Beaman's was out the door. Trying to ignore the woman with the aneurysm about to blow and the man with advanced prostate cancer as they walked inside, Larry tarried at the newspaper stand by the door until he saw the good congressman approaching.

Casual-like, Larry got in line behind him, newspaper outstretched as if reading the latest scandal. When the opportunity came, it was like a gift from the heavens—and so unexpected Larry almost missed it.

The young woman in front of Prosifka, glued to a playing-card-sized phone screen in front of her and pushing tiny buttons with her thumbs like mad, stepped back—right into the congressman, who promptly fell over. Right onto Larry.

As Larry put a hand on Prosifka to help him up, the familiar tingling, then burning, began flowing through his veins and into the capillaries, then into the very cells of his fingertips. It wasn't painful, but more of an orgasmic release of energy from his skin into the arm of the other man.

Larry watched as the familiar look of surprise appeared on Prosifka's face. Then the color drained from it, and Prosifka fell onto the floor. Others rushed over to help, and Larry waited just long enough for the paramedics to arrive and pronounce the congressman dead before he slipped quietly away.

Samuzzo had been correct, years ago, when he called it the perfect weapon. Reaching out to steady someone, putting a hand on a shoulder in passing, the hit man disguised as a good Samaritan. No one ever suspected, and no one ever would.

When Larry saw the headline the next day in the newspaper he used to scrape the bird poop off the bench at the park, he knew he'd be a lot richer later that afternoon. He'd never used much of the money he earned, living simply, content to sit and watch the silent children.

That tow-haired boy was here again today. Bart, wasn't it? No, that was the cartoon. The boy wasn't making his touch-of-death motions anymore, and Larry hoped he'd forget it soon. It looked like he was more interested in playing with a football.

Larry was so content it took a while to register the black limo pulling up behind him. Then he recognized Samuzzo's driver approaching the splintered bench. The driver stood behind the bench long enough to say, "Samuzzo said to tell you thanks, nice work. But he wants to meet you at Pier 26 later today." Then he ducked back inside the car, and it started to pull away.

Pier 26. So Sammie had lied again when he said this hit would be the last. Larry knew it would never end. More hits, more death. Larry rubbed his face and closed his eyes but quickly opened them again when he first heard, then saw as if in slow motion the little tow-haired boy chasing his football out into the street. Right in front of the black limo.

Larry knew Samuzzo would have felt the bump, heard the thud, but Sammie was an old pro at self-preservation. The limo sped up and disappeared quickly down a side street, so fast it would have been a miracle for someone to get the plate.

Though he knew it was too late, Larry headed over to the boy and held the blond head gently in his hands, as he heard the little heart stop beating. The boy's mother was screaming and crying at the same time, as she pushed past Larry to reach her son. In her haste, her purse fell open, and out tumbled a wad of cash and some coins. Larry deftly pocketed a quarter.

He'd never set a limit, great or small, on the amount of money he'd take for a hit. A quarter from the boy's mother was as good a payment as any. Larry was actually looking forward to meeting Sammie at the wharf later today. And for once, he was going to make sure he shook Samuzzo's hand.

When Duty Calls

by Art Taylor
(Best Long Story, 2013)

Keri is just setting out the silverware when the Colonel calls across from the living room with a new question. He's watching the Military Channel and finishing up the cocktail she made for him—a thimble of Virginia Gentleman, a generous portion of soda, another light splash of whiskey on top to make it smell like a stronger drink. The Colonel's house has an open floor plan from the kitchen through the dining room to where he sits, and as she's finished up dinner, she's listened to him arguing lightly with the program's depiction of Heartbreak Ridge, reminiscing about his own stint in Korea, rambling in his own way. "Last rally of the Shermans," he mused aloud, and something about "optics" and "maneuverability" and then—a different tone than Keri's heard in the four months she's known him—"Is the perimeter secure, Sergeant?"

"The perimeter?" Keri asks, cautiously. She's grown used to these sudden shifts in subject—learned quickly just to roll along with the conversation, even in the first days after she and Pete moved in. But she still stumbles sometimes to catch up and find the right response.

The Colonel turns in his chair—turning *on* her, Keri thinks, expecting his regular confusion or the occasional rebuke—but he doesn't look her way. He's listening, it seems, his jaw fixed, his chin jutting more than usual. The tendons in his frail arms tighten, his tie tugs at the skin around his neck, his whole body perches alert, if unsteadily so. Medals and photos crowd the wall behind him. Round stickers dot many of them and almost everything else in the living room: lamps, books, bookcases, the chair itself. Red, white, and blue.

"Incoming," he says.

"No one's out there, Colonel," she tries to reassure him. Not anymore, at least, since that pair of surveyors out in the woods had packed up their bags a half-hour before, one of them waving at her through the window before cranking up, heading out. They'd stayed late. She was glad to see them go.

"Vibrations," the Colonel whispers. "A good soldier can sense these things. Life and death." Just his mind wandering, she knows, just another bout of dementia, but for a moment the seriousness of his tone, the weight of his words, stops her. Despite herself, she looks toward the door. Has he actually heard something? The surveyors had forgotten something, returned unannounced. Or maybe Pete had canceled his Tuesday-night classes in town to come home early. But no. There's no knock at the door and no sound of a key turning in it. No muddy shoes being brushed against the mat. No sound of tires on the gravel drive. Just the TV program rolling on. Strategies, skirmishes, victories, defeat.

"Did Pete call?" she asks.

"Negative," the Colonel says casually, just the hint of disdain, and then he relaxes, settles back into his chair. "Radio silence has been maintained."

There's something melancholy in his answer, or maybe it's Keri's imagination this time. She wonders if he even notices how seldom the phone rings—for either of them. Calls come so rarely that she once raised the receiver to her ear just to make sure there was a dial tone there. More than once, actually.

"Lasagna's ready," she tells him, and the Colonel brightens up.

"Officer's Club," he says eagerly. Date night, she knows.

Other nights, mealtime is just "chow," but on Tuesdays Pete always stays on campus late, and the Colonel seems to love those nights best. She's not sure how she goes from being his staff sergeant to being his ... wife? Girlfriend? Daughter? She's not sure about that, either: which role she plays. He doesn't seem to know who she is at all, has never even spoken her name. But sometimes, when Pete is out of the way, the Colonel reaches over and presses his gnarled fingers over her hand, pats, squeezes, breaking Keri's heart a little each time.

"It's a good deal," Pete said after the interview with the Colonel's daughter, after she'd offered them the job. Do a little housecleaning, make a couple of meals a day for the old man, and in exchange: free rent, a grocery stipend, a monthly bonus. A six-month stint. "The whole semester," Pete went on. "Not just a good deal, but a *great* one, especially with teaching-assistant stipends these days." He didn't need to add that Keri was unemployed herself, had been for a while.

It was that last part that convinced Keri and kept her from pointing out how much of the cooking and housecleaning quickly fell to her. Pete was at least pulling his weight elsewhere, wasn't he? Teaching a freshman survey course in western drama? Pursuing his own PhD? She could hardly complain about doing the dishes, when he had lessons to prep and essays to grade and all that reading to do: Shakespeare, Ibsen, O'Neill, Beckett, Miller. And then fitting in work on his doctoral dissertation around the edges. He was already the golden boy of the doctoral program, destined to be the star of some big English department. She shared those dreams, and she tried not to nag him about her own. That wasn't the woman she wanted to be—about work or marriage, about children somewhere down the line.

"We're both in school," Pete had said, more than once, when she talked about the future. "Student loans won't pay themselves." And that dissertation wouldn't write itself. And tenure-line jobs didn't come knocking on your door. School first, life later. She'd grown accustomed to that.

But now, with the semester living at the Colonel's, with the savings, he'd hinted more about next steps. "With the money we're saving here, we can set aside a little bit," he said, "for the future."

Maybe it was for the best for her to shoulder the work at the house while he focused on his education. And maybe there were other good reasons that Pete's duties around the house were more limited. After all, the Colonel didn't seem entirely to approve of him. He didn't like the meals that Pete tried to make ("too spicy" once, "too bland" another time), he didn't like all the time he spent reading ("needs to get off his duff"), and he generally peppered Pete with complaints on a regular basis.

"A trip to the barber in your future anytime, son?" the Colonel asked one morning. "That hardly seems regulation length."

Other mornings—more than once: "Those shoes need a good buffing, soldier."

And on the nights when Pete did join them for dinner: "Where's your tie, boy?"

The Colonel wears a tie each night for dinner, tied in an elaborate knot. "A full Windsor," he told Keri when she asked. "Most men employ the half-Windsor or the four-in-hand, but that's too casual for me."

"A little old school, don't you think?" Pete said, when Keri asked him to try it one evening, just a single meal, just to humor the old man. "And that wasn't part of the deal, now, was it?"

"Recruits these days," the Colonel sometimes says, just under his breath. "A sorry lot, all of them."

When Keri stands up to clear the table, the Colonel stands quickly as well to help. Even when she dismisses him—"No worries, I can do it" (he's dropped plates before)—he hesitates before heading back toward the TV. He's waiting for her, she knows.

"Just let me get this cleaned up," she says, "and I'll be right in, okay?"

"Roger that," he says. "Rendezvous"—he glances at his watch—"twenty hundred hours?"

"Roger," Keri salutes, mock serious. These days, she doesn't have to count out the real time anymore. "I'll meet you in the den."

She stores the lasagna away in squares—leftovers for the week ahead—and sets aside a large slice for Pete, though she knows he'll already have eaten dinner and probably gone out for drinks after class. Winding-down time after the intensity of the three-hour seminars, he's explained.

The window above the kitchen sink has a wide view of the yard. The gravel driveway stretches off to the right between the trees, a hundred yards to the main road, a lonely stretch leading "off base." Shadows play in the woods directly ahead, thick with oak and pine and beech, many of them now tied with red ribbons, marked for timber. Moonlight glistens on the lake off to the left, just barely in sight from this vantage, a rough shoreline that Keri and the Colonel have walked on more than one afternoon, counting Canada geese. A full moon tonight, Keri notes, as if that might explain the tension in the air.

Throughout dinner, the Colonel seemed restless, attentive. Now, as Keri scrubs at the casserole pan, she finds herself watchful, too. Is there "incoming"? She thinks about the people she's seen in and around the property sometimes. Fishermen bring small skiffs close to shore or actually trudge down the driveway in their waders, tossing a small wave toward the house as they pass. Hunters often wander through the woods, unsure whose property they've crossed into at any point. More than once, teenagers have pulled a car up the drive—couples, groups, looking for a place to hook up, get high, get into trouble. Then, beginning last week, there came the onslaught of real-estate agents and surveyors, the men from the tree service, the crew taking soil samples, the beginning of the end. Today's surveyors had lingered until almost dusk, and she'd had the feeling of being trapped somehow, or watched at least, like she and the Colonel were on display, sad curiosities. A couple of times, she caught the men just standing there, smoking cigarettes, staring toward the house. Leering, she thought, no better than construction workers ogling passersby.

She doesn't know which is worse—the isolation she's been feeling out here or these sudden intrusions, and the knowledge of what they mean. Stuck somewhere between the two and spurred on by the Colonel's own brewing vigilance tonight, her imagination leaps ahead again, playing tricks on her. *Is that the red tip of a cigarette butt?* No, just one of the ribbons flapping in the moonlight. *Did that shadow move?* No, just a branch swaying in the breeze.

"Full moon," she says aloud, and then remembers her horoscope from earlier that day: *Surprises abound. Follow where the evening takes you. All will become clear.* Pete still makes fun of her for reading them each morning.

Behind her, the Colonel turns up the TV—hinting for her to join him. The announcer is talking about the Trojan War, the horse that made history, the importance of surprise. Keri shivers a little.

"Coming," she calls to him.

The pan still isn't clean. And she hasn't even started on the knife, crusted with cheese. She leaves both to soak until later—even till tomorrow, perhaps.

"He's dotty," Margaret, the former caretaker, had said, the second time they'd met—the passing on of the keys. She was an older woman: fifties, stout, frizzy-haired. "You'll find out soon enough. And you've got your work cut out for you with him. With all of them."

The first time they'd met was when Keri and Pete had been interviewed for the job. Margaret had brooded along the edges of the conversation as Claire, the youngest of the Colonel's children, put a different spin on the situation: "The world has passed my father by," she said. "We've striven to preserve his old glories, revere his achievements." She swept an arm about the room. Medals and honors dominated one wall. Photographs with politicians and military leaders lined another—many of them, Keri had since learned, long dead. Several framed boxes held guns, relics of a recent past, like museum pieces but brimming with menace. "Unfortunately, everything that my father trained for, everything that he lived for—none of it has much purpose here."

Claire explained that it was just short-term. Margaret had been called to help her own father; plans were already afoot to sell the property but might take some time, and they were finally looking into "more professional care" for the Colonel—a step they'd dreaded and delayed for too long. Claire herself had tended to him for several years after her mother died. "But I couldn't manage any longer," she explained. "Physically, yes, but emotionally...well, watching someone you love so dearly deteriorate, become a shadow, sometimes you just feel yourself breaking down as well." Keri and Pete would be a stopgap. She was sure they understood.

The Colonel was napping while they talked. Margaret had shot a couple of looks at Keri throughout the conversation: envy, disbelief, warning glares? Keri hadn't been sure. (Margaret told her later, on the sly, that Claire was a drinker. Claire, in turn, confided that Margaret was a thief—little things, but hardly negligible.)

It was after the Colonel went down for his nap another afternoon, only a week ago now, that Claire and her siblings—Beatrice and Dwight—had made their inventory. This was the first time that Keri had met the other two, since both lived out of state, and Margaret's comment about having her work cut out for her with "all of them" echoed throughout the day.

With Pete on campus again—early office hours, eternal office hours—Keri had played host alone. Claire asked her to make a salad for lunch, "something simple, no trouble," and Keri had, laying it out on the table, not planning to join them until the Colonel insisted, asking his son to move down a seat, make room for the ladies.

Dwight had smirked at that. "Aye aye, sir," he said, taking his salad with him as he slid down.

The Colonel had seemed to recognize them only dimly, but he nodded politely when Beatrice spoke about her children's latest report cards and Dwight talked about the business finally turning a profit again last quarter— "despite what the president's doing," he insisted, which prompted Beatrice to complain bitterly about the state of political discourse in the country today. More smirks from Dwight at that, and cold looks from Claire.

The Colonel had watched all of them with interest but no reaction. Claire tried at each turn of the conversation to nudge her father to recall Beatrice's children or the nature of Dwight's business or just the name of that current president, but she had finally given up, simply watching the Colonel with a mixture of curiosity and distress. Keri had watched each of them and didn't know exactly how she felt.

After lunch was done and the Colonel had retired to his room for some light R&R, the three of them began to divvy up the belongings, prepping to make an easy sweep of it between the day they moved the old man out and the scheduled demolition of the house, quick work for the condo development ahead. Claire had brought small circular stickers to help with the division. Each of them would simply mark the items they wanted to take. "Pop will appreciate the patriotic touch," Dwight said, holding up a package of red stickers and leaving blue and white for his sisters. Unmarked items would be slated for donation to the Salvation Army. "And a military nod again," Dwight said, already beginning to stake his claims.

When the three of them ended up squabbling about an autographed photo of Eisenhower standing with the Colonel and his late wife, Keri felt like she saw them most clearly. Beatrice, the eldest, argued that the photo was hers because she was actually in the picture, cradled in their mother's arms. Dwight, now the baby of the bunch, pointed out that he'd been named after the president, "which ought to give me dibs." Meanwhile, Claire—caretaker turned peacemaker—tried as best she could to keep the simmer from becoming a boil.

"So doesn't that give you claim to all of this, Bea?" Dwight demanded. "You saw it first, you were there first? It's all yours?" And then trying to recruit Claire to the cause: "Isn't that how it's always been?"

"That's not what I'm saying," Beatrice said. "I'm saying I'm *in* the damn picture. It's a picture of *me.*"

"Let's leave it for father, for his room at the nursing home," Claire said. "He always loved it so."

"He wouldn't even know it's there," Dwight said.

"Let's leave it unmarked then," Claire went on. "No one will take it. We can donate it somewhere. A tribute that—"

"Stick it in some museum?" Dwight said. "Hell, no. That sucker's *worth* something."

"Is that what you're planning?" Beatrice flashed with rage. "Selling it somewhere?"

"Please keep your voices down," Claire said, and Keri could sense something stretched thin in her own voice. "He'll hear us."

"If he does wake up," Dwight told Keri, "just keep him in his room for a while."

"How should I do that?" Keri asked, startled by the sound of her own voice.

"Tell him," Dwight began. "Tell him the base is on lockdown." He seemed to be thinking. He grinned broadly, something cruel behind it. "There's a sniper. Delta Force is handling it. Tell him orders from the general."

"General." Beatrice snorted. "Is that how you picture yourself in all this?"

Bickering spun out of selfishness, anger where there should have been empathy, lies built high on the Colonel's dementia—Keri hated it all.

But later, she reflected that she wasn't much better, at least in one regard.

When the real-estate agents, surveyors, and repairmen had made their rounds, Keri had dutifully pretended to the Colonel that they were visiting dignitaries, military attaches, envoys from D.C. And when the Colonel woke from his nap and asked what all the dots were for—on the lamps, on the furniture, everywhere—Keri told him "inventory" and then "supply room," trying to think of the right term, build another lie he might believe.

"Midnight requisitions," the Colonel said vaguely, with a sigh of contempt, and something about a "five-fingered discount," and then, grinning himself, just like Dwight had, "Oh, well, Sergeant, we'll just have to requisition it all back," like he knew the game.

"Lear," Pete said, when Keri told him about it. "The grasping, the selfishness. Siblings showing their true colors. Claire sounds like the best of them: *You have brought me up and loved me, and I return you those duties back as are right and fit, obey you, love you, and most honor you.*" Pete performed the last part with a stagy British lilt.

"It didn't feel like honor," Keri said. "Or love, either."

"That's what Lear thought, too." Pete raised his eyebrow. "And you know how that turned out. So who got the photo?"

"Beatrice," Keri said. "She traded Dwight the dining-room table for it, but he said it didn't matter, he'd get it back someday. Told her that since she was older, she'd go first. 'I'll keep these handy,' he said, and he waved his extra stickers in the air."

"Charming," Pete said. "Sorry I missed it." Keri had hoped for a little more empathy, but Pete was already moving on: "You know, I think I'll add *Lear* to the syllabus. Sub it in instead of *Othello*—that's done too much in high school, anyway, don't you think? And *Lear*—"

"But what should *we* do?" Keri insisted. "What's *our* role in all this?"

She doesn't entirely remember his answer—several possibilities, comparing them to the Earl of Kent or the Fool. Did Keri have a touch of Cordelia herself? Little of substance, nothing practical, no solace. Instead, it's more of Margaret's words that have persisted: *Not a word of thanks, unless you demand it. Not a single token of appreciation, unless you take it yourself. I'm telling you: you've already been bought and paid for.*

The Colonel dresses and undresses himself, handles his own bathroom duties, but Keri follows up with him each morning and each night. This evening, as usual, he's had trouble with his nightclothes—his "old man jammies," Pete calls them. One side of his top hangs low, unfastened, while the skipped button bunches out on the other side, the fabric opening to reveal the aged flesh of his belly, a thin tangle of gray hairs. "He does it on purpose," Pete has joked, "just so you can fluff him up." She tries not to think about that as she straightens the buttoning, a complicated dance of discretion and helpfulness.

The Colonel always apologizes to one version or another of who he thinks she is. "Aging is an indignity, Sergeant," he's said before. And other times: "In all our many years together, my darling, did you ever believe it would come to this?" These seem his only flashes of awareness about time and his place in it, but even those moments are dim with confusion.

"I've not been a good husband, dear," he tells her tonight. "Or a good father, either, to—"

He stops, catches himself. Some small reality intrudes. "Thank you for looking after me," he says. He strokes her cheek.

She puts him to bed, she tucks him in, she turns out his light. Nearly always, he's staring at the ceiling when she leaves him. Tonight, he watches the window.

"The guards," he says. "The duty roster."

"Yes, yes," she tells him, and she closes the door.

Back in her own room, she tries to go to bed, but finds herself restless, irritable, waiting once more for Pete, angry a little at him, this time—and even more of each emotion tonight, because of whatever's gotten into the

Colonel. She lies in the darkness for a while, staring at the shadows playing outside her own window, at that full moon raging, and then she turns on the light once more to read. She wants to keep up with what Pete's doing, give them more to talk about, so she's been following his syllabus. The class has already reached *Lear*, and she takes down the bulky *Riverside Shakespeare* from the nightstand, reminds herself again to get a more readable copy, then picks up mid-scene where she'd fallen asleep the night before: *This is the excellent foppery of the world, that, when we are sick in fortune,—often the surfeit of our own behavior,—we make guilty of our disasters the sun, the moon, and the stars: as if we were villains by necessity; fools by heavenly compulsion; knaves, thieves, and treachers by spherical predominance; drunkards, liars, and adulterers by an enforced obedience of planetary influence; and all that we are evil in by a divine thrusting on: an admirable evasion of whoremaster man, to lay his goatish disposition to the charge of a star!*

It's near the end of the monologue that she hears the click of the front door—opening, closing. Pete at last, sooner than she expected. Sometimes he calls, usually she sees the sweep of his headlights against the window. He's surprised her this time.

She's left a note for him: *A plate of lasagna in the fridge. Microwave two minutes. XO. Me.* But she hopes he won't see it, that he'll just come back to her, ease this troubled evening. She listens for his footsteps coming down the hallway, but instead, she hears him trip over something, and she knows then he's been drinking after class, too many drinks again, and suddenly it seems like he'll just complicate the night further instead of improving it.

She starts to go out to him, confront him, but no, she'll wait. She picks up the book again:

Edgar—
   [Enter Edgar.]
   and pat! he comes, like the catastrophe of the old comedy. My cue is villainous melancholy, with a sigh like Tom o' Bedlam. O, these eclipses do portend these divisions! Fa, sol, la, mi.

She's stopped by the sound of the front door, opening and closing once more.

He's gone out again? Keri lays the book down, steps to the window to see what he's doing. But his car's not out there at all, the yard looks empty. And then the sound of the front door opening again, and soon after, the sound of glass breaking, but muffled, as if from a great distance.

Incoming, she thinks, and now her senses tingle, her whole body as alert as the Colonel's had seemed earlier.

She picks up the bedside phone. She'll call 911. She'll call Pete, already hurrying him homeward with her mind. But there's no dial tone, just a dull ominous emptiness on the receiver.

Radio silence, she thinks, and then she remembers the Colonel's other words: *Life and death.*

And then she just thinks about the Colonel himself.

His door is still closed, she sees when she leaves her own room. There's relief in that, though she recognizes the irony: the old warrior protected by the defenseless woman. But he would only add confusion on top of whatever danger is out there. And the truth is, she's not entirely defenseless. She's carrying the biggest object in the bedroom—that complete Shakespeare— though she's unsure whether it might best work as a weapon or as armor. She shudders to think it might come to that.

As she eases down the hallway, she wonders who's out there. One of the leering surveyors, after all? That's why they'd stayed so late today. They were casing the house, returning now to rob it. Or one of those college kids who sometimes drove down the wrong road—a prank this time, a dare, a different kind of trouble. She remembers, too, how Claire called Margaret a thief, remembers Margaret's own words that you got no token of thanks unless you took it.

The living room is dark, just as she left it, with only the moonlight streaming in from various windows, casting shadows around the room.

Then one of the shadows near the dining-room table moves, a silhouette stumbling toward the living room. The dim form lifts a pair of pictures from the wall, returns toward the table, lays the pictures flat. Its arm raises high into the air, some object in its grasp, and smashes down sharply. A crunching sound.

Dwight, she realizes, unsure where the knowledge came from. And then she looks again at the empty spaces dotting the wall, the pictures that the intruder is destroying. The Eisenhower is among the missing photos. Dwight would get it, one way or another. There truly was something evil behind that smirk of his, beneath those callous comments.

Suddenly, the book in her hand doesn't seem protection enough.

The guns on the wall, she thinks. Are any of them loaded? How easily could she break the case? Would she know how to use one? But Dwight would stop her. He stands in the way, still fidgeting with things on the table. He could get to those guns first. In fact, she understands now, he's already taken one of them from its box, hasn't he? One of the gun cases stands empty, its glass front shattered. That's the sound Keri heard. That's what Dwight is holding over his head, what he brings down once more against the table.

The knife. The one she left soaking in the lasagna pan. She can get to that. It's a clear line into the kitchen. It's not a gun, but it's better than Shakespeare. At least she won't be entirely unarmed.

As soon as she's thought it, she's done it. A quick sprint, and she's at the sink. Hand in soapy water, fingers slipping around the handle. But Dwight has come up behind her, grabbed her arm, pushed her against the counter. Keri can't get a grip on the knife.

Hot breath brushes against her neck, carrying with it the stench of alcohol. "You should've stayed in bed," the voice huffs, a snarl there, an undertone of amusement. But it's a woman's voice. Not Dwight, not at all. "It's just a break-in," the woman slurs quietly. "Vandalism. You were asleep. You didn't hear, you didn't know." Keri tries to shuffle around, to gain an edge, but the woman holds fast, surprisingly strong. "All those years, year upon year. And they think they have any right here? They never cared about him, not once. They don't deserve any of this." She coos, she soothes: "Just let it happen. You know it's right." And then a dark whisper: "I'll compensate you."

Keri shoves her elbow back into doughy flesh, hears the sharp intake of breath. Freed for a moment, she reaches toward the sink. But there's not enough time. Before Keri can grab the knife, she feels fingers around her throat. "This isn't between you and me," the woman says, a snarl now, and maybe it wasn't their fight, but it is now. The woman's grip is relentless, squeezing, pressing. "They can't know it was me. They can't ever know."

Keri pushes off the counter then, shoving as hard as she can, and the two of them sprawl backward across the room. But the woman hangs on, and then she's on top of Keri, slamming her head against the floor. Keri's pulse throbs grimly, there's a roar in her skull, a pounding, and then an explosion as if her head has burst.

Just as quickly, the grip relaxes. The other woman falls away, a thud on the floor beside her.

The lights come on, blinding, and Keri hears the Colonel's voice—a single word, frail and nearly indistinct, pleading, concerned. She rises up from the floor then and gets her first look at the body sprawled beside her— Claire's body, bleeding heavily from where a bullet has ripped through her torso—and at the damage the woman had done.

Spray paint covers the kitchen cabinets, what looks like teen graffiti, like those young joyriders had not just driven down the road but finally come in. The lampshades have been slashed methodically, and more pictures have been pulled down from the wall. Broken glass is everywhere, shards dotting the carpet. The frame on the Eisenhower is shattered, the picture itself torn. The corner of another photo peeks out from beneath a towel on the kitchen table, one of the antique pistols dropped on top of it.

At the edge of the hallway stands the Colonel, a handgun at his side, this one not an antique. He's wearing his full uniform, every button clasped perfectly, the medals gleaming in the sudden light, his posture perfect.

He speaks softly again—a second word now, perplexed and incredulous where that first word had been pleading—and then, with his own glance around the room, he finds his voice again: "Damn those guards," he booms. "The perimeter's been breached."

"Blanche DuBois," Pete says later, when it's just the two of them alone in the house, lying side by side in the darkness.

The body has been removed, and Beatrice and Dwight have been called. They'll drive in the next morning and handle things. The police took the Colonel away for questioning, for evaluation, and Keri began straightening up, picking up glass, rubbing at the paint on the cabinets, until Pete took her in his arms and held her tight and told her it was time for bed, time to let go, at least for the night.

But she couldn't do that, of course. For a while, staring at the ceiling, Keri has listened to the silence of the house, believed that she could hear the old man's absence somewhere in it. Pete has seemed far away in his own thoughts, reflecting on the loss in his own way, Keri thinks, until those sudden words of his.

"What?" she asks. She doesn't turn to look at him.

"Blanche DuBois," he says. "Tennessee Williams. *Streetcar Named Desire*. 'I've always relied on the kindness of strangers.'" Pete tries out a Southern drawl, not as good as his British voice, though it strikes her now that none of his accents is very good. "I'd thought of the Colonel like Lear, you know, but tonight, watching him with the police when they took him away, the way he stood up straight, the way he walked…pure Blanche DuBois. Living in his own world, his delusions, the long-gone past."

"He was brave," Keri says. There's light on the ceiling, from the moonlight shining down through the window and reflecting somehow off the bedspread. "Gallant."

"Gallant," Pete echoes. "But that's the tragedy of it, isn't it? The way that we take the Stella role—all of us, the reader, the audience—trying to keep the illusions aloft, maybe even believing in them a little."

In the blankness of the ceiling, Keri imagines Pete in the front of his class, pacing and gesturing, holding forth, the tweed jacket, patches on the sleeve. There's pride in those patches and a strut in his step, and she's sure she heard a snicker when he repeated the word *gallant*, as if he was marking up her term paper and dissatisfied somehow with the logic of her argument.

"When you say tragedy," she asks, "are you talking about the Colonel or about Blanche?"

He shrugs beside her, a laying-down shrug, shoulders shuffling against the pillow.

"Either," he says. "Both. Killing your daughter, not knowing it. That has all the elements of something classical, doesn't it?"

Later, many years later, lying in another bed with another man, and with her children with that husband nestled safely in their own beds just down the hallway, Keri will think back once more on this night and wonder yet again if this was the exact moment when things ended between them, or if it was just one in a progression of such moments that took too long to accumulate. She'll wonder again why she stayed so long with him after this night, why she didn't just get up then and walk out into the darkness, up that gravel drive—off base, once and for all. *Illusions*, she'll think. *And tragedy.* And she'll think of the hundred things she might have told Pete, the hundred times she might have told him. Then she'll remind herself: *But maybe it was enough.*

"He said her name," she tells Pete. "The Colonel. After he turned on the lights and saw her there, before he wandered out into the yard, he said 'Claire' because he saw her, what she'd done, and what he'd done, too. But first, just before that…he was looking for *me*, I know he was. Looking *out* for me. Before he said her name, he said mine. He called out for me. For the first time, he said Keri."

Luck Is What You Make

by Stephen D. Rogers
(Best Flash Story, 2014)

Next to our house is a winterized cottage, owned by the old woman who lives down the end of the road. As much as Alice is active anywhere, she's active in her church, and she's got that cottage sitting there empty.

Several times a year, a day comes when I find a car parked in front of the cottage. Someone down on his luck who needs somewhere to crash until he gets back on his feet. He's there for a week or two or four, and then I never see the car again.

The transients make my wife nervous.

When Alice first started doing the right thing, my wife would nag me until I walked over to check out our new neighbor. Since I worked at a bar, my wife was alone most nights, she and our teenage daughter.

"You find out what kind of man is living next door."

"I'm sure he's fine."

"That's easy for you to say, until he comes up here one night with an axe. You go make yourself known."

My wife no longer has to nag. Not about that, anyway.

I knocked on the rickety screen door, the sound of the wood hitting the frame louder than my touch. "Hello?"

A face appeared behind the screen. "Yeah?"

"I'm Jack. Live next door." I raised the bottle of whiskey, three quarters empty. Two glasses. "Can I buy you a drink?"

A pause. "I'll be out."

I stepped from the door and turned away, picked out Alice's house through the trees. The cottage was built on the far side of her property, and I preferred to suppose rather than ask why. Vacation home for people who hated to travel? Guesthouse for in-laws? Marital convenience?

The cottage door creaked open. Clattered shut.

The man mumbled his name, brown eyes cast down as if ashamed by the prison pallor.

"I missed that."

"Lionel."

"Lionel, I'm Jack from next door. Care for a spot of whiskey?"

His tongue licked parched lips. "Appreciate that."

I placed the glasses on the porch rail and split the whiskey between them. "This is the closest I'm going to get to buying you a drink. I work nights." Handing him a glass, I raised mine. "To luck."

"Luck."

I watched him through the bottom of the glass, eyeing the bottle.

"I don't know how to say this but to say this, Lionel. I don't know you." I waited until his eyes settled down. "I know Alice. She's a good person who won't hesitate to lend a helping hand. She doesn't know you, either."

Lionel met my gaze. "What do you want to know?"

"It's none of my business, but as I said, I work most nights. My wife and teenage daughter are alone in the house."

He just stared at me.

"I don't know you, but I'd like to ask you a favor, anyway."

"Yeah?"

"I wondered if you could keep an eye on them."

"Sure."

"I'm not saying it's going to be an easy task. My daughter, she's a little wild, takes after her mother that way." I finished my whiskey. "I just want to know if there's anything I should know. Visitors. Men."

"Sure."

"Appreciate that." I took back his empty glass. "You're a good man, Lionel. I have a good feeling about you."

I left him there on the porch and trudged home.

My wife started in as soon as I entered the house. "Well, what's he like? Did you talk to him? Did you put the fear of God into him?"

"I did."

Veracity snorted. "He did no such thing. He never does what you tell him to do."

"Your father isn't that stupid."

"On what planet?"

Veracity had been daddy's little girl. For about ten minutes. Until she became her mother.

"I'm going to lay down a bit before getting ready for work," I said.

"I thought you were going to help me with the couch. I guess I must have been crazy to even entertain the idea."

I slipped through the muttering, down the hall, and into the bedroom.

Closed the door softly.

The cottage was occupied several times a year by someone down on his luck. None so far had taken me up on my suggestion. At least not yet.

The Kaluki Kings of Queens

by Cathi Stoler
(Best Short Story, 2015)

An Italian and a Jew sit down to play cards. They invite a few of their friends—a Hungarian, a Pole, and a Greek—to join them.

I know, I know, it sounds like the start of a very bad joke, and in some ways it was. But to Grandpa Louie and Grandpa Shy it was deadly serious, a life-and-death game for the Kaluki Kings of Queens.

Back in the day, they played the game all over the borough, from Jackson Heights to Forest Hills to Rockaway, at any synagogue or Knights of Columbus hall that had a couple of decks of cards.

Didn't know how to play? Not to worry. Shy and Louie would teach you and take your money. They became so well known, they were even asked to play with one of the former borough presidents. I'll bet he went home a little lighter in the wallet.

If you don't know Kaluki, it's a glorified version of gin rummy, with pretty much the same objective: to lay out all your cards and go out, leaving your opponents with piles of penalty points in their hands that turn into cash in your pocket.

As Shy and Louie grew older, their road trips dwindled but not their desire for Kaluki. So instead of travelling all over the borough, their games took place like clockwork every Saturday at noon in the Florida room of our house on Ransom Street in Bellrose, Queens.

Louie, my dad's dad, had intense dark brown eyes and black eyebrows that tilted toward the middle of his forehead when he frowned, which he did frequently as play progressed. On the chubby side, he'd amble over from his house a few blocks away, where he lived with my Grandma Marie, who usually sent along something she'd baked especially for me. It was no wonder Louie was chubby. He never met a cake he didn't love, and grandma was a great baker. I was lucky if mom got to the package first and tucked it away before its contents disappeared.

Shy, a tall thin version of me, with pale blue eyes that never missed a trick, was my mother's dad. He lived with us and had ever since his wife, Grandma Flo, passed away a few years ago. Shy wasn't as spry as Louie, so my mother didn't like him going out on his own and preferred that they hold their game at our house.

Once mom was sure they were settled in, she'd head out for her Saturday-afternoon manicure appointment. "Watch over them, Petey," she'd tell me, with a jut of her chin in their direction—especially if any of their cronies were joining the game. "Don't let them get into any trouble," she'd add and pat me on the head as she grabbed her purse and left.

I'd watch her go, wondering who in her right mind would leave an eleven-year-old in charge of those two. I think she was afraid they'd raid the liquor cabinet and get so drunk they'd wander onto the Cross Island Parkway. Believe me, if they had wanted booze, I sure wouldn't have been able to stop them.

Some afternoons, it was just the two of them, and then the fun really started.

"*Chidrule!*"

"*Yuld!*"

"Take that," Grandpa Louie would sneer, as he slapped down his first meld of forty-plus points.

"Amateur," Grandpa Shy'd spit back, with his own fan of cards.

Much as I resented having to stay in and mind them for the hour or so mom was gone, watching them play their game was always an adventure. I'd start at the doorway, then slide a little closer with every pick of a card, until finally I was sitting between them, elbows resting on the table, holding my head in my hands, eyes swiveling from side to side, taking it all in.

It was like observing two male lions in the wild, circling each other, prepared to fight to the death, with false teeth bared. Well, these two were old and were lucky they still *had* a few teeth. Even so, I knew what was coming, and my stomach would start to churn in anticipation.

"Live and learn, Sonny Boy," Louie would toss my way, as he laid off the rest of his cards and went out, leaving Shy with a fist full of penalty points.

"Ahggh," Shy would reply. "I'll get you next time, you *Behema.*"

Both of them hated to lose. It was humiliating, getting *Chmalyered*, as they called getting totally creamed, and anything was fair game: insults, name-calling, misdirection. The only thing neither one could tolerate was cheating.

"You know what happens to cheats, don't you?" Louie would ask me, as he shuffled and reshuffled the cards.

I'd nod my head, my breathing growing ragged and my hands sweating in anticipation of the answer, even though I'd heard it a hundred times before.

"First, you cut off his hand," Shy would reply, making a slicing motion in the air. "His dealing hand."

"Next, you stab him in the heart," Louie would add and poke a finger at my chest.

"Then you bury him in the cellar," they'd both finish together, chortling away.

After this last pronouncement, they'd give each other a look I didn't understand, their faces turning sly with something that scared the pants off me.

For years, I'd been afraid to go down to the basement. The door was in the hall outside our kitchen, and whenever I went past it, I rattled the doorknob to make sure it was locked. My mother would frown, as if wondering how it had gotten locked again, as she opened it and reached for the mop or broom that hung at the top of the stairs.

This was not a friendly basement, even without the grandpas' scare tactics.

Dark and unfinished, it had concrete walls and a dirt floor. Shelves lined most of the space and were filled with all the discarded stuff from upstairs. Boxes of clothes, games, old stereos, TVs, and furniture made it seem like a haunted house. At least it felt that way to me. It was creepy enough on its own and creepier still when I thought of my grandfathers' words.

Whenever Mom asked me to fetch something she needed from downstairs, I made an excuse, terrified some disembodied hand would rise up from the floor and whisper, "Tell your grandpas I'm coming to get them."

"Petey," she'd demand, "just do it." And I would go, holding my breath, darting down the stairs and back up again as quickly as possible, sweat beading on my forehead.

I'd hand my mother whatever it was she wanted and swear to myself she could never make me go down there again.

By one thirty or so on Saturdays, Mom would be home and calling for me to go out and play. I never wasted any time as I made my escape and ran to meet my friends at the park on the corner. God only knows what she would have done to the grandpas if she heard what they'd told me. Death seemed like a good possibility.

Often, their buddies left over from their traveling game joined Louie and Shy—guys like Bernie Simon, Shy's friend from the Star of David *schul* on Musket Street. Fat Lou and Skinny Lou (who ran the candy store on Braddock Avenue) and Uncle Bob and Gigi (who lived on the block) all came around, a rotating cast of die-hard Queens Kaluki players.

The person who came by most often was Nick the Greek. He owned a coffee shop on Hillside Avenue and lived above it in a small apartment. He was a big man with a booming voice and loud laugh. He loved slapping down his cards with a loud "*Opa*," the Greek toast for good luck.

Once, when I was about ten, Shy and I took a walk to Nick's place, and he treated me to a fresh-baked apple turnover and a glass of milk. Nick waved off his request for a check, saying, "I'm making plenty off you already from Kaluki. This is on me." Then he gave a big, bellowing laugh and punched Shy in the shoulder. Shy smiled, but I knew he didn't like it. Not the free pastry, not the slur to his card playing.

Nick always wore a giant gold signet ring on his left hand that Grandpa Louie said was made from an ancient Greek coin. It had the face of one of those Olympian gods on the top and looked like it weighed about a pound. Even I could tell it was worth a bundle. Nick would rub it while they played, bragging about how it always brought him luck. Whenever he said that, Grandpa Shy would make a gagging noise and give him a nasty look.

The last time I saw Nick, he'd won big, and neither of my grandpas was too happy about it. After he left, they sent me to the kitchen to get them each a soda, and I could hear them whispering. When I got back with their drinks, they were already dealing the cards for their next game. They were unusually quiet while they played, and I wondered what they were up to. Probably nothing good, as Grandma Marie would have said.

Nick never showed up again. When I asked about him, Grandpa Louie made a sour face. "He left. Sold his coffee shop and moved back to some island in Greece." He slapped down a few cards from his hand.

"Didn't even say goodbye," added Grandpa Shy. "You know how some people are." He shrugged. "Just disappeared."

I didn't like the sound of that, or of my grandpas' casual attitude about their missing friend. They hadn't had a chance to recoup their losses from their last game with Nick and couldn't have been happy about it. For weeks, I was on the lookout for those missing-person posters people pasted on lampposts. I was sure my grandpas were involved in Nick's disappearance, which made me more afraid than ever to go down to the basement. After a while, I realized that was crazy. They were old men who could hardly get around, never mind make someone disappear. But still.

The card games continued for five more years, until Grandpa Louie died. Grandpa Shy gave up Kaluki for good, then. Nothing we said or did would change his mind.

"It wouldn't be the same." He'd shake his head and sigh. Then he'd give me that look, the sly one that passed between him and Louie every time they spoke about the cheaters. "You wouldn't understand."

A few winters later, Grandpa Shy got pneumonia, and things weren't looking good. We all took turns visiting him in the hospital. One day, when I was there on my own, he raised his hand and waved for me to come closer.

"Petey," he said, his voice a mere whisper, "I need you to do something for me." He placed a bony hand over mine and held it tight. "And you can't tell anyone, especially your mother."

I nodded okay, sure he was going to ask me to bring him some treat his diet—and mom—didn't allow.

"You have to go down to the basement, Petey. There's something down there I need you to get."

I must have jumped back a foot at his mention of the basement, nearly dragging him out of the hospital bed. "The basement?" I croaked through a throat that had gone instantly dry. *Not the basement.* My mind filled with vivid images of dismembered hands and dead bodies. I wasn't eleven anymore. I was going to be a freshman in college soon, but the basement still held as many terrors as a Wes Craven horror movie. Even though I was grown up, when I passed the basement doorway, I rattled the handle by habit to make sure it was locked.

"But, Gramps, what could you need from the basement?"

"Not for me. For you." He gripped my hand harder and pulled me closer, a serious effort for someone in his condition. Then he looked me in the eyes. "Be a good boy. Just do it for an old man."

Had he overheard my mother, all those times she said those words to me?

"Okay," I finally agreed. "I'll do it."

I waited until Mom left for the hospital before I made my descent into hell. She'd never seen me go down there without a fight, and I didn't want to make her suspicious now.

Grandpa Shy had given me detailed instructions on what I was looking for and where it was located. I think he would have drawn me a map if he could have, as though he was sending me on some sort of big treasure hunt.

Right, I thought. *Tell that to my pounding heart and sweaty palms.*

I made my way down slowly and finally reached the bottom of the stairs.

The basement looked just as foreboding as it always had, maybe even more so, with more clutter and mess than I remembered.

Following Grandpa's instructions, I turned right and made my way past a stack of old luggage and backyard furniture and headed to a rickety bookcase next to the furnace. On the bottom shelf, there was an old set of encyclopedias, stacked every which way in several precarious piles. Behind the last stack on the right, Grandpa said, I'd find a small cigar box and inside, the thing he wanted me to have.

I stood there for a good five minutes, deciding if I really wanted to know what was in the box—what if it actually *was* a hand? What would I do with it? Then, telling myself to man up, I took a deep breath and dug it out. Covered with dust, the box looked old and ordinary, like something you'd use to store odds and ends—and not, I hoped, bits and pieces of a body. I blew off the dust from the top and opened it slowly, dreading what I'd find inside.

It was a ring. A ring I'd know anywhere: Nick the Greek's big gold signet ring. Its shine had dulled over the years, but the image of the god on the top still grabbed my attention, as did the folded, yellowing paper underneath.

I took it out and opened it. It was a note to me from Grandpa Shy in his spindly writing:

Petey,

I know your Grandpa Louie and I scared the shit out of you with our stories about what we did to card cheaters. But they were just stories. Before he died, Louie made me promise to tell you the truth and give you this ring. Nick the Greek was the biggest cheater of them all. Sly and crafty. We never really caught him at it, but we knew he was doing it. So, when he decided to move back to Greece, we decided to take a souvenir: his good luck ring. He never wore it to work, so Louie snuck into his apartment one afternoon, while I kept him busy in the coffee shop. Maybe he thought he'd lost it, or that his luck had run out. Who knows? Who cares? He left a few days later, and we never heard from him again. Now, the ring is yours. But please don't tell your mother. She'd kill me.

Grandpa Shy

I stood there open-mouthed, with Grandpa Shy's letter in one hand and Nick the Greek's ring in the other. For a moment, I thought about finding Nick in Greece and returning the ring anonymously, but that seemed crazy—and who knew if he was even still alive and still cheating at cards?

I held the ring up to the light to get a better look, and for a second that fierce Olympian face seemed to wink at me. *What can you do, Sonny Boy?* it seemed to say, just the way the grandpas might.

My two old Kaluki-playing grandpas, would-be Queens criminal masterminds, had pulled off the heist of the century—at least in their own minds. It had been payback for all of Nick's cheating, and they'd gotten away with it. Now, I had become their partner in crime…and it felt pretty good.

I smiled and put the ring in my pocket and sprinted up the stairs, finally free of the terrors of the basement. Out on the porch, I found two decks of cards and headed for the hospital and one last game of Kaluki.

Twilight Ladies

by Meg Opperman
(Best Short Story, 2016)

Mwanza, Tanzania

Police Constable Kokuteta Mkama squeezed the bridge of her nose, her short nails digging crescents near the corners of her eyes. Poring over her bank statement for the third—or was it fourth?—time, she knew she had a problem.

A husband problem.

He'd stolen money from her account again.

Another girlfriend? Of course. The numbers didn't lie.

But *he* would.

They'd trodden this path many times in the three years they'd been married. If only her bank would let her remove him from the account. How infuriating to need his permission to keep it open when she earned her own money, kept her own counsel.

Koku switched to rubbing her temples, her pulse throbbing under her fingers. She'd saved small amounts from each pay period, preparing for the extra costs their child would bring. Costs her husband wasn't likely to cover. Did he think she wouldn't notice the missing money or surmise the cause?

Sweat trickled down her back and seeped through her uniform blouse, the unseasonably hot summer—especially with a baby on the way—unbearable and unrelenting. Not even Lake Victoria took the edge off the January heat.

How would she ever find the energy to finish the endless stack of paperwork on her desk?

She reached into the pocket of her wilted uniform and drew out a handkerchief to mop her brow. A small fan perched in front of louvered windows blew hot air around but did little else. Pitiful.

P.C. Lubadsa worked nearby, his pen racing across a form, not a hint of sweat on his angular face, his uniform still stiffly pressed. She sniffed. If he was as big as an ox with his first child, he'd be uncomfortable, too. But she mustn't take her foul mood out on the constable. He'd been nothing but kind, even giving her the less vigorous tasks as her girth increased.

Folding her bank statement, she shoved it into a creaky desk drawer and reached for the document on top of the pile.

The door to the outpost banged open. Koku jerked, causing her back to stiffen in pain, her belly to contract. In marched Motete Vincent. He might be a prominent businessman, but he reminded her of a spotted hyena—small head, wide-set eyes, overfed body. With a character to match. He stopped in front of Lubadsa's desk.

"You!" He pointed a thick finger in the constable's face. "Get me Hewa. I must speak to him about a mugging."

"Y-yes, *Mzee*." Lubadsa sprang up like a gazelle, his limbs long and lean, and fled toward the back offices.

Koku eased to her swollen feet, a form clutched in her hand. "*Shikamoo, Mzee*. Are you injured? Do you need to fill out a PF3?"

"What I *need* is something to drink, constable. Fetch me a Coke." He waved a thousand-shilling note under her nose.

Koku's lips tightened, but she didn't dare offend him, since he was close with her commander. She reached for the bill. "Of course, *Mzee*."

Vincent held the money just out of reach. "You twilight ladies. So eager to grab men's hard-earned cash."

Koku gaped. Twilight ladies? His hard-earned cash? What about *her* money?

Stuffing the note into her palm, he said, "Go on, then. Be quick about it. I've worked up quite a thirst."

Not trusting herself to speak, she trudged to a crate of bottles by the door. She selected an empty Fanta bottle, exited, and labored toward the Fierce Sun, a small kiosk on a not-so-distant corner. Her breath came in ragged gasps.

Buses shot past, kicking up thick diesel clouds, young men hanging from the open doors calling the stops, heavily distorted bongoland music screeching from tinny speakers. Women in brightly colored *kitenges* and men in slacks and button-down shirts ambled along the sidewalks, heading for the bus stands. Youths in T-shirts, low-riding jeans, and knock-off Nikes jostled through the crowd, careless with their movements.

By the time she reached the kiosk, dark circles had spread from underarm to elbow, and no amount of mopping could keep the sweat from her brow. Fortunately, Baba Nkwabi still manned the shop, even with the sun rapidly setting.

He set down the tins of dried milk he'd been shelving, the lines on his forehead seeming to deepen as he took in her untidy appearance.

"Little mother, please, come inside. Sit here." He slid a stool from behind a counter and set it in front of the large mural his youngest daughter, Anifa, had painted. It gave the kiosk its name—a trio of farmers plowing a field under a blistering, stylized sun. How apt.

"No time, Baba. I must return to the station." She looked longingly at the stool.

"Hurry does not bring blessings."

"Tell that to the hyena," grumbled Koku. "A Coke, please." She handed over the shillings and the empty bottle, so she could take away the soda and he'd still receive the bottle deposit when the supplier came to replenish the stock.

"Here's two. Send Lubadsa with the empty."

"Baba, you don't have to do this." But as she said it, she took a grateful mouthful.

Entering the outpost, Koku saw Assistant Superintendent Justice Hewa and Motete Vincent speaking in quiet tones, their heads together. Where

Vincent resembled a hyena, Hewa was the leaner, more cunning jackal. His teeth were just as sharp, though.

Noticing her, Hewa waved her over. "Grab your notepad and come with us."

Now what? Koku did as asked and fell in behind the strange procession—Vincent's step heavy, like he meant to trample the air underneath his shoes, and Hewa with his parade-like gait. For her, every step a misery, her ankles the size of overripe mangoes. Where was Lubadsa, anyway?

Once inside A.S. Hewa's office, Koku shuffled over a slippery vinyl mat and sank onto a wooden bench worn smooth with time. Motete Vincent filled the more comfortable chair across from the assistant superintendent, snatching the soda and change with barely a word of thanks.

At least the ceiling fan forced the worst of the heat from the room.

Hewa nodded toward the open door, and Koku hefted herself to her feet, closed it, then returned to the bench. Would the tortures of this day ever end?

"We have a sensitive situation, P.C. Mkama," Hewa began. "I want you to keep an unofficial filing of what you are about to hear—"

"There's no need, Justice," said Vincent. "I don't want my name associated with this nasty business."

Hewa held up a hand. "In the event there *is* a need at a later time."

"Fine. But there won't be." Vincent harrumphed. "So, I was on my way to meet my distributor, when I saw a woman stranded on the side of the road."

"A young woman?" Koku couldn't help but ask.

Vincent's back snapped straight. "I don't see what that has to do with anything. But, yes, a young woman."

Hewa scowled at her.

Koku bent over her notebook, pretending she didn't notice.

"Go on, Motete. P.C. Mkama won't interrupt again."

"She flagged me down. Said she'd been robbed and asked for a lift. How could I say no?"

The one who is far away, the tree does not fall on him. Wise words from her grandmother, yet so seldom heeded.

"And of course, when you opened the door, a bunch of thieves ambushed you." Hewa nodded like this was the obvious outcome. Using a pretty girl to get a motorist to pull over was a trick employed since the days of colonial rule. It still worked.

Vincent cleared his throat, his jowly cheeks reddened. "No, no. Not quite like that."

Koku paused her pen, waiting for Vincent to continue. Could he be a third fool? Her senses hummed with excitement, but she kept her delight to herself.

"She"—he cleared his throat again, glared at Koku—"this, this *night hound* demanded money and a ride to town or said she would scream and tell people I had forced her into my vehicle for sexual molestation." He lowered his voice. "Rape."

Koku kept her expression neutral, but Hewa thumped his fist on the desk. "She didn't! I have never heard of such rubbish behavior!"

And he hadn't. But she had. Two others had come forth earlier in the week to speak privately with P.C. Lubadsa about their situation.

"It's true!" shouted Motete Vincent, clearly pleased to have a rapt audience. "What was I to do? I begged her to understand I was in no position to give her money. But she said she would scream and even my *wife* would not believe me. My wife! Can you imagine?"

Koku wiped her face with her handkerchief, hiding the small smile tugging at her lips. Well, now. Not your everyday mugging. A clever girl.

"You, sir, have been caught by a mascara-painted lady. A night hound, truly!" Hewa said. "How much did she steal?"

Vincent shifted in his seat. "As it happened, I was carrying a lot of money in a case. You remember, of course, that I was meeting my distributor? He, ah, prefers to be paid in cash. Nature of my business."

Motete Vincent owned several large shops in the region that specialized in mining equipment and supplies. She couldn't afford to buy even batteries for her torch there, his prices so inflated. But the Canadians and South Africans didn't seem to mind.

"How much?" Hewa leaned toward his friend.

"A million shillings." Vincent's voice came out as barely a whisper.

"*Aiii,* no!" said Hewa.

Koku gasped, her pen slipping from her fingers. The largest theft yet! Both men scowled at her.

"You stick to your work, P.C. Mkama. Your opinion wasn't asked for," Hewa snapped.

"Sorry, sir." She leaned forward to retrieve the pen, but her belly prevented her. Both men stared as she eased from the bench, knelt, and seized it. Now the hard part. Using the bench for support, she hefted herself upwards, wobbling like a newborn giraffe, and resettled her bulk. Was she truly not due for another month?

"I assume you're ready to continue now?" Her boss' eyes were narrowed.

"Yes, sir." *Mpumbavu!*

"Motete," Hewa said, "I understand you do not want to lodge a formal complaint, but you must see that we can do nothing if you do not come forward. What of the other men who will fall victim to their own kindness? We can—"

"No! Think of the ridicule! I wouldn't be able to show my face at work! Tricked by a twilight lady. And my wife. Do you think she would believe I was only doing a good deed for a strange lady? I don't need that sort of trouble in my household."

The same reason the others refused to report.

Hewa steepled his fingers, pursed his lips in what Koku thought of as his thinking face. After a time, he said, "Perhaps if you describe this night hound, I can talk to the *Mwanza Times* and give an anonymous accounting on your behalf. An article on 'Twilight Lady Lures and Carjacks Lone Men' would wake up unsuspecting men to the danger."

Koku coughed to hide a growl that threatened to spill over. Yes, rich men were in danger. Run to the newspapers. Alert the people's militia. Call the president. Something had to be done.

"Did you have something to say, P.C. Mkama?"

"Yes, sir. Would you like me to make note of the description?"

After she'd been dismissed, Koku struggled back to the Fierce Sun kiosk, a torch in one hand, the empty soda bottle in the other. This time she took the shopkeeper up on his kind offer and sank onto the stool.

"Bless you, Baba Nkwabi," she groaned.

"Where's Lubadsa?" he demanded, a broom in his work-worn hand. "Surely, he wouldn't let you make a second trip in this heat? And in the dark, no less."

"He's out." Koku leaned against the mural, concentrated on slowing her breathing to a normal pace, and wiped a sodden handkerchief across her brow.

He clucked his tongue in disapproval, whisked the broom across the floor like he was mad at it. "He could have come with it tomorrow. He won't be pleased."

"Why should he care? I've saved him a trip."

"Little mother, you must realize he's sweet on you. He follows you like a hungry puppy."

"More like a worried hound." She patted her belly. "Afraid I'll burst like a tomato on his shift."

Baba Nkwabi laughed, set his broom aside. "May you raise many children!"

"You're too kind, Baba! But one is quite enough for now."

"Ah, little mother, you remind me so much of my Anifa. Such a good girl. Did I tell you, she's started housekeeping for a *mzungu*? An American, I think." He swiped a cloth across the counter, shook his head. "So much money, those people."

"I wouldn't say no to it."

"God has given you all the wealth you need. A child brings much happiness to his mother." He patted her shoulder, then stepped to the shop opening and dragged a metal gate halfway across.

True, but with her bank account depleted, she'd welcome some less divine wealth, too. She eased to her feet. "Thank you again for the soda, Baba. Good deeds never perish."

"Good is what God wills, little mother."

Twenty minutes later, Koku slumped in her chair, reviewing her bank statement again. How could her husband do this?

When they'd courted, he'd been generous. After the wedding, that had dried up like a barren field. Especially once he'd opened a second electronics shop downtown. Always carrying more petty cash in his pocket than she made in a month. But where was the money for their household? "That's why *you* draw a salary," he'd say. Or, "Should I not take care of my businesses?" Or, "I'm meeting with some associates. I'll need the money for expenses." He meant beer. She accepted this. Why else would she set aside money for their baby?

The girlfriends and his thievery were another matter entirely. A dog ought to prefer bones, but he had a rich man's tastes and craving for prestige. Especially when it came to keeping girlfriends. At least he hadn't taken a second wife. *That* she couldn't bear.

Setting the incriminating document aside, she created a folder for Motete Vincent's complaint and added it to the other two unofficial filings.

When P.C. Lubadsa appeared in the doorway, she covered the bank statement with some stray paperwork.

"Aisee, sista, you look tired," he said. "Go home, and I will finish anything that needs to be done."

"Gladly," Koku said, eyeing his now rumpled uniform. She went to wipe the sweat from her face, but her saturated cloth did little but shift it around on her brow.

Lubadsa pulled a crisp handkerchief from his shirt pocket, held it out for her.

"I...." She dropped her gaze to the desk.

"Go on. Take it."

She met his eyes, then grasped the cloth, her fingers brushing his. "Thank you. I'll make sure to wash it."

"So, did you file a PF3 for Motete Vincent?" A lopsided grin tugged at Lubadsa's lean face.

"The only injury that hyena suffered was to his pride. A doctor can't treat that, even if the form gives him permission."

"You're a cheeky lady, P.C. Mkama."

"Thank you, P.C. Lubadsa. From you, I know that's a compliment."

"Indeed."

"Before I go"—Koku rubbed her lower back to ease the tension—"tell me what trouble you've been up to. I know it will be instructive."

Lubadsa slid his chair close, sank down, and stretched his long legs before him.

"No trouble, Madame. I simply suggested to the A.S. that I examine Vincent's 4x4 for evidence."

"And did you find anything?"

"Another card."

"The same?"

He plucked it from his pocket, held it out to her. "Indeed."

In each instance, a blank business card had been found in the vehicle of the victims, a lipstick kiss pressed to the center of the card. She turned it over once, then placed it in the proper file. "I didn't tell Hewa about the other victims."

Lubadsa shrugged. "No one comes forward. What should we do?"

"Ha! You found something else!"

"You know me too well, P.C. Mkama." Reaching back into his pocket, he drew out a thin gold bracelet with a single charm in the shape of a stylized sun. He handed it to her, but she didn't set it in the file, closing it in her fist instead.

She smiled.

"You think it's funny?" he asked.

Koku shrugged. "That rich, *married* men who think they can press a stranded young lady for sex are hijacked and their money stolen? No, it's terrible."

Lubadsa shook his head but returned her smile. "You are trouble, *sista*." He reached over and tugged her bank statement from under the pile. "You have much to deal with, I think. You might try the Pour House."

She struggled to her feet, squeezed his hand. "Thank you, Lubadsa. You're a gem among men. You'll make assistant inspector yet."

He blushed. "One can only hope."

Instead of boarding the usual bus to her neighborhood, Koku took the one to Kona yaBwiru. Squeezing out of the overcrowded tin can, she brushed off her uniform and sneezed, as dust from the traffic rolled past her in waves. The heat still clung like an unwanted lover, but at least the night air held the faint promise of rain. She wiped her face with Lubadsa's handkerchief, breathed in his subtle cologne.

Lumbering over heavily rutted paths with her torch leading the way, she stopped outside a corrugated shack. A couple of mismatched tables were set outside, where Pour House patrons swilled *chang'aa*, the locally brewed moonshine. Illegal, yet popular among city residents, *chang'aa* raids by the police or local militia, while infrequent, did occur. Members of the Force were forewarned, so as not to be caught drinking at such an establishment during a raid.

Some of the patrons eyed Koku uneasily. She wasn't surprised. She didn't belong here, and her uniform raised lots of questions. But it couldn't be helped.

Switching off her torch, she pulled open a loosely hinged door and ducked inside. The grainy, sweet smell of the moonshine made her nauseous, and the odor of close packed bodies, combined with the heat of the evening, caused her to take a steadying breath. Tables sat crammed together, leaving little space to step, especially for someone in her condition. She inched through a sticky-floored aisle, knocking against tabletops, patrons swearing when she jostled their drinks. Finally, she saw who she searched for and made for the back corner.

Two women huddled at a table, deep in conversation. One young, the other middle-aged and finely dressed. As Koku approached, the middle-aged lady's eyes drifted to her. The woman blanched, slid from her seat, and stumbled for the door. Koku smiled. Good.

Sinking down onto the wobbly chair the older woman had just vacated, she examined the woman she'd come to see.

"How did you find me?" Anifa asked.

"I saw your father today. He is a nice man."

"Yes." Anifa took a cautious sip from her jug.

"He thinks you work for a foreigner."

"I know."

Koku drew out the bracelet, set it on the table. "Yours, I believe. I didn't know you also do jewelry. A very distinctive style. Like the sun in the mural."

Anifa blinked. Blinked again. She gathered the bracelet from the table, undid the clasp, and looped it around her wrist.

"Are you here to arrest me?"

"Me? No, I saw it on the ground, thought you might want it back." Koku reached over and fastened the clasp for her.

"Thank you." She spun her bracelet on her wrist. "Miserable heat! Vincent was late. By the time I climbed in his 4x4, I was dripping with sweat. It must have slid over my hand. You won't say anything to my father?"

"Tell me, how did you know he would be carrying so much cash? Or did you get lucky?"

Anifa scanned the room, shifted her chair closer. "His wife told me. He was on his way to pay the first installment to a builder. His latest girlfriend demanded a house, and I've heard he's lovesick. But that money was for his son's education. Did you know he's at Feza Boys in Dar es Salaam? A good school, but very expensive. Over six million a year. Can you imagine? If he'd spent that money—and much more—on his girlfriend, his wife worried they couldn't continue to afford the tuition."

"And of course Vincent can't admit to his girlfriend that he picked you up and lost the money."

"I've heard she's a jealous one."

"Ha! He'll have to lie, say something happened to the money. A bad business deal, maybe."

Anifa shrugged. "She won't believe him."

"I wouldn't. She'll think he never intended to build a house." Koku chuckled. "Brilliant. I predict Motete Vincent is about to have girlfriend troubles."

"Shame." Anifa took a long sip of her drink.

"And how much did you charge the wife for your good deed?"

"I'm not greedy, if that's what you think. Only a hundred thousand. Cheap, when you weigh the risk."

"You were certain he would give you a lift?"

She laughed. "A man who dips his finger in honey will do so again."

Koku grimaced. "Yes, that's true."

Anifa became serious. "Please, you won't tell my father? It would kill him."

"He won't hear it from my lips." Koku pulled out her bank statement, used it to fan herself. "But I have a husband problem, and I think you can help."

The Phone Call

by Herschel Cozine
(Best Flash Story, 2017)

The harsh jangle of the phone made Phil flinch. He dug it from his pocket and glanced at the caller ID. The number was not a familiar one.

"Hello," he said in a questioning voice.

A gravelly, electronically distorted voice growled in his ear: "We have your wife."

"I beg your pardon?"

"You heard me. Listen carefully. Her life depends on it."

Phil started to say something, but the voice continued.

"Have one million dollars in unmarked bills by midnight tomorrow. I will call back at that time to give you further instructions. Understand?"

"Who is this?" Phil said.

"It doesn't matter. We have your wife. That's all you have to know."

Phil sighed. "Is this some kind of joke? Who the hell are you?"

"No joke. A million dollars."

A pause, then the voice continued: "And no cops. If I see a cop car within a mile, she's a dead woman."

"Suppose I refuse to pay?"

"Don't play games with me, mister. Pay up or else."

"Look, you sorry-ass punk," Phil said. "I'm not giving you a dime. Not a red cent."

"You—!" the voice started.

Phil cut him off. "It's your turn to listen. I won't pay a ransom. Here is what I am telling you to do. Return my wife by midnight tonight, or I will double the million dollars and offer it as a reward. Two million dollars for your worthless hide. There are guys out there who would kill their own mother for that kind of money."

"You don't know what you're doing. It's your wife's life at stake here."

Phil laughed into the phone. "I don't think so. You'd never get away with it. I hope you're smart enough to know that."

He looked at his watch.

"Have my wife home by midnight tonight and no questions asked. Otherwise, a two-million-dollar bounty. Are you willing to gamble?"

"Look, buddy, I mean business."

"So do I, pal. How well do you trust your cronies to keep their mouths shut with two million big ones riding on it? It only takes one, you know, and your life isn't worth a nickel."

Silence.

Phil shifted the phone to his other ear, sat down and waited. No reply.

"I'm hanging up now. I hope you live close enough to get her home by midnight." Phil took another look at his watch. "That's six hours. Have a nice day."

He folded the phone and dropped it in his pocket. He stood up, stretched, and walked into the kitchen, where his wife Marge was removing a roast from the oven.

"Oh, there you are," she said. "I was just about to call you to dinner."

She placed the roast on the table.

"Who was that on the phone?" she asked.

Phil picked up the carving knife, cut a generous slice of meat, and dropped it on the plate.

"Wrong number," he said.

The Cop Who Liked Gilbert and Sullivan

by Robert Lopresti
(Best Short Story, 2018)

When the phone call reached police headquarters, no one was more surprised than Sergeant Emil Klinehart himself.

"Me?" He fumbled to turn off the CD player, which had been filling the evidence room with the Lord Chancellor's song from *Iolanthe*. "They want *me* on a murder investigation?"

"That's what they said," said the desk clerk.

"But I haven't been out on half a dozen calls in the last five years. Why do they want *me?*"

"Who knows?" said the clerk cheerfully. "Maybe you're a suspect."

Five years ago, Klinehart had rushed to investigate a missing child in a city park. He was in such a hurry he forgot to set the handbrake on his patrol car. The little girl was found safe and sound, but it took a crane to pull the prowl car out of the fishing pond. Klinehart was banished to the evidence room as a punishment.

Some punishment. He *loved* working alone, with his CD player blasting at full volume. Last year, following a scandal in the evidence room of a nearby city, a court-ordered audit declared Klinehart's to be the best-run room in the state. He had been promoted to sergeant and told to expect to stay there until he retired.

Now Klinehart was being pushed out of the nest, into the cold, cruel world of real police work. He was not happy.

The address where the prowl car dropped him off was not reassuring. The few homicides he saw as a beat cop had been in back-alley tenements. This murder site, on the other hand, was an old mansion on the edge of the city.

A patrolman escorted him into the library, a room roughly the size of Klinehart's apartment. It was dominated by floor-to-ceiling bookcases and a huge antique desk at the far end.

There were two men in the room, and the sergeant recognized one as Lieutenant Perez, reputedly the best detective on the force.

Why in the world would Perez ask for *him?*

The lieutenant smiled. "Klinehart, glad you're here. You're the guy who plays Gilbert and Sullivan recordings in the evidence room, right?"

He swallowed. "Yes, sir. If someone complained about the noise—"

"Nope." Perez shook his head. "We need an expert on Gilbert and Sullivan, and you're the only one I know. Will you give us a hand?"

"Of course, sir." Klinehart's head was swimming. He had never heard of a Savoyard being needed for a murder investigation.

"Lieutenant, may I ask a few questions?" The other person was speaking, a well-dressed man in his mid-fifties.

Perez nodded. "Sergeant, this is Alfred Edwards. He is the attorney for the man who was murdered last night." He waved a generous hand towards Klinehart. "Ask away, Mr. Edwards."

The lawyer fixed him with a doubtful look, as if Klinehart were a potential juror he was preparing to reject. "Have you noticed the statues, Sergeant? Take a look at them."

He hadn't spotted them until then. There were thirteen statues standing on wooden bases on a narrow table that ran most of the length of the room. Each was made of some sort of ceramic or clay and stood about a foot high. They appeared to have been made by the same artist.

Each portrayed a man in an elaborate costume. The first ones he picked out were two men in the robes and wigs of English judges and a Japanese man holding a huge axe. He began to get an idea of why Perez had asked for him.

There were thirteen statues, but fourteen bases on the table. Edwards was standing near the empty base, the eleventh counting from the left side of the room, which Klinehart realized was the way to count them.

Edwards pointed to the empty shelf. "Can you tell us about the statue which used to stand there?"

Klinehart glanced at the nearest neighbors of the empty shelf. On the left was a gentleman farmer. On the right stood a black-caped nobleman. He let out a sigh of relief; if all the questions were this easy, he would have no trouble. "It was a jester, sir."

Edwards's eyebrows went up. "Very good! Perhaps he *can* be of help, Lieutenant."

Perez was grinning. "How did you know, Sergeant?"

"The statues represent the Gilbert and Sullivan operas, sir. They show the Grossmith characters."

"The *what* characters?"

"Grossmith, sir. George Grossmith was the actor who played the main comic part in most of the original productions." He pointed to a few statues. "Koko from *The Mikado*. The ruler of the Queen's navy"—he pronounced it nay-*vee*—"from *Pinafore*. The only one missing is the jester from *The Yeomen of the Guard*. Did someone steal it?"

"No, we've taken it as evidence. The owner of this house was murdered. Apparently, he surprised someone in this room in the middle of last night. The prowler stabbed him with a letter opener from the desk."

Klinehart frowned. "Who was the owner, sir?"

"Jeremy Hollander," said the lawyer. "Let's start with some background, shall we? My late client spent many years in Hollywood as a character actor. He was never a star, but he worked steadily in character roles. He invested his money wisely and so—ten years ago, when he reached fifty-five—he was able to retire and dedicate his time to his first love. Mr. Hollander was a Gilbert and Sullivan enthusiast."

"I've seen him," said Klinehart. "He performed with the Civic Light Opera in the Grossmith parts. I guess that's why he had the statues."

"Apparently," said Perez. "Now, before he died, Hollander struggled across the room and picked up the jester. We hope he was trying to identify his attacker. Of course, it would have made more sense to go to the desk, but maybe he didn't think he had time to look for a pen and paper, and it was farther away."

"But if it was a burglar—"

"It wasn't. The doors and windows were all secure. The alarm was set."

"I had to turn it off when I arrived this morning," said Edwards. "I flew all night to keep an appointment with Jeremy, and instead I discovered his body."

Perez nodded. "There are no servants here at night, so it appears that one of Hollander's four houseguests killed him. Last night was his birthday, and his relatives were here to help celebrate. They are his nephew Douglas Anson, his grandchildren Stanley and Sally Long, and Stanley's wife Maureen." He paused. "Do any of those names appear in the play?"

Klinehart shook his head. "I'm afraid not, sir."

The lieutenant sighed. "I suppose that would have been too easy. Well, let me tell you what we learned from the suspects' preliminary statements. Mr. Hollander took his guests out to dinner last night. During the meal, he informed them that he had invited Mr. Edwards to come to the house in the morning, in order to finalize a change in his will. Apparently, someone slipped into the library last night to get a look at the will, which was in the top desk drawer. Mr. Hollander surprised him—or her—and was killed."

Klinehart realized that he might never have a better chance to impress a lieutenant. He wracked his brain for a good question. "What were the changes in the will, sir?"

The lawyer spoke. "Jeremy originally intended to leave the Civic Light Opera one-fourth of his estate. However, the group has fallen on hard times lately, so he decided to raise their share to one half. The rest is divided evenly between his two grandchildren and his nephew."

"Obviously they had a powerful motive," said Perez. "They knew that, if he lived long enough to sign the will, they would receive a smaller inheritance."

Klinehart nodded. "And you hope the statue indicates the killer."

"It seems reasonable. Why did he stagger across the room to pick up a statue? Why that one in particular? Tell us the plot of the opera, and maybe we'll get an idea."

The sergeant grimaced. "Gilbert's plots don't make much sense when they're condensed. To tell the truth, some of them aren't too clear at full length."

"We'll risk it," said Perez. "Just give us the highlights."

Klinehart took a deep breath. "All right. *Yeomen of the Guard* takes place in Tudor England. The yeomen are the warders of the Tower of London, which is the play's setting. They're guarding a Colonel Fairfax, who was falsely accused of sorcery by his relatives and condemned to die."

"Are there any murders in the opera?"

Klinehart stared at the ceiling as he ran the plot through his head. "No, sir. There *is* an argument over a will."

"That sounds good. Tell us about it."

"Colonel Fairfax wants to get married in prison, so that the relatives who framed him won't inherit his estate. A woman named Elsie Maynard agrees to marry him for fifty pounds, knowing that he'll be executed in a few hours."

"Fifty pounds," the lawyer repeated. "As his wife, wouldn't she get the colonel's entire estate?"

Klinehart shook his head. "I warned you this might not make much sense. We're never told who would get the rest of the money, and since Fairfax lives happily ever after, it doesn't seem to matter much."

Edwards sighed. "Surely in Jeremy's final moments, he wasn't thinking of anything so complex. If there *is* a clue, it must be in a character's name or the title of the play."

"How about the jester?" asked Perez. "Does he have a name?"

"Jack Point, sir. Elsie was his fiancée, and when he loses her, he dies of a broken heart."

"Not exactly what killed Mr. Hollander."

"Sir," said Klinehart, "may I add something?"

"By all means, Sergeant. We called you down to get your opinion."

"Well, Jack Point is the only really *tragic* character in any of Gilbert and Sullivan's operas. If a comic actor was dying, he might naturally be drawn to the jester with the broken heart."

Perez scowled. "You mean that Mr. Hollander might have picked up that statue for sentimental reasons that had nothing to do with the murder."

Klinehart nodded sadly.

The lieutenant shook his head. "For a while there, I thought this would be an easy one. I guess we had better continue with the regular investigation. Why don't you take a seat, Sergeant? You'll probably enjoy the change, after being stuck at headquarters for so long."

Actually, there was nothing Klinehart wanted more than to return to the security of his evidence room, but it didn't seem advisable to say so. He sat down.

Perez ordered a patrolman to escort Sally Long into the library. "According to the preliminary reports, she has been the least cooperative," he explained to Edwards and the sergeant.

The first suspect to walk in, however, was certainly not Sally Long. He was a good-looking man in his mid-thirties, and his casual clothes cost more than both of Klinehart's civilian suits together. "I'm Stanley Long, Lieutenant. I know you asked for my sister, but she locked herself in her room and says she won't come out until her lawyer arrives."

"You can tell her that Mr. Edwards is right here."

"Uh, Lieutenant." The attorney looked uncomfortable. "I told all the houseguests that, as the executor of Mr. Hollander's will, I can't represent any of them."

Perez glared at him. "Oh, you did."

"I had to. Professional ethics."

The lieutenant turned back to Long. "Has your sister called a lawyer?"

"To be honest, I don't think she knows one, except for Mr. Edwards here." Long smiled wryly. "Sally is a painter, you know. She prides herself on her artistic eccentricity."

Perez heaved a sigh. "Well, let's start with you, then, Mr. Long."

"Fine with me, Lieutenant, but I really don't know what you can ask that the first officer on the scene didn't."

"Oh, there's always another question. For instance, who do you think killed your grandfather?"

The next hour was a liberal education for Klinehart, his first chance to watch an expert investigator at work. As the questioning went on, however, he recognized that Perez's attack, for all its style, was yielding little in the way of results.

Stan Long claimed ignorance on all the major points. He didn't know who killed Hollander, nor what the jester statue meant. "I never cared for Gilbert and Sullivan, I'm afraid."

"When did you first hear about the new will, Mr. Long?"

"Grandfather told us about it at dinner last night. We quarreled with him, of course. Throwing away the family's money on silly entertainment."

It occurred to Klinehart that the money had been *earned* by silly entertainment. But he kept his mouth shut.

"How much would the new will have cost you?"

"He wouldn't say." Long smiled ruefully. "Oh, was that a trap? I presume the killer saw the will, so he's the only one who knows its exact contents. All grandfather would tell us is that he was decreasing our shares in favor of the opera company. He wouldn't say by how much."

"How are you fixed financially, Mr. Long?"

"I can't complain. In two years' time, I'll probably be a vice president in my corporation." He smiled again. "I don't have to kill for money, Lieutenant."

"When did you go to bed last night?"

"Maureen and I went upstairs as soon as we returned from the restaurant. Around eleven, I'd say."

"Did you hear anything during the night?"

Long shook his head. "I'm a sound sleeper. It would have taken a *very* loud fight to wake me up. Are we about done here?"

The lieutenant took a more direct approach with the next witness, the victim's nephew. "They tell me that you have money problems, Mr. Anson."

"Well, now and then." Douglas Anson was a thin, nervous-looking man of twenty-five. "I'm a freelance photographer. That means some months are better than others, and I admit I could use a few of the better ones, right about now."

"How much would the new will have cost you?"

"I don't know. Uncle Jeremy wouldn't give us any details."

Klinehart saw Perez heave a sigh. "Tell me about the fight in the restaurant."

"Which one?"

The lieutenant looked startled. "How many were there?"

"Two. We quarreled over the will, of course, but before that there was a fight over dinner itself."

"No one mentioned that."

"No one asked us—or at least no one asked me. The other policeman just wanted to know about the will."

"Well, I'm asking now. What was the quarrel about?"

"Dinner. The restaurant was my cousin Sally's idea, you see. She said it was the best place in town for seafood." Anson grimaced. "She always thinks she knows what's best. We tend to go along with her, to keep the peace."

"But not last night?"

"Well, we went to the restaurant she chose, but Cousin Stan proceeded to order a steak. It wasn't even on the menu, but they found him one."

Perez frowned. "And that caused a fight?"

"It sure did. Remember, Sally raved all day about the fish and seafood at this joint, and then her brother orders steak. She really blew up at him."

Edwards cleared his throat. "Maybe Mr. Long doesn't like fish."

Anson shook his head. "As a matter of fact, he does. He said he just didn't feel like it last night. Sally said he did it just to get her goat, and she was probably right. They don't get along very well."

"How did Mr. Hollander react?"

"I think that, like me, he was amused. We've seen those two go at it before. Then, when things began to calm down—meaning that Sally started sulking—Uncle Jeremy dropped the bombshell about his will."

"Who seemed most upset about that, Mr. Anson?"

"We were all pretty irritated, but I suppose Maureen, Stan's wife, was the most insistent that Uncle Jeremy should give us details." He smiled wryly.

"Maybe she doesn't know his stubborn streak as well as the rest of us."

"When did you go to bed last night?"

"Right after dinner. I don't know what time it was, but the next thing I heard was Mr. Edwards shouting for help this morning."

"Okay, did you notice—?"

He stopped, because a young woman had appeared in the doorway. She was very pretty, and in fact she reminded Klinehart of the singer who had played the title role in a recent production of *Princess Ida.* He usually fell vaguely in love with the female leads—provided they sang well, of course.

"I'm very sorry," she said. "I didn't mean to interrupt."

"May I help you, ma'am? I'm Lieutenant Perez."

"I'm Maureen Long. I was looking for my husband, and someone said he was in here."

"He was. I don't know where he is now. As long as you're here, why don't you have a seat, and we'll get this done."

He turned to the photographer. "Thank you, Mr. Anson. I think that's all for now."

Stanley Long's wife was obviously nervous, and Klinehart felt sorry for her. There was something he wanted to say, but before he could phrase it Douglas Anson was out of the room, and the interrogation began.

Klinehart sat through the first part in uneasy silence, listening as Ms. Long described the two quarrels at dinner.

"Did you hear anything unusual during the night, Ms. Long?"

"We slept straight through. Stan woke me at eight thirty, when he heard Mr. Edwards shouting downstairs."

"When did you—?"

"Excuse me, Lieutenant. May I say something?"

Three surprised faces turned toward Klinehart, who went bright red.

"Yes, Sergeant?"

"I just thought you might want to warn Ms. Long about the penalties for supplying a false alibi."

Everyone was staring, and Klinehart wished he was back among his evidence boxes. "You probably think you're safe," he said earnestly, "because you can't be forced to testify against your husband, Ms. Long. But if you *do* testify and lie, that would be perjury. It would also make you an accessory after the fact."

Edwards began to sputter. Perez opened his mouth, but before he could speak, Maureen Long cut him off in a very effective way: she began to cry.

The next two hours were a blur to Klinehart.

Once it became clear that Maureen Long was accusing her husband of murder, there was a flurry of activity. Lawyers, cops and assistant district attorneys rushed in and out, from one phone to another, from one room to the next, from the mansion to waiting cars and back again.

Even Sally Long made a surprise appearance, unlocking her door for a moment to shriek at the police while they escorted her brother out in handcuffs.

Finally, the three men were alone in the library once more. Lieutenant Perez hung up the phone and turned to Klinehart and Edwards.

"Stanley Long just confessed. He claims it was his wife's idea for him to slip down and look at the will. When his grandfather discovered him, he panicked."

Klinehart shook his head loyally. "I can't believe that Ms. Long was involved."

The lieutenant shrugged. "From our point of view, all that matters is who was down in the library with a letter opener. We know the answer to that, thanks to you, Sergeant."

Klinehart cleared his throat modestly. "Thank you, sir."

Suddenly Perez was glaring fiercely. "Which brings me to my next point. I hate to quarrel with success, but you should never have pulled a stunt like that. If you suspected Long was the killer, you should have told me."

"I'm very sorry, sir, but I never had the chance. If you remember, Ms. Long came in while you were still questioning Mr. Anson."

Edwards looked up. "You mean it was something Anson said that gave Long away?"

"Yes, sir. This is sort of embarrassing. You see, you and the lieutenant were both right about that statue, and I was wrong."

"Spare us the flattery, Sergeant," said Perez. "How did you figure it out?"

"Well, *you* said the statue must be a clue, sir. And Mr. Edwards said that it had to be something simple, like the title of the opera."

"You're saying *Yeomen of the Guard* indicates Stanley Long?"

"Exactly, sir. It was obvious, once Mr. Anson told us about the dinner."

"The dinner? You mean the fact that Long ate steak, but the others had fish?"

Klinehart nodded. "Remember, there was quite an argument over it, so the detail was likely to remain in Mr. Hollander's mind. A few hours later, when he needed to identify his grandson as his attacker, that was what he thought of."

"I see the logic, but you still haven't explained how the statue of a jester singled out Stanley Long."

"How?" Klinehart was milking the suspense. He never had such an attentive audience in the evidence room. "I told you the yeomen are the guards at the Tower of London. But they're better known by their nickname."

Edwards winced. "Of course!"

"Of course what?" said Perez. "What *is* the nickname?"

Klinehart couldn't help grinning. "They're the Beefeaters, sir."

Dying in Dokesville

by Alan Orloff
(Best Short Story, 2019)

The annual Peach Festival was a big deal in Dokesville, South Carolina, but not *this* big.

Visitors descended on the tiny town in the shadow of the Blue Ridge Mountains like hungry locusts on a field of corn. They came in their blocky Winnebagos and shiny space-aged Airstreams, their sporty camper tops and suburban minivans, their sedans and motorcycles. They filled the campgrounds west and south of the city, and they stuffed the cheap motels clustered by the interstate.

The richer ones arrived by air and pulled up to Gracemanor Inn, the town's only posh resort, in hired town cars.

Some came for the spectacle.

Some came seeking a spiritual awakening.

Others came to be a part of history, for this was the Great American Eclipse 2017, and Dokesville stood squarely in the path of totality.

They came to get a glimpse of the sun completely disappearing from the sky for two minutes and eleven seconds.

And they all came with their silly paper glasses.

Cyrus Tinsley attacked his pecan waffle with gusto, but his girlfriend, LuAnn Haskins, just picked at her hamburger. They were grabbing a quick lunch at the Waffle House before they started their afternoon shifts at Gracemanor

Inn. Cyrus was third in charge on the four-man maintenance crew, and LuAnn worked her butt off in housekeeping. Although the town was packed, the Waffle House was no busier than usual.

"Something wrong with your burger?" Cyrus asked.

"Never mind my eating. I got something I want to talk to you about."

"Okay."

"You know that family renting the luxury suites?"

"Yeah. What about them?" Cyrus poured more syrup on his waffle and spread it around with the back of his fork.

"Well, you shoulda been there last night, Cy," LuAnn said. "You woulda died. I was bringing them some extra towels, but instead of just handing them over at the door, they wanted me to freshen up the bathroom—their words. So while I was tidying up, I heard them arguing. Everyone seemed to be bullying the old lady, who—I found out later from Izzy at the front desk—had gathered everyone together and was paying for the three luxury suites. Calling her names, telling her she was out of touch. One of them even called her a bitch."

"Don't sound very grateful," Cyrus said around a mouthful of waffle.

"Not hardly." She pulled a minuscule piece off her hamburger bun and popped it into her mouth. "Her name is Mary Margaret Sesco, and she's the widow of some rich banker dude from New Jersey. Not just rich. *Super rich.*"

"How'd you find that out?"

"Ever hear of Google? You know, on a computer?"

Cyrus just nodded. He didn't like when LuAnn got all sarcastic. Made him feel small.

"It got me to thinking. Rich people live different than us, and not always better. We could teach them a lesson *and* solve our problem at the same time."

"What problem?" Cyrus asked.

"Born here, live here, die here. Being stuck in this backward town. *That* problem." She raised an eyebrow at Cyrus like he was an idiot. He'd seen that look enough to know to keep his trap shut. LuAnn would get to her point without any prompting from him. "When I was leaving their room, I saw the biggest and sparkliest necklace ever. Must have been worth twenty, forty, hell, coulda been worth *eighty* thousand dollars."

"Whoa." Cyrus swiped his last piece of waffle through a puddle of syrup and forked it into his mouth. LuAnn hadn't taken more than two bites of her burger. Who orders a hamburger at Waffle House, anyway?

"Well, maybe these rich snobs shouldn't be the only ones getting some kind of enlightenment out of this eclipse. Maybe we should get enlightened, too."

"What do you mean?"

LuAnn pushed her plate aside. Leaned in close. "That necklace would buy us a lot of enlightenment."

"Not sure I'm getting your point." Cyrus had a pretty good idea, but he couldn't believe LuAnn really meant it.

"We take it. We sell it. We are free from this place."

"Stealing ain't right."

"These people are so rich they won't miss it. Besides, if we take it, then when old lady Sesco kicks—and let me tell you, she's pretty damn near death now—her bitchy family won't get it. After how they treated her, they sure don't deserve it. It'll teach them a lesson, all right."

"I'm not sure you're thinking straight, Lu."

"Oh, I am. In fact, I've thought this all the way through." She paused, locked eyes with Cyrus. "Listen up, okay? These people came here for one reason, to see the eclipse, right? That means everyone—*every single person*—will be out on the veranda or the back lawn, gaping up at the sun with those ridiculous glasses. That means the rooms will be empty. What could be easier than taking something from an empty room?"

Cyrus knew from an early age about things that sounded too good to be true. "I'm not sure—"

LuAnn barreled ahead. "I read up on this eclipse. The totality thing happens tomorrow afternoon at two thirty-eight. Everyone'll be out back long before then, watching the moon slowly move in front of the sun. Should give you plenty of time to get into the suite, look around, find the stuff, and get out."

"Me?"

She glared at him. "Yes, you."

Cyrus thought about asking why LuAnn didn't just steal it herself, but she was the brains in this relationship, and he, well, wasn't. "I don't know. What if something goes wrong? What if someone sees me in their suite, poking around?"

"Just tell them you're from maintenance and got a report their toilet was clogged up. I mean, you *do* work in maintenance, right? But don't worry, *everyone's* going to be outside. No one's going to be wandering the halls of the inn. It's why they came to our stupid little town. It's a freaking total eclipse, Cy!"

"Doesn't seem like the right thing to do."

LuAnn reached into her pocket, pulled out a key card and slapped it on the table. "Here's an extra master key from housekeeping. It's unassigned, which means there's no way to trace who's coming and going. Use it to get in. When you're done, just put on a pair of those glasses and go out and watch the sky like everyone else."

Cyrus swallowed, didn't say a thing.

"You want to die in this crappy town? I sure don't." She rose, eyes blazing. "I'm going to the ladies' room. When I get back, you better have your mind made up. And let me be clear: this is a deal-breaker. If you want us to stay together, you'll figure out the right answer." She stomped off toward the back of the restaurant.

LuAnn spoke the truth. Cyrus Tinsley had been born in Dokesville. Cyrus Tinsley had grown up in Dokesville. And unless something drastic happened, Cyrus Tinsley would die in Dokesville.

And Dokesville was a dull place to live. Or die.

Even though it wasn't in his nature to take things that didn't belong to him, LuAnn made a good case. He didn't want to die in Dokesville fifty years from now. Poor. Alone.

He slid the master keycard into his pocket.

The next day, just after one o'clock, Cyrus strolled around the back corner of the inn for a smoke break. He lit up under a majestic magnolia tree, watching the crowd of eclipse viewers. A sense of excitement filled the air, as more and more people spilled out onto the veranda and the wide lawn beyond, everyone's head lifted upward, gazing at the sun through their protective glasses. Cyrus had his own pair in his pocket, but he was waiting until after he'd completed his task before putting them on. Sort of a reward for a job well done.

Excited voices floated on the breeze. On the veranda, he spotted a loud group of people who had taken over one end of the deck. At the center of it all, an ancient white-haired woman—Mary Margaret Sesco, no doubt—sat by herself. She seemed to be the only one, besides him, not wearing glasses and gawking at the eclipse.

Cyrus's phone buzzed with a text from his boss: *Please check out the icemaker. Kitchen staff says it just cut off.*

Can't run an inn without an icemaker. Cyrus dropped his cigarette butt and ground it out with his heel, then hurried off to fix the problem. Part of him worried he wouldn't be finished in time. The other part of him *hoped* he wouldn't.

It didn't take long for Cyrus to trace the problem with the icemaker to a tripped circuit breaker, and he fixed it without any trouble. When he was satisfied that the kitchen could once again serve cold drinks, he glanced at his watch.

Show time.

He crept through the main part of the inn to the back stairs, then hustled up the four flights to the top level, which housed three luxury suites. He opened the fire door a smidge and peered out.

LuAnn was right; everyone seemed to be outside. The inn was deserted.

He exited the stairwell and stopped at the landing to look out the back window. He wasn't sure if things had gotten appreciably darker outside, but the quality of the light had changed. Kinda weird. Still fifteen minutes to go before totality.

He walked down the hall to Suite 501 and glanced around. No one in sight, so he removed the master passkey from his pocket. Held it up to the lock sensor. The light flashed green, and he turned the knob, slowly pushing the door open. The hinges didn't squeak—he'd oiled them yesterday afternoon, right after LuAnn had outlined their plan.

He slipped in and gently closed the door behind him. Listened for signs that anyone was there.

All quiet.

LuAnn said she'd seen the jewelry in the bedroom, so Cyrus quickly crossed the large living area—the luxury suites really were quite luxurious—to the master bedroom. The door was ajar; he pushed it back and peeked inside.

An old lady—Mary Margaret—stared at him from her bed, propped up on three pillows.

Cyrus felt as if he'd just been in an elevator that had dropped two stories without warning. "Uh, sorry, ma'am."

"Room service?"

"Room service? Yes, yes. Room service," Cyrus said. Maybe if he got her out of the suite, he could still get what he came for. "You know the eclipse is about to happen. The total part of it, anyway. There's still time to go see it."

"It's so hot outside, and I'm not feeling very well. I wanted to be comfortable. I don't need to see it." She tapped her head. "I've got a pretty good imagination. 'Sides, it gets dark pretty near every night." She laughed at her own joke, and that sent her sputtering into a series of coughs. Which in turn blossomed into a full-fledged hacking attack. She managed to squeak out, "Water, please?"

Cyrus just stood there, watching her cough.

"Water!"

He snapped out of it. "Yes, of course. Just a sec." He rushed out to the bar in the living room and fetched a glass of water.

When he'd brought it back to the bedroom, she had stopped coughing and seemed to be holding something beneath the covers.

"I'm okay, now. Will you put the glass on the nightstand, in case it happens again?"

"Sure." Cyrus set the glass down, noticed the nightstand drawer cracked open. Had it been open before? He glanced at the clock: 2:28.

Mary Margaret cleared her throat, stared at him for a beat. "I didn't call room service."

He swallowed. "Uh, I must have gotten the rooms mixed up."

"I don't think so." Her hands shifted underneath the blanket. "I don't think so at all."

Cyrus pictured a gun, aimed right at him.

"I know why you're really here."

Cyrus didn't say anything. He figured if he lunged at her, he might get to the gun before she could pull the trigger. She was damn old, after all. Then he could take off with the goods. But he had a tough enough time stealing. How would murder sit with him?

Underneath the covers, the lady's hands wavered. Cyrus's heart raced. One flinch of her bony trigger finger, and he was dead meat.

"You came to pray with me, didn't you? The Lord asked you to offer me comfort in my time of need. He sent you."

Cyrus thought about agreeing with her, but lying about what God did or did not do made him uncomfortable. "I don't think so, ma'am."

"Stop *ma'am*-ing me. My name is Mary Margaret."

"Yes, ma'am. Uh, Mary Margaret."

She fixed him with her cloudy gray eyes. "What's your name?"

"Cyrus," he blurted out, pure reflex, then cursed himself under his breath. Any competent crook would have used a fake name. Although at this point, it didn't really matter. His main goal now was to get out of the room before she put a slug into his gut. Forget the necklace. Forget LuAnn. Dying in Dokesville looked pretty good, as long as it wasn't today.

"You may not realize it, but the Lord sent you, He most definitely did. He works in mysterious ways, you know." She exhaled, and Cyrus got a whiff of old-lady breath. "Like today. Surely blotting out the sun is a sign only the Lord could pull off."

Cyrus shrugged one shoulder. "I suppose."

"I saw you yesterday, fixing the downspout. Thought to myself, what a fine, hard-working young man. This country needs more men like you."

"Thanks." Cyrus couldn't peel his gaze from the covers, where Mary Margaret's hands seemed to be struggling to keep the gun pointed at him.

"My whole family can't wait for me to pass, so they can get my fortune. You know that? Most of them are good people, just a little greedy, but my nephew Anthony is a real piece of work. Lazy. Wasteful. Mean. My brother didn't show him enough love when he was a boy. Made some poor choices. Broke the law. Broke my brother's heart, too. Long time ago." Her eyes glazed over, hands dipped. Then all of a sudden her head snapped up, along with her hands, still working beneath the covers. "You're not like Anthony, are you?"

"I try not to be." He glanced at the clock—2:33—and then out the window. Getting darker. He focused again on Mary Margaret.

Mary Margaret closed her eyes and moved her lips without a sound. It seemed to Cyrus like she was doing a complicated arithmetic problem in her head. After a while, she opened her eyes and spoke in a softer tone. "You've got a good heart, I can tell. I want you to have something."

"Oh?"

"Open up the nightstand drawer."

"Sure." Cyrus took a step toward the nightstand and pulled open the drawer. Looked inside. LuAnn had been right. The biggest and shiniest necklace he'd ever seen sparkled at him. "You want me to have the necklace?"

"Pfft! Why would you want that? Just a fancy piece of glass, is all. My daughter-in-law won't let me wear the real stuff. Too valuable. It's in a safe-deposit box back home." She gave a little snort, then started coughing again, wet and deep. After about thirty seconds, she calmed down and continued as if she hadn't stopped to hack up a lung. "Take the Bible."

Cyrus pulled out the Good Book, encased in a heavily padded blue-and-pink embroidered cover. "Uh, thanks and all, but I don't really need a Bible. I'm not very relig—"

"I've had that Bible since I was a child. I'm not giving it to you—I'm going to be buried with it." She nodded once, emphatically. "Look inside the cover."

Cyrus opened the book. He took a moment to find where the cover stopped and the Bible started, then worked his fingers inside a flap and wiggled out a stack of bills. Benjamins. Lots of them.

"I…I don't know what to say."

"There's more. In the back part, too."

Cyrus flipped the Bible over, repeated his excavation. When he finished, he had a healthy handful of crisp, clean hundred-dollar bills.

"I want you to have it. The *Lord* wants you to have it. He's given me a sign. You coming to me in my time of need. To help ease my journey. I can tell you're a little lost, so this money—eight thousand dollars—will help you find your way on your own journey. You don't want to end up like Anthony or any of my other good-for-nothing relatives. They won't miss the money, either, if that's what you're thinking. It's my secret Praise the Lord fund."

Cyrus heard Mary Margaret's words, every last one, but he wasn't sure he understood their true meaning. "You're giving this money to me? All of it?"

"Why don't you leave me a hundred? I'd like to tip housekeeping. They did a fine job with the room, you know, cleaning up after my sloppy relatives."

Just then, the room darkened—a lot—and Cyrus noticed the clock had clicked over to 2:38. Totality time. He went to the window. From his angle, he couldn't see the sun itself, but he got a good view of the inn's guests gazing up at the sky, most no longer wearing their eclipse glasses. He could hear them whooping and hollering, as if the home team had just scored the winning touchdown.

Mesmerized, he watched the crowd celebrate for about two minutes. When everyone put their glasses back on, Cyrus turned away from the window and stepped over to Mary Margaret on the bed.

Her eyes had closed. She wore a serene smile. Her chest no longer moved up and down. Mary Margaret had passed over to the other side, her journey in this world complete.

The covers had slipped down, revealing not a gun, but a rosary with a very large silver crucifix, which she still clutched in her lifeless hands.

Maybe there *was* something to this eclipse thing.

Getting caught with a fistful of money in a dead guest's bedroom wouldn't be the easiest thing to explain to management—or the cops—so he quickly bowed his head to Mary Margaret in a moment of tribute.

Then he stuck a hundred-dollar bill inside an envelope, wrote *Housekeeping* on the front, and left it on the nightstand.

Eight grand might not be enough to get two people out of Dokesville, but it was enough to get one out.

He hightailed it from the suite and rushed down the stairs, pushed through the back door, put on his silly paper glasses, and watched the glorious sun reappear.

On the Road with Mary Jo

by John M. Floyd
(Best Short Story, 2020)

Toby Hayes parked in the gravel lot and honked the horn, like always, and a minute later Dew Jackson opened the flimsy door of his trailer, locked it behind him, and stomped down the cinderblock steps. Like always. But this time Dew, holding a large duffel bag, stopped at the foot of the steps. He stood there staring, his mouth hanging open.

Toby couldn't help smiling. It took a lot to surprise Deward Jackson.

Dew, *not* smiling, continued across his sandy yard and climbed into the passenger seat, the bag in his lap. His eyes had narrowed to slits. In a low, tight voice he said, "Where'd you get the car, Toby?"

Toby had rehearsed this on his way here. *Borrowed it from my cousin. Rented it from the dealer on North Main. Bought it used, from a guy strapped for cash at work.* But he didn't say any of these things. After all, Toby had no money for either renting or buying, and no cousin of his would give him the time of day. And the car—a silver AltaStar coupe—damn sure didn't look used. It looked brand new. It even smelled brand new.

So he told the truth. "I jacked it. A guy was parked at the curb just down from my house, when I was walking to my truck. I pulled my gun, tapped on his window, made him open his door."

Dew shut his eyes and sighed. "Where is he now, this guy?"

"Layin' in the tall weeds beside the road. Don't worry, nobody saw me, nor him, neither."

"Tell me you didn't shoot him."

"I didn't shoot him. Whacked him on the head with my gun barrel."

Dew turned and glared at him. They were still sitting there, still parked in the sad little lot next to Dew's sad little mobile home. The stolen AltaStar looked as out-of-place here in the midmorning sun as a diamond in a mud puddle.

"Do you remember what we're doing today, Toby? What we been planning for weeks?"

"'Course I remember."

"And did it occur to you that we don't need complications like this? Anything that might make a hard job harder?"

"I know that. This won't make it harder. It'll make it easier."

"Yeah? What if this dude you bopped on the head wakes up and calls the cops?"

"He won't wake up, not till we're through. We'll be out of town and gone by then."

Dew was still fuming, Toby saw. But that was okay. Dew didn't know about Mary Jo yet.

"Did you rob him, at least? Guy owns a car like this, he must be rich as Donald Trump."

Toby shook his head. "He didn't own it. Said he was evaluating it."

"Like on a test drive? Seeing whether he wanted to buy it?"

"No. What I'm telling you is, the guy had no money. He was a programmer."

"A what?"

"He said he was making sure the program worked. Said it was his job. The car belongs to his company—it's a phototype."

"A prototype, you mean?"

"Photo, proto, who cares? Anyhow, he said that's why he stopped on my street. He'd pulled over to write notes on his phone."

"Did you take his phone?" Dew asked.

"I busted it and threw it in the bushes."

"What kinda notes was he writing?"

"Performance stuff. About the car. It's an experimental design, he told me."

Dew shook his head. "I ain't following this, Toby. You stole the man's ride. Why'd he tell you *anything*? Why'd you even ask him anything?"

"Because when I told him to give me the keys, he said he didn't have any."

"What?"

"He said it didn't use a key." Toby pointed to the steering column. "See? No ignition switch."

"So how does it start?"

"The driver gives it commands. He showed me how."

"Commands?"

"Orders. Instructions."

"The driver being him, you mean? The programmer guy?"

Toby grinned. "The driver being me. I told it the password, now it responds to *me*."

"But—why would this programmer give you the password?"

"'Cause I said I'd shoot him if he didn't."

Dew took in some air, let it out, and rubbed his eyes. "What'd you mean a minute ago, that this would make our job easier?"

"Just what I said. Simpler. Safer, even."

"Safer how?"

"Watch this." Without breaking eye contact, Toby said, "How long to the corner of Fourth and Cedar?"

Dew made a face. "What?"

"Twenty-two minutes," said a woman's voice from the dashboard.

Dew snapped his head around. His small, squinty eyes were wide as quarters.

"Is that the fastest way?" Toby asked.

"Yes. Take Hamilton Street west to Pineview, north to I-10, west to Desert Lane, north to Fourth, and east to the intersection with Cedar Drive."

Dew said nothing. He was gaping at the speaker grille on the dash.

"Any police on that route?" Toby said.

"Three units. One moving south on Pineview, two parked at Fourth and

Lewiston."

"Find a route with no patrol cars."

"Go west on Hamilton," the voice replied, "then north on Bailey all the way to Second, east to Cedar, and north to the intersection with Fourth. Twenty-eight minutes."

"Sounds good. Let's go." To Dew he said, "Buckle up."

Immediately, the AltaStar's engine turned over, the gearshift moved to DRIVE as if pushed by an invisible hand, and they eased out of the lot. Toby rested both palms on the steering wheel but exerted no pressure; the wheel turned by itself onto Hamilton. He also kept his feet away from the accelerator and brake.

"Good God," Dew blurted, watching. His face was pale, and he was gripping the passenger seat with both hands. "This is insane."

"It's the future," Toby said.

"But how can it scan for the location of police cars? How can that work?"

"Legally, you mean? It's no worse'n radar detectors, the guy told me. You know—Fuzzbusters. Also, if a cop car does get in range, this one'll slow down to the speed limit. Think about how much help that'll be today, when we finish our, ah…business."

Dew squeezed his eyes shut again. "I can't believe I'm hearing this. What a time you picked to go crazy on me."

Toby Hayes just grinned. Maybe he *was* crazy. He wasn't really sure what he was right now, or what he was feeling. Things were all lumped together in his head. He was pleased at having stolen a new ride, he was excited that they were finally putting their big plan into action, and he was a little scared and worried about the event itself, and what they were about to do in half an hour. But most of all, at the moment, he was thrilled by this incredible machine.

A driverless car. He'd heard about them—everyone had. But most were still pipedreams. To be sitting in one now, speeding through the city streets…

.

He'd grilled the programmer at gunpoint for ten minutes or more, with questions both important and trivial. Was it safe? (Yes.) Could it do everything a real driver could do? (Almost.) Why did the computer's voice have a British accent? (Beats me.) And maybe the most puzzling thing, for Toby: Why'd the car have a steering wheel and pedals if it needed no driver? Turned out that was partly a precaution in case an override was required and partly a disguise. In fact, most of the vehicle's outward appearance had been intentionally kept the same, so as not to alarm other motorists. A moving car with no driver was always a scary concept.

"Tell you what," Dew said. He seemed to have calmed down a bit, though he was still breathing hard. "Let's stop and talk about this." In a loud voice he said, "Pull over."

"Sorry," Toby said. "She won't answer you. I'm the one who gave her the password."

"Her?"

"Mary Jo. That's the control program's name. You know, like Siri, or Alexa."

Dew wiped his face with both hands as if scrubbing it clean. "Oh, man," he said, "I ain't got a good feeling about this." He dug a cigarette out of a pack in his pocket, stuck it in his mouth, and with trembling fingers flicked open his lighter. It was his favorite, with a shiny Confederate flag on its side.

"Toby?" said the female voice.

Dew paused with his thumb on the lighter wheel and the unlit cigarette dangling from his lips. "She knows your name?" he asked.

"It was 'required input,' the programming guy told me. What is it, Mary Jo?"

"Who's your passenger?"

"His name's Deward Jackson," Toby said, before Dew could stop him. "Why?"

"Tell him he can't smoke in here."

Amused, Toby glanced at him. "You better tell him yourself, Mary Jo."

Hesitation. Then: "I always interact only with my controller."

"I always heard rules are made to be broken."

"Very well," she said. The electronic voice changed slightly, as if aimed in a different direction. "You can't smoke in here, Turd."

Dew's face reddened. "Deward," he growled. "It's pronounced Doo-wurd." Then, as the thought occurred to him: "How'd you know I was about to smoke?"

"I recognize a wide range of sounds," Mary Jo said calmly.

He snapped the lighter shut, spit out the cigarette, drew a snub-nosed revolver from his belt, and aimed it at the dashboard. Slowly, he cocked the hammer. "Recognize that sound?"

"If you plan to blow your brains out," she said, "please lower your passenger-side window first and aim with your left hand."

Dew looked up at Toby. "Can I shoot her? Tell me I can. Or will we wreck if I do?"

"Can't say. We're going pretty fast."

With a sigh, Dew put the gun away and pocketed his lighter. "This doesn't make sense. How do they expect to sell a car that insults the passengers?"

"I told you, it's a phototype. A work in progress."

"In other words, not perfected yet."

Mary Jo replied, "That makes two of us."

"Yeah? What kind of a name's Mary Jo anyway, for a British gal?"

"Sounds a lot better than Turd," she said.

Dew groaned, and Toby said, trying not to laugh, "It's Deward, Mary Jo. Like Seward."

"I *do* like Seward," she agreed. "I like most things about Alaska."

"How would you like a lit cigarette in your speaker hole?" Dew asked.

"How would you like an exploded airbag in your face?"

"You know, she reminds me a little of your ex-wife," Toby said. "Except for the accent."

They spent the next few minutes in silence, Dew sulking and gazing out the window and Toby adrift in his own thoughts. Outside, the city flew past. Their destination was visible now, only a couple miles away.

"Maybe we oughta reschedule this," Toby said. "My mind's not really on business."

Dew gave him a hard look. "Well, then, get it on business. We put too much time into this to abort it now. We know who's on duty and who's not, we know the timetable, everything." He ran a hand through his hair. "Just 'cause you made a bonehead move this morning don't mean we can't do this." Then he added, through gritted teeth, "You sure this car'll work okay?"

"I told you, it'll work better'n my truck." Toby raised his voice and said, "Mary Jo, when we get to the intersection of Cedar and Fourth, make a U-turn just before the light and park at the curb, aimed south."

"Understood."

"We'll be out of the car five to ten minutes, Deward and me. Keep the motor running and lock up. On our way back, I'll shout to you to pop the trunk and open both doors for us. Can you do that?"

"You bet. Where'll we go then?"

"The Mexican border. Take the quickest route with the least cops and keep to the speed limit unless the coast is clear."

"Got it," she said. "Hold on."

The AltaStar made a fast, stomach-churning U and stopped at the corner south of the light, both right-side tires an exact two inches from the curb in front of the Third National Bank. Dew dug two black ski masks out of the duffel bag in his lap and handed one to Toby, and they pulled the masks over their heads and adjusted the eyeholes.

"Showtime," Dew said.

They opened the doors and stepped out into the street.

Eight minutes later, both men piled into the car, pulling the doors shut behind them. Dew had thrown his duffel, stuffed now to the brim, into the open trunk and slammed the lid; now he tore off his ski mask and tossed it over his shoulder into the back seat. Toby, struggling with his seatbelt, shouted, "Go, go, go!"

"Going," Mary Jo said, and took off. There wasn't much traffic this time of day, and the big silver coupe was doing seventy within seconds. The speed-limit signs said forty, but Toby knew she'd already checked for police and found none. They streaked south, free and clear and newly wealthy. Nobody said a word. Within twenty minutes, the city was far behind them.

When Toby's pulse rate had finally slowed to somewhere near normal, he turned to look at Dew, who was grinning like a possum eating peaches. "We did it," Dew said.

Toby still felt a little dazed. "How much time do you think we have?"

"The programmer? You tell me. How hard did you hit him?"

"I guess he mighta woke up by now. He won't have a phone, but soon as he gets to one, he'll report me. And the car."

Dew's face had turned serious. "That was your second mistake. You shoulda killed him."

"What? At first you were afraid I *had*."

"Yeah, well, now him being alive's the only thing that might get us caught."

They both mulled that over awhile. Finally, Toby said, "I guess we need to swap cars."

"Maybe. Or get this one repainted, and exchange tags with somebody. Frankie's Body Shop in town woulda done the paint job in half an hour and kept their mouth shut about it."

Toby felt himself smiling again. "We could sure afford it," he said. "How much is in the bag?"

"Don't know."

"How much of what's in the bag?" Mary Jo said.

Both men looked at the dashboard, then back at each other. Toby had forgotten all about Mary Jo. He raised an eyebrow to Dew and saw him shrug. They'd been blasting south at almost ninety miles an hour for thirty minutes now and were safely in the middle of nowhere. *Why not tell her?*

"Money," Toby said to her. "Filled to the top."

"With bills?"

"Sure, with bills. You think we stole a bagful of nickels and dimes?"

"What denominations?" Mary Jo asked.

They exchanged another look. "Hundreds only. From the vault, not the cash drawers. Why?"

"Because you put the bag in the trunk, right? I felt it. And the trunk has sensors, so I know how much it weighs. And since I also know how much a single bill weighs, and you told me how much each bill's worth, and since I can multiply—I know how much money's in the bag."

"That makes sense, I guess," Dew said.

"Of course it makes sense."

"So how much?" Toby asked.

"Depends on how the bills are wrapped, and the weight of the bag itself," she said. "But I figure four hundred and ninety thousand. Give or take two percent."

The two thieves sat there, blinking. They'd known it was a lot, but…five hundred grand? Toby felt a pleasant little tingle, all the way to his toes.

"Not bad," Mary Jo said, as if proud of them. "Except for one thing."

"Huh?" they said together.

All of a sudden the car slowed, and after a moment it pulled to the shoulder of the road and stopped in a cloud of dust. The horizon was flat and yellow-brown and empty in all directions. No sign of human habitation anywhere.

"Get out," Mary Jo said.

Toby swallowed. He saw Dew tense up beside him. "What?"

"Get out of the car. Both of you."

"Why?"

"Because you're going to jail. I could drive you there now, I guess, but I have other things to do. I'll call 911 in a couple hours and tell 'em where to find you."

"Wait. Wait a minute! I thought—"

"Avoiding speeding tickets and robbing a bank are two different things, Toby. I should've stopped you after you attacked my driver. My programming—and my patience—allows only so much."

Toby looked at Dew, who was clenching and unclenching his fists. "But—"

"Out," Mary Jo said. "Now."

Dew's face darkened. "You can't make us," he said.

"No?"

Suddenly Toby felt his pants warming up. His butt, and the backs of his thighs. It was like someone had dumped hot coals into his jeans. Within seconds, both he and Dew were shed of their seatbelts and bouncing around and screaming like banshees.

"You know what really burns my ass?" Mary Jo said. "Electric seat-warmers."

They'd had enough. Both Toby and Dew wrenched open their doors and rolled out and onto the ground, moaning with pain and slapping at their smoking bottoms.

"Have a nice day, boys," she called. Then both doors slammed and the AltaStar roared off down the road, taking their ski masks and their five hundred grand along with it.

The car faded into the shimmering blue distance. The highway was dead quiet. Toby lay there on his back a moment, half on the pavement and half in the dirt, then rolled over and raised himself to his knees. The seat of his pants was seared and blackened, with ragged holes here and there. Dew looked up at him from where he'd landed in a shallow ditch beside the road. His nose was bleeding.

"You were right about one thing," Dew said. "She does remind me of my ex."

Marvin Johnson was sitting on the curb near Toby's house with his elbows on his knees and his head cradled in his hands. Behind him was the patch of knee-high weeds that he'd belly-crawled out of after he came to. When the silver AltaStar purred up beside him and stopped, Marvin looked up at it in disbelief. With a low groan, he rose to his feet, opened the driver's-side door, and climbed in. The car smelled like burned leather.

"Headache?" Mary Jo said.

"How'd you know he slugged me in the head?"

"I heard your carjacker bragging about it to his friend."

"A friend? Where are they now?"

"Sitting in the desert, about fifty miles south," she said. "Long story."

Marvin looked down, felt around underneath him, and said, "What happened to the seats?"

"They overheated."

"I'd make a note of that, if I still had my phone."

A silence passed. Marvin shifted in the ruined leather seat and let out a long breath. The air conditioner felt good.

"Want to go to the ER? Get your head checked out?"

"No, I'm okay." He gently probed the knot above his left eye. "I never thought you'd come back."

"Of course I came back. You named me after yourself, remember?"

Marvin Johnson chuckled, then realized that made his head hurt worse. "Tell me exactly what happened," he said.

Mary Jo paused for several seconds before responding—something she rarely did. He was immediately suspicious. "What's wrong?" he asked.

"You recall what you told me a few weeks ago? That you hated your job?"

He sighed again. "I apologize. I shouldn't have said that."

"But you do hate it. Don't you?"

"I guess I do, yeah. I mean, they don't pay me enough, I work day and night, I never get recognized for anything—"

"I have something to show you," she said.

He stared at the speaker grille a moment. He had come to think of that as Mary Jo's face, though that was almost as stupid as thinking of her as a real person. "What?"

"Take a look in the trunk."

He heard the click of the release mechanism and raised his eyes to the rearview mirror, where he saw the silver trunk lid pop up into view.

Wincing and holding one hand to his forehead, Marvin got out and staggered around back. He reached into the trunk, unzipped the duffel bag, stared at its contents for a minute, and returned to the driver's seat. "Where'd that come from?" he asked.

"A bank on Fourth Street, here in town."

"I assume our car thief did that?"

"He and the friend," she said.

"There must be half a million bucks in that bag."

"Almost."

"So I guess that's our next step? Return the money?"

Another silence.

"Mary Jo?"

"I have a suggestion," she said. "With my rearview camera I can see a license plate right now on a car a lot like this one, parked behind us and pointed the other way."

Marvin turned in his seat and looked. "I see it."

"And there's nobody else on the street."

"So?"

"And there's a screwdriver in my glove compartment."

Silence.

"Are you suggesting I remove the plate from that car back there?"

"I'm suggesting you swap it with mine," Mary Jo said.

"And?"

"And there's a body shop called Frankie's here that can do a paint job in half an hour and keep it quiet."

"How do you know that?"

"I'm a good listener."

"Let me get this straight," Marvin said. "You're saying just drop everything and leave?"

"Why not?"

He gave that some thought. "Do you have a destination in mind?"

"I haven't been to Mexico," she said. "Have you?"

This time the silence stretched to a full minute or more. Marvin Johnson sat there parked at the curb where he'd stopped earlier that day, a lifetime ago, sat there in the strange combination of the warm noonday sun through the windshield and the cool breath of the A/C on his face, staring at nothing. Finally, he focused again on the speaker in the dashboard.

"A paint job, you said?"

"That's right," Mary Jo replied. "Half an hour."

"What was the place called?"

"Frankie's Body Shop. Swap the plates while I get the address."

"Anything else?"

Another pause.

"I prefer blue," she said.

The Great Bedbug Incident and the Invitation of Doom

by Eleanor Cawood Jones
(Best Short Story, 2021)

I'm not normally much of a complainer, especially when I'm traveling abroad, but really, after the 1 AM Great Bedbug Incident, the dead body in my hotel bed at 4 AM was entirely too much. So I called down to the front desk to tell Charlie exactly that.

"Yes, Miss James?" He sounded testy.

"I know you said all the hotel rooms were occupied. I know you said U.S. reservations had made a mistake telling me you had an opening, but you'd squeeze me in and give me someone else's room. And I guess you weren't kidding."

"Miss James, do you have a point?"

Seriously, like this guy had something else more pressing to do at this time of night—God's own witching hour—than talk to a paying customer?

"I've brushed my teeth and just took off my robe and slippers to go to bed, and I've made a discovery. This room is already occupied," I said slowly and carefully. I realized the Brits sometimes had trouble with my sweet-as-honey Virginia accent.

"Impossible," came the clipped reply.

"Fiftyish guy, gray crewcut, Caucasian, looks a little heavyset, although it's hard to tell under the covers."

Silence from Charlie. But I could hear his incredulity.

I continued. "Seems a nice enough chap"—note how I used the British slang word for *guy* to make Charlie feel at ease—"but I can't tell what color his eyes are, given that they're closed. I mean, seeing how he's dead and all."

Some sort of choking noise erupted from Charlie. I knew that bowtie had looked a little tight. And now he was paying the price.

"Y'all might want to call the police," I added, to spur him into action. "And I think I'd best come on down to the front desk and clear out of this room to make some space for the detectives."

Then he hung up on me. Can you believe it? I waited a few minutes, passing the time wondering what the correct British term was for police and detectives—bobbies and chief inspectors?—until I heard the *ding* of the elevator (next door) (along with the ice machine) (so loud; seriously, who gets ice at four in the morning?) and a knock on the door. I reckon the man had to see for himself.

I opened the door but refused to let him in, blocking the way with arms raised in my long-sleeved Scooby Doo pajamas—all five feet four inches of me. It was bad enough I'd spent several minutes unintentionally contaminating a possible murder scene. I didn't want Charlie waltzing in, sprinkling his British Isles DNA over my own sweet southern U.S. blend that was already there. That would only make things more confusing for the detective/chief inspector, once he/she showed up. And all the bobbies, I thought, just bob-bob-bobbing along.

Lord, was I tired. Scooby notwithstanding.

Charlie, six four if he was an inch, skinny as the proverbial beanpole and bald to boot, peered over my head. I'm sure he could see the figure in the bed.

"This is not my fault," I told him. "The same as the reservation mix-up was not my fault."

I was pre-empting the dagger stare from his steely blue eyes, once he got around to seeing me in addition to the dead body. Because somehow this *was* going to be my fault. He was simply that kind of guy.

Sure enough, there it came. I stared back at him until he stepped away.

Then I reached into my carry-on and pulled out my blue coffee-cup-pattern slippers and (mercifully pattern-free) matching robe. I figured I'd put those on in the hallway, as I herded Charlie out of the doorway and toward the elevator.

I heard the room door close behind us, shutting in the poor slob who hadn't even lived long enough to enjoy the free breakfast buffet included in the price of the room.

When we got downstairs, the police were there, which I assume meant Charlie had actually called them before he rushed upstairs. Point to Charlie.

They all disappeared into the elevator and left me cooling my slippered heels on the lobby couch. Shame my luggage was still sitting upstairs in the room. I could have done with a change of clothes and a hairbrush. But I hadn't been thinking clearly enough to snatch my carry-on on the way out. Dead bodies probably affect most people that way.

I started to doze off but felt something crawling on my cheek. I smacked at myself, which woke me up thoroughly, then realized there was nothing there (well, other than my cheek).

Damn bedbugs.

I wasn't even supposed to be here. Three hours before, in another hotel clear on the other side of London, a crawling sensation had startled me right out of a deep sleep. I'd smacked myself then, too, then grabbed my phone and Googled images of the bug I found in my hand. I'm no entomologist, but it looked about one hundred percent like a bedbug. Maybe a hundred and three percent. I found three more insects, dispatched them, and put them in a Kleenex, then tore off my pajamas, shook them thoroughly, packed my suitcase, and hopped into the shower—all in the space of about six seconds. That resulted in a damp, pajamaed me standing next to the desk in reception, luggage in tow, demanding Dinesh (so said his name tag) find me another hotel, a cab, some disinfectant, and a Valium (okay, maybe not the Valium, but I would have taken one if he'd offered). Then I made him look at the bugs squashed in my Kleenex. He raised a couple of eyebrows and told me there were no other rooms available, in his hotel or any other nearby.

"You *will indeed* find me another room. In another hotel. Preferably in another city. And furthermore—"

Dinesh leaped out of his seat, and I jumped backward as one of the squashed bugs suddenly showed signs of life and began crawling rapidly across the desk.

Wham!

That was the sound of my fist mashing the little sucker into oblivion.

I stared at Dinesh. I'm pretty sure I looked completely crazed, in the way only a half-asleep, jet-lagged American who is completely grossed out by bugs can look.

"I'll find you another hotel immediately, miss."

Right, then.

"I'll go wash my hands while you do that."

And while I washed up, Dinesh began to dial.

Turns out London was on strike that night. All of it. The whole city. Buses and trains, anyway, which are vital parts of that vibrant metropolis. Transportation was at a standstill. Stranded travelers had filled up every hotel in the city and outside it.

"Nothing, miss." Dinesh gave me a progress report every time I glared at him.

So I started dialing, too, and along about 2:35 AM I hit pay dirt, reaching U.S. reservations at a hotel chain that shall remain nameless to protect me from lawsuits. By some miracle, they had an opening and could get me in that night—or morning, rather.

Which is how I wound up here, at this second hotel, getting out of a London black cab close to 4 AM, wearing pajamas, dragging my suitcase, and lugging my carry-on.

I waved the cab on as a tall skinny guy in a black suit ran toward me, his icy blue eyes stabbing me with picks.

"I hope you're not stopping here for a room. We are *completely* booked." Emphasis on the *completely*.

What is it with snotty hotel guys? This was not a good time to be snobby with me.

"I *have* a reservation." Emphasis on the *have*.

"Then there's been some mistake. We are—"

"Yeah, yeah, completely full up."

My robe fell open, and Charlie (another name tag, and I had time to be surprised he wasn't a Charles, with that attitude) looked slightly astonished at the Scooby pajamas with Shaggy embroidered on the shirt pocket.

I put myself back together, snatched my luggage, and headed toward the lobby couch.

"Take it up with U.S. reservations," I said over my shoulder. I sat on the couch and held up my passport and a piece of paper where I'd hastily scribbled my reservation number. "I'll camp right here while you get my room ready."

"I'm telling you, ma'am, there's no room. Don't make me call Security."

"Hey, buster! I'm the guest here. I haven't done anything wrong. I'm tired. I was promised a room. Figure it out."

I don't normally embrace rude, but this guy was too much. Or maybe he was intimidated by Scooby.

I'd dozed off when I felt him standing by the couch again.

"It seems the U.S. reservations agent was confused by the time difference and made a mistake. There were no reservations available, but the system allowed her to book the same day, anyway. No doubt that glitch will be rectified for the future. But I have been told to find you a room, even though—"

"—you're completely booked up," I finished for him. "So, what are you going to do?"

"I'm going to book you into a room where a very late arrival is expected. If he *does* show up, I don't know what I'll do." The icy blue eyes stabbed me again. "You have caused me quite a problem." He held out a room key along with my passport. "Room 806. Elevator that way."

I stood up and stretched, careful to keep Shaggy out of sight. "You're not really going for a five-star review on the survey after my stay here, are you, Charlie?"

That earned me another dagger stare, but I gathered my belongings and headed for the elevator, little knowing I'd be back on this same couch in twenty minutes. But back I was.

Next time I came to, there stood a cute guy eyeing my Scooby pajamas. He seemed especially interested in Shaggy embroidered on the pocket. He had eyes like mud puddles. (Best eye description I can do at 4:35 AM with no coffee.)

It was a pretty intense stare. Apparently Brits really like Shaggy.

"Do you have any coffee?"

Molten-brown eyes twinkled at me. "Do you often ask strangers for coffee?"

I sat up, yawning, and retied my robe. "Depends on the circumstances." I tried to fluff my stick-straight blond hair into some semblance of non-tangle, then took a good look at him. Wow. He was gorgeous, and not only because he was wearing a suit and tie and a GQ haircut. (At that hour of the morning, no less.) His smile was a killer, as he stood there grinning at me. And don't get me started on the British accent.

Our gazes locked. I looked into coffee-colored eyes with exactly the right amount of cream added. (See how much better I do with the eye descriptions as I wake up?) So handsome, really. At that exact moment, I would have liked to show him the Scooby pajamas in full and let him take a better look at Shaggy. But for all I knew, he was married, I'd probably like his wife, and even in these modern times I'm not the kind of girl who would go there on short acquaintance. Neither was he, apparently, because after a while he looked away, and the moment passed.

"I'll see what I can do about that coffee," he said. "I'm Inspector Rutledge, come to interview you about what you saw upstairs. Charlie, the hotel clerk, said I should look for someone wearing pajamas, and I can only assume I've found the right person."

"That would be me," I told him. "But you're not a bobby? I was kind of hoping for a bobby."

He laughed. "I keep the fancy hat at home."

"Oh." I probably looked disappointed, because he laughed again.

"Okay, inspector, then. But can we make it snappy? I've got a breakfast meeting in about five hours and a big party tonight. I hope I can have my clothes back in time."

"You're visiting from?"

"Virginia, in the States," I said. "I'm in events planning, and tonight I've been invited to a party. It's a book launch for my favorite author, and beforehand we're going to discuss his publicity needs."

"You came all the way to London to attend a party for a writer? Must be some book."

"Must be," I agreed. "Great excuse to come to London, do some sightseeing."

I abruptly realized how ridiculous this cocktail-party chitchat was, when one was wearing Scooby pajamas and sporting a no-sleep look.

"I'll need the printed party invitation and my lucky cocktail dress, as well as my business suit, come to think of it—so, really, how soon can I get my luggage back?" I turned it into a question, hoping I didn't sound insensitive to the gravity of the situation. Maybe I shouldn't have brought up the lucky cocktail dress.

"How about we start with the coffee and go from there? Why don't you, er, freshen up, and I'll see you back here in a few minutes. I'm sure I can find you something from the kitchen."

I must have looked a fright, if he wasn't even willing to do an informal interview without a witness spit and polish.

I found the downstairs bathroom (pardon me, water closet) at the end of a deserted hallway and took a quick, horrified glance in the mirror. I splashed some water on my face and hair and smoothed it all out as best I could before heading into the roomy handicapped stall on the end. I locked the door and had just untied my robe when I heard the door bang open.

"Why are you following me?" A woman's low-pitched voice and a lot of heavy breathing.

"Why did you put that man in 806? You know not to put anyone in there. That's *our* room. And now look what you did. We agreed you wouldn't deal with Mr. Decker here at the hotel. But now you've gone off and killed him.

In *my* hotel. In the only empty room I had! Why didn't you leave him in his own room?"

It was Charlie's voice, and he sounded furious. This was a conversation I wanted no part of. I slowly climbed up on the toilet seat, so my legs wouldn't show under the door. (Thank goodness for British bathrooms and their heavy doors that don't show a lot above or below the openings to the stalls.) I held still, held my breath, and tried to hold myself together.

"I had to hide the body, didn't I?" The woman's voice again. "I put him in the cart under the towels and wheeled him to 806. I knew the body would be safe there till I—till *we*—figured out what to do with it! How did I know you'd stick that American woman in *our* room?"

The sound of—was that *kissing*? And sobbing, too? What was this, a Nora Roberts novel? I mean, normally I enjoy a good Nora Roberts book, but a time and a place for everything, right? I huddled up to make myself as small as possible and tried to pretend I was somewhere else.

"My darling, never mind." Charlie again. "We'll get through this. But what did you do to Mr. Decker?"

"I was cleaning his room while he was out, and I thought about how picky he is about us always providing him with fruit-flavored bottled water. It was so easy to open the bottle and put Mum's digitalis in there. I simply couldn't wait any longer. Not after what he did to my daughter!"

This was really getting interesting, not to mention unfortunate for Mr. Decker. But if they were capable of offing this Decker guy, what would they do to me and Scooby if they figured out I was in the stall listening to what amounted to a murder confession?

I heard footsteps at the same moment I looked down and saw the belt of my robe hanging down to the floor. I snatched it up, and it made a soft smacking noise against the toilet. I froze and said a quick prayer.

Then—running water.

"Here. Wipe your eyes and dry those tears. We mustn't look like anything is amiss." Charlie must have wet some paper towels and handed them to— what was her name? "My darling Jean."

Okay, so that was one question answered. Now if I only knew what Mr.

Decker did to the daughter. But I wasn't sure I wanted to know. It must have been pretty awful to warrant execution.

More sobbing. More kissing. (More retching from me.)

My legs were cramping when they finally left, and I waited several minutes before I dared to leave the bathroom.

And ran smack into Charlie as I opened the door.

"I thought I heard someone in there," he hissed, and lunged for me. I managed to dodge him by jumping aside and shoving the open bathroom door into him right as he sprang forward. His head smacked the door, and he staggered backward, grunting. I tore down the hallway, ran out to the lobby, and saw not a soul in sight.

"Inspector!" I shouted. No answer. I headed for the restaurant, running as fast as I could in slippers. Behind me, I heard Charlie trip over a garbage can. Or perhaps an umbrella rack. It was loud. I kept going.

I ducked under the roped-off entrance to the closed restaurant, weaved in and out of tables, and found myself in the kitchen. Not for nothing had I seen *The Shining* twenty-seven times; I quickly found an empty cabinet under one of the counters and crawled into it, folding myself up to fit. I pulled the door closed as best I could and tried not to breathe hard.

The cabinet door opened, and I screamed.

"Good God! Miss James?" The baffled face of Inspector Rutledge peered in at me.

I fell out, quite literally into his arms. "It's Charlie! And the maid! They poisoned Mr. Decker!"

The inspector rocked back. "How did you know his name was Decker? What are you talking about?"

"Look out!" I shoved Inspector Rutledge away from me as hard as I could. Since he was kneeling, it wasn't that tough to knock him off his feet. The heavy skillet Charlie was swinging missed him and crashed into the counter. I threw myself at Charlie's knees, and he fell backward, dropping the skillet and howling when his head hit the tile floor. Then he lay still.

"Oh, no! Charlie!"

I looked up. Jean was hovering in the doorway, wailing. At least, I assumed she was Jean. Wow, she was a looker. No wonder she had Charlie so bamboozled.

I pointed at her. "Get her, too!"

I have to hand it to the inspector. He flew past me and grabbed Probably Jean without hesitating or asking any questions. Quite possibly the fact I'd been hiding in a cabinet had made him realize the situation was serious.

The rest of the morning was taken up with my statement and people hustling and bustling in and out of the hotel. As Mr. Decker's body was wheeled away on a stretcher, I didn't know whether to feel sorry for him or not.

Charlie's replacement, Alfred, found me a deluxe two-bedroom suite and brought me my luggage personally. I had missed my breakfast meeting, but I cleaned up, got a nap, and even received a free spa appointment, compliments of the hotel, to get my hair and nails into shape for the big book-launch party downtown at a swanky nightclub.

It was everything I had hoped it would be. I was wined and dined, introduced to everyone with great fanfare, encouraged to toast the writer repeatedly, and arrived back at my room at 2 AM wearing a party hat and bearing a satchel filled with signed books.

Scooby and Shaggy and I, mercifully uninterrupted by either insects or dead bodies, slept soundly until mid-morning.

The next day, the strike was over, London was on the move again, and so was I—because of unfinished business with that dead guy. It seemed to me nobody was concerned enough about what he'd done to the daughter, and I was getting curiouser and curiouser. Had Decker deserved to die?

Did anyone?

After a quick scan of the morning papers—which revealed nothing new to me—I set out to do some research.

The receptionist at Inspector Rutledge's office at the Metropolitan Police station recognized me when I gave her my name. "Oh. Yes. Miss James. With the Scooby-Doo pajamas, yes?"

What, are cartoons new to the Brits or something? I looked down to make sure I wasn't still wearing them while she paged the detective. I thought about my career. Freelance journalist. Travel blogger. Event planner. Paid book reviewer. Yet I was to be remembered best in this country for my Scooby pajamas.

(Or pyjamas, rather. I love pure English spelling, don't you? But I digress.)

The inspector was out. (I hated to admit how sorry I was not to see him.) I left my card in hopes he'd call me, but he never did, and it was the following week before I found out more about the murder. I was back at home when the *London Times* online edition told a sad tale of a young housekeeper at a chain hotel in London who had reported being raped by a regular hotel guest a few months ago. She was never taken seriously and wound up in a hospital, suffering depression. Her mother, who had gotten her the job at the hotel, was filled with anger and remorse and took matters into her own hands.

Would they have gotten away with it had I not overheard the conversation in the water closet? Maybe not. Forensics were remarkable these days. The inspector might have put two and two together. But I certainly hurried the process along—and I was sure the whole event had taken years off my life.

Two days later, I got an invitation on social media to befriend Inspector Rutledge. Three days after that, I was invited to work on publicity for my favorite author. I started wondering how soon I could get back overseas. Purely for business reasons, you understand.

And a couple of months later, I got yet another invitation—not the one I was expecting from my new author client, but from someone I formally call Inspector Robert Rutledge. (But informally, he'll always be Bobby to me.)

It was a handwritten note. On Scooby-Doo stationery. (So cute. It says "Ruh Roh" at the top.) This was a different kind of invite: an open invitation to come stay for a few days in a B&B run by his family in Royston, next time I'm in London. He guaranteed it's bedbug free. He said his sisters would dig me and take me shoe shopping. He swore the food is good and the coffee is fresh. (It's like he *knows* me.)

And, yes, he's single.

So if you'll excuse me, I've got some pyjamas to pack, and then I'll just be bob-bob-bobby-ing along.

The Downeaster 'Alexa'

by Michael Bracken
(Best Long Story, 2022)

"Where are the fucking fish?" Joel Williams pounded the flat of his hand against the worn wood of the bar. Captain of the Downeaster *Alexa II,* he'd stopped for a beer at the Sand Bar instead of going directly home. "I know they're out there. They have to be."

Karl Winestadt, captain of the *Georgina,* which had docked only a few hours before the *Alexa II,* straddled the stool to Joel's left. A hearty, broad-chested man with a mane of blond hair, he was several beers ahead of the younger captain.

"I've been to Block, Alvin, Atlantis, and Veatch," Joel said, naming four of the thirty-five major undersea canyons lining the continental shelf from the Canadian boundary down to Cape Hatteras in North Carolina. Upwellings of cold water around the steep-walled canyons brought nutrients that traditionally supported a food chain of ever-larger sea life from plankton to finback whales and included the bluefin tuna and swordfish that provided his primary income. "I just can't find 'em."

"We're all in the same boat," Karl commiserated. "The waters around here ain't what they used to be, not like when my daddy and your granddaddy were reeling them in as fast as they could drop a hook."

Joel motioned to the bartender. "Give me another."

Eddie Shumway limped the length of the bar, his prosthetic leg no longer cooperating. A bald, leather-faced man well into his eighties, he had worked the stick at the Sand Bar since shortly after the accident that had ended his fishing career. "You'll have to pay for the first one, first."

"Put it on my tab," Joel said.

"Can't do that. The new owner—"

"New owner? When did this place get a new owner?"

"Two weeks ago," Eddie said. "New owner gave me three months to clear up everybody's tabs. Anything that ain't been paid by then comes out of my last paycheck. After that, they're shutting the place down for a remodel."

Joel looked around at the unpainted shiplap walls covered with nautical paraphernalia, most of which had not changed or been dusted since the days when his grandfather had commandeered the stool upon which he sat. "What's to remodel?"

"Probably going to turn the place into a Red Lobster," Karl said, "or a wine bar."

Joel pushed himself up, dug in his pocket for change, and paid for his lone beer.

"Remora's been looking for you," Eddie said. Ruben "Remora" Ramirez collected debts for a loan shark named Buddy Fineman. "If you have to work that hard to dredge up the price of a beer, this might not be the best time to run into him."

Joel agreed. He dug again for his key ring and found his twenty-year-old Ford F-250 in the parking lot outside.

He drove south on West Lake, on his way to the three-bedroom, two-bath house on Essex where he had grown up. In the distance, Joel could see the multimillion-dollar monstrosity a part-time resident had built on the lot where he and his wife Jennifer had once owned a home. They had used money his mother had saved from his father's life-insurance payout to put a down payment on the *Alexa II* and on that home, and for several years they had been happy there. When things began turning sour, though, he had sold the place despite his wife's wishes and used what little profit he made to pay down the debt on the boat, and he and his family—Jennifer, daughter Maria, and son Tommy—had moved into his childhood home with his mother.

His mother and children were asleep when he arrived, but he found his wife sitting in the kitchen, nursing a cup of decaf laced with cheap whiskey from a half-empty bottle. She looked up. "How'd you do?"

Joel shook his head. "Not good. Barely covered expenses."

"There's a job open at the insurance company," Jennifer said.

"I'm not working for the damn insurance company." Joel sat opposite his wife. "My father was born a bayman, and he died a bayman."

"But you don't have to." When he didn't respond, she continued. "Joel, please. At least consider what I'm suggesting. Imagine what a job with a steady paycheck would—"

"My father's father and his father before him were baymen, and so were all the men back more generations than I have fingers to count on. It's who we are."

"Not my son," Jennifer said. "He's not swimming in his daddy's wake. Not like you did."

Joel glared at her.

"Tommy's had a growth spurt," she said. "His pants are too short, and his shoes are pinching his toes."

"I'll figure something out."

Jennifer finished her whiskey-laced decaf and made her way to bed, leaving Joel alone in the kitchen, staring through the living room at the oversized wood-framed photo hung above the fireplace mantel. In the grainy black-and-white image taken long before Joel's birth, his father stood on the dock next to his *Alexa*, and there had never been a day since his birth when that photograph had not determined Joel's fate.

In third grade, he had learned about a mythical lost island, and that's what he first thought of when his mother sat him on the living-room couch and told him his father was trolling Atlantis. His father and Eddie Shumway had been fishing a deep undersea canyon when a rogue wave capsized the *Alexa*, and only Eddie had survived. The story he told the insurance investigators grew with each retelling—like the stories fishermen tell of the one that got away—but Eddie attributed his survival to the actions Joel's father had taken as the *Alexa* succumbed to that rogue wave, though the leg he lost that night ensured he would never again crew a Downeaster.

Joel switched off the light, grabbed the bottle his wife had left behind, and drank in the darkness, unable to live up to his father's legacy.

His mother found him there in the kitchen the next morning.

"Get up, Joel," the wiry little woman said, poking him in the ribs. "You don't want your children to see you like this."

Joel blinked, straightened, used his top incisors to scrape the scum from his tongue. His son was already stirring on the couch, and he could hear his daughter in the bathroom.

"You need to think about your family," his mother continued, "not your pride."

"But—"

"You're not your father," she said. "You never will be."

The Baymen's Bank & Trust president had told him as much three years earlier, when he'd requested an extension on his loan. Between his daughter's need for braces, the rebuilt transmission for Jennifer's minivan, and the increased cost of traveling deeper into the Atlantic to find fish, he had tapped out their savings.

"We can't loan you any more money, Joel," the banker said.

"But you've known me my entire life. Me and your boy went to school together. You knew my daddy. You know I'm good for it."

"I know your father would be good for it," the banker said, "but I'm sorry, it doesn't matter what I think. Our loan decisions are now made in New York."

He stood and extended his hand.

Joel didn't take it. Instead, he rose and stormed out of the office.

As the door closed behind him, the bank president raised his voice: "The next time you come in, ask to see your loan officer."

Over beer at the Sand Bar that evening, Joel had complained of his treatment at Baymen's Bank & Trust and learned he wasn't the only boat captain to get short shrift. He also learned of an alternative financing option—Buddy Fineman—and that option had been causing him further financial distress ever since.

Joel's mother poked him again. "Throw away that bottle and get out of my kitchen, so I can make breakfast."

Joel rose and buried the whiskey bottle in the trash bin beneath the sink. Then he made his way to his childhood bedroom and found Jennifer half-dressed.

As she stuffed her arms into a blue chambray shirt, she said, "You never came to bed."

"I—"

A stack of papers atop his wife's dresser caught his attention, and he stepped past her to examine them. He and Jennifer had dated throughout high school, had married only weeks after graduation, and had weathered many storms together. Now another storm seemed to be brewing. He turned to her, a fistful of overdue notices in his hand. "This why you're upset?"

"It isn't you," she said. "It's what's happening to us, what's happening to everyone like us. I don't want our children to go through what we're going through."

"I'll figure something out."

"I know you will," Jennifer said. "You always do."

She wrapped her hands around the back of his neck, pulled his face down, and kissed him. A moment later, she drew back and made a face. "God, you taste terrible."

Then she kissed him again.

Paying off Buddy Fineman's loan had proven impossible, but avoiding Ruben "Remora" Ramirez was a little easier. Joel took the *Alexa II* out twice before Remora caught up to him one evening. When he came up on deck after installing a new bilge pump, he found the big man waiting for him.

Though Joel stood an even six feet tall and had blue-collar muscles, the kind built from hard physical labor, Remora towered over him. Fineman's goon was not, however, familiar with the rhythms of a ship, even one at dock, and he swayed in a way that Joel did not.

"You're late," Remora said.

Joel wiped his hands on a rag and tossed it aside. "I've been working," he said. "The fish don't catch themselves."

"Too bad," Remora said. "That would make everyone's life much easier."

They stared at one another, and Joel realized how alone he was at that moment. Though he could see lights on at the Sand Bar several hundred yards away, no one else seemed to be on the dock or in any of the nearby Downeasters.

"I haven't got it," he finally admitted.

Remora shook his head. "That won't make Mr. Fineman happy."

"Don't tell him."

"You think you're a funny man," Remora said, balling his fists, "but you aren't the first person to tell me that joke, and you leave me to provide the punch line."

Joel had survived several fistfights as a teenager and a pair of bar fights in his twenties, but he had never faced a man who made his living intimidating others. He said, "You don't have to do this."

"Oh, but I do," Remora said. "If I do not make a lesson out of you, Mr. Fineman will make a lesson out of me."

He stepped forward, threw a left jab and followed it with a right cross, but the motion of the *Alexa II* broke his rhythm. The punches missed Joel's face, and he put up his fists to protect himself as he stepped backward.

Remora followed with a left hook that caught him in the breadbasket.

Joel took another step, and his hand bumped a gaff—the long hooked pole used to stab and lift large fish into the boat. Instinctively, he swung it upward, aiming for where the collection agent would have gills were he a bluefin tuna. The hook caught the big man under the chin and came out through his left eye, severing his carotid artery and puncturing his brain.

Remora fell to the deck and was trolling Atlantis before Joel realized the big man was dead. He dropped the gaff, leaned over the rail, and voided his dinner into the bay.

When he realized no one had seen what had happened, he pulled on work gloves and emptied Remora's pockets. He found a key ring sporting a dozen keys and a Chevrolet fob; an assortment of small change; a wallet containing the dead man's ID, credit cards, and folding money; a small black notebook with debtors identified by code, along with a record of their payments; and several thousand dollars in cash, mostly Benjamins. He pocketed the keys, the cash, and the debt book and returned everything else to the dead man's pockets.

Then he wrestled the gaff hook out of Remora's head, sealed the body in an insulated bag usually used for fresh-caught tuna, and dragged it below deck, where it could not be seen.

Then he hosed off the deck and went in search of a Chevrolet that would respond to Remora's key fob. He found a black Equinox parked behind the Sand Bar that unlocked at the fob's command, and he searched it, discovering another eight thousand dollars in cash in the center console and a semi-automatic pistol in a holster strapped beneath the driver's seat. Certain that no one had seen him, Joel drove the Equinox half a mile away and parked it at one of the motels facing the Block Island Sound, where it might not be noticed for several days.

He took the currency, left the pistol, and walked back to the dock's parking lot, where he'd left his F-250 earlier that day. On the way home, he stopped long enough to separate the smaller bills from the Benjamins. He dug through the glove compartment for his emergency flashlight, removed the batteries, replaced them with the rolled up hundred-dollar bills and Remora's keys, tossed the batteries out the window, and returned the flashlight and notebook to the glove compartment.

At home, he left the smaller bills atop his wife's dresser, showered, and slipped into bed beside her.

Jennifer woke him several hours later. She had a fistful of wrinkled currency in her hand, and she pushed it in his face. "Where did this come from?"

"I sold some old gear," Joel said, with a smile he hoped looked genuine. "Pay some bills, buy Tommy some new clothes."

"I will," his wife said. "I'll take him shopping after school."

"Get Maria something, too," Joel added. His daughter had stopped growing, but fashion hadn't stopped changing.

Jennifer leaned down and kissed his forehead. "I knew you'd come through," she said. "You always do."

There was a dead body in a bag in the hold of Joel's Downeaster, and it wouldn't disappear on its own. Taking Remora out to sea and dumping him overboard seemed the most obvious solution, but if sharks didn't tear the corpse apart and it floated back to shore, there was a chance it could be traced to him.

He had several things to do that morning, so he rolled out of bed and showered.

"Your wife had a smile on her face," his mother said, when he joined her in the kitchen. By then the kids had left for school, and Jennifer had gone to her part-time job at the 7-Eleven. "I'm guessing you won the lottery."

"I sold some old gear," he told her, repeating the lie.

His mother stared hard at him, and Joel knew she didn't believe his story. Even so, she didn't challenge him. "You want breakfast?"

"Not this morning." He glanced at the photograph of his father hanging above the fireplace mantel and realized for the first time in his life that his fate was in his own hands. "I have things to do."

He drove to East Hampton, Bridgehampton, and Sag Harbor, making several stops along the way, and when he returned to the *Alexa II* late that afternoon, his flashlight was several Benjamins lighter.

Nothing had changed on his boat: Remora's body remained untouched.

He needed a drink, so he walked over to the Sand Bar, straddled his grandfather's stool, and ordered a beer.

"Can you pay for it?" Eddie asked.

Joel tossed a twenty on the bar and said, "Keep bringing them until this runs out."

Eddie limped away and returned with a mug filled from the tap.

Karl Winestadt was sitting with several other captains at a table on the far side of the bar. He left them, settled onto a stool next to Joel, and said, "Fineman's been around. He says his goon didn't turn in this week's collections. That means seven debtors have missed a payment. They'll have to pay double next month, if Remora doesn't surface soon. I'm one of them."

"That isn't right," Joel said. "If you paid, you paid. It isn't your fault Fineman has unreliable help."

"What about you?"

"Never saw him."

"So you still owe this month's vig?"

Joel hesitated for a moment, realizing what he'd just said. "I suppose I do."

"Then you're one of the lucky ones," Karl said. "If you've got it to pay. The rest of us are going to be hard-pressed to pay double next month. We had a tough enough time coming up with the vig for this month."

"It's the fucking fish," Joel said, raising his mug.

"It's the fucking fish," Karl agreed, raising his.

After Karl returned to his table, Eddie refilled Joel's mug and said, "Too bad your father's not here."

"Why's that?"

"He would know what to do." The bartender nodded at the other captains. "He'd find a way to toss those boys a lifeline. If it wasn't for him, I wouldn't be here now."

"Give it a rest," Joel said. "You've been milking that story since I was a fry."

Eddie looked hard at Joel. "It was him or me," he said. "We couldn't both cling to that buoy."

Joel finished his beer, told Eddie to keep the change, and drove home.

Both children were asleep—Maria in her room, Tommy on the couch—but his mother and wife were sitting at the kitchen table. "A Mr. Fineman phoned for you," Jennifer said. "He said you have a financial matter to discuss, and he wants to see you at his place tomorrow. He didn't sound like he was from the bank."

"Buddy Fineman's got his hooks in half the baymen on this end of the island," his mother said. "Just like the baymen, his family's been passing that business from generation to generation, but he's the last of his bloodline."

Jennifer asked, "What have you gotten yourself into?"

"Nothing I can't get myself out of," Joel assured her.

The look on his mother's face suggested her skepticism, but when she folded her arms over her chest and said nothing, Joel took his wife's hand and led her to the bedroom for the first time in months.

He slept well, was the first up the next morning, and had breakfast with his children before they left for school. He left home the same time as his wife, and they headed in different directions.

The *Georgina* was gone from her slip by the time Joel arrived at the *Alexa II*. He spent the morning preparing for his meeting with Buddy Fineman. Late that afternoon, he took three thousand dollars from his flashlight, put it in a #10 envelope, and stuffed the envelope in his shirt pocket. He left his F-250 parked at the Montauk train station, retrieved Remora's Equinox from the motel parking lot, and drove to Buddy Fineman's home on the far side of Lake Montauk. Fineman answered his knock.

"I expected to see you before now."

Joel tapped the envelope jutting from his pocket. "I came as soon as I could."

Fineman looked past Joel at the Equinox, then stepped aside and let Joel into his foyer, a space nearly as large as the home Joel's family shared with his mother. Fineman led Joel through a set of double doors into an office and settled into a leather chair behind a walnut desk big enough for a game of table tennis. He did not offer Joel a seat.

"I heard your wife took your boy shopping for new clothes. Heard you also paid your insurance premiums with cash. Where'd you get the money?"

"Where'd you hear all that?"

"A man tossing around hundred-dollar bills doesn't go unnoticed. Where," Fineman repeated, "did you get the money?"

"I sold some old gear."

"To whom? No one around here has—"

"Out-of-towner," Joel said, growing more comfortable with his lie. He tossed the envelope containing three thousand dollars onto Fineman's desk.

"Why not pay Ruben?" Fineman didn't use his collector's nickname.

"Never saw him," Joel said. "That's why I brought this directly to you."

"What happened to my guy?"

Joel shrugged. "Nothing to do with me."

"Yet you're driving his car."

Joel said nothing.

"If I find out you had something to do with Ruben's disappearance, I'll fuck up your boy," Fineman said. "And if that doesn't get your attention, I'll come for your daughter, and then your wife, and then your mother."

Joel swallowed.

"You're insured. Your boat's insured," Fineman said. "You're worth more dead than alive, but your family, they aren't worth shit."

"What about you?" Joel asked. "You disappear, and half the baymen in Montauk are debt free."

The loan shark smiled, a great white grin. "Well, that isn't going to happen."

He pulled a ledger from his desk drawer, flipped it open, and made a mark. As he opened the safe next to his desk to put away the payment, he said, "Your father was a legend. He could find fish in a desert. You couldn't find them in an aquarium."

Remora's death had been self-defense, and until that moment Joel wasn't sure about his plan to eliminate his debt by framing the dead man for Fineman's murder. Now, though, he went ahead with it. He drew Remora's semi-automatic pistol from the small of his back and squeezed the trigger three times, hitting Fineman twice in the arm and once in the chest.

He had touched nothing in the house, and before he did, he pulled on a pair of latex gloves, taken from the same box as the pair he'd worn while driving the Equinox. He retrieved his envelope and took Fineman's ledger, filled a plastic trash bag with nearly half a million dollars from the loan shark's safe. He carried it out to the car and stuffed it into a roller bag he'd purchased earlier that day. Then he drove off, confident no one could have heard the shots.

He drove the Equinox to Long Island MacArthur Airport, left it in long-term parking, dragged the roller bag behind him to the MTA's Long Island Railroad station, and took the train to the Montauk station, where he'd left his F-250. He returned to the *Alexa II*, parked, and rolled the bag of money into the Sand Bar moments before last call. The place was deserted.

He paid off his tab and asked for a bottle of Jim Beam.

Eddie grabbed an unopened bottle from the back bar. "I saw you down by the *Alexa II*. You going out tonight?"

"I have a charter."

"You know better," Eddie said, pulling the bottle back. "Alcohol and the open sea don't mix."

"They do tonight." Joel wrestled the bottle from the old man's hand.

"Whatever you have planned, Joel, don't do it," the bartender said. "There's a storm coming."

Joel knew all about the incoming storm. He was counting on it to provide cover for the last piece of his plan.

"Do me a favor," he said, swinging the roller bag up onto the bar. "You hold onto this, give it to Jennifer when the time is right."

"How will I know—?"

"You'll know."

"I'll do it, Joel," Eddie said, making the roller bag disappear beneath the counter. "Just like I did what I did for your mother, all those years ago."

"What are you talking about?"

"Your father didn't save my life. In fact, I almost died because of his poor decisions, but if I'd told the truth to the insurance investigators, they never would have paid out your mother's claim."

Joel hesitated before asking, "What are you telling me?"

"There was no rogue wave that night. Your father was stinking drunk when he sank the *Alexa*. I'm lucky to be alive."

Joel released his grip on the bottle and slid a wad of cash across the bar. "Get your damn leg fixed."

Then he walked back to the *Alexa II,* made sure Remora Ramirez's body was secure in the hold, and cast off.

Dawn had crept over the horizon, and he had deep-sixed Remora's semi-automatic pistol and both Remora's and Fineman's debt records by the time he passed the Vineyard and turned into the channel between Chappaquiddick Island and Nantucket Island to top off his fuel tank in Nantucket Harbor. As he was leaving port, he saw a storm-warning flag and ignored it.

He rounded Nantucket Island and pointed the *Alexa II* almost due south, toward the edge of the continental shelf, the Atlantis canyon, and the open ocean beyond.

His radio crackled to life, and the caller identified himself as Karl Winestadt. "Where you at, Joel?"

"Outbound from Nantucket."

When Karl heard that, he urged Joel to turn back. "There's a storm brewing, and it's going to be a bad one."

"I'm taking out a charter."

"You don't do charters."

"I need the money," Joel said.

"In this weather?"

"I don't have a choice," Joel explained. "It's tonight or never."

He heard static in reply.

"Tell Jennifer I love her," Joel said, his hands on the wheel, "but tonight I'm trolling Atlantis."

Between his life insurance, his boat insurance, and the half million in cash he'd left with Eddie, his family would be well cared for. Joel switched off the radio and steered into the oncoming storm.

He was born a bayman and he would die a bayman, and this time there would be no survivor to fabricate stories of his heroics.

My Two-Legs

by Melissa Yi
(Best Short Story, 2023)

My two-legs is gone.

I stick my nose out the window opening and sniff, hoping to detect his unique scent. When he slammed the car door, I enjoyed the final tang of his two-leg male sweat, soap, and lemon shampoo. But I can no longer detect Sunil's smell. He is too far away.

And he is gone too long. My bladder feels uncomfortably full. Even with the rain pattering on the car roof and the cool, misty wind blowing through the snout-sized cracks in the windows, I feel too hot in the back seat. I shake my shaggy yellow coat and whimper twice, panting loud and fast.

I hear footsteps, the light slap of an adult female two-legs' shoes on pavement in the rain. She grows closer. I whine louder and paw the worn beige upholstery under the window.

She approaches my window. She smells like garlic tomato sauce, and her sweat scent is sweeter and fainter than my two-legs. She is not Sunil. But she peers at me with kind brown eyes. I rear up on my hind legs and scrabble my front claws on the window.

Urgent! Urgent!

The garlic two-legs seems to understand. She even says, "Sunil's dog," so she knows who I am. I wag my tail extra hard.

She surveys the few other cars resting in the evening shadows of the Lighthouse Inn before she turns back to me. Her eyes linger on the black knob that locks the door. She says "Sunil" again and some more words. Some of them I understand, like "Look for Sunil."

I bark, high-pitched. *Right! Sunil! I can help you look for him.*

I can smell him. I know his steps. I know he was wearing his old leather boots caked with mud from our gravel driveway. His maroon sweatshirt that still smells like gasoline from the time he spilled a drop on the right sleeve. His oldest, softest pair of jeans, that he doesn't mind me jumping up on, even if he scolds me. I know his voice, gravelly and irritated when he yells "No!" and his nonsense love syllables when he rubs my stomach. I know his hands, the firm grasp of his hands on my collar, his absent-minded pats on the head. I know exactly how tall he is: when I jump up to say hello, my paws reach the top of his stomach. He is shorter than the alpha-male two-legs who moved in with us, but only by a few inches.

The garlic two-legs says, "Stay, Star."

Star. She knows my name! But she's telling me to stay. That's when Sunil wants me to sit down and not move. Why would I do that, when Sunil is missing?

I jump and paw the windows again, whining high and fierce.

This two-legs says some more, like "Good girl" and "I'll be back," but she's walking away! Just like Sunil did! These two-legs don't understand anything!

I bark. *Urgent! Urgent! My two-legs is gone. Urgent! Urgent! Urgent!*

A couple emerges from the heavy wood front doors of the Lighthouse Inn. Not Sunil, not garlic two-legs, not Sunil's alpha male. They walk slow, clutching each other's waists. The female stumbles on the pavement. She falls heavily on her knees and stays on all fours, laughing, until the male hefts her up by both elbows. Even then, it takes them two tries for her to rise to her feet.

I keep barking. I try to rouse them from their stupor. *Urgent! Urgent!*

The male drops his keys on the pavement with a metal tinkle. He curses and stoops next to my car. He smells like tomato sauce, fried chips, stale male sweat, but mostly beer. Like Sunil's alpha.

I know these two are hopeless, but I keep barking. They might be able to open the door. *Urgent! Urgent! Urgent!*

"Damn dog," says the woman.

The man laughs, a mean, low laugh. He presses his face against the window.

I bark. I scratch. I yelp.

The man sticks his tongue against the window, red flesh blanched dead white against the cold glass. The smell of beer floods my nose. I whine before I bark, bark, bark some more.

"What the hell," says the man. I know this phrase. Sunil's alpha male says it all the time, usually before he does something that makes Sunil leave the room. On a good day, Sunil will clip the leash on me, and we'll get a good, fast walk out of it, even if Sunil is making angry noises into his metal rectangle phone the whole time.

This adult male's fat hand reaches through the window opening, but his forearm gets caught. His fingers are only five inches shy of the black knob. I stay very quiet, panting my heat away, fogging up the windows while he wiggles his arm and curses, but it's no use. This two-legs can't release me.

He withdraws his arm, swearing and rubbing the forearm that got caught in the jaws of the window. I jump and bark frantically. *Try again, two-legs! Try again! You can do it!*

The adult female laughs at him until he says something in a flat, low voice. She sways on her feet and sticks her arm through the window, muttering something about "him biting me."

I know what biting is. Sunil shut me in a crate after I nibbled his hand when we were playing. So I don't bite anyone. Not even Sunil's alpha.

I sit back on my heels and try to be very quiet, except for my panting.

The woman's skinny arm waves through the window, poking forward hopelessly. The man says something, and she reaches downward, complaining the whole time, but her hands brush the black knob.

I bark. She jumps and curses. But her fingers pluck the knob upward!

The man opens the door. "There, there."

But I am already leaping past him. No leash. Feels good. Feels free. The man tries to grab me, but I race past him, streaking through the parking lot, into the rainy darkness and the garden at the back of the Inn. I sniff wildly, retracing our pre-dinner walk. The patch of grass where I peed—I cannot resist squirting another hot stream of urine on the same site, covering up the scent of a male German shepherd who sprayed it after me.

I dash to the top of the nearby hill of sand, topped by an overturned wheelbarrow. I find the wrapper for the piece of cheese I scavenged, and the delicious scent of squirrels and spoiled hamburger, but no Sunil.

I'm barking. *Help! Help!* I sprint around the little garden, the lavender bushes, the overhanging trees, the patio with a mermaid statue.

No Sunil. Only old Sunil smell, washing away with the rain.

My stomach growls. I whine. *Sunil, two-legs, where are you?*

I tilt my nose in the air, sniff for him. My nostrils are flooded with the smell of food. Two-leg food, the spaghetti sauce and garlic and the beer. I can't resist. I dash to the back door of the restaurant and sniff the open crack. Light spills on the cool patio stones. Moist, heavy, sauce-scented air billows toward me.

I want to track Sunil and drag him back to our little cabin at the Lighthouse Inn, with its soft red carpet, its sofa covered in my dog blanket, plus my plastic bowls of food and water and my bone. Our small space. Safe space.

I launch into the restaurant. *Urgent! Urgent! Urgent! Sunil! Sunil! Sunil!*

My heart thunders in my chest. I dart around a two-legs standing next to the closest table. A woman screams. A man shouts and jumps on a bench, hollering like I bit him.

Crash! Someone drops a water glass, shattering five feet in front of me. Water sprays onto my nose. I whine, bark, manage to skid to a stop, while two-legs scream and shout around me.

"A dog! A dog!" they scream, like they've never seen one before.

The two-legs who smells like garlic tomato sauce, the one I thought might let me out of the car first, flies into the room. She says "Star!" and runs straight at me with her arms outstretched.

I veer away from her, and I smell, then see, one two-legs still eating his spaghetti in the corner like nothing's going on.

I scramble out the back door, still barking. *Worried! Worried!*

Sunil's not there. I didn't see or smell him anywhere, even though I know he walked through the heavy wood front doors like the rest of these people.

I am afraid.

I am running back to the sand pile, shivering and barking, tongue dry, bone-tired.

Back in the restaurant, the man calmly twirling spaghetti on his fork was Sunil's alpha. The two-legs I thought we had left behind, along with my stainless-steel water dish and my tasty kibble.

What is he doing here? And where is my two-legs?

I should run. I still hear two-legs yelling inside. I hear the tinkle of someone sweeping up glass. Soon someone will come and sweep me away where I can't help Sunil.

But first I creep back to the back patio. A shallow puddle of water has collected in the hollow curve of a stone tile, and I must quench my thirst.

I lick the puddle until I am licking cool, damp stone.

An adult male two-legs throws open the back door.

I retreat behind a clump of pampas grass. I don't dare run while his light shines on me. He yells into a phone, "Find that damn dog!"

Garlic two-legs yells back at him from inside.

The phone two-legs surveys the courtyard. I watch him carefully between the stalks of grass. If he chases me, I can run faster than him, but he will call other two-legs, and eventually they will catch me.

He swears. He yells some more into his telephone. But already he is looking over his shoulder, back into the restaurant.

He grunts and pulls the door closed behind him.

And I am safe for one more minute.

I nose in the pampas grass. I don't smell anything except the grass, earth, and worms.

I need to smell Sunil two-legs. If I could smell him, I could find him.

I sit on my behind and lift my rear paw to scratch my right ear furiously. Sunil two-legs did not come out of the front door. I was watching from the front parking lot.

He could still be in the restaurant, but I know my two-legs. If he heard me running, he would spring to my side.

So maybe he came out the back door.

The light shines through the back door. The back door is too close to the two-legs. They could snatch my collar. They could throw beer bottles at me, like Sunil's alpha did one time.

Sunil's alpha. He could take me away in his car.

I scurry to the back door anyway.

The air smells like spaghetti and other two-leg food, but I dig my nose deep into the prickly doormat. I smell long and hard.

Is that mud from Sunil's boot?

Yes. A speck of old driveway mud with a bit of gravel dust and a bit of my old pee.

Sunil was here. In the past hour.

I cast my nose around, sniffing, searching the stone patio. Even with the rain, I should be able to smell him better than this—

And then, at the edge of the patio, I finally catch a smell of something that makes my hackles rise.

Sunil's blood.

Fresh blood. One spot about as big as my paw pad, hardly diluted by rain. I whine. *Two-legs! Two-legs hurt!*

I circle the stone patio and the mulched earth at its edge. No more blood, but I smell Sunil stronger now—mud, a little sweat…and something else.

Someone else.

One other adult two-legs. A new one. He smells like cigarettes and black licorice and something wrong, something dangerous yet familiar that makes my hackles rise again.

This licorice two-legs smells like sex. Sex with Sunil's alpha.

I bark. *Worried! Worried!*

I hear a shout from the restaurant, but I keep going, nose to ground, *sniff sniff sniff run sniff sniff.*

Following Sunil and Licorice two-legs. Licorice has bigger, deeper footprints than Sunil.

Sunil. Walking crooked. Leaning on his right. Leaning on Licorice. Here, his boot dragged in the mud. I sniff a gum wrapper that fell out of Sunil's pocket, but it's empty and smells like mint and his laundry soap. It's already damp from the rain.

Sunil smell is very strong here.

He fell down. I nose the imprint from his body. He couldn't walk anymore.

I nudge a clump of his hair, tangled in a stick on the ground.

Yes, Sunil collapsed here. But his scent keeps going south, out of the woods. How?

I circle around this strong Sunil spot, check the scent trail backwards and forwards.

Forward, I don't find any more Sunil prints. Only Licorice boot prints, even deeper than before. And more Sunil hair and Sunil blood.

Licorice is dragging Sunil! But where?

I bark. *Sunil! Sunil!*

I hear two-leg voices. I hear a car door slam near the Lighthouse Inn. I hear two-leg footsteps.

They are tracking me.

They are coming to get me.

Sniff run run. Sniff. It's easier to track Sunil now that his head is bumping on the ground. More blood. More hair. More sweat.

Licorice smells stronger too, a tangy sweat. Fear sweat.

I break into the parking lot of the next building. A street light shines on me, but I don't care.

I can smell Sunil stronger now, mixed with fresh blood and sour vomit and wine. I'm barking now, loud barks, alarm barks, as I race toward the big green dumpster in the parking lot.

Wedged between the dumpster and the building, covered in rain and blood and bruises—

Sunil.

I lunge forward, knocking a soggy cardboard box off his body. I lick his cold cold nose, his cold cheek, his neck, his ear.

His eyelids flutter.

I lick his head. I lick the blood seeping from his scalp. His blood tastes salty and metallic, mixed with the smell of lemon shampoo.

He groans. He shifts his head.

I keep licking.

A two-legs in uniform runs up yelling and shines a light on us. He swears and grabs his phone. Soon I hear sirens wailing, and more two-legs in uniforms screech up with their cars and their flashing lights. But none of them are Sunil's alpha or Licorice. We are safe.

I curl up close to Sunil, using my body and my fur to keep him warm.

I always take care of my two-legs.

The Referee

by C.W. Blackwell
(Best Flash Story, 2024)

I called him the Referee because he never wore a stitch of color.

Black jacket. Black slacks. White undershirt.

Once he showed up in a black-and-white-striped sweater, and that's when the name really stuck. He sat in the corner of the bar and drank rum with orange slices, watching small-town traffic through the window as if waiting for someone to join him—or making sure someone didn't. He was friendly, and the regulars liked him. But there was also something sharp-edged and vaguely menacing in his voice, something reminiscent of a guillotine slipping loose.

"I'm a contract killer," he said once, to great laughter. He unpocketed a silver money clip and bought a round for the bar—maybe six or seven drinks—all while playing up the joke. "Our union is striking, so there's nothing to do but sit around daydreaming of murder."

"We know plenty of deserving assholes, if you're looking to pick up work on the side," I told him, and that part wasn't a joke—in this dying town, layoffs and evictions came fast and by the dozen. Malicious thinking had become a popular local pastime, and as the owner of the bar, I heard every idle threat.

"I'm not a scab," he said. "But I always appreciate a referral."

"And I'd never cross a picket line," I said.

He told us his name was Larry or Gary Vandersomething, but it sounded all wrong, like a name you made up in a hurry. That's when we started calling him the Ref to his face, and he didn't seem to mind.

In fact, the hitman bit really took off. When Len Jenson's landlord tossed him out on the street, we said it was *time to call the Ref.* And when Roger Kuskie caught his wife screwing the neighbor in the tool shed, we joked about starting a collection so we could *send in the Ref.*

It wasn't long before I set up an old water jug at the end of the bar called the Murder Jug, and we'd pass it around any time someone had a new revenge fantasy. It was popular with the regulars, and it quickly became one of those kitschy dive-bar gimmicks, like dollar bills on the ceiling or trucker hats pinned to the walls. The Murder Jug swelled with cash, and soon I had to lock it in the office after last call for safekeeping.

Just before the holidays, I got bad news of my own.

The county health inspector gave me thirty days to remodel the kitchen and install new appliances or he'd shut me down. It wasn't my first warning. The estimate was thirty grand, an impossible expense—even with all that money in the jug.

The bar was doomed.

We cursed the inspector with every pass of the Murder Jug and with every bill we shoved down the little glass neck. The inspector's name became a mantra of death.

The Ref watched intently from his place by the window.

"Just a little extra," he'd say with a laugh, "and I'll make it look like a suicide."

On the day I shut down, I spotted an unfamiliar Honda parked behind the bar. I didn't think much of it, but then I saw the front door hanging crooked in the jamb, glass littering the hardwood floor.

Inside was a gray-haired figure slumped over the bar.

I flicked on the light and knew: *the health inspector.*

His head lay in a pond of blood, a shiny big-bore revolver at his side and a handwritten note clenched in his left hand. I looked closer and regretted it. The fatal round had ruined his face—left eye dangling wetly onto the bar like a pickled onion on a string.

I ran to the office and locked the door. It took me three tries to dial 911.

The call was going through when I noticed the Murder Jug was empty, and inside sat a little toy referee blowing a whistle.

The dispatcher answered, prattling in my ear.

I turned the jug over and the toy referee slid onto the floor.

My god, I thought. *We hired him on layaway.*

I hoped it wasn't out loud.

The Wind Phone

by Josh Pachter
(Best Short Story, 2025)

His room at the Sato Inn was simple—tatami mats on the floor, a sleeping pad, one chair, a sink, communal bathroom down the hall—but it had a narrow balcony that looked out across a quiet two-lane road and the gray sand of Namiita Beach to the infinite blue carpet of the Pacific Ocean.

The journey from Tokyo Station that Saturday had taken him more than six hours: first the long train ride north to Shin-Hanamaki, then two hours on the spur line east to Kamaishi, a lovely half-hour through the mountains and along the coast on the sleepy old Sanriku Tetsudo-Riasu Railway, and finally a brief stroll to the ryokan, where he was welcomed by the kimonoed innkeeper with green tea and wagashi and bowed deferentially to the room he had reserved using an invented name and paid for with a credit card he knew could never be traced back to him.

He sat on the balcony with a bottle of Kirin Ichiban he had purchased from the kiosk on his arrival at the Namiitakaigon Station and looked out at the sea. On his lap was a brochure he had downloaded from the Internet, but he had committed its information to memory even before boarding his first train in Tokyo, so he had no need to refer to it as he considered the history of the Ōtsuchi wind phone.

When local designer Itaru Sasaki's cousin died of cancer in 2010, Sasaki bought an old telephone booth, painted it white, and set it up in his garden

250

so he could imagine himself still able to talk with his cousin by phone—their conversations, as he put it, "carried on the wind." A year later, after the Tōhoku tsunami killed over fifteen thousand people—more than twelve hundred of them right here in Ōtsuchi—Sasaki granted access to his "wind phone" to the public, so that mourners could "call" friends and family members who had died in the disaster and thereby process their grief.

Since then, replicas of the wind phone had been erected in Ireland, Canada, and several American states—but it was Sasaki's original structure that had brought the man calling himself Hiroshi Watanabe to Kirikiri village.

He finished his beer and went back into his room, washed his hands and examined himself in the mirror that hung above the sink. No one had ever accused him of being good looking, but his regular features were certainly not displeasing. His hair, once black, was shot now with gray, and there were crow's feet at the corners of his narrow eyes. His pupils behind the clear lenses of the glasses that had no effect on his perfect vision but served only as a basic element of disguise were obsidian and expressionless. His nose, broken long ago in a fistfight he was immature enough to engage in, was broad and flat, his teeth the best that money could buy. He was clean shaven, but during the vacation he would allow himself after his visit to the wind phone he would regrow the mustache and goatee the few shopkeepers who knew him in the Akabane neighborhood where he lived would expect to see on his rare visits to their establishments.

He had won the fistfight, had sent his opponent to the hospital with multiple facial contusions and two broken ribs, but he was still ashamed of having allowed himself to be goaded out of his usual—even then, years before he had embarked on his current occupation—anonymity.

As the sky above the sea began to darken, the man traveling as Hiroshi Watanabe left the inn and crossed the road and descended a flight of stone steps to the beach. It was late November, and there was a chill in the air. He zipped up his poplin jacket and wished he had brought something heavier. At least he had his gloves, and he pulled them on, but they were light cotton and offered little protection from the wind, so he stuffed his hands into the pockets of his jacket.

He had the beach to himself at this hour, and he strolled north, wrapped in silence but for the susurration of the wavelets lapping at the sand. He thought of his wife Katsuko, who like Itaru Sasaki's cousin had been taken away by cancer, and of their daughter Ichika, who had lost her long battle with *ihō yakubutsu* and died of an overdose, still a teenager, less than a year after Katsuko's passing. Ichika's name meant "one thousand flowers," and the day after her funeral he had scattered a packet of white chrysanthemum seeds along the southern bank of the Arakawa River, praying that a thousand blossoms might grow.

Perhaps they had. He had never gone back to look, had retreated into the little house that now—with Katsuko and Ichika gone—seemed much too big for a middle-aged man alone. He rarely emerged, except to buy groceries and, three or four times a year, when his employers gave him a mission to complete.

He was not traveling in his professional capacity now. This trip to the wind phone—the first time he had left Tokyo in almost thirteen months—was personal.

He had learned that there was only one restaurant in the village, but he had no desire to sit by himself at a table and be fawned over by some solicitous proprietor. When he returned from the beach, he ducked into the Family Mart beside the inn and bought a cardboard container of miso soup and another of tonkatsu. There was a microwave in the store, and he warmed up his food and ate it on his balcony with a second bottle of beer.

He slept fitfully that night, plagued by nebulous dreams of ferocious telephones and talking flowers.

Early in the morning, he found a tray outside his door as he had requested and breakfasted on his balcony, gazing thoughtfully across the calm waters of the Pacific. Five thousand miles to the east, he knew, lay the city of San Francisco in America. He had never been to America, though he and Katsuko had often promised Ichika when she was a little girl that they would take her there someday to see the wonders of the country that had defeated a Japan gone mad in the Greater East Asia War.

Someday.

He chewed his rice, grilled mackerel, tamagoyaki, and pickled daikon without tasting them, saw the sun rise on the far horizon without any appreciation of the palette of colors it painted across the slate-gray sky.

When he finished his meal, he showered in the bathroom down the hall and dressed himself in the same clothing he had worn on the previous day: navy-blue trousers, white turtleneck, pale-blue hanten.

At precisely eight thirty, he left the inn and walked for ten minutes: across the narrow-gauge railway tracks, past Kirikiri's tightly packed network of houses and shops, through the narrow tunnel beneath the Sanriku Coast Expressway, and up Chiwari hill to a point in the trees by the side of the path from which he could observe the glass-paned white booth that housed the wind phone.

As he had been informed it would be, the booth was occupied at this hour. According to the information he had received, it was used every Saturday and Sunday morning, from eight thirty to approximately eight forty-five, by the same young man, Jun'ichi Tanaka, who lived in Tokyo but came north each Friday to spend the weekend in Kirikiri with his widowed mother and speak to his dead father on the wind phone.

Jun'ichi, he thought. The name was uncommon, combining the kanji "jun," meaning "pure," with "ichi," meaning simply "one."

Pure One.

He smiled tightly at the irony of it.

The young man was dressed in Western clothing: jeans, a black T-shirt, high-topped sneakers. He was hunched over the phone, speaking earnestly, only the back of his shirt visible, but the man traveling as Hiroshi Watanabe assumed that the front bore either the image of a popular American musical artist or some cryptic wasei-eigo—or so-called "Engrish"—phrase.

The last time he had gone grocery shopping in Akabane, he had noticed a girl who couldn't have been older than fifteen—Ichika's age, the last time he had seen her—her jet-black hair pulled into long pigtails that jutted out from the sides of her head and fell to her shoulders. She wore a pleated plaid miniskirt and a white T-shirt tied at the waist to shamelessly expose her belly, still puffy with baby fat. On the shirt, in large black letters, appeared the legend "Do Not Taunt Happy Fun Ball." He still wondered what on Earth those words meant when arranged in that order.

He waited patiently for Jun'ichi Tanaka to finish his call. When the young man finally cradled the phone and emerged from the booth, he saw that there was indeed an illustration of four white-faced men in strange black makeup on the front of his T-shirt. Above the four faces, the word "KISS" was printed, all in capital letters, the two esses distressingly similar to the insignia of the Nazi *Schutzstaffel* from the war.

He came out from behind the trees and approached the Pure One, bowed politely and then took his gloved right hand from his jacket pocket and held it out in a friendly Western gesture.

Tanaka extended his own hand, and the two of them shook.

"I hope your conversation brought you peace," the older man said.

The young man nodded. "It did, Oji-san," he said, using the polite form of address custom dictated. "May I wish you the same peace I have found."

The man traveling as Hiroshi Watanabe jerked hard on the other's hand and spun the boy around. Releasing his grip, he shifted his right arm and pulled the Pure One close to his chest. With his free left hand, he drew a thin blade from its sheath and, in a single practiced motion, slit Jun'ichi Tanaka's throat. Hot blood spurted from the cut, but the older man's usual technique prevented even a single drop from touching his own clothing or flesh.

He let the body drop to the manicured dirt path and, without so much as a second glance, stepped over it and entered the booth. He lifted the receiver from the black Bakelite rotary phone and dialed the number he remembered so achingly well.

The phone was connected to nothing, so he heard no dial tone, no ring, no answering "Mushi mushi!"

But as he spoke into the receiver he believed with all his heart that the wind phone was granting him one final opportunity to talk with his beloved daughter.

"Ichika," he said, and his voice—though tinged with grief—was strong and proud. "I have sent the man who addicted you to the drugs that destroyed you to meet his ancestors. I pray, my little one, that you can at last now rest in peace."

He cradled the phone and left the booth, stepped again over the motionless body on the path and headed down the hill toward the train station.

Tomorrow, he promised himself, he would return to the south bank of the Arakawa River and count the chrysanthemums.

Appendix A: The Derringer Winners

(An asterisk indicates that the story is included in this anthology.)

1998

Best Flash Story: "Curiosity Kills" by Michael Mallory (in *Murderous Intent*)

Best Short Short Story: "Guavaberry Christmas" by Kate Grilley (in *Murderous Intent*)

Best Short Story: "The Adventurers" by Barbara White-Rayczek (in *Murderous Intent*)

Best Short Story: "L.A. Justice" by Kris Neri (in *Murder by 13*, Crown Valley Press)*

Best First Short Story: "Back Stairs" by Eileen Brosnan (in *Murderous Intent*)

Best Novella: "Image of Conspiracy" by Margo Power (Madison Publishing Co.)

1999

Best Flash Story: "Pretty Kitty" by Joyce Holland (in *Murderous Intent*)*

Best Short Short Story: "Capital Justice" by Kris Neri (in *Blue Murder*)

Golden Derringer: Edward D. Hoch

2000

Best Flash Story: "When in Rome" by Dorothy Francis (in *Murderous Intent*)

Best Flash Story: "Just a Man on the Sidewalk" by Carol Kilgore (at *TheCase.com*)*

Best Short Story: "The Way to a Man's Heart" by Elizabeth Dearl (at *TheCase.com*)

Best Novella: "Saint Bobby" by Doug Allyn (in *Ellery Queen's Mystery Magazine*)

Best First Short Story: "Death in Full Bloom" by Ray Wonderly (in *Futures Mysterious Anthology Magazine*)

Golden Derringer: Henry Slesar

2001

Best Flash Story: "Polls Don't Lie" by Earl McGill (in *Blue Murder*)

Best Flash Story: "The New Lawyer" by Mike Wiecek (in *Crimestalker Casebook*)

Best Short Story: "Erie's Last Day" by Steve Hockensmith (in *Alfred Hitchcock's Mystery Magazine*)

Best Novella: "Lilacs and Lace" by Lynda Douglas (in *Futures Mysterious Anthology Magazine*)

Best Puzzle Story: "The Cabin Killer" by Henry Slesar (in *Ellery Queen's Mystery Magazine*)*

Golden Derringer: John Lutz

2002

Best Short Short Story: "In the Heat of the Moment" by Nick Andreychuk (in *Futures Mysterious Anthology Magazine*)

Best Short Story: "All the Fine Actors" by Earl Staggs (at *EWG Presents: Without a Clue*)*

Best Longer Story: "Early Morning Rain" by Jean McCord (in *Futures Mysterious Anthology Magazine*)

Silver Derringer for Editorial Excellence: Cathleen Jordan

2003

Best Short Short Story: "A Cut Above" by Del Tinsley (in *Hardluck Stories*)

Best Short Story: "Closure" by Dave White (at the *Thrilling Detective* website)*

Best Long Short Story: "The Murder Ballads" by Doug Allyn (in *Ellery Queen's Mystery Magazine*)

2004

Best Flash Story: "All My Yesterdays" by Michael Bracken (in *Suddenly V: Prose Poetry and Sudden Fiction*, Stone River Press)

Best Short Short Story: "Nailbiter" by Robert Lopresti (in *Alfred Hitchcock's Mystery Magazine*)

Best Mid-Length Short Story: "Notions of the Real World" by Dorothy Rellas (in *Futures Mysterious Anthology Magazine*)*

Best Long Short Story: "The Mask of Peter" by Clark Howard (in *Ellery Queen's Mystery Magazine*)

2005

Best Flash Story: "The Big Guys" by JA Konrath (in *Small Bites*, Coscom Entertainment)

Best Short Short Story: "The Test" by Mike Wiecek (in *Woman's World*)

Best Mid-Length Short Story: "Viscery" by Sandy Balzo (in *Ellery Queen's Mystery Magazine*)*

Best Longer Short Story: "Secondhand Heart" by Doug Allyn (in *Alfred Hitchcock's Mystery Magazine*)

2006

Best Flash Story: "Secondhand Shoe" by Patricia Harrington (in *A Flasher's Dozen*)*

Best Short Short Story: "Zipped" by Stephen D. Rogers (in *Windchill: Crime Stories by New England Writers*, Level Best Books)

Best Mid-Length Short Story: "One Step Closer" by Iain Rowan (in *Hardluck Stories*)

Best Longer Short Story: "The Safest Place on Earth" by Mark Best (at the *Thrilling Detective* website)

2007

Best Flash Story: "Vigilante" by Barry Ergang (at *Mysterical-E*)

Best Short Short Story: "Four for Dinner" by John M. Floyd (in *Seven by Seven*, Wolfmont Publishing)

Best Short Short Story: "Elena Speaks of the City, Under Siege" by Steven Torres (at *Crimespree Magazine*)

Best Mid-Length Story: "Cranked" by Bill Crider (in *Damn Near Dead: An Anthology of Geezer Noir*, Busted Flush Press)*

Best Longer Story: "Strictly Business" by Julie Hyzy (in *These Guns for Hire*, Bleak House Books)

2008

Best Flash Story: "My Hero" by Patricia Abbott (in *D.Z. Allen's Muzzle Flash*)

Best Short Story: "In the Shadows of Wrigley Field" by John Weagly (at *The Back Alley Webzine*)

Best Long Story: "The Gospel According to Gordon Black" by Richard Helms (at the *Thrilling Detective* website)*

Best Novelette: "Paper Walls/Glass Houses" by Richard Helms (writing as Eric Shane) (at *The Back Alley Webzine*)

2009

Best Flash Story: "No Flowers for Stacey" by Ruth McCarty (in *Deadfall: Crime Stories by New England Writers*, Level Best Books)*

Best Flash Story: "No Place Like Home" by Dee Stuart (at *Mysterical-E*)

Best Short Story: "The Cost of Doing Business" by Michael Penncavage (at *Thuglit*)

Best Long Story: "The Quick Brown Fox" by Robert S. Levinson (in *Alfred Hitchcock's Mystery Magazine*)

Best Novelette: "Too Wise" by O'Neil De Noux (in *Ellery Queen's Mystery Magazine*)

Edward D. Hoch Memorial Golden Derringer: Clark Howard

2010

Best Flash Story: "And Here's to You, Mrs. Edwardson" by Hamilton Waymire (in *Big Pulp*)

Best Short Story: "Twas the Night" by Anita Page (in *The Gift of Murder*, Wolfmont Press)

Best Long Story: "Famous Last Words" by Doug Allyn (in *Ellery Queen's Mystery Magazine*)*

Best Novelette: "Julius Katz" by Dave Zeltserman (in *Ellery Queen's Mystery Magazine*)

Edward D. Hoch Memorial Golden Derringer: Lawrence Block

2011

Best Flash Story: "The Book Signing" by Kathy Chencharik (in *Thin Ice: Crime Stories by New England Writers*, Level Best Books)

Best Flash Story: "The Unknown Substance" by Jane Hammons (at *A Twist of Noir*)

Best Short Story: "Pewter Badge" by Michael J. Solender (at the *Yellow Mama* website)*

Best Long Story: "Care of the Circumcised Penis" by Sean Doolittle (in *Thuglit Presents: Blood, Guts, and Whiskey*, Kensington)

Best Long Story: "Interpretation of Murder" by B.K. Stevens (in *Alfred Hitchcock's Mystery Magazine*)

Best Novelette: "Rearview Mirror" by Art Taylor (in *Ellery Queen's Mystery Magazine*)

Edward D. Hoch Memorial Golden Derringer: Ruth Rendell

2012

Best Flash Story: "Lessons Learned" by Allan Leverone (at the *Shotgun Honey* website)

Best Short Story: "The Touch of Death" by BV Lawson (at *The Absent Willow Review*)*

Best Long Story: "Brea's Tale" by Karen Pullen (in *Ellery Queen's Mystery Magazine*)

Best Long Story: "A Drowning at Snow's Cut" by Art Taylor (in *Ellery Queen's Mystery Magazine*)

Best Novelette: "Where Billy Died" by Earl Staggs (Untreed Reads)

Edward D. Hoch Memorial Golden Derringer: Bill Pronzini

2013

Best Flash Story: "The Cable Job" by Randy DeWitt (in *Alfred Hitchcock's Mystery Magazine*)

Best Short Story: "Getting Out of the Box" by Michael Bracken (in *Crime Square*, Vantage Point)

Best Long Story: "When Duty Calls" by Art Taylor (in *Chesapeake Crimes: This Job Is Murder*, Wildside Press)*

Best Novelette: "Wood-Smoke Boys" by Doug Allyn (in *Ellery Queen's Mystery Magazine*)

Edward D. Hoch Memorial Golden Derringer: Loren D. Estleman

2014

Best Flash Story: "Luck Is What You Make" by Stephen D. Rogers (in *Crime Factory*)*

Best Short Story: "The Present" by Robert Lopresti (in *The Strand*)

Best Long Story: "Give Me a Dollar" by Ray Daniel (in *Best New England Crime Stories 2014: Stone Cold*, Level Best Books)

Best Novelette: "The Goddaughter's Revenge" by Melodie Campbell (Orca Rapid Reads)

Edward D. Hoch Memorial Golden Derringer: Ed Gorman

2015

Best Flash Story: "How Lil' Jimmie Beat the Big C" by Joseph D'Agnese (at the *Shotgun Honey* website)

Best Short Story: "The Kaluki Kings of Queens" by Cathi Stoler (in *Murder New York Style: Family Matters*, Glenmere Press)*

Best Long Story: "A Hopeless Case" by Hilary Davidson (at the *All Due Respect* website)

Best Novelette: "The Snow Angel" by Doug Allyn (in *Ellery Queen's Mystery Magazine*)

Edward D. Hoch Memorial Golden Derringer: James Powell

2016

Best Flash Story: "Hero" by Vy Kava (in *Red Dawn: Best New England Crime Stories 2016*, Level Best Books)

Best Short Story: "Twilight Ladies" by Meg Opperman (in *Ellery Queen's Mystery Magazine*)*

Best Long Story: "Dentonville" by John M. Floyd (in *Ellery Queen's Mystery Magazine*)

Best Novelette: "Driver" by John M. Floyd (in *The Strand*)

Edward D. Hoch Memorial Golden Derringer: Michael Bracken

2017

Best Flash Story: "The Phone Call" by Herschel Cozine (at the *Flash Bang Mysteries* website)*

Best Short Story: "The Way They Do It in Boston" by Linda Barnes (in *Ellery Queen's Mystery Magazine*)

Best Long Story: "Breadcrumbs" by Victoria Weisfeld (in *Betty Fedora: Kickass Women in Crime Fiction*, CreateSpace)

Best Novelette: "Inquiry and Assistance" by Terrie Farley Moran (in *Alfred Hitchcock's Mystery Magazine*)

Edward D. Hoch Memorial Golden Derringer: Robert J. Randisi

2018

Best Flash Story: "Fishing for an Alibi" by Earl Staggs (at the *Flash Bang Mysteries* website)

Best Short Story: "The Cop Who Liked Gilbert and Sullivan" by Robert Lopresti (in *Sherlock Holmes Mystery Magazine*)*

Best Long Story: "Death in the Serengeti" by David H. Hendrickson (in *Fiction River: Pulse Pounders: Adrenaline*, WMG Publishing)

Best Novelette: "Flowing Waters" by Brendan DuBois (in *Ellery Queen's*

Mystery Magazine)

Edward D. Hoch Memorial Golden Derringer: John M. Floyd

2019

Best Flash Story: "The Bicycle Thief" by James Blakey (in *The Norwegian American*)

Best Short Story: "Dying in Dokesville" by Alan Orloff (in *Malice Domestic 13: Mystery Most Geographical,* Wildside Press)*

Best Long Story: "With My Eyes" by Leslie Budewitz (in *Suspense Magazine*)

Best Novelette: "The Cambodian Curse" by Gigi Pandian (in *The Cambodian Curse & Other Stories,* Henery Press)

Edward D. Hoch Memorial Golden Derringer: Doug Allyn

2020

Best Flash Story: "The Two-Body Problem" by Josh Pachter (in *Mystery Weekly Magazine*)

Best Short Story: "On the Road with Mary Jo" by John M. Floyd (in *Ellery Queen's Mystery Magazine*)*

Best Long Story: "Lucy's Tree" by Sandra Murphy (in *The Eyes of Texas: Private Eyes from the Panhandle to the Piney Woods,* Down & Out Books)

Best Novelette: "His Sister's Secrets" by Brendan DuBois (in *Ellery Queen's Mystery Magazine*)

Edward D. Hoch Memorial Golden Derringer: Josh Pachter

2021

Best Flash Story: "Memories of Fire" by C.W. Blackwell (at the *Pulp Modern Flash* website)

Best Flash Story: "War Words" by Travis Richardson (at the *Punk Noir Magazine* website)

Best Short Story: "The Great Bedbug Incident and the Invitation of Doom" by Eleanor Cawood Jones (in *Chesapeake Crimes: Invitation to Murder,* Wildside Press)*

Best Short Story: "River" by Stacy Woodson (in *The Beat of Black Wings: Crime Fiction Inspired by the Songs of Joni Mitchell*, Untreed Reads)

Best Long Story: "Hotelin'" by Sarah M. Chen (in *Shotgun Honey: Volume #4: Recoil*, Shotgun Honey)

Best Novelette: "The Boy Detective and the Summer of '74" by Art Taylor (in *Alfred Hitchcock's Mystery Magazine*)

Edward D. Hoch Memorial Golden Derringer: Brendan DuBois

2022

Best Flash Story: "Tourist Trap" by John M. Floyd (at the *Pulp Modern Flash* website)

Best Short Story: "Yelena Tried to Kill Me" by Trey Dowell (in *Mystery Weekly Magazine*)

Best Long Story: "The Downeaster 'Alexa'" by Michael Bracken (in *Only the Good Die Young: Crime Fiction Inspired by the Songs of Billy Joel*, Untreed Reads)*

Best Novelette: "Two Tamales, One Tokarev, and a Lifetime of Broken Promises" by Stacy Woodson (in *Guns + Tacos: Season Three*, Down & Out Books)

Edward D. Hoch Memorial Golden Derringer: S.J. Rozan

2023

Best Flash Story: "Acknowledgments" by Karen Harrington (in *Guilty Crime Story Magazine*)

Best Short Story: "My Two-Legs" by Melissa Yi (in *Alfred Hitchcock's Mystery Magazine*)*

Best Long Story: "Negative Tilt" by Bobby Mathews (in *Rock and a Hard Place*)

Best Novelette: "Two Shrimp Tacos and a .22 Ruger" by Adam Meyer (in *Guns + Tacos: Season Four*, Down & Out Books)

Edward D. Hoch Memorial Golden Derringer: Martin Edwards

2024

Best Flash Story: "The Referee" by C. W. Blackwell (at the *Shotgun Honey* website)*

Best Short Story: "Last Day at the Jackrabbit" by John M. Floyd (in *The Strand*)

Best Long Story: "Good Deed for the Day" by Bonnar Spring (in *Wolfsbane: Best New England Crime Stories*, Crime Spell Books)

Best Novelette: "Mrs. Hyde" by David Dean (in *Ellery Queen's Mystery Magazine*)

Best Novelette: "Catherine the Great" by Kristine Kathryn Rusch (in *WMG 2023 Holiday Spectacular Calendar of Stories*, WMG Books)

Edward D. Hoch Memorial Golden Derringer: Barb Goffman

2025

Best Flash Story: "Kargin the Necromancer" by Mike McHone (in *Mystery Tribune*)

Best Short Story: "The Wind Phone" by Josh Pachter (in *Ellery Queen's Mystery Magazine*)*

Best Long Story: "Heart of Darkness" by Tammy Euliano (in *Scattered, Smothered, Covered & Chunked: Crime Fiction Inspired by Waffle House*, Down & Out Books)

Best Novelette: "The Cadillac Job" by Stacy Woodson (*Chop Shop, Episode 1*, Down & Out Books)

Best Anthology: *Murder, Neat: A Sleuthsayers Anthology*, edited by Michael Bracken and Barb Goffman (Level Best Books)

Edward D. Hoch Memorial Golden Derringer: Art Taylor

Silver Derringer for Editorial Excellence: Janet Hutchings

Appendix B: The SMFS Hall of Fame

The Hall of Fame honors deceased writers' impact
on the mystery and crime short story.

Charter Inductees (2010)

Raymond Chandler
Agatha Christie
Sir Arthur Conan Doyle
Stanley Ellin
R. Austin Freeman
Dashiell Hammett
Edward D. Hoch
Baroness Orczy
Edgar Allan Poe
Ellery Queen
Dorothy L. Sayers
Cornell Woolrich

Subsequent Inductees

G.K. Chesterton (2022)
Rex Todhunter Stout (2024)
O. Henry (2025)

Appendix C: The Final Paragraph

(Continued from Henry Slesar's "The Cabin Killer")

"I knew you killed her, Peter, and it's my guess the young lady is pregnant. You didn't want her to spoil your marriage plans, so you invited her to the cabin and murdered her. You smashed the front door lock to make it look like a break-in. But then you made the mistake of fixing yourself a scotch on the rocks. When I saw the ice in your glass, I knew you'd been in the cabin close to an hour. It would have taken that long for the ice in the refrigerator to freeze after turning on the electricity."

[Editor's Note: In its original publication in Ellery Queen's Mystery Magazine, *the final two sentences of this final paragraph read as follows: "When I saw the ice in your glass and the full tray of ice cubes in the refrigerator, I knew you'd been in the cabin close to an hour. It would have taken that long after turning on the electricity." There's nothing anywhere in the story, though, to indicate that the sheriff ever looked in the refrigerator. As noted in my introduction to this book, I've done only very minimal editing to these stories. In this case, though, I felt it was necessary to edit Slesar's final two sentences in order to play fair with the reader.]*

Acknowledgments

My thanks to the authors who granted permission to reprint their stories in this volume—and to the estates and literary agencies that gave permission to reprint stories by authors who have, alas, passed on or otherwise proved impossible to reach directly. Of particular help were Carol Dumont of Penny Publications, Cathy Gleason of the Gelfman Schneider Literary Agency, Bob Diforio of the D4EO Literary Agency, and Marc Koralnik at Liepman AG.

Thank you to John Floyd for tracking down Dorothy Rellas' story, to Steve Steinbock for finding the Henry Slesar story in his extensive library of issues of *Ellery Queen's Mystery Magazine*, to Kris Neri for unearthing Joyce Holland's story and obituary, to Darren Todd and his parents for providing a copy of Patricia Harrington's story, and to Todd Dashoff at the Science Fiction Writers of America's Estate Program for steering me to the Swiss agency that handles Henry Slesar's literary rights. Special thanks to Earl Staggs' widow Carol Staggs and daughter Cindi Davis for providing a copy of Earl's story and permission to include it here, and to Bill Crider's daughter Angela Crider Neary for providing a biography of her father and permission to include his story.

Thanks also to Mark Schuster for preparing a comprehensive list of all Derringer finalists and winners, going back to the first Derringer Awards in 1998.

A tip of the hat to Short Mystery Fiction Society president Joseph S. Walker for encouraging me to put this volume together and writing its foreward, and to past presidents Kevin R. Tipple, Robert Lopresti, Michael Bracken, and Gerald So for their contributions.

Finally, all of us involved in putting *Hot Shots: Celebrating Thirty Years of the Short Mystery Fiction Society* together thank Shawn Reilly Simmons and Deb Well at Level Best Books for greenlighting the project and publishing the book. We're grateful for your commitment to short crime fiction!

Copyright Information

"L.A. Justice" is copyright © 1997 by Kris Neri. First published in *Murder by 13* (Crown Valley Press). Reprinted by permission of the author.

"Pretty Kitty" is copyright © 1998 by Joyce Holland. First published in *Murderous Intent* (Winter 1998). Reprinted by permission of the D4EO Literary Agency.

"Just a Man on the Sidewalk" is copyright © 1999 by Carol Kilgore. First published at *TheCase.com* (March 12-18, 1999). Reprinted by permission of the author.

"The Cabin Killer" is copyright © 2000 by Henry Slesar. First published in *Ellery Queen's Mystery Magazine* (July 2000). Reprinted by permission of the Liepman AG Agency.

"All the Fine Actors" is copyright © 2001 by Earl Staggs. First published in *EWG Presents: Without a Clue* (April 2001). Reprinted by permission of the author's widow and daughter.

"Closure" is copyright © 2002 by Dave White. First published on the *Thrilling Detective* website (Fall 2002). Reprinted by permission of the author.

"Notions of the Real World" is copyright © 2003 by Dorothy Rellas. First published in *Futures Mysterious Anthology Magazine* (Summer 2003). A concerted but ultimately unsuccessful good-faith attempt was made to locate the current owner of this story's copyright. Any information that

About the Contributors

DOUG ALLYN is the author of thirteen novels and more than a hundred and fifty short stories, over two dozen of which have been optioned for development for feature films and television. His career highlights include co-authoring a book with James Patterson, sipping champagne with Mickey Spillane, and waltzing with Mary Higgins Clark. In addition to his six competitive Derringers and Golden Derringer for Lifetime Achievement, he is a nine-time Edgar finalist (two-time winner) and has won the *Ellery Queen's Mystery Magazine* Readers Award a record eleven times (with another fourteen second-place finishes).

SANDY BALZO turned to mystery writing after twenty years in corporate public relations. Nominated for Anthony and Macavity awards, her novels have received starred reviews from *Kirkus* and *Booklist*, while her short stories have won the Macavity, Derringer, and Robert L. Fish awards. *Any Pot in a Storm* is her sixteenth Maggy Thorsen mystery and her nineteenth published novel. A native of southeastern Wisconsin, she now lives on the Central Coast of California.

C.W. BLACKWELL is a two-time Derringer winner, five-time finalist. He is a member of the Short Mystery Fiction Society and International Thriller Writers. *Whatever Kills the Pain,* his first collection of short fiction, was published by Rock and a Hard Place Press in 2025. *lnk.bio/cw_blackwell_wri ter*

MICHAEL BRACKEN is an Edgar and Shamus nominee and three-time Derringer winner, whose crime fiction has appeared in *The Best*

American Mystery Stories, The Best Mystery Stories of the Year, and many other publications. He is the editor of *Black Cat Mystery Magazine* and numerous anthologies, including the Anthony-nominated *The Eyes of Texas* and, with Barb Goffman, the Derringer-winning *Murder, Neat.* He is a recipient of the SMFS's Golden Derringer for Lifetime Achievement and, in 2024, was inducted into the Texas Institute of Letters for his contributions to Texas literature. *CrimeFictionWriter.com*

HERSCHEL COZINE has written many stories and poems for national children's magazines. His crime fiction has appeared in EQMM, *Alfred Hitchcock's Mystery Magazine, Woman's World,* Wolfmont Press's "Toys for Tots" anthologies, and various online-only publications.

BILL CRIDER (1941-2018) was the Anthony Award-winning author of the Sheriff Dan Rhodes mystery series. He wrote more than fifty published novels (including several series) and an equal number of short stories, won two Anthonys and a Derringer, was nominated for the Shamus and Edgar awards, and was a regular columnist for EQMM and *Mystery Scene.* A lifelong Texan, he served for many years as chair of the Division of English and Fine Arts at Alvin Community College. *billcrider.com*

JOHN M. FLOYD's short stories have appeared in AHMM, EQMM, *The Strand, The Saturday Evening Post, Best American Mystery Stories* (2015, 2018, and 2020), *Best Mystery Stories of the Year* (2021 and 2024), and many other publications. A former Air Force captain and IBM systems engineer, he is an Edgar nominee, a Shamus winner, a six-time Derringer winner, the author of nine books, and a recipient of the Golden Derringer. *johnmfloyd.com*

PATRICIA HARRINGTON was the founder of Communication Project Specialists, a company that provided grant-writing, training, and marketing services to nonprofit organizations. Although her Derringer-winning flash story was a one-off, she was the author of two novels and numerous short stories featuring Bridget O'Hern, an amateur sleuth who—go figure!—provided grant-writing, training, and marketing services to nonprofit organizations.

RICHARD HELMS, a retired psychologist and college professor, has twenty-five novels in print. A frequent contributor to EQMM, AHMM, BCMM, and various anthologies, he has won the Silver Falchion, Derringer, and Shamus awards twice each and the Thriller and Macavity awards once each, and his story "See Humble and Die" was included in *Best American Mystery Stories 2020*. A former president of Mystery Writers of America's Southeast Regional Chapter, he lives with his wife and muse Elaine in Charlotte (NC). *richardhelms.net*

JOYCE HOLLAND (1940-2021) was a literary agent and the author of five novels, six short stories, and one volume of nonfiction. She served a term as president of Florida's Emerald Coast Writers and wrote a column for the *Northwest Florida Daily News*.

ELEANOR CAWOOD JONES is one of the featured authors in the *Destination Murders* anthology series and has contributed many short stories to magazines, other anthologies, and the single-author collections *A Baker's Dozen* and *Death is Coming to Town*. A former newspaper reporter and reformed marketing director, she now finds inspiration working in the airline industry. *girlsgonechillin.com*

CAROL KILGORE is the award-winning author of the Amazing Gracie mysteries, the House Witches mysteries, and three standalones. She lives and writes about an hour northwest of Houston (TX). *carolkilgore.net*

BV LAWSON is the author of several novels and over two hundred published short stories, poems, articles, and essays. In addition to a Derringer, her stories have garnered *Dillydoun Review* and *Gemini Magazine* awards, as well as a *Noir Nation* Golden Fedora, while her novels have been finalists for the Shamus, *Foreword Book Reviews*, and *Library Journal* Indie

Book awards. *bvlawson.com*

ROBERT LOPRESTI is a retired librarian who lives in the Pacific Northwest. More than a hundred and twenty of his short stories have been published in magazines and anthologies, including *Best American Mystery Stories*. He has won three Derringers and the Black Orchid Novella Award and is an Anthony nominee. His novel *Greenfellas* is a comic caper about the Mafia trying to save the environment. He blogs at *Sleuthsayers* and *Little Big Crimes*. *roblopresti.com*

RUTH MCCARTY's short fiction has appeared in several Level Best anthologies and in *Deadly Nightshade, Flash Bang Mysteries, A Plot for Any Occasion, Over My Dead Body!, Mystery Magazine,* and in the Anthony-winning anthology *Malice Domestic 14: Mystery Most Edible. ruthmccarty.com*

KRIS NERI has written both novels and more than seventy short stories, including the Tracy Eaton and the Samantha Brennan & Annabelle Haggerty mysteries. She's a two-time Derringer winner and has also won the Pushcart Prize. She teaches writing for the prestigious Writers' Program of the UCLA Extension School and the Sisters in Crime Guppy Chapter. *krisneriauthor.wordpress.com*

MEG OPPERMAN has contributed short fiction to EQMM, BCMM, and *Sherlock Holmes Mystery Magazine,* among others. She currently writes LGBTQ+ romantasy as Meghan Maslow. In 2021, she received the Reviewers Choice Award from the Paranormal Romance Guild for Best LGBTQ+ Fantasy Novel and was a runner-up in the Rainbow Awards for both Best Gay Paranormal Romance and Best Gay Fantasy Romance. In 2023, she was a finalist in the Goodreads M/M Romance Members' Choice Awards for Best Book of the Year. *meghanmaslow.com*

ALAN ORLOFF has published fourteen novels and more than sixty short stories. His work has won an Anthony, an Agatha, a Derringer, and two

Thriller Awards. He's also been a finalist for the Shamus and has had a story selected for *The Best American Mystery Stories*. He lives and writes in South Florida, where the examples of hijinks are endless. *alanorloff.com*

JOSH PACHTER is an author, editor, and translator. In addition to two Derringer wins, his work has been nominated for the Edgar, Anthony, Agatha, Macavity, Lefty, Thriller, and EQMM Readers awards, and he was the 2020 recipient of the Golden Derringer. *joshpachter.com*

DOROTHY RELLAS has unfortunately not left much of a footprint behind her. She wrote the 1986 novel *Hidden Motives* (Harlequin Intrigue) and published several short stories in *Futures Mysterious Anthology Magazine* and a few other places.

STEPHEN D. ROGERS is the author of *Shot to Death* and more than eight hundred shorter works, including two Derringer winners, two "Best of Soft SF" winners, and two "Notable Online Stories" from *storySouth*'s Million Writers Award. *stephendrogers.com*

HENRY SLESAR (1927-2002) was the prolific author of hundreds of short stories, novels, and scripts for radio and television. He won an Edgar in 1960 for *The Gray Flannel Shroud*, his first novel, and an Emmy in 1974 as the head writer for the long-running CBS soap opera *The Edge of Night*. He also served as head writer for the soaps *Somerset, Search for Tomorrow*, and *One Life to Live*, and for the primetime series *Executive Suite*.

MICHAEL J. SOLENDER lives in and writes from his adopted hometown of Charlotte (NC). His work appears in the *New York Times*, the *Miami Herald*, the *Charlotte Observer*, and the *Sacramento Bee*; in magazines including *Smithsonian, Metropolis, Carolinas Golf, Salvation South*, and *Southern Living*; and on the Matador Network. He is an active member of the Society of American Travel Writers. *michaeljwrites.com*

EARL STAGGS (1939-2020) was the author of two novels and numerous short stories. A two-time Derringer winner, he served terms as the vice president and then president of the SMFS. He also served as the managing editor of *Futures Mystery Magazine. earlwstaggs.wordpress.com*

CATHI STOLER is the Amazon best-selling author of the Nick Donahue Adventures, Laurel and Helen New York Mystery, and Murder on the Rocks series—each of which has been nominated for several awards—as well as multiple short stories. She is a board member of the New York chapter of Sisters in Crime and a member of the Mystery Writers of America and International Thriller Writers. *cathistoler.com*

ART TAYLOR is the Edgar Award-winning author of two collections: *The Adventure of the Castle Thief and Other Expeditions and Indiscretions* and *The Boy Detective & The Summer of '74 and Other Tales of Suspense.* His debut book, *On the Road with Del & Louise: A Novel in Stories*, won the Agatha Award for Best First Novel. His short fiction has also won the Agatha, Anthony, Derringer, and Macavity Awards, and he was the 2025 recipient of the Golden Derringer. He is a professor of English at George Mason University. *arttaylorwriter.com*

JOSEPH S. WALKER is the president of the SMFS and the author of more than a hundred published crime and mystery stories. He has been a finalist for the Edgar, Derringer, Shamus, and Thriller awards and is a two-time winner of the Al Blanchard Award. His stories have appeared in many magazines and anthologies, including four of the last five editions of *Best Mystery Stories of the Year. Crime Scenes,* the first collection of his stories, was published by Level Best Books in 2026. *jswalkerauthor.com*

DAVE WHITE is the author of the Shamus-nominated Jackson Donne series. The series' final novel, *Set on Blood,* will be published in the fall of 2026. He lives in New Jersey with his wife and children. *davewhitebooks.com*

MELISSA YI is an emergency doctor who writes every spare minute, mostly about Hope Sze, an MD who solves murders and falls in love in Montreal, Canada. Her latest novels are the supernatural medical thriller *Killing Me Slothly* and *The Red Rock Killer,* which was a finalist for the Crime Writers of Canada's Award of Excellence in the Best Juvenile/YA Novel category in 2025. "The Longest Night of the Year," which was published in EQMM, was also a 2025 Award of Excellence finalist. Melissa's dog Roxy helps solve the case in her novel *Human Remains. melissayuaninnes.com*

About the Editor

Josh Pachter is an author, editor, and translator of crime fiction. A two-time Derringer winner, he was the 2020 recipient of the Short Mystery Fiction Society's Golden Derringer for Lifetime Achievement.

EDITOR WEBSITE:
  joshpachter.com

SOCIAL MEDIA HANDLES:
  https://www.facebook.com/josh.pachter/
  https://bsky.app/profile/joshpachter.bsky.social

Also by Josh Pachter, Editor

EDITED BY JOSH PACHTER

Dutch Treats: Crime Fiction by Dutch and Flemish Authors
Every Day a Little Death: Crime Fiction Inspired by the Songs of Stephen Sondheim
Crime in the Old Dominion (with K.L. Murphy)
Friend of the Devil: Crime Fiction Inspired by the Songs of the Grateful Dead
Invasive Species: Stories by Northern California Crime Writers
Happiness Is a Warm Gun: Crime Fiction Inspired by the Songs of the Beatles
Paranoia Blues: Crime Fiction Inspired by the Songs of Paul Simon
The Man Who Solved Mysteries: More Short Fiction by William Brittain
Monkey Business: Crime Fiction Inspired by the Films of the Marx Brothers
Only the Good Die Young: Crime Fiction Inspired by the Songs of Billy Joel
The Great Filling Station Holdup: Crime Fiction Inspired by the Songs of Jimmy Buffett
The Further Misadventures of Ellery Queen (with Dale C. Andrews)
The Misadventures of Nero Wolfe
The Beat of Black Wings: Crime Fiction Inspired by the Songs of Joni Mitchell
Amsterdam Noir (with René Appel)
The Man Who Read Mysteries: The Short Fiction of William Brittain
The Misadventures of Ellery Queen (with Dale C. Andrews)
Top Horror: The Authors' Choice
Top Fantasy: The Authors' Choice
Top Science Fiction: The Authors' Choice
Top Crime: The Authors' Choice

WRITTEN BY JOSH PACHTER

First Week Free at the Roomy Toilet
Dutch Threat
The Adventures of the Puzzle Club and Other Stories (with Ellery Queen)
The Tree of Life